FUSION FIRE

Books by Kathy Tyers

FUSION FIRE

The Firebird Series — Book Two

Kathy Tyers

PUBLISHING

Fusion Fire by Kathy Tyers
Published by Enclave Publishing
5025 N. Central Ave., #35
Phoenix, AZ 85012
www.enclavepublishing.com

ISBN (paper): 978-162184-0411

Published in the United States by Enclave Publishing, an imprint of Third Day
Books, LLC, Phoenix, Arizona.

This is a work of fiction. Names, characters, places, and incidents are products of
the author's imagination or are used fictitiously. Any similarity to actual people,
organizations, and/or events is purely coincidental.

Cover illustration by Cory Clubb, Go Bold Designs
Typesetting by Margaret Stroud

Printed in the United States of America

DEDICATION

To WTG
I am grateful *indeed*
To God and to you
For our new life together.

TABLE OF CONTENTS

1

NIGHT ATTACK

notturno minore
night piece in a minor key

Even rain on wet leaves can sound ominous after midnight.

Firebird stopped walking and listened intently. The dark hours were slipping away, but she'd awakened with both calves bound up in excruciating muscle cramps. Pausing on her third lap around a long, windowless training room, she felt positive she'd heard something—someone—out in the passway.

She would've known if it were Brennen.

Barefoot, she crept across the cushioned mat. Once a storage area, this room bristled with weapons, simulators, and exercise equipment. A home-security master board glimmered behind the flight simulator. She bent toward it.

One of her unborn sons kicked her ribs in protest.

Firebird straightened and pushed red-brown hair back from her face. She'd hoped to command a star cruiser someday... she'd never hoped to resemble one. Now, six and a half months pregnant with twins, she suspected she did.

She snugged the belt of her flimsy nightrobe. On the security board, an image of their two-story hillside home gleamed in pale yellow holo. Each entry and window shone red, fully covered by sensors and dispatch circuits. Brennen had invested his Federate severance pay in a lovely, defensible location near Thyrica's primary military base, then installed the best available home sec system. In ten years of intelligence work, he'd made enemies.

The board showed no sign of intrusion.

Firebird glanced over her shoulder. Blame pregnancy hormones, but she wasn't convinced. She despised this maternal jumpiness, this urge to protect herself at all cost. She'd been a military pilot, qualified on advanced fighter-craft and small arms.

Still, these days she must protect two other lives. She needed to be jumpy.

Brennen had merely rolled over when she'd slipped painfully out of bed. She wondered if she ought to go back and wake him now. She'd done that two nights ago, when she thought she heard noises. They'd found nothing wrong.

Deciding she didn't want her pride stung again, she opened a weapons cupboard. She bypassed several training knives, a broadsword, and two deadly service blazers. A bulky shock pistol—her weapon of choice, a gift from her husband—lay behind the blazers. Hefting it expertly, she thumbed a stud on one side of the grip and quickly checked its charge.

Husband. Unbelievably, she had a husband. Last year, she'd forsaken her homeworld, with its holy laws and traditions that demanded her death, and married Field General Brennen Caldwell. An expert telepath and her enemy when they met, he won her trust and introduced her to faith… and Firebird had never dreamed of love like Brennen gave her, day after night after day. Eight months ago, they had pair bonded in his people's way, linking their lives and their feelings in a marriage only death could end.

She reached for the door control, then hesitated again. She really would rather Brenn didn't find her prowling armed. If she stepped out into that passway quivering with nerves, her worry would wake him. The Ehretan pair bond sensitized each of them to the other's strong emotions, even though she was no trained telepath.

Quiet my heart and mind, Mighty Singer… and help me, she prayed. Her determination, her jumpiness, and even her fond concern for her twins ebbed away. She touched the door control.

The steel panel silently slid aside. She braced against it until her eyes adjusted. Across the passway, diffused city light filtered up Trinn Hill into their second bedroom. She peered out its glasteel window-wall.

Rain had softened into thick fog. Two tiny red eyes shone out for a few seconds, then extinguished. Thyrica's planetary developers must've had quite a sense of humor to create those fist-sized, oozy night-slugs.

She steadied the shock pistol between her hands. Trying to move as serenely as the deep night, she shuffled toward a bend in the passway. She adjusted her grip on the pistol and then peered around the corner.

Her breath caught. Silhouetted by a floor-level luma, a wiry stranger stood facing into the master room. He braced against the doorway with his left arm.

She couldn't see his right hand.

She squeezed her pistol's grip.

The stranger whirled, brandishing a black energy blazer in one blackened hand. He thrust his other hand toward her too, palm outward.

Firebird knew that gesture too well. "Brenn!" she shouted. She shot a wild burst—

Then toppled sideways, dropping her pistol with suddenly limp fingers. The intruder had a telepath's power of voice-command. Her right shoulder hit the wall, and she pitched toward the floor. She mustn't fall hard—must not miscarry—but her arms turned to jelly. She couldn't catch herself.

As she flopped on the carpet, barely missing her pistol, she felt Brennen come fully awake. His confusion burst into the back of her mind. Less than a second later, the hall flashed blood red with blazer fire. The prowler's attention shifted to Brennen. Freed from command, Firebird groped for her pistol.

"Mari!" Brennen shouted. "Stay down!"

She raised her head. A four-armed silhouette danced wildly atop their bed, grappling and kicking. She crawled forward on her elbows and knees. If she could get into the room quickly, she might stun both men with one burst and hit the house alarm.

Too late! Deadly red lightning flashed again. Half the silhouette flew toward the bedroom window-wall, and then—unbelievably—glasteel exploded. "Brenn!" she cried, pushing up on her knees just outside the door, struggling for balance. An alarm klaxon blared. Flood lamps activated outdoors.

"Stay there," he called again from the bed. His combat focus throbbed in her awareness, but his voice sounded steady. "He's gone. Don't come in, though. There's glasteel everywhere."

Warm light flooded the master room. Her husband perched on the foot of their bed, dressed in drawstring trousers and aiming a blazer out into the night through a gulf that had been their security window-wall. Middle-sized, muscular without any extra bulk, he stared down the blazer's sights as if he'd been welded to the weapon.

Firebird lumbered to her bare feet and backed into the extra bedroom to look outdoors. Under the flood lamps, fog dripped from fragrant, evergreen kirka tree limbs onto soggy undergrowth. The night-slug had left a gleaming slime trail, but she saw no footprints. Damp, resin-scented air drifted into the house. The klaxon's tritonal wailing shut off.

A warm hand touched her shoulder. Brennen's concern wrapped around her, warming her much better than her flimsy nightrobe could do. His pale russet hair drooped over one ear, flattened by six hours of sleep, but his cheeks looked flushed, and his intensely blue eyes showed no drowsiness. He still gripped a blazer down at his side. "Are you all right?" he asked.

"I'm fine," she said, catching her breath. "Just a little bounced around. But are you?"

"Yes. Stay out of the bedroom. I'm calling Alert Forces."

Stepping back, she clenched a fist. Thyrica's Alert Forces tracked the lawless Shuhr, renegade cousins of Brennen's telepathic kindred. She had wondered if someday those enemies might attack Brennen just because he was the strongest Sentinel of his generation. "I'm coming with you," she declared.

"Well—yes. You could lie down in the study." He paced up the hall, comforting her with his presence but keeping both hands free, on the off chance the intruder might come back.

Firebird followed. She hated feeling vulnerable. At any other time, she might've gone out the window chasing that prowler.

Brennen jabbed the com console near the steel door, then raised one eyebrow. "No contractions?" he murmured. "You're sure you're all right?"

Sensing his worry, actually feeling it secondhand on the pair bond, she let him feel her own concern... and spotted a reddening streak on his right forearm. "He grazed you!"

A male voice blared through the room speakers, reverberating off duracrete walls. "General Caldwell, your alert's lit up. False alarm?"

Brennen turned away, hiding his scorched arm, but now she spotted blood trickling down his left shoulder and side. "Real thing. We're all right, but we'd appreciate backup."

"On its way. Your location?"

"Downlevel, secure room. Intruder's gone, we think."

"Stay there."

Brennen paced back to the half-open steel door, still gripping that blazer. Misty air seeped along the floor.

Shivering, Firebird crossed to the weapons cupboard. She was too full of adrenaline to sit down, and only starting to realize they'd survived a murder attempt. Had the intruder wanted Brennen, or her... or both? "What happened to your shoulder? Your side?"

He craned his neck. "Oh? Glasteel, probably. Not serious." He'd taken life-threatening injuries in intelligence work. He'd also saved her life. Twice—no, three times. "I'll get you to college," he said. "Master Spieth can watch you for complications."

"Good idea." She bent over to seize one of the other blazers and a half-used spool of medical biotape and was soundly punched again.

All right, then, I don't resemble a star cruiser. A cruiser-carrier. "I guess our secret's about to come out," she complained. She'd gone into hiding as soon as her pregnancy showed, hoping to shock her family with the news just before their twins arrived... and Netaia's nobles would be deeply shocked. Brennen, blessed with a knack for avoiding danger, had agreed she should vanish for a while.

"You've stayed out of the public eye long enough. Ex-princess," he said tenderly, raising an eyebrow as he cupped one hand over his forearm.

"I never was a princess," she insisted through gritted teeth. "Let's tape that burn."

He swept her long hair back over her shoulder. "Well... no. It probably needs more than biotape. I'll let Master Spieth treat it."

"That was close." He nodded. "Hurting?"

"It's blocked." Among other Sentinel skills, he could cancel nerve impulses. "I'm more worried about you."

"Let me clean your shoulder, Brenn."

He craned his neck. "Still bleeding?"

"A little."

"It doesn't hurt. Just leave it."

"Did you pick up any clue as to who that was?"

"No." He strolled back to the door—standing guard, she assumed, but wanting not to worry her.

Good try, Brenn.

"What woke you up?" he asked.

"Leg cramps. Again," she groaned, massaging her left calf.

He peered out. "I never thought I would thank the Holy One for your leg cramps."

Neither had she. But if she'd been asleep a few minutes ago, they might both be dead. She shivered again and snatched a high-protein bar off a shelf. Medical Master Spieth supplied these nourishing snacks by the crate.

Two of his Sentinel colleagues arrived four minutes later. "Mistress Firebird," one exclaimed.

"Hello, Dardy." She extended a palm to Air Master Damalcon Dardy, whose massive frame belied a boyish face. Hoping he wouldn't feel her hand shake as he clasped it, she said, "Haven't talked to you in months."

"Are you all right?" he asked. Then he took a second look. "Oh my," he said softly. "Are you *sure* you're all right?"

"So far as I know. Thanks for coming."

Dardy and his partner walked them around the house. Built by a retired star captain who'd spent too much time traveling between the two Federate regions in a tiny messenger ship, the hillside home had a rambling upper story and a long deck that overlooked central Soldane and distant Kyrren Fjord, and a double rooftop landing port. Dardy's partner's instrument scan plainly showed large shoe prints leading up to—and through—its airlock-type main entry.

Firebird shuddered. So much for advanced security.

As she reentered her home, Soldane city police arrived. The officers took statements, low-light images of the intruder's entry and getaway, and more scans. Though they addressed Brennen respectfully, Firebird noticed they never stood close to any of the three Sentinels. It had taken her, too, a long time to trust these hereditary telepaths, Brennen's kindred.

Standing at the foot of the bed, she tapped one foot, now booted. "How did he get through that window? It was reinforced glasteel."

"This was etched in advance." Sentinel Dardy pointed at a rim of glasteel that protruded bladelike from the windowbar.

"Squill!" she exclaimed. "He was here before, setting us up." She must've heard him two nights ago. She felt like a target. These days, she would be hard to miss.

Brennen stepped out of the freshing room. He carried a medium-sized duffel. "Anything else you want, Mari?"

No one else called Firebird by that name. Brennen had given it to her last year, helping her hide from a hostile regime. When they married, she made it part of her legal identity. "Mari" meant her new life.

She shook her head. Finally, she felt safe enough to realize she was terrified. "I don't need anything but you," she insisted. "Nothing."

● ● ●

Inland, beyond the craggy Dracken Range, at the small town of Arown, the Sentinel College maintained one of the Federacy's best medical facilities. Master Sentinel Aldana Spieth laid her soft sonoscope on an examining room counter. "You'll be fine," she said, "all three of you, but I'd like you off your feet for a day."

Relieved for her twins, and glad Spieth didn't need to give her any injections, Firebird swung around to sit up on the table. Master Spieth's lovely, laugh-lined face was framed by silver hair, and a gold star adorned her white tunic. Its eight rays proclaimed her a Master Sentinel like Brennen, one of Thyrica's most powerful telepathic refugees.

"How's Brenn?" Firebird clutched the internally warmed table's yielding edge. "Where's he gone?"

Master Spieth scribbled on a recall pad with one fingernail. "Kyrie probed out the glasteel shards, and that flash burn's not dangerously deep. He's all right. He's busy for a while, though. You get to finish your night's rest."

"It's morning." Firebird glanced out the window. Beyond three rounded, red stone buildings, a new band of clouds turned orange-maroon. Dawn was racing the next eastbound storm inland. "There's a murderer out there—"

"You will rest," Spieth said flatly. "For two more months, you have a higher priority than chasing—"

"I can't lie down and let Brennen take all the risks—"

"Yes, you can." Spieth laid down her recall pad and narrowed her iron gray eyes. "Your balance is completely out of whack. You could take a dangerous fall just by stepping down wrong. Couldn't you?"

Firebird barely got her mouth open.

"Yes, you could," Spieth snapped. "If you won't promise to cooperate, I'll either put you under voice-command or else lock you in. Which will it be?"

Firebird shook her head. She had no intention of risking her babies' lives. She was determined to keep them safe too—but she hated acting timid. "I can at least help Brenn. He won't rest."

"He'd do almost anything for you, but he can't carry a baby until you deliver." The master touched a call button. "You're young, Firebird. You're strong and healthy, but a twin pregnancy has extra risks. You've just been stressed. You will rest. I'm ordering you an early breakfast as well. Eat it all."

Firebird folded both arms around her belly and those unborn sons, barely resisting the temptation to roll her eyes. She was eating six times a day and napping twice—ridiculous, but... but Spieth was right. She needed both. She felt like a cruiser, but she couldn't seem to gain enough weight to suit the medical master or her staff.

She tired quickly too. So far she didn't think much of motherhood, even if her children-to-be carried the genes of a tremendously gifted family. "Find me a bed," she said curtly. "I'll rest."

• • •

Brennen eyed a newscan screen in the med center's third-floor lounge. As soon as Spieth had treated his cuts and his burn, he'd called his mother, wakening her to explain what had happened before she heard it from some other source—and sure enough, here it came over the net:

• • •

Master Sentinel Brennen Caldwell, new General Coordinator of Thyrian Forces, was attacked last night in his home by an unknown assailant. Neither he nor his wife, Lady Firebird Caldwell nee Angelo of the occupied Netaia Protectorate Systems, was seriously injured. Alert Forces and Soldane Police are investigating.

• • •

Brennen's mother would've spotted the message and worried. Her parting words were, "Please call your brother." He nodded, though he and Tarance didn't get along.

He cleared the connection and touched in a call code. He hated to wake Tarance's family. Once Destia bounced out of bed, Tarance and Asea might never get back to sleep. That would lay one more small grudge in the weighty basket Brennen's older brother carried so proudly.

Still, he didn't want Asea worrying.

The call light flashed for several seconds, then repeated. Brennen frowned. Normally Tarance jumped on night calls. They could be medical emergencies, and Tarance zealously guarded Asea's sleep. Tarance's medical practice, subsidized by the college, earned him general respect among even the non-gifted.

Brennen canceled his call, hustled up the passway's blue shortweave carpet to Firebird's room, and stepped in. Beneath a battery of deactivated sensors, she lay curled away from the door. Sensor deactivation was a good sign. Spieth didn't think she or either of his sons was in danger.

They would both be relieved when she delivered those twins. He endured most of her discomfort and frustration right along with her, including the mood swings. He laid a hand on her shoulder.

Her eyes opened. "Hm?" Then, instantly, "Brenn!" She pushed up onto her elbows. "What's happening?"

Muting his concern, he kissed her forehead. "I just contacted Mother. She wants me to check on Tarance."

She wrinkled her forehead. For an instant, she looked almost childlike.

Brennen knew her toughness, though. This small woman had nearly beaten a deep mind-access interrogation and faced a firing squad. Scarred though she was by her cruel upbringing, she was literally part of him now, as he was part of her. "I know you're frustrated," he said, "staying here like this. It won't last forever. I'll give you an oil rub when I get back. Fair enough?"

Smiling, she shut her eyes, and as she sighed once more, her alert state faded in his senses. In less than a minute, she slept again.

She did need the rest, with her body changing so quickly. Six months ago, neither of them had known about a twin pregnancy's physical demands. Brennen caressed her shoulder, then returned to the lounge and tried Tarance's personal-carry line. Tarance kept that close, even when traveling.

Air Master Dardy poked his head through the door and eyed the com screen. "Everything all right?"

Brennen nodded. Dardy's aggressive deference made Brennen feel like an icon, instead of a talented human who was as guilty as the rest of the starbred—including the renegade Shuhr—of carrying artificially altered genes. Their ancestors were created by scientists who hoped telepathy would create lasting peace on Ehret, their original home world. Instead, the first telepathic Ehretan starbred matured into normal, selfish young men and women whose power cravings touched off a devastating civil war.

"I'm just trying to reach Tarance," Brennen answered, "and let him know we weren't hurt."

"Heavy sleeper?"

"No. He could be on vacation." Or... *Holy One, is he all right?*

• • •

Brennen and Dardy hurried across Dr. Tarance Caldwell's rooftop landing pad. The coastal drizzle soaked moss-hung trees far below, down on the avenue. Early commuters guided streamlined groundcars through puddles. Their headlamps made glittery streaks in the rain.

Eleven years ago, after eight years of college and medical training, Dr. Tarance Caldwell had bought a compact home in this area, one of Soldane's pleasant urban neighborhoods, settling into a life as comfortable and secure as Brennen's had been unpredictable.

No one answered Tarance's entry bell. Dardy frowned.

Brennen turned inward for his epsilon-energy carrier and sent a quest pulse indoors. The home felt eerily empty.

They could all be asleep, he reminded himself. A quest pulse would only locate alert minds.

"Could they be on vacation?" Dardy asked.

If Dardy sensed Brennen's unease, he must've diffused his epsilon shields. Sentinels normally surrounded themselves with mental-frequency static so they wouldn't sense the constant assault of others' emotions. "He would've taken his personal-carry," Brennen objected. Tarance hated it when he let himself in, but he felt he had no choice. He keyed up the unlock sequence.

Dim gray daylight filtered onto Tarance's longweave carpet and the overstuffed furniture down below on his main floor. Cushions lay everywhere. Tarance and Asea's three children often stayed up late. Brennen paused at the foot of the stairs and dropped his own epsilon shields.

He still felt no one awake but Dardy. "Hello?" he called. "Tarance? Asea?"

Dardy paced into the kitchen to open the cold cabinet. His concern rose to answer Brennen's, and now—without epsilon shields—Brennen felt it with excruciating accuracy. "Full of perishables," Dardy said, shaking his head. "They haven't gone far."

Disquieted, Brennen strode up the hall. He turned left, into the master room. On the bed in half darkness, plush covers draped two forms. "Tarance," Brennen called. He repeated, louder, "Tarance." Neither body moved.

Brennen waved on the room light. Tarance lay on his back, Asea on her side. Their eyes remained shut, their faces peaceful, but neither breathed. Brennen froze, as helpless as if he'd been caught in voice-command. "No," he croaked.

Dardy hustled around the bed. Brennen reached toward his older brother's throat to check for a pulse, then saw the scorched left ear. Blazer, point-blank range. Death would have been sudden and silent.

Dardy laid down Asea's wrist, shook his head, then pulled up the bed sheet to cover both faces. "Get out of here, Caldwell. Go sit down."

"I've seen death before," he said, but his hands felt numb. "Let me help." Then he exclaimed, "The children!" and flung himself across the passway.

The boys, Brit and Kether, lay on narrow beds on either side of a smaller room, two gangling teenaged bodies that showed no sign of pain, struggle, or life.

Dardy met him in the hallway. "Destia?" Brennen cried, wheeling toward the third bedroom.

Dardy shook his head. "The girl's... dead too. Go sit down. I just called Soldane police."

Brennen sank onto a lounger and pressed both trembling hands over his eyes. Twice in eighty years, someone had tried to wipe out his ancient bloodline. Did this make a third attempt, or had Tarance's family fallen to someone's private vendetta?

He slumped. His breath came in puffs. He was trained in emotional control, but he couldn't squelch this storm of grief.

No, not grief. Guilt.

Stop, reason insisted. *You aren't responsible. You merely survived— because Mari was awake.*

Then who struck here? The Shuhr?

According to Alert Force reports, none of their renegade cousins cared about the Sentinels' ancient faith. Surely the Shuhr scoffed at prophecies about the Carabohd-Caldwell family, although—as a precaution—the Sentinel kindred tried to keep most of those prophecies secret.

Who else would've done this?

Tarance's dim living room seemed light-years away from Brennen's point of consciousness. *You're going into shock*, reason observed. *Lie down. Get your feet up.*

He obeyed. *Tarance*, he groaned again, this time into the invisible realm. *O Holy One, welcome him. Make him content, as Asea and I could never do in this lifetime.*

Another memory stabbed deep. Only two dekia ago, twenty all-too-short days back, they had celebrated Destia's spiritual coming of age by consecrating her into the faith community.

Twice before, one... only one... adult male in his line had survived.

But Destia was only twelve! And what about Asea? They'd never killed women before. Or was this someone else's work?

Agony choked him. He was too numb to weep.

2

ECHOES

morendo
dying away

Two days later, Firebird stared out a barred, trapezoidal window. Five stories down, pounding rain soaked an enclosed lawn of jujink, a primitive blue-green ground cover. Red stone walls dotted with other windows surrounded the courtyard. These high-security campus apartments housed medical patients' families from all over the Federacy, including—now—four of the five surviving members of Brennen's extended family. The Caldwell murders had scandalized Soldane and landed her back in protective custody, just like when she was a Federate war prisoner. Brennen could still commute to work, but last night even he stayed indoors. They'd packed yesterday, escorted by half a dozen hurrying college staffers and Alert Forces Sentinels. Today, the first home she and Brennen had made together would go back on the market—as a killer walked free.

Unspeakably frustrated, she turned away from the window. This apartment was too small for a full cooking unit. It had a servo table linked to the building's provision facility, a small living space, and two even smaller bedrooms. Last night, she'd unpacked only a few clothes and her clairsa, then stayed up past midnight, playing her sorrow and frustration on the small Netaian harp. She knew an enormous repertoire of traditional ballads, plus a dozen of her own.

Brennen squeezed out of the inner bedroom, threading a path around boxes and moving crates while he adjusted the cuffs on his midnight-blue uniform. He'd taken only one day of bereavement leave. As the first shock of grieving faded, she felt more of the pain squeezing his heart and mind, keen and sharp on the pair bond.

The preliminary police report stunned her too. Tarance, Asea, and the boys died without waking up, but Destia had been bound and forced to kneel for her execution. The only blessing was that Dardy—not Brennen—found her body. What had that black-handed stranger planned for her and Brennen?

"I don't understand," she murmured. The empathetic pair bond was helping her and Brennen learn to communicate, despite vastly different upbringings. Her grief and outrage should be all the clues he needed to catch her meaning. "It isn't right," she added.

He halted in the narrow hall. His hair looked damp, with fair dry wisps over his forehead and ears. She caught a whiff of herbed soap. "I agree," he said. "Destia didn't deserve that. No more than any wastling on your world deserved to die horribly and young."

Firebird tilted her chin. "But that's different. They serve the Powers." Raised to sacrifice herself for those merciless Netaian demigods, though even as a child she doubted they existed, Firebird had finally forsaken them. "Reverence for the Powers holds our government together," she said, "but that's Netaia. Why would the Holy One let this happen to one of His young people, unless He's powerless—too?"

Brennen's forehead furrowed. "Terrible crimes happen every day, throughout the Whorl. Flawed humans are free to commit them."

"That seems wrong." She shook her head. She'd learned so much since leaving Netaia. "Our God is vast, He's... infinite, ancient, and wise."

"You want to know," Brennen said slowly, "why evil and pain can exist."

"Yes," she exclaimed. Someday, the galaxies' Creator would mend the evil and injustice she hated so deeply. His books made that promise. She hoped to play a part in its fulfillment. "How could Netaian noble families order their own children's deaths?" she demanded. "Why is there pain and terror, why are there Shuhr, and why, why are they doing this to your family?" A tear spilled down her cheek. That poor child...

Brennen caressed the teardrop away. "Even pain can be a blessing if it wakes us up to danger."

Yes, her leg cramps had saved her, and Brennen, and both their unborn sons. But that hadn't helped Destia.

He shook his head. "As for evil—it exists, and we've all partaken."

Now he was quoting. They'd argued about this, one night after her Path instruction session. Sensing his feelings didn't mean she always agreed. How could Brenn's people believe even the best of them were tainted? She didn't feel evil. She'd found mercy and peace in the Eternal Speaker. She never would've murdered a twelve-year-old girl.

"The existence of evil isn't a question anyone should have to settle before work." Brennen quirked an eyebrow. "Can you wait for this evening?"

"Of course. But Brenn, answer one question. Why Tarance's whole family? It wasn't to punish you, because he came to kill us next. Do you think it's the prophecies?"

"Yes." Brennen had been voice-commanded not to explain those predictions to anyone who hadn't formally joined the faith community. She only knew that he and Tarance were the last heirs to important promises.

Intrigued, and enthralled by the One who replaced her guilt with mercy, Firebird had finished Path instruction. Whether or not she felt soul-tainted, his people demanded a formal consecration for full membership. She'd set a date. The rite would be private, since she wanted to avoid publicity. Only Brennen's family would attend.

Yesterday, she'd canceled. She couldn't put Brennen's widowed mother through another consecration ceremony less than three weeks after Destia's. "If the Shuhr are attacking your family," she murmured, "then they know what you won't tell me."

"I can't," he reminded her. He walked to the barred window. "Unfortunately, one of the minor promises is fairly well known. Evidently, some descendant of my ancestors will destroy a so-called nest of evil that sounds—in one of the prophecies—like it's probably the Shuhr world."

"Oh," she said softly, "oh." If the renegades thought they were threatened, that was reason enough to kill Caldwells. Some descendant... maybe Brennen himself, avenging this quintuple murder? "That's a minor promise?"

He nodded, turning back to stare with those startling blue eyes.

She guessed that he wanted to read her thoughts. Like all military Sentinels, he swore to respect others' privacy unless security was at stake.

Should she offer him mind-access?

Later, maybe. For now, she just hoped he would keep talking. "Do they follow some rival god?" she pressed.

"As far as we know, they serve no one but themselves. But that selfish attitude does honor the Adversary. He has strong servants. We must be stronger."

Firebird crossed her arms, which wasn't easy these days. "Absolutely."

Still, if Tarance had died for those prophecies, she and Brennen were in danger. She glanced at the locked entry.

"College has a Class-One security net. You're safer here than in base housing."

"I know," she said.

He caught her in an embrace, kissed her gently, then strode out.

"You be careful," she muttered. A queer little contraction rippled across her taut belly. "Good morning, princeling." She stroked the spot. She felt like a dance hall these days, with all those little limbs kicking and punching.

It had been more than a century since her dynasty produced a male child. Hoping to give Brennen the son he obviously wanted, Firebird had visited this medical center even before they'd tried to conceive. She'd thought the Sentinels might diagnose some reason for her family's odd history. Master Spieth found—and treated—Mazo syndrome, a hereditary disorder that sometimes arose among Thyrica's small Ehret-descended enclave.

The notion sent Firebird spinning. She was no Ehretan descendant! She was of royal blood... pure Netaian...

Bending over Spieth's data desk together, she and the medical master had accessed Netaian historical records. The last Angelo male, Prince Avocin, had married outside the ten noble families. His wife, Sharah Casvah, was allegedly born in Denford, on Netaia's southerly continent.

Master Spieth had craned her neck to look up at Firebird. Her iron gray eyes shone out of their net of creases. "Casvah is an Ehretan name," she announced. "If this woman was a full-blooded Ehretan refugee, she could've easily inserted a birth record into the Netaian register. She had none of our Privacy and Priority Codes to keep her from manipulating data. As soon as she set her eye on Prince Avocin, nothing stood between her and the palace."

Firebird laughed shortly. "We were taught that this sudden lack of male heirs was the Powers' lasting judgment on Prince Avocin for marrying out of the noble families." One more blow to Strength, Valor, and Excellence; Knowledge, Fidelity, and Resolve; Authority, Indomitability, and Pride— the nine holy Powers, who weren't gods after all.

Two days after that visit with Spieth, Firebird had come out of shock and asked Brennen if she could attempt Sentinel training, if she carried even a few altered Ehretan genes. Even before she conceived, she had vowed to learn to protect her children.

Truth to tell, she was already a little afraid of raising them. Brennen tried gamely to dissuade her, calling Sentinel powers a mixed blessing, the result of illicit research—and a burden besides. *No sensible person would want them,* he claimed.

She passed two qualifying tests immediately. First, Master Spieth confirmed epsilon potential in her midbrain. Then, character examiners awarded her a passing score (though not without warning her of her faults). She'd barely started studying for her final qualifying test, a memorization exam over the Privacy and Priority Codes' first volume, when— to her delight and chagrin—she found herself pregnant. She couldn't travel daily from Soldane to Arown for training and keep her pregnancy secret, so she took up other studies and pursued them at home on Trinn Hill, overlooking Soldane.

Suddenly, she lived at college. She'd suspected, ever since Spieth diagnosed twins, that she would end up living here. The best medical care in the Federacy was moments away... and so was the best training.

Eyeing the packing crates, she tried to remember where she'd buried that Code book.

3

TALAS OIL

legato
smoothly

Before leaving for Base One in Soldane, Brennen spent an hour with six members of the special Alert Forces, closeted in an office under the college's administration building. He sat at midtable, surrounded by supportive colleagues.

It was hard to leave Mari alone. He couldn't shake the sense that he ought to be home defending her and their sons. His wife, trained by the Netaian Planetary Navy, could probably fight off most assailants—even pregnant—but if the Shuhr had decided to wipe out his family at last, she was in danger.

"About one-seventy centimeters," he answered Dardy's first question after they'd offered condolences... and sincere congratulations. These six were all consecrants. With Tarance and his sons gone into eternity, these men and women had been relieved—delighted—to learn that the Caldwell family had twins on the way.

Brennen strengthened his affective control and continued, "Wiry. Short curly hair. Cleft chin."

"Black hair?"

"He'd blackened his face and hands," Brennen reminded the other Sentinels. "His hair looked black."

"Epsilon strength?"

"I didn't have time to test. But he was strong. He tried to put me under voice-command." Without any outsiders present, the codes would have allowed this group to subvocalize—speak mind to mind, sending and receiving words on epsilon waves. That wasn't commonly done, though.

Whenever a Sentinel used the epsilon energy-producing region of his or her brain—the ayin complex—it aged slightly.

"Good." The woman next to him poised her hands over a specialized recall pad. "Now that he's firmly in your mind, let me see." Her fingers swept the pad. Brennen felt her access probe study the mental image. By the time she finished, a portrait gleamed on the pad's surface.

"Yes," Brennen said. "That's him."

She touched the SEND key. Alert Forces would post the image at all locations.

In the eighty years since the Shuhr colony was discovered, all attempts to negotiate with that other major Ehretan remnant had ended in one-sided massacre. *Shuhr* meant "enemy" in the holy tongue.

"I've studied the records," Dardy said. Seated across from Brennen, watching him on behalf of a concerned medical master, Dardy rested muscular forearms on the table. "If they've really committed most of the unsolved piracies, they have everything from metals to museum pieces on that world of theirs. And who knows how many murders we could trace to them."

"I'd guess," an ethics instructor said slowly, "most of us who've vanished."

"All right." Dardy stared at Brennen, who felt a gentle emotional probe follow the stare. "Then why are they killing the Caldwells so doggedly? The Shuhr have never walked the Path. Why would they try to thwart prophecy?"

"Exactly," said the artist.

Brennen spoke up. "I have a theory." He'd scarcely slept, thinking this through.

"You have the floor." Dardy opened a hand on the table. "You're the one in danger. We'll back you, whatever it takes."

Brennen thanked Dardy subvocally, then spoke aloud. "Wealthy, secure people crave excitement."

Dardy raised an eyebrow.

"It's as you said," Brennen pressed. "They don't care about prophecies. So out of boredom, or maybe on a dare," he added bitterly, "someone has taken up a devilish challenge."

"Three times in seventy-eight years?"

"This time," Brennen reminded Dardy, "it was different."

"He tried to kill all of you, including the women."

Brennen's emotions escaped control again. Destia had been the lively young flower of Tarance's family. Why *had* the Holy One let that happen? It was one of the most difficult issues that honest, thoughtful worshipers faced. How could the Eternal Sovereign allow suffering and death? It had caught Mari square on, and she lacked his twenty years in the faith.

Guide her, Holy One. Give me words to explain. Your ways are perfect and your wisdom is eternal, but I hear you so faintly sometimes.

Dardy rubbed his chin. Brennen sensed that Dardy had raised his epsilon shields, probably to block out Brennen's private feelings. "If you're still targeted," Dardy said, "our best hope is to lure him out again, then bring him down. But that will have to be done carefully."

"Lure him out," echoed the ethics instructor, who had also shielded to let Brennen grieve. "Yes, but how?"

Brennen rejoined the conversation. "For myself, I'm willing to risk setting a trap. And Firebird is a fighter. But the children must be protected." He'd never felt so exposed, so easy to attack. "They would only be truly safe back at sanctuary, at Hesed House."

"Then go," urged a woman down the table. "Leave today. If you hadn't left Hesed after your wedding, maybe this wouldn't have happened."

"Unless we'd come here," Brennen reminded her, "unless Spieth had treated her Mazo syndrome, we couldn't have conceived them."

She nodded somberly. These unborn lives, heirs to so many prophecies, were now even more precious to this kindred than before—if that were possible. "We'd be vulnerable between takeoff and slip if we tried to get back there," Brennen said.

"We can't risk them," the instructor agreed. "Not unless it's a last resort."

The woman added, "With unlimited wealth, the Shuhr could chase you across the Whorl."

Dardy's eyes narrowed. Again Brennen felt him probe. *I'll be all right,* he insisted subvocally.

Silence fell. In his mind's eye, Brennen saw Tarance as he'd crowned Destia with a beribboned garland of yellow and white flowers, only two dekia before. He clung to the image for a moment, reaching into his belt pocket to touch a small bird-of-prey medallion Tarance had given him years ago. He'd carried it all over the Federacy. He would never part with it now. It still seemed impossible that he would not spar with Tarance or laugh with Asea again. Not in this lifetime.

"One Shuhr agent," the instructor murmured, "masquerading as one of us, could turn the Federacy against us. Then we would all have to run for Hesed, or else be annihilated."

"We're the Federacy's best defense against them," said Dardy. "As long as the Shuhr pose a threat, the Federacy needs us."

"So we hope." Brennen too had faced fear and jealousy from non-gifted individuals. If the Federates ever turned on the Sentinel kindred, his people would not survive. "Then we must set that trap. Make it look as if I'm fleeing offworld..."

• • •

Four hours later, Brennen stood on an observation deck and peered down at ocean breakers nibbling a long, stony beach. No matter how many planets he visited, the vast Thyrian ocean always filled him with awe. Less than a sixth of this planet's surface was dry land; the rest was ocean and ice. Clouds swirled against the base's clear zone. Here, Thyrian Forces tenuously controlled the weather systems this huge ocean flung onto a peninsula between two deep fjords.

The onshore wind stung his face. Northward, to his right, sea-beaten cliffs bent westward into an inlet and then faded into haze.

Midafternoon, his spiritual father had arrived on base and suggested they speak alone, outdoors. Shamarr Lo Dickin's snowy hair and ministerial tunic whipped in the wind. Gray-blue eyes glimmered beneath his furrowed forehead. A direct heir of Mattah Dickin, the Ehretan Shamarr whose family had saved fifty-one starbred orphans from planetary destruction, Dickin was the spiritual leader of Thyrica's starbred community. He'd taken Brennen as a protégé during Brenn's Sentinel training, and they'd grown closer during the seven years since Brennen's father died.

"Show me," Dickin said simply.

Brennen dispersed all epsilon static. He glanced aside just long enough to welcome another access probe, then relaxed against the glassite railing, clenching his hands while his mentor looked into his mind.

The Shamarr's epsilon touch rested on the tragic murders and their discovery. He paused to spread comforting warmth over Brennen's grief, then lingered to examine this morning's exchange with Firebird Mari. Then his warm presence withdrew. "Tell me your fears," he said. "Speak and release them to Him."

Brennen hadn't seen Destia's body, but he had read the report. "I'm afraid they could catch Mari," he said, grappling with his emotions. "That they would be cruel, for sport. That they'd watch her terror from inside her own mind, while they... killed our sons. And then destroyed her."

When Brennen fell silent, Dickin frowned. A seascape of parallel waves formed on his forehead. "Go on," he said.

Brennen exhaled. Really, he hadn't expected Dickin to let him escape without voicing this too. "Father, she knows enough now to ask the deep questions. She was raised in a false faith that molded her thinking. She might find satisfying answers in her own mind instead of the Speaker's words. She might step off the Path." A detour could be agonizing for the wanderer and everyone close to her.

"Now," the Shamarr said, "let Him take those burdens, as He promised."

Brennen squinted out to sea. "I can objectively. But can I sincerely?"

"Are you the only one watching over her soul, Brennen Caldwell?"

He exhaled. "No."

"Be careful, Brennen. Your tremendous accomplishments tempt you to rely too much on yourself. In His will, Firebird Mari and your sons are safer than you or I could keep them. Of course," he added, raising his head, "that doesn't mean we'll let down our guard."

"I won't," Brennen murmured, "believe me."

"And the holy Word to Come," Dickin added, "remains in the One's mighty care. Don't confuse yourself with fear. That would be wasted effort. Fulfill your duties to Thyrica. You are still in the heart of His will."

"Truly, Father?"

"As you said this morning, if you hadn't left the Procyel system, they could not have been conceived. Your presence here is part of a plan."

The plan. Centuries before Ehret's destruction, believers were promised that one day, a Caldwell—Carabohd, in the old language—would father a king with the power to destroy and renew the universe, who would replace the symbolic covering of ancient sacrifices with soul-deep purification, and finally bring peace to guilty humanity. That holy messenger would have been born on Ehret, but when the Ehretans genetically altered their children, they delayed His advent. This Word to Come, King of the New Universe, would wait until they re-qualified themselves by serving unaltered humankind. The Sentinel community now realized that even their fall had been prophesied in their older holy book, *Dabar*.

Dark gray rain slanted down from a cloud bank out at sea. At the corner of Brennen's vision, Dickin drew a blue-green vial from a tunic pocket.

Brennen straightened, surprised. He'd seen this vial before, when Dickin commissioned a teacher to lead the faith community on Caroli. It held the purified oil of a spice called *talas,* once grown on Ehret.

Dickin poured his left palm full of oil and corked the vial one-handed.

Then he laid both hands on Brennen's head and looked toward the gray clouds. "For the trials ahead, Mighty One, strengthen this man, your servant. Give him wisdom and courage and mercy. Speak clearly to him, the eldest of your holy lineage. Let him carry that burden honorably. So let it be."

In that moment, Brennen realized Dickin had come not just to counsel, but to anoint him as the eldest surviving heir of his family. He hadn't known there was such a rite. Some of these heirs experienced sacred dreams, even waking visions, in dangerous times. He squeezed his eyes shut and added a heartfelt prayer to Dickin's. "I'm no perfect servant, Holy One. Carry my fears, as you promised. Let me hear and obey you in all things. So let it be."

He stared into Dickin's eyes for a few more seconds, drawing strength and peace. Despite the sea wind, he caught the sweet fragrance of talas oil. *Soon,* he prayed silently, *let me tell her what one of our sons might become. What one of our descendants will be.* That, he guessed, would be all she ever needed to walk the Path steadily, until death took her across to His presence.

• • •

Firebird sat at their new apartment's small data desk, which was also their servo and dining table. Brilliant blue letters gleamed on a darker blue field. She sipped a cup of bland herbal tea Master Spieth had prescribed.

MIN OF JUDIC, she keyed in, scowling. REDUCE FREEDOM COEFF TO 20%.

As the program returned a result, her spirits sank again. This simulation was her link with Soldane University. For four months, hiding behind a pseudonym, she'd studied governmental analysis. Her home world was repressed by a noble class that claimed to represent the nine holy Powers, deified attributes from an ancient mythology. Netaia was now subdued and occupied by the vast Federacy, but those electors refused to step down. They believed ruling was their ordained right... whether or not they were capable, Firebird reflected bitterly, whether or not they cared squill for any of the people they claimed to protect.

Netaia's class system, and its steel-fisted electoral monopolies, denied almost a quarter of its populace basic rights that most Federates took for granted. Even before Firebird left Netaia, she'd sat in back rooms where her sisters never dared to go, listening to illegal ballads. Her clairsa had been her entrée to those clubs and warehouses, her deep love for her people's songs her shield. No one had ever assaulted her. She'd heard songs and seen crowd reactions that would've made other electors tremble, but she guessed no other elector ever heard them.

Now Soldane University's analysis program confirmed her fears. The Netaian low-common and servitor classes had suffered too many harsh judgments, too much hopelessness and inequity. They wanted to participate in the vast wealth and culture Netaia's nobles and high-commoners took for granted.

Could change come peacefully? Occupation Governor Lee Danton had implemented reforms, but Firebird hadn't simulated one reform program that eased interclass tensions in time to prevent a greater than eighty percent chance of civil war breaking out. Netaia's noble and generous populace might never recover from such a catastrophe. Its high culture might become easy prey for others who wanted its wealth.

Not the Shuhr! she begged. *Have mercy on my homeland!* She bowed her head, remembering how she'd plunged with her oldest sister Carradee through feathery snowfields outside the winter palace. At tropical Sitree that same week, she'd nearly drowned proving she could swim farther underwater than their middle sister, Phoena.

The next year their father had died on a hunting trip. Without Prince Irion, their mother led no more family vacations. All Firebird's later memories were of Citangelo. She recalled sitting in an ornate balcony at the Conservatory's symphony hall, savoring every note of a viol concerto's premiere performance... and sitting before the Electorate, performing an original ballad at all of eleven years old.

•   •   •

Netaia, Netaia,
Green mountains and blue oceans,
Mighty Tiggaree, roll, roll along...

•   •   •

The main entry whooshed. Wholeness and union, contentment and strength washed away her homesickness. She looked up, gladly welcoming her partner in the pair bond. Brennen stepped around moving crates between the main door and servo table. Outside the trapezoidal windows, daylight faded.

"Long day," he said softly.

"Long," she agreed.

He sank down beside her. Instead of reaching out, he kept both hands in his lap, comforting with waves of tender assurance. She didn't need to be touched. She felt whole again now that he'd entered the room. Already, the sweet emotional stereo of feeling his emotions along with her own seemed completely natural. Once, she'd been as fiercely independent as Netaia itself. Now she knew the downside of pair bonding. She never would feel complete, as long as she lived, unless Brennen was with her.

"I should apologize," she said slowly. "You didn't need a dose of my doubts this morning, on top of your grieving."

"I'm glad you're honest. Now let me be honest with you too."

She shut down the blue screen.

"I'm deathly afraid that the Shuhr will attack us again," he said.

She didn't like to think that Brennen could be afraid, but she had to understand. Even a crack shot could be surprised and murdered. He'd ordered a voice-activated, supplemental security system for this apartment, which should be delivered tomorrow.

"I worry that this time," he went on, "they'll target you before me."

She laid a hand on her stomach. "Because they've found out."

"Yes. But now that I've said it, I have to tell you I've been reprimanded for worrying." He smiled sidelong.

"Reprimanded?"

"Shamarr Dickin came to the base today," he said. "He counseled me, prayed for me."

"I am in awe of that man," she admitted. "Has he always been your spiritual father?" That relationship must've been a little like calling the queen her mother.

Brennen shook his head. "You know how young I was when I won my master's star. Too young for that much responsibility."

Seventeen, she recalled, catching a whiff of something sweet.

He stared at the nearest wall. "When they vested me in the Word, I got the shock of my life. Shamarr Dickin himself stood to declare himself my sponsoring master. I almost burst with pride. Then he explained at great length, before all the masters who were attending and my family," he added, putting more love and regret into that word than Firebird would've thought possible, "that this was no honor but a strict discipline.

I would answer to Dickin for any misconduct. That raid without orders, at Gemina, earned a penance to go with the Federate Service Crest." He turned his head. One side of his hair looked oddly dark, as if wet.

"What did you lean against?" she asked.

"Nothing. That's oil, from when Shamarr Dickin prayed. Smell it." She stretched her neck and sniffed. Slightly sweet, slightly... green. Not what she smelled a minute ago. "Do you still want to talk about why evil exists?" he asked, and she felt his willingness.

"Not really." She squared her shoulders. "At the moment, I just want to fight back."

"I thought you would. I brought you something," he added, raising his hands. Now she realized he held them cupped around something.

"A new weapon?" she wished out loud.

Laughing, he opened his fingers. His hands cradled a blossom. Eight intensely blue-green petals framed its yellow center, and its heady, honey-rich odor made her blink.

"Oh!" She leaned her head against his shoulder. "What's it called?"

"Mira lily. They grow at Hesed."

Her memories of Hesed House, on Procyel II where they married, were splendid but vague. After she'd recovered from bonding shock, they hadn't stayed long. At Hesed, Brennen had received a fateful communiqué. Regional command, reprimanding him for disobeying a direct order, had dismissed him from Federate service. Intoxicated by finally touching the depths of his strength, and sustained by his supreme, careful tenderness, Firebird hadn't cared a skitter's fin for the Federacy's rebuke. She now guessed that her attitude had helped him cope with the setback.

He was ambitious, though he hid it well.

"It'll stay fresh indefinitely in this damp climate," he said, "if you give it enough light. It only needs air and a little moisture." He tipped the lily off his hands onto hers.

"Thank you," she whispered. Gingerly, she examined the delicate blossom. Behind the bloom curled a short pale green root covered with net-like brown lines.

"If we're careful, you can wear it in your hair." He reached into a pocket of his wide belt and pulled out a silver clip, took back the lily, and wove its succulent root through half the clip. Firebird held her breath while he pinned the bloom over her left ear. "There." He arranged her long hair about her shoulders.

She felt his wash of approval and returned fervent gratitude. He knew... he felt... how it roused her when he toyed with her hair. For a moment he pressed into her mind, caressing her with his very existence, and she felt as if she were floating on a tropical sea flooded with sweet incense.

Then he reached into a deep tunic pocket and handed her a thin parcel. "And this was delivered just before Dickin arrived."

Firebird lifted its pressboard lid. Inside, a spiraling ebony handgrip protruded from a supple black sheath. "Ah!" she exclaimed. She tipped the dagger out of its box, caressed the beaded pommel, and exclaimed again, "Brenn!" The grip felt so comfortable that she guessed he'd ordered it for her small, broad hand. She drew the blade. It too was finished in flat black, to be invisible at night, tapering gracefully from narrow waist to symmetrical point, with a wicked double edge.

"It'll split hair." He smiled down the blade. "I tried it. I reserved a training room for this evening. I'd like to see if you remember what I taught you. A dagger's easier to conceal than a shock pistol—or a blazer."

Truly, she never should go unarmed now, not even at home. Maybe especially not at home.

"...And then maybe a foot rub?" he offered.

That was incentive! "I remember," she insisted. Exercise, and then a massage... glory, that would feel good! She sheathed the dagger and carried it into their crate-crowded bedroom. "I'm just not sure I can still do it. I'll show you after dinner," she called, laying the dagger beneath her dressing mirror under a small, square pendant hung on a fine gold chain. Mounted inside that pendant was Brennen's first gift, a microcopied document that once guaranteed her Federate asylum.

He appeared in the doorway. "What?" he teased. "Not this instant? You're not hungry, are you?"

To think that she tried to refuse that asylum!

Gently she slapped his cheek. "We, sir, are starving."

4

SHUHR

allargando
slowing down and growing louder

At the heart of an underground colony known to its population as the Golden City, Eshdeth Shirak's black-haired grandson approached on dragging feet. Beneath a ceiling fused *in situ* from space-black obsidian, Shirak had displayed a massive Kellian tapestry, once worked in brilliant colors, but faded by six and a half centuries; three fused-silica artworks by a deceased Elysian master; and his new favorite, a three-dimensional curtain of mist that was six meters long and three high. Inside, icicles of light and stalagmites of darkness thrust and parried, battling for mastery. His desk was another masterwork, laser sculpted by one of his uncles from the City's native obsidian. On this Ehretan colony of Three Zed, every significant settlement had been blasted, tunneled, domed or fused on a tube-riddled surface of lava, obsidian, basalt, and dusty gray pumice.

Shirak's grandson, Micahel—now twenty—was a favorite among City girls for his curly hair and impish face with cleft chin and high cheekbones. Today, though, Micahel walked with his head down, emanating disgust and faint dread. He held his right arm against his side.

Shirak tapped a stylus against his desk's gleaming surface. Micahel halted several meters away—maintaining his epsilon shields moderately well, despite the leakage. Youth made him strong.

At Shirak's right shoulder, his Testing Director waited at relaxed attention. Tall, slim, and muscular, wearing his silky black hair long over a red collar, Dru Polar stood surrounded by the dense epsilon cloud of his own shields. Shirak could almost see them, they deflected so strongly. Dru Polar looked thirty. He was sixty-eight.

Ninety-six himself, Eshdeth Shirak had ruled the Golden City for seventeen years. Before he died, the unbound starbred would finally conquer the Federacy. Millions of Federates would die in that war, but to Shirak, their lives were worth precisely nothing. When his people's bioscientists finally tapped the Federacy's resources, all projections showed that the Ehretan unbound would achieve immortality. A genetically superior race deserved deathlessness—and with unlimited wealth, who would ever grow tired of living?

Also, without the non-gifted competing for resources, Shirak's people could finally multiply freely. The cost would be sterilizing settled worlds, one at a time, of inferior human life. Eshdeth Shirak was prepared to exact that cost, and he had the means to do it. He'd built up this colony through long-range planning.

Dru Polar kept it strong by eliminating weakness. Polar had spent two years training Eshdeth's grandson—and others. Micahel's final training mission should have sounded a death knell for the Federacy's dominance of the Whorl and its Sentinels' oh-so-smug complacency.

Flicking his thumb, Shirak signaled his grandson to diffuse his shields.

"You failed?" He spoke aloud, partly out of disdain, partly to rest his epsilon centers. His carrier had started to falter, despite hundreds of ayin treatments. The injectable hormone was harvested from his own cloned offspring by extracting their undifferentiated embryonic brain tissue. Postponing the dreaded epsilon waning was Three Zed's second greatest medical accomplishment after life extension.

An epsilon torrent of information scrambled with anger coursed out of the boy.

"Sit down," Shirak ordered, ignoring Polar's subtly projected approval of the way he spoke aloud. On many occasions, vocal speech did convey insult. "You're babbling. Organize your thoughts."

Micahel folded his body into a hard black chair. He kept that right arm close.

"Hurt yourself?" Polar asked, also disdainfully vocal.

Micahel addressed his grandfather by title. *Yes, Eldest, I failed,* he sub-vocalized to them both. *I missed one of the pair.*

Testing Director Polar stepped around Micahel. His black eyes—lashless, top and bottom—narrowed in his long face. *The arm. What happened?*

Micahel touched his elbow with his left hand. *Shattered,* he grumbled. *Went through a glasteel window. They just fused it down on Second South.*

Pity, Polar sent blandly. *Ending that line would've made a dramatic opening statement.*

Micahel glared up at his trainer, then frowned across the desk at his grandfather.

Eighty years ago, Eshdeth Shirak's father had made a critical discovery. Though most of the Ehretan Sentinels still called themselves a chosen people, they'd altered their names when they agreed to use the Whorl's trade language. The ancient Carabohd family became Caldwell. Hiding, probably, but the unbound starbred found them. Their mythical significance made them splendid targets.

I matched your record, at least, Micahel sent. *And raised you two female bystanders.*

"How?" asked Shirak.

Four out of five, with clean head shots in their sleep. Micahel's cheek twitched.

Dull, Polar agreed, *but permanent. And the fifth?*

Micahel smiled sidelong at Polar. *Young, unbreached, and alone, with her family dead. I had time to force her mind open and show her what I'd done. How I intended to finish.*

An answering smile spread across Polar's long face. *Ah,* he sent appreciatively. *Lend me the memory someday. Especially how she reacted.*

Steepling his fingers, Eshdeth Shirak frowned. "Never forget," he said, "that this family doesn't really threaten us. Striking there simply impresses the faithful."

But someday, Polar answered, *when the last of that family lies cold in his grave, that won't simply end their idiot hope for a messiah. It will prove that their so-called god never existed.*

Micahel squeezed his left hand into a fist.

Polar's determination to disprove old theology puzzled Eshdeth Shirak. He couldn't bring himself to care about Ehretan religion, with its blood memories and unintelligible prophecies.

On the other hand, they'd sent Micahel to Thyrica to prove himself, not to enjoy himself. "May we assume you missed the younger one?" he asked. "The Master Sentinel?"

Of course. The one who's trained in self-defense.

Ah well, Polar projected mockingly. *Did you muddy your tracks?*

Micahel managed a smile. *Remember Paxon, who was thinking about defecting to their camp?*

Shirak frowned. *That's not something we forget.*

I left him under deep command, to wait a week and then attack the college.

That, at least, met Shirak's approval. The Sentinels' College at Arown had the largest number of Sentinels anywhere, except for their impenetrable sanctuary. Every Sentinel dead left the Whorl safer for Shirak's immortal, unborn great-grandchildren.

And if Paxon survives, Micahel added, *he has my memories of that night.*

Then if they catch and access him, they'll think the murderer's in custody. Polar quirked an eyebrow. *This with a shattered elbow?*

Micahel squared his shoulders.

"With that," said Shirak, "your family is pleased."

But I have news. Micahel's epsilon sense darkened. *Master Caldwell's woman is already pregnant. With twins. And I missed her.*

Shirak groaned. Pregnancy was an unspeakably vulgar topic. "Then you could've left them three males, not one."

What happened at his house? Polar demanded. *What went wrong?*

Micahel rested his chin on his left hand and shook his head. Plainly he wished Polar hadn't asked. *The woman was awake and out of their room,* he sent at last. *She roused him before I could get him under command.*

Polar stroked his long face and taunted, *Undone by a breeding woman. Shame, Micahel.*

Micahel glared.

Polar raised his head and stared sideways, up at the ceiling. *Wasn't she Netaian royalty?* he asked, seemingly out of nowhere.

"Why would that matter?" asked Shirak.

Netaia, Polar projected. *Recite, Micahel.*

Their student turned toward a transparent tank near Shirak's desk. Inside, an arch of shimmering stars mapped the local Whorl, which trailed its arm of the galaxy in slow rotation around the hub. Without gesturing, showing off a new epsilon skill, Micahel swept a blue indicator dot off their own golden pinpoint. He drove it counterspinward toward a pale yellow star near the Whorl's end. *Netaian system,* he projected. *Absorbed by the Federacy only last year. Twelve planets, two colonized, with three deep-space modules in orbit nine. Two subjugate "buffer" systems,* he added, flicking the dot side to side. *And yes, Director. Mistress Firebird was born to Netaia's ruling matriarchy. One of three sisters, all named for native or historical birds.*

Shirak smirked. "Provincial fancy-bred."

Polar stopped stroking his face. *That wasn't my point. Weren't we in touch, decades back, with one of our own who made planetfall on Netaia and was stranded there? I think she was Casvah family. I know she wanted medical attention for her daughters.*

Shirak shrugged. He worked with the long plan—with the future, not the past. Non-Federate worlds didn't interest him.

Polar switched to vocal speech. "We offered treatment if she would come here, but her last communication said one of her daughters had married royalty, and they had decided to stay. We lost touch with the line."

"A lost Ehretan family?" Shirak pursed his lips. "Adiyn will want to discuss this." The City's chief geneticist had mapped all known Ehretan chromosomal lines. Could they be sure, though, that the Casvah genes still survived, though mingled with local royalty? Shirak made a note to alert his Thyrian agents and the newer ones on Netaia.

Micahel half closed his black eyes. Wounded pride throbbed in him. *I won't disappoint you again.*

"You nearly succeeded," Polar said with unusual generosity. "And you survived the attempt. You'll get another chance."

"Don't fixate on a superstition," Shirak warned Micahel, adding an epsilon nudge for Polar's sake.

"Meanwhile," Polar said, "Caldwell has a new weakness, a pregnant bond mate. We could exploit this and bring in new genes with a simple kidnapping."

Director, Micahel interrupted boldly, *Grandfather—stop thinking like old men. For decades, you've held back, just because there are few of us.*

For good reasons. Polar glowered.

Shirak glared too. They tended to distrust their strong-willed young people. Maybe Micahel would benefit from a year's exile to one of the settlements.

Micahel stood up. He walked to the star tank and stretched out his uninjured arm, as if seizing the Whorl. "Let me hit their college," he said. "Hard. If we started a real fight with the Sentinels, most Federates would trip themselves backing away. They'd abandon the Sentinels like plague carriers. They only half trust them anyway." He held up one finger. "Give me one real attack ship. I'd turn it into a dozen, and those into more. Paxon's feint won't close the college. Every Sentinel trained is one more fighting us." It was the inverse of Shirak's dictum, of course.

Polar eyed his student. *He's fixated, all right. But why not let him try? Tallis might abandon the Sentinels. If it turned on them, that could clear our road straight to Regional headquarters.*

"It's not impossible," Shirak admitted. Breaking up the Federacy would end its ability to defend single worlds. Shirak's son Modabah, administering one of the City's outlying settlements, would enjoy creating several plans of attack.

Polar gripped Micahel's left shoulder. *All we have to lose is Micahel, a few ships, and a few—you weren't thinking of recruiting from the City, were you, Micahel?*

No. The young man's epsilon sense turned sullen. *Settlements.*

We'll talk. Polar gave him a friendly shake.

"Dismissed." Shirak waved a hand. "Congratulations." Micahel hurried out.

Dru Polar sat down on Shirak's desk, hung a leg over its side, and sent the indicator spark spinning around a remote star system, high over the galactic plane: Ehret, the devastated world where their forbears had created genetic telepathy.

Shirak secured his epsilon carrier and wrenched away the spark. Under his direction it whizzed back down into the Whorl, past Thyrica and the Sentinels' sanctuary in the Procyel system, to circle Tallis. "Don't let him strike too hard, too soon," he reminded young Polar. "The armory team isn't ready, and neither are our people on Tallis. Our fathers—your grandfathers—lost their chance to take Ehret because we weren't yet invulnerable—"

"We lost it," Polar interrupted, "because the unaltered cretins resisted. They destroyed it."

"Anger and revenge are fine in your students, but control them," said Shirak. "Don't let Micahel waste too many lives. Not even from the settlements." Until the armory team created impenetrable personal wear, few City adults would venture off Three Zed. No sane, mature person would waste two potential centuries of life on a hazardous mission.

But Shirak remembered his impetuous twenties. He'd tasted a helpless victim's terror. His pass at the Carabohd family had eliminated Master Brennen's granduncle.

Casvah, rejoined with the Thyrian remnant? Juddis Adiyn would be ecstatic. He often ordered heredity lines recombined by his reproductive technicians, hoping to produce new abilities in the next generation. A "lost" line could contain untapped gene sequences, more precious than any jewels. One skin cell, one drop of blood, would give him a gene sample. An intact specimen would yield better data.

Mistress Caldwell, or a relative...

"We can spare a few out there." Polar gestured toward the nearest settlement. Any truly promising youngsters would've left the settlements to be trained in the City. "I'll keep Micahel reined in. He deserves another chance to launch this campaign. He's my top student, and your grandson."

Shirak activated the sonic massage unit built into his chair. "Very good. Send him to recruit in the settlements, send him offworld, and stand back. But don't interfere with our long-term goals, friend. It's certainly vital to take the Federacy, but not to thwart the birth of some mythical future messiah."

• • •

Brennen followed Damalcon Dardy into Corporal Claggett's underground office at the Base One complex. Claggett and Cristod Harris, a military instructor from the college, were pouring hot cups of kass when Brennen entered.

Seven days had passed since the murders.

Harris was a small man of cocksure stance. He laid a hand on Brennen's arm. "I'm terribly sorry about Tarance and his family. How's your mother?"

"She left yesterday for Kyrrenham." Brennen frowned. He'd passed through shock and anger into a new stage of grieving. Whenever he thought of her, his heart and mind silently challenged the Holy One. She'd mourned his father for years. He felt she deserved better.

"That spiritual retreat south of Peak?"

"Her cousin works there."

"And how are you?"

Instead of answering aloud, Brennen diffused his outer shields and looked into Claggett's eyes, then Harris's, again offering full access to his emotional state.

"True," Claggett murmured. "Those four simply awakened on the other side. What an easy way to make the Crossing. And Destia is past all pain now."

But his mother was not. Did she need so much refining?

He restored his shields. "We should begin. Thank you for including me."

"It was time you joined us." Dardy rolled out a wide hardcopy diagram on Claggett's desk. "If you're going to try setting a trap, you'll need this. It's an experimental technology we've named RIA," he said, pronouncing it Ree-a, "Remote Individual Amplification. It's not on record, except for this sheet, because it mustn't be tapped by the Shuhr under any circumstances. So far as we know, they haven't discovered that this feedback cycle can be operated by a single individual."

At the Federacy's Regional command center on Tallis, before his dismissal, Brennen had been a respected Special Operations intelligence officer. Now he coordinated procurement and training, serving as a liaison among base, college, and Federate-service Sentinels. Dull work, especially after Special Ops, but he embraced it. Now his punishment for disobeying an order kept him near Firebird—and soon, his children.

He eyed the schematic. Generally, a Sentinel working alone could sustain an epsilon wave no farther than a room's width away. Brennen could achieve twice that, but he would love to extend his range.

"Harris discovered it," Claggett said. Harris smiled slightly at the acknowledgment.

Brennen reviewed the P and P Codes, which he constantly refreshed in his trained memory. He couldn't find any clause that banned extending their working range. "But it's not on any file? Have you kept this secret from the Federacy?"

Harris and Claggett exchanged dubious glances. Claggett frowned slightly. "For now," Harris explained, plainly uncomfortable.

Then they disagreed. "Is that wise?" Brennen asked.

"I'm surprised to hear you say that." Dardy raised one eyebrow. "After they expelled you."

Brennen clasped his hands. "I disobeyed an order. Even though I did that to follow my vesting vows, I expected to be disciplined." When he'd done that, he'd dashed Dardy's hopes—his own, too—to see a Sentinel rise to the Federate High command at Elysia. After ten years on the fast track, he'd had a legitimate chance.

Claggett thrust one hand into a hip pocket. "We're determined to keep this from the Shuhr. That's all."

"I would think so," Brennen murmured. "This has weapons potential." He leaned closer to the schematic. "Show me how it should work."

At that instant, something touched the back of his mind. He whirled away from the schematic and seized the distant quest pulse before it extinguished, then rolled it in his memory, examining its nuances, trying to identify the source. He knew every Sentinel on Thyrica.

This had come from none of them.

He turned back around. Dardy still studied his diagram.

Did any of you feel that? Brennen demanded subvocally. *Quest pulse.*

Dardy raised his head. Claggett and Harris exchanged alarmed glances. "No," Dardy exclaimed.

"Then he wasn't looking for information," Brennen said.

"No." Dardy pointed at Brennen. "He was looking for you." Brennen touched a control on Claggett's data desk. "Central," answered a bland voice.

"Security alert," Brennen ordered. "We may have a Shuhr agent on base."

5

DAY STRIKE

rinforzando
sudden, short crescendo

Brennen keyed Claggett's com over to college security. He knew the woman who answered. "Carola. Possible Shuhr intruder on Base One. Is my apartment secure?"

"I'll post a guard," came the crisp reply.

"Two, if you have them."

"I'll see if we do."

Harris strode out the door as Claggett secured his documents. Dardy stood glancing from the door to Brennen, hesitating until Brennen sprinted after Harris. A feminine voice droned through the passway speaker. "Stage One alert. Possible intruder. Secure classified data. Stage One alert..."

Harris stood holding the lift. Brennen beat Dardy and Claggett inside it and pushed the emergency switch. The door almost caught Harris's foot as it shut, then the cubicle ascended at knee-straining speed toward the ground-level command center. When the doors shot open, Brennen hurried across the clearing area. A smoked glasteel roof curved overhead.

Command and Control, a cliffside room, was walled in the same smoky glasteel. Barely glancing at the awe-inspiring sea view, Brennen strode to the main wall of projection screens and controllers' stations. The base commander, Major General Stieg Moro—a small, florid Thyrian in his fifties—frowned over a controller's shoulder.

A slender young man with a sparse but neatly trimmed beard sat at the number one controller's station. He looked puzzled. "No intruder in this structure," he said.

General Moro wore a row of service and honor ribbons down his left sleeve, the "thread tracks" of a distinguished career. Brennen's thread tracks would have been just as long, but military Sentinels wore no decorations or rank insignia. "I'm having security double check," Moro greeted him. Unlike some nongifted Thyrians, Moro worked well with Sentinels. "Why did you give the alert?"

"Quest pulse," Brennen began.

An angry voice from the main speaker panel interrupted him. "Com One, this is Hangar Two. I've got two MPs down, apparently dead, and an unauthorized startup of one of the FI-2s. Send backup."

A hijacker, inside a hangar full of deadly intercept fighters?

As the bearded controller answered into his collar mike, General Moro scanned the main screen for local air activity. "Scramble the MPs. Have we got a flight up?"

"No drills scheduled until fifteen hundred, sir." A second controller fingered his touchpanels. "Flight Six is in ready room."

Brennen's wartime instincts awoke as if he'd never left Veroh, his first major command. Launching a fighter element would take twelve minutes. By then, that FI-2 could threaten the nearby city of Soldane.

Moro scrambled Six anyway. Brennen stepped back and tried to outthink the intruder. The immediate risk: that he would double back to attack the base and anything that scrambled to pursue him. Evidently Moro thought so too, because his next order raised the alert level, along with full particle shielding. The intercept fighter still could escape, but nothing incoming would penetrate. No missile, no suicide pass.

Now. Try stopping him inside the hangar.

As if he and Brennen were thinking in tandem, Moro turned to his second controller. "Stage Three," he ordered. "Lock us down." Then he leaned on the console. "Status, Hangar Two?"

The controller relayed. Brennen stayed at the second controller's shoulder. "Give me a visual for Hangar Two."

An interior image appeared at eye level. Ten night black intercept fighters stood side by side. Nine cockpits hung open, already prepped for afternoon drill. The third FI-2 from the right had been closed down. Heat rippled from its laser-ion engines, and Brennen spotted a dark helmet moving inside its cockpit. Near the hardened hangar's main entry, two military policemen lay motionless.

He grimaced. The intruder had penetrated the base—not difficult—but he'd also breached a guarded hangar and keyed in the ignition code sequence for an FI-2's generators. Those codes were classified.

His next thought made his neck hairs stand up. Besides the hijacker, there could be a traitor among base security.

Sunlight shone through the hangar's massive main door. Brennen leaned over the controller's shoulder. "Shut down," he ordered. "Contain him."

"Can't" came the answer over the com. "Circuit's disrupted or something."

"Try manual," Moro barked.

The FI-2 rolled forward. A man's figure dashed toward the fighter, drawing his service blazer. He couldn't beat that ship to the main door. Instead, he dropped to a firing crouch behind a power cart and targeted the landing gear.

The FI-2 kept rolling. The second controller caught Brennen's eye. "Flight Six on its way to Hangar Four, sir. Should be airborne in nine minutes."

• • •

Firebird glanced up from her data screen, surprised by a midday knock. It would feel good to stretch, she decided. She walked to the main door and checked its passway monitor. A surprisingly tall, broad-shouldered young man stood just outside, brandishing an ID disk labeled "College Security, Benj Rasey" in his outstretched palm.

As promised, Brennen had installed the secondary security system as soon as its hardware arrived. That door wouldn't open unless she or Brennen touched a control and simultaneously spoke up. The master room had an additional security layer. "Yes?" she asked, keeping her hands at her sides.

The young man raised both eyebrows. "Mistress Caldwell, there's an alert out at Soldane, at Base One. Possible intruder. Nothing's happening here, but I've been asked to stay at your door until I'm given the all-clear. Just didn't want you worrying if you looked out and spotted me."

"Oh." She glanced back at the table. She'd been deep in sociopolitical-economic machinations, surprised to find herself starting to grasp several key concepts. She'd always despised bureaucracy, but every time she ran another simulation, she hoped to find something that might save her people from a bloodbath. College and base security were light-years from her mind. "Thank you, Benj," she muttered. She switched off the passway monitor, turned away from the door, and plodded back to the servo table.

Curious, she canceled her connection with Soldane University and punched up the base's public activity channel. Instead of its usual welcoming animation, a geometric pattern filled the inset screen. Three lines of text announced a Stage Three alert in progress.

Firebird's pulse quickened. *What in Six-alpha?* Stage Three was battle status!

• • •

Brennen watched the largest screen, which displayed an aerial grid of the Soldane quadrant. A threat-red speck swooped out over Kyrren Fjord, north of the base. The bogey's long turn took it back toward populous Soldane.

Moro's florid face paled. This was a base commander's nightmare. He'd just alerted public-defense authorities.

Hangar Two reported again: the hijacked fighter carried no missiles, but its laser cannons were half charged. Moro tried to communicate with the unknown pilot. He got no response.

Brennen glared at the screen. If a threat carried bombs or missiles, an intercept anywhere—even over a population center—would be top priority. In this case, he would try not to intercept over a city. The fighter, not its weapons, posed the greatest risk.

The red speck overflew Soldane, still accelerating. Someone behind Brennen said, "Soldane's safe." It headed inland, aiming for the cleft in the tall, jagged Dracken Range, where air and ground traffic passed through.

Inland. Arown.

The college!

Brennen turned back to General Moro. "Sir, I need an inland line." General Moro gestured him to the vacant third controller's station.

As Moro alerted other land and ice bases, Brennen keyed for college security again. The same operator answered. "Carola," he said, "there's a hijacked intercept fighter on its way toward you. Get the particle and energy shields up. Can you evacuate?"

"ETA?" she asked.

He eyed the map screen and took his best guess. "Thirteen minutes."

Her voice rose. "No. Can't evacuate that fast. We'll call shelter drill. "

"Good." Double shields should keep the civilians safe, even from a suicide dive by this size ship, and the underground shelters would provide extra protection. But if Security had a traitor, the college's shielding couldn't be trusted. Base and college shared security staff.

"Carola," he said, "one more thing. Extra security around the shielding generators."

"On its way, General."

• • •

Firebird's blue screen went red. Out in the passway, an eerie klaxon started to whine. Moments later, black letters filled her screen. SHELTER DRILL. REPORT TO UNDERGROUND SECURE AREA. DO NOT DELAY. USE STAIRWELLS, NOT LIFTS.

She tried a general search. The communications net appeared to be down.

Someone pounded on her apartment door. "Just a minute," she shouted. She pressed to her feet, crossed the small living area in four steps, and seized her clairsa from alongside the lounger. If anything happened to that handmade instrument, she could never replace it. She shoved it into its long, triangular hard case.

Then she had a second thought. Benj Rasey, college security, could be a Shuhr agent. They were here, and they had no mercy. She buckled on her dagger's new forearm sheath and tugged her sleeve down to cover it. Then she hurried to the door, pressed its entry control, and said, "Open." The Security man stood with one hand on his shock pistol. "All right," she said, "I'm coming. Are the other apartments alerted?"

"That's what the siren's for. I'm supposed to get you downlevel."

"We can take ten seconds and beat on some doors," she exclaimed. Another door slid open. A tall, nightrobed woman with craggy features blinked down at her. "Shelter drill," Firebird called. "We have to go downlevel. Use the stairs. Anyone else in there?"

"No. My husband's at the med center."

"Good. They'll get him to a secure area. Come on," Firebird said. Young Benj opened the stairwell's manual door. Firebird glanced at the time lights on her wristband. Two minutes had passed.

• • •

Is that new RIA unit operational? Brennen shot the thought at Corporal Claggett.

Claggett stood several paces back, with Dardy. He shook his head.

Behind them, the deck had started to fill with base staff on extended kass breaks.

Moro snapped at his controller. "Full speed, then. Get it into range. We can't shoot down over traffic."

Brennen followed Moro's glance. On the worldwide forces map, one heavy cruiser orbited far south and slightly east, out over the ocean. The cruiser, *Lance*, had electromagnetic catchfield capability. Its normal orbit would've taken it far west of Soldane, but it had shifted course. If they could get it into range, it might snag the hijacker out of midair, no matter how thick the cloud cover or how low he flew.

He? Brennen canceled that assumption. The last time he called for a catchfield, the enemy's young suicide pilot had been female, Netaian, and of royal blood. Shuhr too came in both sexes.

The controller called over his shoulder to General Moro, "Intercept range, eight minutes, forty seconds."

Brennen's shoulders sagged. With the hijacked ship still accelerating, its ETA at the college had dropped below six minutes.

● ● ●

Firebird's breath came in gasps by the time she had lumbered down two flights of stairs, but she kept going. Benj caught up at the third floor above ground. Leaning on his arm, she hurried through a dark blue blast door into the underground shelter and looked around, panting. He pulled her toward the nearest bench and tapped a man on one shoulder. The stranger looked up and instantly offered his seat.

"Thanks," Firebird mumbled. Twin pregnancy was humbling. She looked helpless, and she knew it. She'd rather be out there in the danger zone, fighting at Brennen's side. "Here," she said to Benj. "Give me that."

He handed down her clairsa and stayed close. Firebird concentrated for half a minute on breathing deeply. Meanwhile, her mind raced. Why had the college been sent underground, why was the net down, and why weren't they being told why? Something had to have happened at Base One. A missile launch botched, a satellite malfunctioning? An attack from space?

Brennen. *Protect him, Mighty Singer! He's your faithful servant, and Thyrica needs him. I need him!*

The brightly lit duracrete shelter looked to be a quarter-klick long, with a double row of benches up its center and bunks along both sides.

Its ceiling curved in a strong-looking half cylinder. It felt hot and close, or maybe that was just her.

The nightrobed woman stood nearby, crossing her arms and glaring around. Firebird spoke up. "I'm sure he's as safe as we are," she said, taking a guess.

"Where's yours?" the woman demanded, making a good guess of her own.

"Soldane."

"This isn't a drill, is it? Something's wrong."

"It's a strange time for a drill," Firebird agreed. She drew a slow, deep breath. If this was another attack on her family, she'd unwittingly endangered hundreds of people by moving to college. Base housing had been considered safer from heavy attack, and the college was safer from infiltration. They'd chosen with both administrators' blessings.

Mistakenly?

This would be her last pregnancy, she vowed. She hated feeling helpless and defensive and responsible.

She looked around the shelter, abruptly realizing she was somewhat responsible for these people too. A year ago, at Federate Veroh, she'd waited groundside for an attack from space. But that had been a military base, defended by Federate squadrons. These were civilians.

Somewhere close, a child wailed. Firebird leaned forward and poked Benj's broad shoulder. She motioned him out between the benches, beckoned him to bend down, then murmured in his ear, "All right. What's going on? I want a report. Why isn't anyone talking to us? Don't you have interlink?"

His eyes widened, then his smile crinkled sideways. "That's right, you were military."

"Yes, and my husband's on base." She said it softly but firmly. Spotting a little local-band interlink on his belt, she reached for it. It was probably off-net. "Come on," she urged. "Get us a report."

He drew it, thumbed it on, and spoke softly. "Rasey in Unit Five. What's up?" Then he held it to his ear. His eyebrows pulled together, then down. His arm dropped. "College just lost particle shielding," he whispered, "and there's a hijacked intercept fighter on its way in. ETA four minutes."

Appalled, Firebird stepped away from him. She glanced around. No particle shielding?

Maybe the hijacker wasn't headed here.

And maybe skitters will sprout finny wings and fly.
A baby kicked. Hard.

• • •

Brennen held his breath as he tracked bogey and cruiser.

"*Lance* can't make it," the controller muttered. He'd done the calculations three times.

Brennen clenched a fist. A cruiser might exceed theoretical max speed, but only with enough advance time to shut down nonessential systems and gradually accelerate. Over his head, the scrambled Thyrian fighters finally roared above the dome and banked eastward. They couldn't catch up, either.

Three minutes, twenty seconds. He'd been decorated for creative thinking under pressure. *Help me now,* he prayed in deadly earnest.

• • •

"Don't let me fall," Firebird snapped at Benj. Seizing his shoulder with one hand, she hoisted her right foot up onto the bench.

"Wait," he protested, "you can't—"

She pulled hard against his shoulder and lunged forward, then up onto the bench. Her momentum almost carried her over its other side. Benj grabbed her hand and steadied her. She waved her other arm, shouting, "Listen! Hey, listen to me." A few voices quieted.

A piercing whistle shrieked near her feet. Startled, she glanced down. The nightrobed woman lowered her looped thumb and forefinger.

Firebird shouted into instant silence, "Listen! This isn't a drill. Take cover. Get back under those reinforced bunks along the walls. That's one reason they're here. They're the strongest points in any shelter. Don't hurt each other, but don't waste time. And don't argue," she added. "I've had some emergency experience." She hadn't given orders since Veroh. To her relief, the shelter's murmuring occupants parted down its center and moved toward its sloping sides.

"Now," Benj growled. "You get down. Carefully."

Firebird's legs wobbled. Ten flights of stairs, carrying this load! Master Spieth was right about her sense of balance. She let Benj and the woman steady her down, then snatched her clairsa case and hurried to an empty stretch along one rounded wall. Feeling as awkward as a fighter carrier in atmosphere, she sank to her hands and knees, then eased down onto the cold duracrete. She wormed sideways under a bunk, dragging her instrument behind her.

Then she had time to imagine herself lying there, buried under tons of rubble, breathing dust.

She spotted an interlink speaker. Why hadn't topside broadcast to them? Had a line shorted, or did topside have worse problems?

Her forehead felt sweaty again. Her ribs itched. One of the twins shifted gear from slow punches to flutter kicking. *Mighty Singer, protect my children!* Not far away, another child whimpered. Firebird guessed this would be an awful memory for that youngster.

Benj Rasey rolled in alongside her.

"You're safer along the wall," she said. "Isn't there room back there?"

"Yes. But if this thing collapses, you're safer if I can help hold up the slab."

"Thanks." She grimaced at the notion. She hated her next thought, but she couldn't afford to reject it. Benj had acted kindly, even aggressively protective, but he could still be a Shuhr agent. She loosened her dagger in its new sheath and pushed her back against the rough wall. *Brenn, whatever you're doing, do it fast!*

• • •

"Base One to *Lance*," Brennen transmitted. General Moro had just authorized an experimental tactic. "Catchfield on narrow beam, max range. Tug that bogey off course."

"Roger. Narrow beam."

Brennen stared at the Dracken Pass screen.

"Look!" The second controller pointed. "He's drifted."

Lance's catchfield had pulled the hijacker south, barely off course. "He's correcting, though," Brennen observed. This seemed to be an experienced pilot, but maybe—he hoped—not quite experienced enough.

"*Lance* to Base One," said the distant voice. "We have low-grade intercept. Bogey's pulling north and groundward to maintain vector."

"Right," Brennen murmured. He'd pulled against catchfields, flying combat. It felt like compensating for a strong crosswind… but crosswinds rarely died as suddenly as a catchfield could be switched off. Let the pilot assume *Lance* really was trying to haul him in.

Raising his voice, Brennen directed, "Hold intercept until I signal. Then cut catchfield. Stand by."

"Roger that."

"Good idea," Dardy said softly. Brennen hadn't realized he stood so close.

"What?" a junior officer whispered loudly. "What's he doing?"

Dardy stepped back. "The bogey's trying to maintain his course by steering hard against *Lance's* catchfield. The field's pulling him up and south, toward *Lance*. He's got to steer north and down to hold his course. But if they suddenly shut off the field—"

"Now," ordered Brennen.

On screen, the red blip bumped north... and vanished. "*Lance*," General Moro called. "Bogey down?"

"Confirm," said the distant voice. "Bogey down. Getting a smoke plume."

Thank you. Brennen's shoulders sagged with his relief. He covered his face with one hand. Someone gripped his shoulder. Someone else cheered.

"Any sign of a chute?" Moro asked.

"Negative, chute," the voice answered. "No sign of evacuation. Looks like a kill."

6

CONDEMNED

mezzo forte
moderately loudly

Firebird waited behind their apartment door as Brennen strode up the passway late that afternoon. Spotting him on the monitor, she hit the door control and exclaimed, "Brenn!" He lunged through, caught her in both arms, and held tightly.

Benj had gotten the all-clear after five minutes under those bunks. Firebird helped reassure scared children and their anxious parents before taking her turn in the crowded lift. Master Spieth sent a courier ten minutes later with a new prescription, some foul-tasting syrup to prevent early labor.

She and Brennen stumbled together into the apartment, still holding each other. He hit the door control. Then he kissed her fervently, pressing hard against her body. Little limbs pushed back.

After a minute she relaxed, and they fell away from each other. She headed for the servo table, pushed aside the snack she'd been munching, and touched in a triple order.

"The pilot's name was Paxon." Brennen followed her. "Emil Paxon. Recent arrival, allegedly from Tallis."

"How in the Whorl did he get an FI-2 into the air?" Firebird knew about security checks, military police, and generator code sequences. This implied a terrible security breach.

"We don't know." Brennen sank into the opposite chair and pushed hair out of his face. Sweat stains marked his tunic. "I stayed long enough to supervise deep-access questioning of every security tech on base. Everyone there came up clean. There are still two to check, but they're off duty today."

"Will they check college people too?"

Brennen pursed his lips. "Same crew. It was beyond coincidence when you lost net and shielding here. Both base and college have gone to heightened alert. They'll stay that way until further notice." He rested his arms on the table, then laid his head on them. "There's one thing I don't understand," he mumbled. "It takes six days for a messenger ship to reach Three Zed. Their leaders couldn't have found out that the original attack failed, in order to command Paxon to try again. Not for five more days."

An exquisite smell drifted out of the warmer slot, distracting her. "Go back to that access questioning," she said. "Remember, I hid things from you under access, back at Veroh."

"Possible." He pushed up off the table. "But only if a subject's extremely strong. There's usually some sense of resistance."

He talked casually about advanced interrogation techniques...

And I still haven't even started learning! she grumbled silently. It was high time she took that last qualifying test. "Aren't Shuhr supposed to breed for epsilon talent?"

"That's only a rumor."

She stared at the digital timer over the warming slot. Ninety-three seconds until dinner. Ninety-two. Ninety-one. "Maybe," she said, "you just proved it. Who's our sec tech for this building?"

"Harcourt Terrell. He was the first one suspected, but the first to volunteer for access. I checked him myself."

Brennen had been the Federacy's top access interrogation specialist. If he hadn't found deception, no one else possibly could.

But just as she'd felt Benj Rasey was no threat, she doubted this Harcourt Terrell. He made such a logical suspect. "Please don't count him out. Keep an eye on him."

"We will."

"Do you suppose," she asked, "that Paxon was our... the murderer?"

As Brennen's eyebrows lowered, she felt the deep rumble of his anger. He too must've stared at the newsnet image of an FI-2 burning on a boulder-strewn slope, inky smoke turning white as the first flames subsided. "I hope so," he said. "If he was, he's no threat now."

• • •

Firebird plunged back into both sets of studies the following day, and the next. On the third, she reported to a tiny, bare cubicle across campus and recited into a monitor for two hours.

The college didn't keep her waiting for the results. Immediately, the test administrator sent her to an office in the same building.

A woman answered the entry alarm. Thin, arched eyebrows almost vanished under her wispy bangs. *What a lovely woman,* Firebird observed. Was she fifty? On second thought, she must be younger... possibly by quite a bit. Sentinels couldn't use youth-implant capsules, which most Federate citizens carried under their skins from early adulthood. An implant released synthetic hormones that forced aging and mutating somatic cells to replace themselves, but by bitter coincidence, that process attacked the genetically altered ayin complex. As a wastling, Firebird had never needed an implant.

"Mistress Caldwell," said the woman, "come in. I'm Janesca Harris."

Firebird followed the Sentinel inside. She reached up out of habit to flick hair over her shoulder, but she'd tied it back today, like she used to do when training for battle. "Good morning, Sentinel Harris."

"You may call me Janesca, Firebird. Congratulations on passing your first memo exam. First of many, I'm afraid—if you're sure you want to proceed." Beneath slightly drooped eyelids, Janesca Harris's clear brown eyes pierced with a brilliance like Brennen's.

"I'm sure." Firebird glanced all around. The office looked out on the college quadrangle, where knife-edged shadows scuttled across the wet jujink lawn. On an interior wall, in Janesca's meter-cube aquarium, primitive green proto-fish slithered between pink and yellow creatures that looked like pompon flowers.

Her stare caught in one corner of the room, where a triangular stringed instrument sat on a wooden stand. "Oh," she exclaimed, "is that a kinnora?" She'd heard of the Thyrian small harp, but she hadn't hunted one down. She'd been sightseeing while she could, studying what she must, and turning the beautiful house on Trinn Hill into a home.

She missed it already.

Sentinel Harris picked up the dark instrument. "Most visitors ask if I play or if it's just for decoration." She strummed the colorful strings with one fingernail. They rang together in a sweet, sustained pentatonic sweep, with no jarring minor seconds. "I understand you're a harper too."

"I've played since I was eight. It's the only thing I owned on Netaia that I still have. I play for the boys when they kick." Firebird stroked the loose skyff she'd put on.

Janesca motioned her toward a simple kirka-wood chair, then pulled a dark blue bound volume off her shelf. No common scanbook cartridge, it matched the Code book Firebird had studied. "Before I issue this," said Janesca, "I must administer a sekiyr's first oath. Our abilities carry grave responsibility. Are you ready to hold yourself accountable to the college and its masters?"

"Of course."

"You understand the consequences if you ever use these skills selfishly? This is your last chance to back down without consequences."

"I understand," Firebird said soberly. "Brennen and Ellet Kinsman both explained that misuse is a capital offense."

"Very well." From a closed compartment, Janesca drew a dull gray object that looked like a dagger hilt. Firebird recognized an Ehretan crystace, the Sentinels' ceremonial weapon. One touch on its activating stud, and sonic waves would bombard the ehrite-shard blade inside that hilt. Two of the blade's axes would elongate, stretching it to arm's length.

"Place your hand over mine on the crystace," said Janesca. Grinning, Firebird grasped the older woman's hand. She loved ceremony. Most Netaians did. Still, she didn't lean too far forward.

"It's a simple vow," Janesca said. "Repeat as I do. 'This is my vow, to use only in the service of others, in obedience to the holy Word, any skills that I learn in this training.'"

Firebird followed phrase by phrase.

"This is the crystace with which I shall keep my vesting vows, if my skills and compliance satisfy my masters."

Firebird felt her eyes widen. Her own crystace? She'd seen Brennen's, even held it and swung it. But her own!

"This is the crystace..." Janesca spoke on, her eyes more solemn. Firebird repeated the words. "...they shall sheathe in my heart, if ever, defying this oath, I use Sentinel skills for capricious or selfish purposes."

Firebird's hand tingled as she echoed the final clause. That was a risk she felt willing to take.

Janesca returned the weapon to her wall compartment. "Congratulations," she murmured. "Never take that oath lightly. It has been done."

"I understand." If Brennen could keep these codes, she could too.

"Well!" Janesca handed her the midnight blue book. "Read the first subheading."

Firebird took it with trembling fingers. Inside, her new name—Firebird Mari Caldwell—had already been scribed on the coverleaf in a flowing, feminine script. Seeing that, she warmed even more to Janesca Harris.

• • •

One. P'nah, The Turn.

The release of mental energy onto a modulated epsilon carrier presupposes an ability to identify and locate epsilon energy and to separate it from background sensory imagery. Turning inward to sense one's self at the primal level was originally considered the best way to begin. Beyond oneself, though, other powers exist, some good and some evil. Proceed with prayerful caution.

At the moment before falling asleep, when thought is stilled, there occurs an inward-chasing of the mind's natural pattern that will lead in sleep to dreams. To consciously follow that chase inward, to sense the energy arising in one's own ayin complex, has proved a practical beginning for this course of study.

• • •

"Ready to try?" Janesca asked.

Firebird didn't quite understand. "What exactly is turning?"

"It is a preparatory mental posture. The epsilon energy we use is already present in certain locations in your nervous system. You must learn to sense it before you can use it."

"I see."

"You'll learn to take this listening, or turning, or grasping stance quickly and smoothly. Then, once you can maintain the turn, you'll learn to control, then project, the wave of epsilon energy."

"Right." Firebird closed her eyes. Determined to succeed, she relaxed toward sleep—or tried to.

The next hour surpassed any day spent with her sister Phoena for sheer hellish frustration. Though Janesca encouraged and offered suggestions, the simple act of mindfully listening inward seemed utterly impossible. Thoughts of food—she'd forgotten to eat while studying (she couldn't face the traditional Thyrian fish breakfast these days, anyway)—new concepts she'd studied, and even the sun playing hide-and-search outdoors all took turns distracting her, though once she thought, almost...

Her leap toward the odd momentary sensation brought her alert and drowned out the faint touch with a chorus of mental comments.

Exhaling, she let her head droop. "Relax," Janesca said. "Rest."

Firebird pulled the soft tie out of her hair. This was unbelievable. The simplest, most basic mental gesture—and she couldn't make it. This would go on her record. She longed to conceal her failure. *Not in this enclave, you won't!* ...And she would have to tell Brennen first, when he came home tonight. That would dent her thickheaded pride. The college's character examiners had warned that she faced a lifelong battle against willfulness, impatience, and pride. She'd gone home that day feeling branded. Tattooed. Brennen hadn't comforted her when he confessed that he too had been warned... of ambition and overconfidence in his abilities.

Pride, one of the Powers, had been drilled into her as a virtue! It still drove her to always, always excel. "Was any of that even close?"

"No," Janesca said. "Like mind-access, it's a specific sensation."

She compressed her lips. "How will I know when I get it?"

"I'll tell you."

"I can't study, can't practice at home."

"Not until you can do this. If you have time at home, start studying the second Code book."

"I'll try again," Firebird insisted. "Once more."

Janesca spread her hands. "I'm sorry, but we've gone past your time. Come tomorrow at eight hundred. Bring your... clairsa," she suggested. She must've found the instrument's name in Firebird's vita. "I've worked several girls through their first turn with music."

• • •

Firebird had barely stumbled back into the apartment when its entry alarm rang again. Startled, she set down Code book Two and took a deep breath. This didn't necessarily mean another attack. Actually, with her thoughts looping around and around, inventing excuses for her failure, she would appreciate a distraction.

On the passway monitor screen appeared a woman wearing quicksilver gray.

Federate messenger service! College security would've scanned both the messenger and her parcel. Firebird sent the door open.

"For you, Mistress Caldwell." The woman handed her a short metal tube. "Prepaid."

For decades, faster-than-light ships had provided the fastest communication over interstellar distances. Firebird laid the roll on an end table and read the source, then shook her head, disbelieving. It had come from Citangelo, her home city. Had another Netaian month passed already? This would be her monthly summons to return and answer charges of high treason, heresy, and sedition.

She leaned against the windowbar and stared out at another Thyrian rain shower. She stood charged with high treason because—very much against her will—she had survived her first and only military mission... and her interrogation.

Heresy? Essentially, Netaians worshiped their government as the Powers' elect presence. Captured during Netaia's attack on Federate Veroh, she had watched her navy slaughter civilians—and in her grief, accepted asylum. Later she had taken Federate transnational citizenship... and by defecting, betrayed the Powers.

They added "sedition" to her charges when she and Brennen—acting against Federate orders—thwarted her sister Phoena's deadly plot to restore Netaian independence. She had killed a researcher... accidentally, but who on Netaia believed that? Instead of charging her with simple murder, they had included that in the grave sedition charge.

She was guilty of all these "crimes." What charge would they add when they learned she was pregnant? That news would arrive on Netaia momentarily, because of the Shuhr attack and the police report.

Angry—that simply by living, she had become a high criminal—she curled up with her new Code book and the first half of lunch. Netaia's electors might've discreetly celebrated if Emil Paxon had killed her and dozens of others.

Such electors deserved to be overthrown. She should just ignore that message roll...

But she couldn't. As minutes passed, she stole one glance at it, then another. In Citangelo, where it originated, formal gardens along the palace's white marble façade would be bursting with early summer's white, scarlet, and gold blossoms. In back, the private lawns would lie like sun-washed carpets. She'd taken dry weather for granted there! She had loved to run barefoot down slope toward the reflecting ponds, flipping somersaults whenever no electoral redjacket followed to make sure she maintained her dignity.

Lady Firebird Angelo, queen's wastling, had tried passionately to serve Netaia, to contribute by life and by death to its glory.

And she'd killed a man. A nobleman, whose wastling children she'd known, and whose father publicly praised her...

Tears blurred her vision. She glanced out the window, upward this time. Shredded gray clouds raced overhead. A hundred klicks north, it was probably snowing. Brennen's soaking wet world was lovely and lush, but it would never be her home.

Pregnancy hormones! Aching, she seized the message roll and twisted its seal.

A bound bundle of hard copy dropped out. Its heavy cover displayed her own scarlet-and-gold family crest, a shield with three stars, above the gold electoral seal. This was no summons, but a legal transcript. The electors had finally tried her *in absentia*.

What was the verdict? she wondered, though she could guess. She flipped past pages of legal exposition to the summation.

• • •

Charge of high treason: guilty as charged.
Charge of heresy: guilty.
Charge of sedition: guilty.

• • •

Surprise, she sighed silently. No elector would defend a royal wastling for obeying her conscience... and by their definitions, she was unquestionably guilty. She'd even committed one more crime, which they'd never proved. She had helped a fellow wastling escape offworld.

She paged backward. Her sister Phoena's name appeared in several places, testifying against her and even suggesting they reopen the old investigation of Lord Alef Drake's disappearance. Her oldest sister, Carradee—married to Alef's brother—had presided but said little.

Firebird turned to the end, oddly nervous. Had they sentenced her? To death, of course. By a sadistically tidy execution protocol known as lustration, in the largest available public venue, should she ever re-enter Netaian space.

She swallowed hard. *No chance of that, noble electors!*

Lustration was an old word meaning "purification," and the sentence was reserved for the apostate. Beginning with fingers and toes, the condemned prisoner's extremities—and, eventually, torso—were compressed by slowly moving metal plates superheated to vaporize flesh and bone. Lustration could last for hours, giving the prisoner ample time to atone for her heinous crime... and maybe to recant.

Nauseated by the thought, she spotted a loose sheet of writing paper and held it up to the rainy daylight. Occupation Governor Danton had exercised his prerogative and granted a full pardon, though he recommended that she not return until the noble electors rescinded her sentence.

Thank you, Governor. Sadly she rerolled the papers. Her fellow electors would never do that.

She whacked the windowbar with the bundle, slapped tears off her cheeks, then compulsively reopened and reread the sentence against her. It carried the official seals of both Crown and Electorate. They'd even forced Carradee to sign it.

She must learn to belong among Brennen's people, or else belong nowhere for the rest of her days. Why should this hurt so much? As a wastling, she had lived under a death sentence all her life.

But in only a few days, Netaia would celebrate Carradee's official birthday, on the same date when all queens had been honored. Last year, the palace's first-floor ballroom had rung far into the night with music and giddy gaiety. She and her fellow wastling, Lord Corey Bowman, had whirled in each other's arms until neither could stand upright.

Corey had died when Netaia invaded Veroh—turned instantly with his tagwing fighter to fusion fire.

Firebird straightened her weary back. She wouldn't cry anymore. Her past had died with Corey, and she lived for a future that would include her sons. Someday—soon!—she would master that epsilon turn. Seizing the code book, she opened it back to chapter one and read, *Shielding in the Presence of the Nongifted: In Service....*

7

PHOENA'S CHOICE

quasi maestoso
almost majestically

For Phoena Irina Eschelle Angelo, the final hours of the queen's birthday had always been the highest point of her year. Tonight, the main palace ballroom—floored in black marble shot with gold—was curtained with Angelo-crimson velvette swaths. Bas-relief portraits representing all nine holy Powers observed from the gilt-crusted ceiling, while life-sized gilded statues of historical electors watched over furniture groups from their periods. Phoena had dressed in her finest. Tonight she would dance with every nobleman on Netaia, young and old, from all ten noble families, receiving their homage. This year the Queen's Ball honored Phoena's sister instead of their mother, but that changed nothing important. Nor did the slightly jealous new husband who hovered nearby with friendly words for her other dancing partners.

She and Count Tel Tellai had married in splendor two months ago. Tel was an elegant little husband, well dressed and well mannered, with a passion for Netaia that almost matched her own, but beauty must be shared, or it would wither. Phoena's honeyed complexion made men blink and stare. She could unnerve the most noble duke with a flicker of hot brown eyes.

She shook out her gold-toned sleeves and took the thin arm of Baron Reshn Parkai. At the far end of the ballroom, below triple ranks of jeweled chandeliers, a fine orchestra filled the dais. Tonight, the Netaian aristocracy ruled a crowd sprinkled with only the best-connected commoners, and not one uniformed Federate was in evidence. Tonight this did not look like an occupied world.

The orchestra played superbly. A pity Firebird couldn't hear it, Phoena observed as she took the baron's half-gloved hand. Music affected her wastling sister in baffling ways. It altered her moods and brought out a perverse inner strength. No rightful heir or heiress had been safe from scornful glances when Firebird lived on Netaia. Obviously, Firebird had hoped to displace Phoena in the succession. She would have tried if she dared, but that crime carried terrible consequences.

How satisfying to know she wouldn't return. With the grim sentence passed, Phoena could finally put Firebird out of her mind. Though she would willingly witness the lustration, she'd voted for lethal injection. Firebird was positively terrorized by needles.

Traitors' executions weren't horrendous just for deterrent value. The more a criminal suffered while dying, the shorter her agonies would be in the horrific Dark that Cleanses, where all evil was purged from offenders' souls before passage was granted to eternal bliss.

Phoena and Parkai bowed correctly to one another. A line of trumpeters strode forward through the orchestra and assembled on the dais steps. Their fanfare called the crowd to assemble and toast Carradee Second.

Phoena summoned her dainty-faced prince with a crooked finger. They joined Carradee and Prince Daithi on a platform near the conductor's podium. Servitors in scarlet livery circulated hastily, balancing goblets on gold trays. As tradition decreed, the queen's future would be saluted by nine people, and then Carradee would answer. Phoena, asked to toast, had declined. She explained to Carradee that any woman would rather be praised by a man than another woman!

And Carradee had believed her. "Carradee the Good" and "Carradee the Kind," Phoena had heard her called.

Carradee the Federate Toady, Phoena pronounced to herself. She loathed insincerity. She couldn't have wished Carradee a long reign.

First Lord Bualin Erwin knelt at the foot of the dais. "It is my sublime privilege..."

Phoena gave her nails a quick buff on her sleeves and displayed her public smile. She knew how to feign gracious interest. Beside her, Tel straightened the fringed formal sash of his new rank by marriage. After the debacle up north eight months ago, Phoena had been forced to arrange repairs to Hunter Height and pay costs from her personal accounts. Then she'd been threatened with a further investigation, as Occupation Governor Danton pressured Carradee for details of Phoena's research. Phoena had needed to distract Carradee. Tel obliged by proposing the wedding.

She eyed her sister. Carradee, tallest of the three Angelo sisters, looked radiant, though she wasn't known for her beauty. Why tonight? It couldn't be the simple blue gown, though that set off her pale gray eyes and camouflaged her tendency to carry an extra kilo or two (or five). Nor her conservative sweep of blond curls. Even with a full staff of servitors, Carradee showed no imagination in clothing or hair. But tonight she wore the delicate Iarla crown, a confection of goldstone and ruby-set arches, and she looked glowingly happy.

It would be lovely to be queen at the Queen's Ball, standard bearer for holy Authority and the three Netaian systems. Phoena kept smiling, but she ached with jealousy. Last year, she'd reached for power and missed. Pacified by Phoena's insistence that she never meant to take the throne—only to help liberate Netaia from the Federacy, which they both wanted—Carradee had apparently forgiven her. But another chance might come, so Phoena had endured her month of house arrest with Tel's devoted help, paid her fines, and then turned back to guiding the secret loyalist movement. One day they would throw the Federates off Netaia.

Carradee rose in her turn, elaborately thanked each person who had toasted her, and drained her glass. Then she raised a hand and signaled the orchestra to wait. "One other thing," she announced.

This is it, Phoena observed. Whatever had Carradee so tickled, it was about to come out. Phoena shook her shoulder-length chestnut hair, which tonight she wore in perfect waves, each lock beaded at the end with a cluster of emeralds. Tel flicked imaginary dust from his black sateen jacket. He too understood the importance of appearances. He had the makings of a very decent portrait painter, and he'd landscaped exquisite gardens at the Tellai estate before she had moved him into the palace.

"We have the privilege," Carradee continued, clasping her short-fingered hands, "of making an announcement no other queen in the history of our great people has made. We do singularly feel the honor, the delight, and the hope that this is only a foretaste of years ahead, as Netaia takes its rightful place among great systems of the Whorl."

Hmm. Well put, for Carradee.

Carradee's gold-jacketed Prince Daithi remained at attention, with his brown curls for once slicked smooth, as Carradee slow-stepped along the dais's edge. "In recent weeks," she continued, "we have been forced into difficult, even impossible decisions."

At the reference to Firebird's death sentence, Phoena narrowed her eyes. She regained her composure, but now she listened suspiciously.

"Yet our great world has entered a new age of great thoughts, great deeds, and great hearts," Carradee insisted. "And so, noble electors, gentlemen and ladies, we rejoice to tell you this. We have received news from

Thyrica, where our youngest sister, Lady Firebird, now lives in enforced exile. Although we have decreed that she may not return, we ask you—our good guests—to rejoice with us on this festive night. Lady Firebird expects a child in less than two months."

For five seconds, if a greenfly had landed somewhere in the ballroom, every partygoer would have heard it. Never had a wastling gone so far. Sacred Disciplines barred even Phoena, as the second-born, from bearing children unless Carradee died without issue... and she had two young daughters.

Other faces showed shock, or disbelief, or delight that was quickly concealed, but Carradee beamed. Then a wave of sound splashed banner-hung walls. Everyone started to speak at once.

Except Phoena. Scandalized by Firebird's new crime against the heritage that should have meant more to her than life itself—should've ended her wretched life almost a year ago—she stood motionless until Carradee reached her and spoke softly over the clamor. "Phoena, I tried to reach you alone, earlier, but you were at the tresser."

Phoena crossed her arms and frowned severely. Tel kept still, as he should. This was an Angelo concern.

"She can't come back, Phoena. You saw to that. Evidently they were trying to keep this a secret, but—"

"I should think so."

"It came out in a newscan. She and General Caldwell were attacked in their home."

"But?" Phoena leaped to the disappointing conclusion. If they'd come to grief, Carradee would have made a graver announcement.

"No, no. They weren't hurt."

"I'm sorry to hear that."

"Yes! One should be safe in one's home." Carradee seemed, or pretended, not to understand. "Phoena, listen to me. Insofar as the Crown is concerned, you and Tel are welcome to have children of your own too. If you and I stood together, I am sure we could persuade the other electors to establish a kindlier law of succession. No other culture practices heir limitation. No estate is worth preserving at such a cost to our beloved children. I truly believe that. Don't you?"

Phoena wanted to shriek, but commoners would hear. Carradee Second, this monarch, this head of the Electoral Council—this Federate puppet!—approved Firebird's apostasies. She offered a chance to commit similar crimes with impunity. Had she too lost all honor? All sense of Strength, Valor, and Excellence... and how about Fidelity? Resolve?

Authority! Those Powers, and all the others, glared down from the ceiling.

Once again, Carradee proved that she didn't deserve to wear that arching, jeweled circlet—with the extra chins it gave her—nor any other crown.

"You'll see what I believe," Phoena answered in a low voice like poison.

Carradee backstepped, wide-eyed, and finally signaled the orchestral conductor. As he directed the opening chords of another dance medley, Phoena gathered her skirts. She whirled from the dais, trailing Prince Tel behind her. Dancers dodged as she strode across the marble floor.

She had almost reached the crimson-curtained doors when a tall man stepped into her path. She glared into his eyes for an instant.

Bowing apology, he ducked aside. She swept out the doors.

• • •

At three hundred that morning Phoena lay awake, irritated to the core by Tel's soft, regular breathing. In privacy, he'd admitted he felt glad for Firebird.

Glad! The little slink!

How could this be happening? Power was slipping away from Netaia's rightfully ordained nobility, the only rulers who could govern with justice and far-future vision. Three centuries ago, outworld invaders had devastated Netaia. Only the noble class, undergirded by a dying religion they altered and revived for this purpose, had restored order and prosperity. Bound to obedience at all social strata, Netaia had achieved cultural glory.

Now, under the Federates, commoners lusted for rights that could undercut long-range justice, even for their own descendants. The Federates surrounded Carradee, poisoning her with low influences. Carradee had even appointed four business leaders—commoners!—to her Electorate.

Carradee had no backbone. If Phoena sat on the throne, by this date she might've thrown off Governor Danton and his minions... but Phoena couldn't challenge the militarily powerful Federates alone.

No, but by Ishma and Delaira and the littlest moon Menarri, she knew who could!

Shocked by the thought, she sat upright in her octagonal bed. Brennen Caldwell's colleagues supposedly had relatives who had never bowed to the Federacy. She'd never considered asking their help for the loyalist movement... until tonight. Why now?

Why not? Phoena wrapped long, bare arms around her knees and stared into the dismal future Carradee was creating. Prosperity, culture, and security would vanish from Netaia, unless someone made a bold move to save it all, to dare—and risk losing—everything that made life satisfying.

She must not leave Citangelo without taking precautions, of course. A pair of loyal house guards, a Vargan stinger—deadly, but easy to conceal—no, two stingers.

She threw off her silken bedcovers. Maybe no one else had the courage to do this, but in future years, Netaia's nobility would recall Phoena's choice and salute her with reverence.

In her private freshing room, she slipped into an unostentatious traveling suit, then gathered a few bits of feminine trivia for her shoulder bag.

Tel stirred on the bed, snorting as he flailed toward the warm spot she'd left empty.

She froze and waited for him to speak, but he rolled over again and sank deeper into sleep. She found a black coat. Somehow she knew exactly where she ought to go. Should she leave Tel a message with her personal girl?

No. He'd try to stop her, and she didn't want to be followed. He would realize soon enough that she'd left him.

And by all nine of the Powers, and for their sake—halting in the doorway, Phoena pressed one hand to the marble wall and vowed it—she would not return until she came home to be crowned.

• • •

By stealth and luck, Phoena left the palace grounds unobserved by her other house guards, by the Federates, and even by a team of Sentinel aides, whose watch was focused at that critical moment on partygoers leaving through the front gate. Two escorts followed her across the park-like lower grounds to a minor gate, unguarded but keyed to family members' palm prints. Without hurrying, she proceeded down a darkened, increasingly dangerous street into a neighborhood between landed estates. Footsore and shivering, she tapped on the tinny door of a ground-level apartment built from graying duracrete blocks, then glanced back up the narrow street. Neither Federates nor criminals had trailed them. Finding the entry alarm, she pressed it and held it down.

The door slid partway aside. "Yes?" an unfamiliar voice asked.

"My name is Phoena Angelo," she muttered. "Let me in."

As the door slid aside, Phoena stepped into a world she rarely visited, the realm of the low-common class. Two meters ahead, up a narrow hallway, shone a blinding yellow lamp. She caught a whiff of old grease and musty perfume and hoped her sense of smell would fatigue quickly.

She beckoned her guards to follow. One drew a shock pistol. The other kept both hands free.

Following this stranger up a worn shortweave carpet, Phoena saw a table and several padded sling chairs. One was occupied.

Penn Baker, a flabby-figured man whose eyes never stopped watering, finally introduced himself and then the lanky man with dark hair and bony cheeks as, "My host Ard Talumah, a traveling merchant." She recognized the long-faced man, a commoner. How was that possible?

On Baker's ceiling, she spotted the compulsory receiving grid, a hand-sized panel installed in one room of every low-commoner or servitor's dwelling. There was always a slim chance that Enforcement was watching or listening. For the first time, it worried her.

"Forget that." Penn Baker waved toward a tiny pyramid on his scarred tabletop. "Compliments of Talumah," he explained.

Phoena eyed the device. "Scrambler?" she asked. "If this room ever comes up for inspection, and there's no image—"

"There'll be an image," Baker interrupted. "Sound, too, with the sonic signatures of people who might actually be in the room. But repeating whatever was programmed ahead of time."

Impressed, Phoena frowned at the device. For now, she would use it. But when she returned as queen, she would eliminate such technology.

The floor rattled for several seconds, startling her. "Maglev train," Baker explained. "We're over the tunnel."

Talumah's stare amplified her unease. "You're offworld?" she demanded. "Here on business?"

"Call it that." Talumah's dark smile was almost a sneer. She decided to ignore him and deal with Baker. It took only a few words to explain what she wanted.

"Of course, I'll represent you to them." Baker rubbed his eyes with a pale hand. "I'd be honored. Who else knows you came to me?"

"No one. That is the only way to keep secrets."

"Well done, Highness." Talumah applauded insincerely with his fingertips.

"These men will come along." She gestured back at her house guards. "I would also appreciate your concealing my presence until I take a few further precautions."

"Naturally, Your Highness." Talumah unfolded himself out of his sling chair. To her surprise, he bowed reasonably well. "I would be honored," he said. "Deeply honored." As he stared, just longer than she would call polite, strange new thoughts tickled her mind. Really, why bother with extra precautions? The unbound starbred would value her as one of their own. She was welcome to bring honor guards, but the Shuhr would not merely respect her. They would revere her.

He smiled. Finally, she recognized him. He'd stepped into her path near the crimson-hung doors as she led Tel from the ballroom, shortly before she decided to go to the Shuhr.

• • •

Talumah left before sunrise. For four days, Phoena showed Penn Baker her public smile, wore borrowed clothing, and paced that stale-smelling hallway. Its duracrete-block walls were so poorly cured that flakes and even gouges had fallen, leaving holes that some previous occupant, amusing himself, had painted the precise shade of orange that represented Excellence—her personal favorite of the Powers—in Netaia's noble-class heraldry. She could've purchased her own ship ten times in four days, but Baker kept claiming he needed more time.

So she tracked the newsnets, none of which carried any word of her disappearance. Carradee undoubtedly was frantic, but afraid to advertise Phoena's disappearance. Not even the cheap channel, which had sunk to new lows of scandal and rumor under Federate governance, mentioned Phoena. Carradee wouldn't go to Federate Governor Danton until it was much too late. She would never know Phoena had hidden within a stone's throw of prestigious River Way, less than three clicks from the palace.

On the fourth evening, Phoena sat in one of Baker's sling chairs, idly watching an evening newsnet broadcast. Danton's spokeswoman claimed that the Federacy was paying fifty percent of the costs to rebuild Netaia's shattered planetary defenses. "Less than that," Phoena fumed. "My friends are selling off resources to pay his new taxes. This is a Federate ploy to disfranchise the noble class."

Baker snorted. "Selling off resources? I'd like to see you try to buy anything technical on my wages, with so many factories blasted away."

She sniffed. "No one's trying to rob you of your heritage. Your very identity—"

"You electors," he interrupted, "gave us the Veroh War. You brought the Federacy down on us. If the Feds only make you pay half to rebuild, that's generous."

"Shut up," she snapped. With one crosstown call, she could send him and all his family to Hinanna Prison.

"You'll see." He glared at the wall screen. "Someday, you nobles will see what your people really think of you."

Her cheeks heated. "Shut up!" she repeated through clenched teeth.

The next morning, when Baker slipped back into his apartment, he seemed properly subservient again. "Are you ready to leave, Your Highness? I've found a ship."

"Good." She sniffed. "I have made my arrangements. It's time we were gone."

She never thought to wonder where her house guards had gone, and she forgot the Vargan stingers.

8

GOLDEN CITY

energico
with energy

Phoena could hardly wait to debark from Penn Baker's six-person shuttle. Years before, Firebird had scornfully labeled her a "groundhog," and on this ten-day slip there were miserable, claustrophobic moments when she wished she too had adjusted to space travel. She hated the constant vibration in her body while the ship and every molecule aboard remained at right angles toward normal space—turned that way by the slip-shield, so they could exceed light speed. Worse, she gasped a little every time she remembered that light-years of vacuum sucked at the ship's shining hull. At any moment, something—some infinitesimal something—could end her mission, and no one would ever know where she had gone or why.

But here they were. She didn't spot her final destination until the last few seconds before landing, when with a pudgy hand Baker pointed to several incongruously smooth strips around an old volcano on this airless lump of a planet. "Shielded entries," he explained. "Not every lava tube on Three Zed is settled, but wait until you see this one." Then he busied himself at his controls. She couldn't understand the splatter of glowing panels on his display, nor did she care to. As inhospitable as that lava field looked, she would prefer solid rock to this flimsy, cluttered lifeboat.

An entry cracked open. They glided through. Penn Baker grounded the shuttle at the center of a small hangar with pocked black walls and said, "We'll pass through into the main bay when we have air."

The hangar darkened abruptly. She seized a grab bar. A second pair of smooth metal doors swept open beyond the shuttle's nose, and Baker followed a stream of light into the cavern.

A minute later, as Phoena walked down the landing ramp, she felt her first qualm about coming to these people. Her suit smelled musty. Their first impression would not be as excellent as she wished. But never mind; they shared a goal. Resolutely wrapping long fingers around her shoulder bag, she watched ten men approach between rows of service machinery under an irregular metal ceiling. Two of them stopped short of her. The rest, evidently service personnel, passed toward Baker's ship.

Phoena eyed the greeters. Both had wavy dark hair and cold, distant brown eyes in nicely masculine faces.

"Your Highness?" The one on the right barely bowed. He wore an edging of gold on the collar of his deep gray-green jumpsuit. It looked like a uniform insignia.

"Yes," she said. "I'd like to speak with someone in authority."

"Those are my orders." He gestured toward a metal door. Baker offered Phoena his arm. As she stepped out, the other greeter paced a few steps behind.

The door slid open. Phoena felt her eyes widen. Beyond the landing bay opened a long, straight tunnel that was roofed, walled, and floored in brilliant, nugget-textured gold. Delighted, she clutched Baker's arm.

He covered her hand. "Welcome to the Golden City," he said. A smile dimpled his pale cheeks.

Phoena tilted her chin, raised her chest, and strode forward.

The gleaming corridor branched several times, sometimes at right angles and sometimes into side passages that curved like tetter tunnels. At last they passed through a golden sliding door into a major chamber. Overhead, the ceiling vanished into an unlit distance. Beneath her feet opened a chasm whose depth she couldn't guess, but over it, a transparent floor of gray volcanic glass had been laid. Inset here and there on faceted walls of gleaming gold, gems and metal filigree sparkled in artful arrangements. A flowering vine clung to trellised supports nearby.

Phoena smiled. She could learn to be comfortable here.

Near a group of chairs, three men stood to acknowledge her. One, stocky and stubby legged, had puffy eyes and a crooked smile. The man who stood centrally was a head taller, broad shouldered, gray at his temples but otherwise impeccably blessed with stunning black hair. He gripped his wide belt with lightly furred hands.

The third man appeared closest to her age. As tall as the one in command, he'd grown his hair to a stunning shoulder length, and from collar to cuffs he wore brilliant sapphire blue, with a black sash belt. His eyes were black, and as she stepped close she saw that he had no eyelashes, top or bottom. Manly confidence streamed from him like a corona. She couldn't imagine a more stunning contrast to her spineless little prince of convenience.

"Your Highness, welcome." The man at the center spoke with a heavy, unidentifiable accent. "I am Eshdeth Shirak, director and Eldest of the Golden City. My colleagues, Juddis Adiyn, whose research continues to extend both our youth and our old age." The stubby man inclined his head, grinning as if she'd brought him a wonderful gift. "Testing Director Dru Polar," Shirak continued, glancing toward the one in sapphire blue. "Director Polar and his staff train our young people in what you would call starbred abilities."

Polar reached toward the vine and snapped off a fantastic bloom. Ribbon-like petals of pink, white, and gold cascaded from its furred purple throat. "Welcome, Highness," he said, offering the flower.

She took it graciously. In Lieutenant Governor Caldwell and his colleagues, those starbred abilities repelled her. In Polar, they drew her like a heady fragrance.

"Your presence on Three Zed honors us." Polar flicked one hand. Footsteps rattled behind her. Turning, she saw Penn Baker—whom she'd already forgotten—and the two greeters exit the cavern through a sliding door.

To business, then! Gripping the flower's stiff stem, Phoena spoke. "Gentlemen, let me introduce my mission without unnecessary formalities. I believe that we face a situation as intolerable to you as it is to me. My home world has been invaded."

"That would be intolerable," said Shirak. "Please, let us be seated."

Polar motioned her to the tallest straight-backed chair. Flattered, she glanced around as they all sat down. What a splendid use for jewels... always displayed, instead of hidden in dark treasure vaults.

Testing Director Polar addressed her. "But I fail to see why you think we would find your position intolerable."

She leaned toward him. "On Netaia, I lead a movement to restore independence, the same freedom your people obviously cherish, and with the same zealous spirit."

"And?" Polar prompted.

"There is more. But first, gentlemen, let me state clearly that I am no friend of the Federacy. Nor of Thyrica."

Director Polar smiled darkly. "You probably mean a fairly small Thyrian population."

"Not small enough," she said, clipping her words. "My youngest sister has married an ambitious man, who obviously means to use our royal heritage for his own gain."

Polar and Shirak shared an oddly intense glance.

"In doing so," she continued, "she has despised her nation and her family. She stands convicted on several capital counts, but we are unable to execute her sentence because of that man and the Federacy."

"Yet we hear that his family was just attacked. Reportedly, some of your people were responsible."

"I won't deny that," said Shirak. "I won't confirm it, either."

Excellent! "I've come to offer assistance."

Polar raised an eyebrow. "Oh?"

"Why do you hate her so, Highness?" Adiyn asked.

Phoena tilted her chin. "I hate no one. But she only pretends to revere our ways." Merely thinking about Firebird put an edge on Phoena's voice. "She is a rebellious, power-greedy child. She always thought she should've been born first, that she should be queen."

"Did she say so?" Adiyn's grin faded to a bland smile.

Phoena felt flushed. "I believe she did. Worse, she convinced others to say so."

Polar looked appropriately pained.

"We gave her everything." Phoena raised the bloom and sniffed its rich, royal purple throat, and then lowered it, disappointed. It gave off a putrid fragrance. "Comforts, the finest education, and best of all, the promise of eternal honor... but even that didn't satisfy her.

"She murdered one of my friends, A researcher," she added, glancing sidelong at the scientist Adiyn, "who was working to give Netaia a future, a weapon that might have restored our independence."

Polar cocked an eyebrow. "Murdered? Personally?"

"Shot him dead at close range," Phoena growled. "She is vile, gentlemen. Greedy, and faithless, and... and spiteful."

Shirak crossed his long legs. Soberly he stroked his chin. "Surely you would expect some favor in exchange."

His prompting made her bold. "Wouldn't eliminating her and her husband be its own reward?"

Shirak shrugged. "You have other desires."

"I mentioned the loyalist movement," she said, "and our desperate hope. But another sister stands between me and the throne. The Federacy has made Carradee a collaborator of the worst type. She must be removed from power. And her daughters—"

"How old?" Adiyn asked.

"Four and one. Innocent of any crime. Perhaps they could be assimilated into your culture. They are lovely girls. They would look charming in this magnificent city." Gesturing with the blossom so that its streamers caressed her wrist, she spotted a constellation of brilliant-cut diamonds—no, a galaxy!—set over Polar's shoulder in the golden wall. She tore her stare away. "I could give you information that would help you accomplish that too."

"Then we put you on that throne?" Polar asked dryly.

"I have no lust for power, gentlemen, but I am the only remaining confirmed heiress. I am both capable of ruling and truly loyal. In fact, our mother Siwann wanted to make me her heiress." Siwann had never said so in words, but she had admitted Carradee lacked the stern will of a monarch. "I am no murderer," Phoena added delicately, "but Carradee is gravely misguided. Something must be done. Quickly."

Dru Polar turned back to Shirak. Again she saw them stare into each other's eyes, and she abruptly realized they must be speaking mind to mind, excluding her. Shirak turned next to Adiyn. The frumpy man's grin broadened.

She frowned at the snub. "I have, of course, left messages." She detected a hint of slouch in her posture and corrected it. "If I should fail to return or send word within this month, Netaian calendar, the Federacy will be notified as to my whereabouts. They consider themselves obligated to guard my family."

Dru Polar stood and offered his right hand. She clasped it and rose, pleased that he didn't let go immediately. "We don't fault your measures for your own defense, of course," he said. "Unquestionably, we can reach an agreement."

She glanced at Shirak for confirmation. He dipped his chin, then said, "Let us discuss your offer and return word to you."

"Meanwhile," Polar added, "you must consider yourself my guest." She brightened, warming to him as he continued, "I shall have you shown to our best visitors' rooms, where you may rest while we discuss your proposal. And..." At last he dropped her hand. As his lashless eyes looked down into hers, she felt a sharp, compelling sensation she couldn't identify. He smiled with one side of his lips. "Thank you for coming, Your Highness," he said.

• • •

Phoena followed the gold-collared greeter down two levels to a suite that seemed small and stark after that high golden chamber. Its walls looked like silver, not gold, with a common, low white ceiling and gray shortweave carpet. Still, the narrow receiving room had such basic appointments as a comfortable lounger, and the inner bedroom seemed spacious. The lack of windows disturbed her, but compared with Penn Baker's ship, this was a palace suite. Obviously, her road to restoring Netaia's noble heritage lay through this golden city.

She wanted to bathe, but she had no fresh clothing. She searched a wall compartment in the back room but found nothing.

Surely the city had magnificent shops. She was Director Polar's personal guest. His hospitality would extend to discretionary credit.

As she crossed the silver sitting room, its door opened. A woman stepped inside—no, a girl. Brazenly voluptuous, she had a sullen face and long, straight hair that hung below her waspish waist. Phoena gaped at the hair. It was black at its roots, then yellow blond, and then red, in a repeating rep-tilian pattern. She carried her head with extraordinary poise for someone so young. "You'd like clean clothes," she said blandly. She signaled behind her with a hand controller. A service cart glided in. "Penn Baker says you brought nothing along. That was wise, if you wanted to vanish mysteri-ously. You are about my size." She looked Phoena up and down. "Director Polar asked me to lend you some things."

"Thank you." Phoena stood her ground for a moment, then realized the girl expected her to unload the cart. She reached for it casually, as though she'd anticipated no more. The first armload of formless blouses smelled faintly of strange sachet.

"Are you related to Director Polar?" Phoena asked between loads, when the silence became uncomfortable.

"We're all cousins of some degree. Why do you ask?"

"I noticed a resemblance." Phoena was so glad to find dresses in the second compartment that she said nothing about the striped-haired girl's impertinent familiarity.

"You look like your sister too." That tone of voice conveyed no open insult, but the girl's stare suggested she knew it would be received as no compliment. "My name is Cassia Talumah. I was born in Cahal, an out-lying settlement near here. Those of us who show particular talent are brought here to the Golden City to train. Why live anywhere else? We have the youth lab, the ayin extractors... and we set policies for all of this world."

Then this was a common power-grabber who must've learned Phoena was born to authority. Moving regally, Phoena transferred the last items onto the lounger. "You've already finished your schooling?"

"By your calendar, I graduated twenty-three years ago."

Phoena narrowed her eyes. "I think not."

Cassia slid both hands up her shapely hips. "Your mistake," she said, smirking. "I'll be seeing you."

Phoena chose a likely ensemble of pale yellow lace and then treated herself to a long, delicious vaporbath in the tiny freshing room. Once dressed, she decided to explore while the men finished talking. There must be other halls as exquisite as the one where they met her.

And had Cassia mentioned a youth lab? Could that girl possibly be in her thirties, or even older? Not even the finest implants would keep anyone so youthful.

Her receiving room's outer door had no handle, no visible control panel. Puzzled, she pushed it. It wouldn't budge.

She stepped backward, bumped into the lounger, and then sat down, fighting sudden alarm with reason. No doubt they would soon finish their council. They would want to be able to reach her immediately. Meanwhile, in the absence of servitors, she would put away her borrowed clothing.

A few minutes later, she heard footsteps and returned to the outer room. Testing Director Polar had entered. His loose blue shirt shone against the silvery walls.

"Well?" she asked, but his smile told her all she needed to know.

"We've accepted your offer," he said. "I am certain we'll value your help, as you value ours. We want everything you can show us concerning Lady Firebird, her personality, habits, and history. We need to be able to predict her most likely responses to several possible attacks. Then we'll evaluate Netaia and our approach to Carradee. You know Citangelo—the palace layout, the travel routes she and her children usually take."

"When I'm queen, you'll be able to keep a close eye on me as well, won't you?"

"We're not worried about keeping eyes on you. We'll have other concerns."

Mollified, Phoena took a seat on the long brown lounger. It felt harder than it looked.

Polar pulled over the smaller of two mock wooden chairs and sat down almost knee to knee with her. "Have you experienced mind-access before?" he asked. His smile looked faintly sensual.

Disgusted, Phoena slid away. "Director Polar, I have every intention of answering your questions. There's no need to make this an interrogation."

"I believe that, Your Highness." He reached for her hand. She drew it away, but he lunged forward and seized it. From the heat of his fingers, she realized that hers had gone cold. "But I do a quicker, more thorough job this way, and it won't hurt... badly."

She snatched her hand free and sprang to her feet, yellow lace fluttering around her. "This is unnecessary. I demand to speak with Eldest Shirak."

"Sit down," he said with a queer quiet tone in his voice.

Phoena found herself obeying. "How dare you," she breathed. He was enjoying this!

"I'm told your sister wasn't eager to be accessed when Caldwell first breached her. Cooperate, Phoena. Those are Shirak's terms. Do as we say, and we'll see you well rewarded."

The throne, she reminded herself. The Crown, the Federates banished from her home world, and that Fire-brat settled forever.

Gathering her courage, she raised her eyes to meet his.

• • •

Phoena came to herself lying on the hard brown lounger with a painfully empty stomach and odd twinges on her scalp and arms, but her awakening impressions were of peace and safety. She'd never known such contentment.

Cassia Talumah brought warm fruit-scented pastries, a hot cup of kass, and another exotic flower in a crystal chalice. Without even rising from the lounger, Phoena grabbed a pastry.

"Oh, Your Highness, one thing." Cassia reached around her striped hair to lay paper and a stylus on Phoena's end table. "Your husband must be worried sick about you. You should let him know you're safe."

The busty little snake was right. Poor loyal Tel would be frantic by now. "Thanks," Phoena said, lounging and eating without the slightest care for propriety. "I'll get around to it."

"Now," Cassia said.

Phoena sat up and reached for the stylus.

• • •

Carrying a recall pad and a full cold-case of tissue samples, Juddis Adiyn walked with Polar toward their apartments. "I think you were right," Adiyn said. "The preliminary scan is mixed-Ehretan."

"Congratulations." Polar kept walking.

"She's positively slavering to believe that we owe her a throne," Adiyn observed. "I never saw a mind more amenable to suggestion."

"Shef'th," Polar swore, "those Netaian implants have devastated her ayin. Of course she can't resist."

Adiyn smiled. Already, royal Netaia was Three Zed's new treasure trove. Baker's shuttle had carried crates full of trinkets from its museums and vaults, procured by Ard Talumah. Adiyn claimed a tiny necklace and bracelet set in graduated emeralds and flawless sapphires, crafted for some long-grown countess or duchess.

Evidently, Talumah had needed only one moment's encounter in a ballroom to set the hook of mind-manipulation deep in his royal prey.

"I'll have Terza map her cell samples today," Adiyn said. "Mitochondrial first, since that should be our Casvah line. Nuclear material will differ in the sister. Carabohd and Casvah," he mused aloud. "The good name has married the vessel."

"Sounds ominous."

"I'm sure they would like us to think so. Evidently the new mistress isn't helpless, even pregnant."

"She murdered a researcher." Polar mocked Phoena's words in a fluttering falsetto.

"Does this affect Micahel's plans for the college?"

"Not at all." Polar shrugged. "I only wish I could be there to watch."

"He's eliminating the unfit for you?" Polar smiled darkly.

"What if," Adiyn said slowly, "General Caldwell comes here?"

Polar glowered. "Have you foreseen that?"

Adiyn adjusted his hold on his sample case. "So long as Netaia is under Federate protection, so is the royal family. They wouldn't dare assign anyone but a Sentinel to try to rescue her. I can see them sending him."

"Possibly," Polar said. "He's been overconfident before."

"It's on two branches of the shebiyl," Adiyn declared. He had a special talent, exceptional clarity in glimpsing the elusive shebiyl. It was a set of branching, alternate paths that the future might take, and studying it was an epsilon skill their Sentinel counterparts swore not to use. They called it *keshef*, sorcery.

Their loss.

Polar transferred his recall pad from one hand to the other. "If he comes, don't waste him on Micahel."

"You want him... for your antipodal fusion work?" As always, Adiyn considered the colony's research programs before endorsing anyone's license to kill.

"Yes." Polar drew out the word's sibilance. "Absolutely."

9

DABAR

vivace
lively

With only a month left before her due date, Firebird's energy level dropped daily. She'd been in excellent shape eight months ago. Now, young and strong though she might be, simply staying mobile took most of her strength.

At least she wasn't confined to bed. This morning, on one of Brennen's days off work, he joined her downlevel for exercise. She missed their training sessions with her new dagger, but she couldn't change directions quickly anymore. Now she had to settle for a long, slow daily walk.

Since it was pouring—again—she trudged around the housing complex's training room, doggedly counting laps by opening her fingers one by one on Brennen's arm, reminiscing...

• • •

Brennen had circled to his right on the springy blue training mat, blanking all expression from his face. Even matching her slower reaction time, he executed the footwork of Carolinian dagger play with a classical dancer's grace. She would've loved to sit down and just watch him.

Playing along usually raised her spirits, even on legs that ached from carrying too much weight, but this time, she had stepped out of stance. "Oh Brenn, maybe not today. Somehow I can't bear the thought of blood." She didn't even like eating meat these days.

"Mari." He crouched. "There won't always be a shock pistol handy. You'd get no second chance in a confrontation. Trust me, if I'm in danger..." He gave her a one-sided smile. "I'll react."

He lunged. Automatically she dodged, surprised by her body's quick reaction to his dulled training dagger, even now. She swiped for his arm but missed. Instantly he spun and cracked her forearm with his handgrip. "Come in *short*." He glared. "That Netaian sword thrust will get you killed."

• • •

Sighing, she sank down onto a bench and puffed out a breath. "I'm a barge," she muttered. "A tanker."

"You are my beautiful bond mate. And Spieth says you're still too small."

"I'm trying to gain weight, Brennen. She says the babies are big enough—I'm just small."

"You want to be able to nurse them," he reminded her.

"Yes," she grunted. "I do." She rocked forward, preparing to stand up.

"Caldwell!" called a husky, disembodied voice.

Brennen hustled toward the door, peered at the passway monitor, then reached up. As the door slid open, Damalcon Dardy stepped through. "Hello," Firebird cried, unashamedly glad to have company.

Then she caught Brennen's unease. Evidently Dardy had already shown him that this was no social call. She leaned back again andtook the weight off her legs.

Brennen snatched his sweater off the floor. "Should we go uplevel?" he asked Dardy.

The big man shrugged. "You're not in danger. It's just bad news."

He strode toward Firebird, lifted another bench, and pulled it out into the room. He sat down facing her. Brennen joined them.

"How bad?" she asked. Her arms felt clammy.

"Your sister Phoena's missing again."

Firebird relaxed slightly, relieved it wasn't worse. "Has Governor Danton checked Hunter Height?" Absently scratching her breastbone, she gave Brennen a wry look. Phoena might be conducting weapons research again. Danton would have to rein her in without their help this time.

Dardy frowned. "He found traces right there in Citangelo. We're afraid the Shuhr are involved."

She drew up straighter. "Evidence?" Brennen asked.

Dardy shrugged. "She wasn't declared missing until eight days after she vanished. Two house guards disappeared about the same time, and at first they were suspected. Danton's people, working with your Enforcement Corps, finally picked up several hairs in a dust tracing outside a recently abandoned apartment."

Leaning forward over clasped hands, Brennen frowned. "Whose apartment?"

"Recently reregistered to a Penn Baker." Dardy eyed Firebird as he spoke the name.

She shrugged. She'd never heard it.

"Netaian born. Low-common class. Took up offworld trading early this year—and then moved in with a roommate," he said. "A trader we've watched with concern."

Shuhr, she understood. But why—

"Mazo syndrome," she exclaimed softly. That condition Master Spieth had diagnosed, which robbed her family of male heirs, occurred only in Ehretan descendants. "Could they have gone after Phoena once they knew about our Ehretan genes?"

Dardy crossed his muscular arms. "Possibly. Or they could want ransom. For now, we're assuming she was abducted. They found no trace of the guards."

"There are thousands of ways to hide a corpse," Firebird muttered. A voice at the back of her mind taunted, *If they're trying to hurt us by harming Phoena, they've got a surprise coming!* Still, she shivered. So many had died: Corey, Baron Parkai, Destia...

"No evidence she was injured?" Brennen actually sounded concerned.

"No blood. Debris analysis said she'd lived there for several days."

Brennen exhaled sharply. "What's been done to protect Carradee?"

"Everything short of putting her under protective custody, like you two. At least until we confirm some kind of motive."

Firebird stared at her aching, sandaled feet. Protective custody? She'd never guessed how desperately she loved open spaces.

Later that night, she lay staring at the ceiling over their bed. If Phoena were dead, she'd be immensely relieved. All personal torment aside, Phoena would've killed millions, even billions of innocent civilians with the fruits of her secret armament research.

But what if she wasn't dead? What if they made her cooperate with the attempt to wipe out Brennen's family?

Why was that woman even born? she challenged the Singer. She had no trouble believing Phoena's soul was tainted!

Brennen rolled over. "Want help getting to sleep?"

"Sorry." Firebird sighed. With a telepathic husband, she couldn't lie there and brood. "No. I'm finished. Good night."

• • •

Phoena's hosts showed her their spotless armory center, squired her out to the weapons testing facility, and let her tour the tunnels devoted to biological research... and several bioformed zones with ecosystems that were so stunningly complex she almost forgot they lay underground... but she never grew tired of her gray-walled rooms. Meals arrived on schedule, and intriguing visitors came to call. This morning, two stepped through her door.

"Welcome!" Juddis Adiyn, the frumpy geneticist, she already knew. He'd visited several times. Who, though, was this tall young man with the strongly cleft chin? He virtually radiated the holy Powers of Strength and Indomitability. She motioned both men toward her lounger and remained standing on the shortweave carpet, showing respect.

"Micahel asked to meet you," Adiyn explained. "Princess Phoena Angelo of Netaia, this is the Eldest's grandson, Micahel Shirak."

The Eldest's grandson? No wonder! And he'd asked to meet her...

Wouldn't Dru be jealous?

"Will you be Eldest someday?" For an instant, Phoena wished Adiyn would get up so she could sit down beside this comely Shuhr prince. Then she remembered her new manners.

"In a century, maybe." Micahel ran a hand over the short black curls that she ached to touch. "We never wish death on our Elders."

"I should think that you..." How odd. Her mind had gone blank.

Micahel crossed his long legs. Stretching out both arms, he sprawled on her brown lounger. "I had a close call with your sister," he announced. "Recently."

Phoena felt her eyes widen. Had Micahel already eliminated Carradee? Was it time to start planning her coronation? "How splendid—"

"Your younger sister. Vastly pregnant." Micahel pantomimed a huge belly with both arms.

Deflated, she demanded, "Where?" She didn't want to even think about Firebird. Thinking about her *pregnant* was almost pornographic.

"On Thyrica. Briefly. I'd just come from visiting her brother-in-law."

"Caldwell has a brother?" That hadn't occurred to her, but surely even a monster could be related to someone. Some of the Powers admittedly showed in his actions. It had taken Strength to escape her at Hunter Height—but now she had allies. And yes, she'd heard something about an assault.

"He *had* a brother." Micahel half smiled.

"Oh?"

Adiyn clasped both hands around his knees. "Micahel made a productive visit to Thyrica. General Caldwell lost his only brother, his sister-in-law, two nephews, and a niece."

"Micahel!" Phoena exclaimed. "I must introduce you to Carradee." She stepped forward, intending to offer her hand for a kiss. Halfway to the lounger, she realized they wouldn't want that. And she must please them.

But she'd learned that they felt her delight. They must have come just to give pleasure… and feel it. "How did you deal with this brother of his?" she asked eagerly. "And why did you bother?"

Micahel laced his long fingers, straightened his arms, and stretched his hands. She imagined him holding a weapon and liked the idea.

Wouldn't Dru be jealous?

"My family and Caldwell's have a history that might surprise you," he said. "My grandfather killed all but one male in his line. My father took his three uncles. This was my turn."

Phoena sighed. "Pity," she said. "You didn't quite finish the…"

Blank.

She tried again. "I wish you success in finishing, sir." She inclined her head in respect. "Have you ever considered visiting Citangelo, Micahel? I'll return, one day—"

Blank again. Longer this time, and deeper. For several seconds, she stood flicking her borrowed skirt, trying to recall what she and Adiyn had been discussing. She only remembered the favor she'd asked him the last time he came. "You promised to read my future," she prompted. "I'll pay for your services when you take me back to Citangelo."

He blinked his odd little eyes. "Highness, I'll tell you what I've seen gratis, because it amuses me. Of course, what I read might not happen. We see possibilities branching in all directions."

He'd tried to explain the shebiyl concept. She found it tiring. One future, that's all she asked. A grand one. "But you saw a destiny? For me?"

"Oh yes."

His nameless young escort, already forgotten, uncrossed his long legs and stared at him.

Phoena clasped her hands behind her back. "Long life?" she asked, smiling expectantly.

Adiyn answered in a flat voice. Simply, "No."

Phoena cocked an eyebrow, wishing she hadn't asked... yet this possible future might not be all bad.

"Neither will you be happy," Adiyn added, staring up into her eyes, measuring her reaction. Evidently she didn't look frightened enough to amuse him, because he pressed the point. "Never again, unless we choose to deceive you. Would you like to know how you will die?"

"I think not." Rattled despite her Resolve, she glanced toward the door that led to her private bedroom. A strategic retreat. "Thank you for the information," she said firmly. "I'll use it wisely..."

Blank.

"Of course, Princess," Adiyn exclaimed, spreading his hands. "You may expect to live long and well. Haven't we begun your longevity treatments?" Beside him, the young man winked.

She didn't remember any such treatments, but with her mind blanking so often here, she must take Adiyn's word for it. She inclined her head graciously. If only she could remember the younger man's name! She'd like to see him again. Judging from the wink and the way he stared, the feeling might be returned.

Wouldn't Dru be jealous?

"I also foresaw plans for your coronation," Adiyn said. "Grand plans. Very grand."

"Ah," she exclaimed, smiling down at... Micahel. That was the name. "I'll make sure you're invited," she told him. "And you." She glanced at Adiyn.

"Imagine how long you'll reign," Micahel suggested. "We live two hundred years, and you are still young—"

"And a glorious death," said Adiyn, "in the name of the greatest cause possible."

Phoena tilted her chin and smiled at Micahel. "I am not ready," she answered, "to speak about dying."

• • •

Benj Rasey escorted Firebird back across campus from another fruitless, frustrating, virtually pointless session with Janesca Harris. She flung her rain cloak over the lounger, stomped to the kitchen's servo unit, and programmed one of the few lunch options that didn't include wretched Thyrian fish. After washing it down with Spieth's foul syrup, she shoved her dishes into the washer, cleaned up in the tiny freshing room, and then dug into a moving crate she still hadn't unpacked.

Phoena could rot in the Shuhr's deepest dungeon for all she cared... and today's second nap could wait. She had a dream to chase.

She'd tried last week to reschedule her formal consecration, but Brennen's mother begged another few dekias' reprieve. Firebird had honored that plea. It moved her to belong to a family that cared for one another.

But as of today, she'd finished waiting to hear those Caldwell prophecies. In Path instruction, she'd learned a little of Ehret's ancient language and how to use a tutorial scanbook.

Willful, she reminded herself. *And impatient.*

Deep in the crate, she found the scan cartridge. She loaded the cube into her bedside scanbook. Then, clutching the flat viewer, she marched back out to the servo table.

Brennen's unadorned copy of *Dabar* stood on a shelf close by. She often stumbled out of bed to find him already dressed, sipping a cup of kass and reading this. Last week he'd said, "Listen to this, Mari," and translated a long lament, a plea that the Speaker might explain why evil men flourish... then destroy them. Some nights, he read to her in bed and then settled in to pray. She was learning almost as much about the Singer from Brennen's prayers as from his books. Once, she'd rolled over at midnight to find him still praying.

Mattah, the newer holy book, had been translated into Colonial. She'd studied it with her Path instructor. Path instruction only outlined *Dabar,* though. Publishing that volume or any part of it in any other language was forbidden. She still didn't understand why.

She sighed, then yawned. *So much to learn, so many questions.* At least now she felt confident that answers existed. As an inquisitive child, she'd pored over Netaia's written Disciplines. She had found little she could grasp, except that the government must be obeyed. The rest seemed like double-talk.

The difference, she realized, was that this God truly existed. He touched everything, unlike the distant Netaian Powers. His mercy had washed away her guilt over betraying their false, legalistic religious system.

She opened Brennen's light-bound volume and laid it beside her scanbook. *Dabar* contained twenty-two books of prophecies, some with over thirty chapters. Setting her chin on one hand, she paged backward and forward. At several places, Brennen had made faint marginal notes in Ehretan.

She selected a marked passage, switched on the tutorial's memory option, then painstakingly started keying in phrases.

Several minutes later, these words gleamed on her scanbook's square screen:

• • •

Send out your light, lead me to your open door,
To your altar, and there make me clean.
Wash me, strip from me
The ashes (note: scum, residue) that fill my dark heart.
At the altar, I shall know
As you always have known.

• • •

Firebird frowned. She had mixed feelings about approaching that altar. The consecration service she'd been promised would include a transfer of memory, handed down from generation to generation, of the last sacrifice offered in Ehret's great temple. She'd been appalled—and nauseated—when her Path instructor had told her that only shed blood assured divine mercy, and only faith in its efficacy bought her salvation. In time, she had begun to grasp the concept of atonement, of a covering for all past offenses.

That didn't mean she looked forward to seeing it happen, even second- or fourth- or tenth-hand from Shamarr Dickin. But she would prove she was willing to join Brennen's community.

And she wanted to know those prophecies. They foretold *her* future now too.

Without bothering to translate Brennen's neat marginal note, she flipped to another marked passage.

• • •

I will be with that remnant.
I will refine and test them as meteor steel
And make them a sword in my hand.
Word to Come, Mighty One, Holy King of the New Universe,
Refine all the worlds and their peoples.
Wield your children in justice, the suns in your truth.

• • •

Better! Word for word, she keyed in Brennen's note. Seconds later she read, *Loose sword useless. Effective only in His hand.*

She scratched her ribs, puzzling over the passage. "That remnant" obviously referred to the Sentinels. "Refine and test them..." Their exile, their vows to serve others? "A sword in my hand" she liked. Meteoric iron made tough, splendid blades. She'd seen one in a museum, at Citangelo. She hated killing, but she did love the understated, deadly elegance of a ceremonial sword.

Brennen had also underlined all three titles for his God but made no note beside them. "Word to Come" had always intrigued her. At first, she'd thought it odd to refer to God in future tense. But an eternal Person had to exist in the past, present, and future. The second aspect of Ehret's *Shaliyah,* the Three, they generally called the Word. Speaker, Word, Voice—three manifestations of the Holy One. She would always think of Him, though, as the Mighty Singer in a dimension beyond space and time. He'd shown himself to her that way one night on Netaia. Facing a lonely death by Phoena's order, she'd seen a brief, compelling vision of His primal music launching time and space on their courses. Instantly, she'd turned from her guilt and doubts to worship Him.

She saved both passages to memory and paged on. Some time later, she was keying in a short verse when a sweet inrush of sensation swept over her. As Brennen walked in, she rocked back from the servo table and watched for a reaction. "Anything new about Phoena?" she asked.

"No." His presence swept deeper into her emotions. "New frustration," he observed gently. "Did things go poorly with Janesca again?"

"No worse than usual." She didn't want to explain until he saw—

He glanced at her scanbook and his open *Dabar.* She felt a surge of delight before he tempered it. "What are you doing?" he asked, smiling wryly. He knew, of course, that she felt his real reaction.

"Research," she said. "I know you're under voice-command, and I don't like to nag. I thought I'd see what I could find for myself."

He sat down beside her and tucked an arm around the small of her back, kneading her perpetually sore muscles. "As long as you don't save to memory," he murmured close to her ear. "That's publishing."

"Oops," she said. "I'll dump the passages I saved. I don't think I found any family secrets," she added.

"They're only clear in the canonical context." He stood again, and joy shone through his eyes. She'd first seen that glow months before, when she first asked about his faith—and again at Hesed, as they stood at the waterside making their vows. "But you're enjoying yourself," he observed.

"Actually, I am." She pushed the scanbook aside and steeled herself. "Anyway, you were right. Janesca tried a different approach today. A visualization, based on a passage in *Mattah*. It was one more disaster."

He encouraged her with his sympathetic silence.

"I tried for an hour. Nothing."

"Give it time," he said. "You've had years to develop thought habits. You can still learn new ones."

"After a month of complete failure? How long did it take you to master the turn?"

"That's not relevant. I was twelve and extremely gifted."

She refused to be sidetracked. "How long? At least let me enjoy your success vicariously."

He looked aside. "I read the section with Master Keeson. He explained, and I tried it. We went on."

He'd turned on his first attempt, as a twelve-year-old. Her shoulders sagged. What should she expect from a boy who won a master's star at seventeen?

Once again a child kicked her, rudely reminding her to sit tall, no matter how weary she felt.

Brennen glanced at her black clairsa case, propped against a wall near the nondescript lounger. "How long did it take you to learn to play a chord?"

"I was eight and a good learner, and... all right, Brenn, I had an excellent ear. We have different gifts."

He smiled, obviously still pleased at finding her knee-deep in *Dabar* and not worried about her failings. "You'll learn to turn."

"I'll turn," she said through gritted teeth, "or die trying."

He raised an eyebrow.

"Just an expression," she muttered.

Later, as she undressed for bed while Brennen finished in the freshing room, a jab of pain and regret caught her from nowhere, like a blow to her solar plexus. Was this grief for Phoena?

Then she realized it came on the pair bond from Brennen. She dropped her day clothes down the chute and closed the window's security slats. That switched on a small, intensely white luma below the bottom slat. By its light, Brennen emerged. He stepped around the bed.

"What?" she asked softly. "Tell me."

"I... no." As he lay down, the anguish ebbed away, but she suspected he'd only shielded it from her.

Emotional shielding—one more ability she would never learn, at this rate. She climbed in beside him, settled in on her side, and stared across her pillow at his straight-nosed silhouette. "Brenn, you can't do all your grieving alone." She stroked his shoulder. "Let me at least listen. It'll help." He was so strong, so capable—and in desperate pain. Having a family that cared also made him vulnerable.

He stared at the institutional white ceiling.

"What were you remembering?" she urged. "I felt it. All of a sudden."

His eyes fell shut, and the dull ache gripped her chest again. "I missed their wedding," he said. "I was in college, on sanctuary rotation, and they decided to marry here. At my next holiday, I came home at my own expense, but Tarance turned me away at their door. I could've gotten family leave, he said. I hadn't known. He said Asea was crushed. I could tell she felt hurt," he added, "but Mari, she was too happy with Tarance to be really upset. They were nineteen."

"So you were fourteen?" Firebird vividly remembered the first intimate days of pair bonding. Lacking Brennen's training, she was plunged by their union of body and mind into a joyous shock state so deep she would've forgotten to eat if Brennen hadn't shared his meals. Nothing mattered, nothing even existed, except keeping Brennen close, and the exquisite new pleasures he gave her. If Asea experienced that, she would've easily forgiven a tardy young brother-in-law. The public ceremony really only entitled them to seal the pair bond privately.

Tarance had simply been spiteful. Nineteen and full of himself. "You were just a child, Brenn. You didn't know you could get... family leave."

"No," he said, "but I didn't ask, either."

"Your parents didn't tell you to ask? Your teachers?"

"It happened quickly. They married about three weeks after a friend introduced them."

That was normal. Telepaths could tell quickly if they found a connatural mate. Brennen, still single in his late twenties—past thirty on the Federate calendar—had almost given up when they met.

"I... wish I'd taken the trouble to apologize, later."

"Seems to me," she said, "he should've apologized to you."

"I could've made the first move. He was always jealous of my abilities, especially since he was five years older. I passed him by at college."

"I see. I understand."

"I don't think you do. We loved each other as boys. Losing his love was my first deep pain. It would be easy to hate the man who killed him. I mustn't."

"Why not?" Self-sacrificing love might be a virtue, but so was justice. "Glory, Brenn. I hate him."

"It's forbidden." She watched his silhouetted lips move as he whispered, "Anger's allowed, but not hatred. We all need mercy. Eleven million Ehretans died for each one who survived."

"That's ridiculous. You didn't kill those people."

"I've killed others. My squadron killed your dearest friend. Freedom is a terrible gift, and so is power. Especially ours. What if we tried to take the Federacy?"

He'd resisted her mood swings, but she couldn't fight his grief. "You wouldn't," she said bitterly. "Evil people started the Ehretan war. And," she wondered aloud, "why did the Speaker let that happen? Fifty million deaths?" Those numbers suggested an enormous weight of suffering.

"Evil exists," he said, "and we've all partaken. We've all broken our fellowship with the Holy One. We need atonement—"

Abruptly the twins tried to rearrange themselves, pushing and kicking in all directions at once. There was no longer room for that. She carried the stronger kicker high, on her right. The less active twin now rode low, left. "Oof!" She groaned, arching her back. "Oh, Brenn. Carradee used to complain, and I never gave her any sympathy. I wish I could talk to her. I wish I could get out of this apartment. Between babies and walls, I can hardly breathe."

Brennen pressed his body against hers, as he loved to do when the babies moved. She sensed a dim light of hope dispelling his grief. "It will end, Mari. Probably sooner than Master Spieth is predicting. And maybe," he murmured, "they'll get along better than Tarance and I did—or you and Phoena."

10

TELLAI

risoluto assai
very resolutely

Janesca Harris didn't give up. Two days later, Firebird sat with her eyes closed, trying again to concentrate on a visualization that might enable her to turn. Simply listening for the epsilon energy hadn't worked, so Janesca and Medical Master Spieth had conferred.

"Try this," Master Spieth had said. "It may sound strange, but all this has to happen at the mental level. Try to imagine a wall. A wall standing between what you once were and what you are in our community. Loved and secure in the Speaker's will and fully qualified to tap into significant power. 'You are no longer the Adversary's prisoner, for I have purchased you,'" she quoted. She extended both hands, palms out. "Push through that prison wall, where you waited for death, into your new life."

Janesca added, "This might also help fine-tune your ability to concentrate on a distraction image. You'll want that for childbirth."

It had sounded good, but it wasn't working. Again Firebird sat in Janesca's office. Again she vividly remembered the outwall at Hunter Height, on Netaia... where she truly had waited for death. Maintaining the image, and closing out all memory of Phoena's firing squad, should help her ignore all distractions.

Weathered but solid, the wall's granite surface had crusty, irregular splotches of green and orange lichen. She recalled its roughness and the iron handrail icy cold in the moments before dawn. Instead of an execution site, she tried picturing it as Master Spieth suggested, as a final barrier separating her from the glorious life, the depth and strength she hoped to achieve.

She imagined the wall crumbling to gray gravel. She tried pushing it down. She recalled scrambling over the top, escaping with Brennen. She prayed over and over for guidance.

Nothing happened.

She opened her eyes. "I'm sorry, Janesca. I still can't see the energy... or hear it."

Today they sat alone. The dark-haired woman reached toward her instrument stand. "That's not bad, but you still focus more tightly on your music. Let's play."

Relieved to escape Hunter Height once again, Firebird picked up her own small harp. Beside Janesca's lyre-like equilateral kinnora, Firebird's Netaian clairsa looked as if it had been stretched almost to breaking. Its longer strings were spun from brass-toned metal alloy, its curving upper arch hand-carved from a rare russet-colored Netaian wood with a design of intertwined knots. She steadied it against her shoulder and belly, placed her hands, and then spun off a cartwheeling arpeggio.

Janesca struck up a stately Thyrian melody. Firebird listened once through, resting her forehead against her instrument's soundboard. As the melody repeated, she placed her fingertips, then joined in. Instinctively she twined cascades of chords and high, tinkling appoggiaturi around the pentatonic folk tune. One verse of this melody suggested green Thyrian hills that rolled toward a rain-blurred horizon. Another, the broad Tigga-ree River that flowed over multicolored stone through Citangelo.

A weird little contraction gripped and released, then grabbed her again. Distracted, Firebird let her hands fall from the strings. Mister High-and-Right started kicking.

"You're getting close," Janesca observed. "They'll be early."

"Twins often are." Firebird wasn't ready, not really. The longer she managed to carry them, the healthier they'd be.

Janesca laid a hand on Firebird's clairsa, smiling. "If they're early, they may be small. You might have an easy delivery. And our neonate facility is excellent."

Firebird frowned. She would be glad to shed all this weight, to escape leg cramps and short breath and indigestion, but she dreaded labor— unmedicated, to prevent damage to the infants' fragile ayina, their epsilon centers. She'd been taught all kinds of distraction techniques too. But once the babies arrived, these training sessions would end. She'd be much too busy with infant care.

Sighing, she leaned her head against her clairsa's top arch. "Am I your most difficult student ever?"

"Pride, Firebird."

Oh Janesca, I'm pregnant and irritable. Don't scold me.

"Inverted pride can be as dangerous as self-exaltation. Most of the time, you'll fall somewhere between top and bottom. Be content with that."

Firebird gripped both edges of her clairsa's sound box, willing herself not to react. She would always aim for the top rank in everything she attempted. "Are you sorry you agreed to train me?"

"Never."

Firebird laid her clairsa back in its case, yawning mightily. It was high time for her morning nap. "Shall I come back tomorrow, or shall we end this... until after?"

Janesca's eyebrows lifted. "Which do you want?"

Firebird flicked two closures, then hoisted the case onto her left shoulder, cramping her ankles and calves one more time. "To come back," she said. "Who knows? Tomorrow could be my last chance for months."

• • •

Brennen found a disturbing report in the midday intelligence summary.

He framed the report, keyed for hard copy, then leaned back on his desk chair to commit it to memory. Overhead, clouds whisked inland above his smoked glasteel ceiling. As General Coordinator of Thyrian Forces, he had a ground-floor suite, more prestigious than Claggett's underground office. Heightened base security meant an extra ten to fifteen minutes' wait at the landing area each morning while MPs checked each arrival's credentials and vehicle. It was a small price to pay for the confidence that no more FI-2s would be hijacked.

But according to this report, a Second Division training flight had vanished from maneuvers with the Federate fleet. Twelve one-year-old ships, deadly even when carrying dummy missiles, were gone without a trace.

Brennen fingered his cuff. Another hijacking... and this one succeeded. Back on Tallis, Special Ops would be comparing reports from all over the Whorl and assigning Sentinels to investigate.

That was no longer his job, but it was his grave concern. The Shuhr were raiding again.

Tarance. Phoena. Now this.

The vanished craft were Narkin Flightworks 316 Fighters. From another well of memory he dredged up specs: Dual-drive and maneuverable in vacuum or atmosphere, they could be flown against space convoys or used to attack planetside facilities. To his knowledge, their only weakness was what his fellow intercept-fighter pilots called "stodginess." A little slow and not particularly maneuverable.

Holy One, not the college again.

He blinked. He still had stunned moments when all thoughts seemed unclear except his memories of Tarance, Asea, his nephews, or Destia—and moments when he couldn't remember their faces at all. He'd served the Federacy for ten satisfying years, but now he wondered if anything he'd done had lasting value. What did military intelligence matter, with eternity one heartbeat away? He must protect Firebird and their sons from an adversary that waited to devour them.

The Speaker did allow suffering, to refine and strengthen his people, but evil was strong. So was hatred. Brennen could've found targets, if hating were allowed. Destia's murderer. Firebird's family...

A light pulsed on the communications panel recessed into his glass-and-leather-surfaced desk. A message from Captain Frenwick, who sat beyond the near wall at her station, followed in five seconds. "Man to see you," vocalized the desk's circuitry. "No appointment, claims urgent."

Brennen pressed an ACKNOWLEDGE panel. With a flicker of epsilon energy aimed through one hand, he cleared away several papers, some into a scribebook and some, memorized or rejected, into a sonic shredder. The desk's leather matched the coppery ironbark wood that lined his interior walls, and like his office, it was almost embarrassingly expansive. He didn't need opulence to do his job well.

A transport roared over on low approach. Distracted, he thought back to the unsettling news. For thirty years, the Shuhr had successfully attacked convoys with old-line interceptors.

Absently, he pressed another series of panels to answer Captain Frenwick. "Name, business, query?" He stared again at the transport, now parting Thyrian fighter groups on afternoon drill. Thyrica's Home Forces didn't fly NF-316s yet. The Shuhr could attack here with devastating consequences. With new Narkin VI slip-shields, NF-316s could travel short distances at faster-than-light speeds. They were also hard to destroy with a shot to the shields' critical point, aft of the engines—

"Tellai-Angelo, Tel," Captain Frenwick answered. "Home world Netaia. Won't state business. Shall I spell the name?"

Speaking of Firebird's family! Brennen lunged toward the touchboard. He had last seen Count Tel, now Phoena's husband at all of twenty-two, eyeing Firebird over the muzzle of a deadly D-rifle at Hunter Height. *You may not hate!* he reminded himself. In Tellai's case, pity was more appropriate. "Audiovisual confirmation, query?"

Captain Frenwick's husky voice filtered through the com console's speaker. "Look this way, sir, for an identity check."

A screen lit in the desk's near corner. On it, a slight human silhouette stood under the smoky dome's curve. The stranger stepped into indoor lighting and appeared as an individual, small nosed and almost girlish in his face, with large, soft eyes as dark as his hair.

This was Tellai, all right. Disbelieving, Brennen pressed his TRANS-MIT key and said, "Send him in."

He heard a clatter as Captain Frenwick replaced her remote lens in its slot, and then, "The door on the right, sir."

Brennen finished clearing his desk before Tellai stepped through. "Sit down, Your Highness," he said, dispersing his epsilon static to read Tellai's emotions quickly and clearly.

The new Prince Tel took a deep chair. Brennen caught fear and hostility, but not the determination there would've been in an assassin's emotional state. Tellai eyed the curved ceiling of smoked glasteel, the ironbark walls, and memfiles that held most of the Federacy's historical, industrial, and intelligence records. His long-lashed eyes stared up at a mounted pair of silver dress daggers, surrounded by a squadron of training certificates with the framed Federate Service Crest flying lead, then down at the massive desk. When Tel finally faced him, Brennen grudgingly thanked his office's extravagant designers. The young popinjay had been taken down several levels before he even spoke, and by then Brennen had made a chilling guess.

"Have you heard from Princess Phoena?"

Tellai groped into a breast pocket and drew out a folded paper, but he held it tightly. "General..." He cleared his throat. "I read this to Governor Danton, who sent me to you. It is from Phoena, in her scribing, but something's wrong." Brennen read disdain beneath Tellai's judiciously arched eyebrows. "Danton said if anyone in the Whorl could help me, you could." He shrugged. "So. I've come to you professionally, knowing you have no personal reason to help me. I suppose I owe an apology, if I mean to seek your help."

Help? Brennen would've liked to refuse before even hearing Tellai's request. He would like to call two MPs to escort him off the base. But he respected Netaia's occupation governor, Lee Danton, who had helped him and Firebird finish that unauthorized mission to Netaia. "All right," he said quietly. "For the present, I'll forget your politics and what happened at Hunter Height. But I must demand one condition before we discuss anything." He met and held the stare of the proud brown eyes. "I can't trust you blindly, Tellai. You're Phoena Angelo's husband. I have to make sure you aren't here to murder me, nor Lady Firebird."

Tellai smoothed a black velvette sleeve. "I expected that."

"Then you'll allow me access to confirm your motives."

Tellai blanched.

"Didn't you assume I would want that?"

"I hoped you had better manners than to ask. What guarantee do I have that you won't do more than look around once you get inside my mind?"

"What are you hiding?"

Tellai turned away. Brennen waited silently. Another flight of intercept fighters buzzed the dome, and Brennen wished he were flying one, instead of interviewing a spineless aristocrat. He fingered the edge of his desk top.

The prince probably had plenty to hide. Count Tel had supported Phoena's plots even before Netaia fell to the Federacy. Finally, Brennen spoke again. "You're free to leave, Your Highness."

"I can't," Tellai mumbled. "What must I do?"

"Only look this way. Then don't fight me."

Brennen caught him, held, and probed gingerly at the surface emotional layer of Tellai's alpha matrix. He confirmed the hostility and terror of himself, dominant in a web of plans and dreams that was utterly tangled and uncontrolled. Tellai didn't know his own heart any better now than when Brennen first read him, back in the lieutenant governor's office at Citangelo. Something in Tellai's misplaced pride also recalled the labyrinth that had once been Firebird's emotional state. Even now, sometimes she baffled him by clinging to vestiges of that graceless Netaian mindset.

He couldn't hate this man, and for the moment he didn't need to fear him. Withdrawing the probe, he brushed delicately at Prince Tel's suspicion. With Tellai slightly calmed, they could get through this business with less anger on both sides.

The prince shook his head. He probably hadn't liked the sensation of access. "That's all the time it takes you?"

Brennen closed his eyes for a few seconds, resting, then said, "I know your motives, but little else in that time. Now tell me why you came."

As Tellai exhaled, the supercilious arch of his eyebrows softened. "I never thought I'd be glad of your abilities, but they've saved me a long convincing speech. Here." He handed Phoena's letter across the black scribing pad.

Brennen unfolded it to book-page size and flattened it against a glass inset. "I'd like to duplicate this for my records."

"Granted," Tellai said stiffly.

Brennen turned the sheet over, pressed a concealed panel with his knee, then picked up the letter again.

• • •

Darling Tel,

I'm safe and can write you now. We have friends at Three Zed with the power we need to reach all our goals. Keep C. calm. Don't let her go rushing off to Danton. She needn't.

• • •

Phoena was alive, then, but confirmed in Shuhr hands. Disturbed, Brennen read on.

• • •

They're treating me respectfully, so you needn't worry. Soon we'll be together, and Netaia will be put to rights.

Till then,

Your love,

P.

• • •

Brennen rested his chin on one hand. He knew Phoena well enough to agree with her husband: This letter's tone was odd. "Do you have anything else that she scribed?" he asked. "Something older?"

Tellai blushed vividly. "I do, sir, but it's extremely personal."

"I won't copy it, then. But I need to see it." Brennen stared up into Tellai's soft brown eyes. Having just held him under access, he could read his emotions easily. Tellai struggled transparently between hope and indignation. Brennen waited. One man would walk away from this meeting as the acknowledged dominant.

Finally, the nobleman drew a tri-D from his pocket and slid it across the desk. Brennen accepted it in both hands. It was a head-and-shoulders portrait of Phoena in goldstone tiara and orange velvette robe, scribed with a message that accepted his marriage proposal and promised revenge together on the Federacy and other enemies, including Firebird. Ignoring the texts, Brennen placed them side by side to compare scripts.

He frowned. "Come around, Tellai. Let me show you something." Tel hurried up to stand by his shoulder.

Brennen pointed out several short words that occurred in both texts. "Look at the difference in the rhythm of her strokes. The hand is the same, but its cadence has changed."

"Didn't she write this, then?" Tel touched the new missive.

"I think she did. If it's a forgery it's excellent, but I think we can believe she is alive."

Tellai rested a trembling hand on the desk. "Have they done something to her mind, Caldwell?"

"I'm afraid it's likely." He couldn't deceive a frightened husband, not even this one. "That would account for the changed cadence and for the tone of the text, which reads 'not Phoena' to both of us."

"What?" Tel demanded. "What could they do?"

How much to tell him? Watch-link, memory blocks, subvocal seduction—even implanting false memories—all were possible. The Shuhr had no Privacy and Priority Codes. "I'd guess," he said slowly, "that they've simply lulled her to keep her under control."

Tellai swallowed hard. He pocketed the portrait. "Then I'll tell you what I think, Caldwell. I think she went to them out of anger, when we thought it was rather nice that Firebird was having a baby."

Brennen started. "Who did?"

"Carradee and Daithi and I."

Brennen studied Tellai through narrowed eyes. Incredibly, he sensed no sign of evasion. Tellai told the truth. Despite Netaia's vile wastling traditions, Tellai was happy for Firebird. He liked her, even admired her.

Oblivious to the sea change he'd just caused, Tellai went on. "Phoena could intend to help these people kill Firebird and... maybe Carradee. That's what I'm really afraid of," he admitted. "Carradee and her girls stand between Phoena and the throne. I tried talking to her, but she wouldn't listen. And she has a bad habit of underestimating other people. These Shuhr..." Shrinking from his speculation, Tellai walked away.

As Brennen waited, he formed his own theory. A Shuhr agent could've found the vindictive princess easy prey. One offer of illicit power could have brought her down.

Tellai spun around. "Once they take what they want from her, will they keep her alive and leave her..." His hands trembled. "Leave her... herself?"

"They might, if they think she could be of use to them."

"Make her a puppet queen?"

"Possibly." But even as he said it, Brennen guessed the Shuhr needed no symbolic ruler for Netaia or any other world.

Tellai squared his narrow shoulders. "Danton thought you might be able to help."

"I can't promise anything," Brennen returned carefully. "What did you hope I could do?"

"That you'd help me try to get her away from these people."

Brennen resisted the impulse to laugh.

"Rescue her," Tel plunged ahead. "I have resources. The cost of fuel would be no problem—"

"Why did you come to me?" Stung by this flaunting of wealth, Brennen pressed both forearms against his desk. "You could've joined Phoena at Three Zed. Why do you now think that they're dangerous and we could help? What changed your mind?"

Tellai addressed the sturdy memfiles across the room. "That's not easy to answer, Caldwell. It's more a matter of what you haven't done than anything you have. I know more about you Sentinels now, and you in particular, than I did before. All I can say is that you've played very discreetly, compared with what you could've done. I can't side with you, but I respect you as an opponent." He wheeled suddenly. "Powers, Caldwell, isn't it enough that I've swallowed my guts and come to you? They'll probably destroy my wife if you won't help me!"

Rescue Phoena Angelo? The idea turned Brennen's stomach. "Your Highness, I'll do nothing for Phoena that endangers Firebird. Maybe you're aware that we're at risk ourselves."

"I heard that." Tellai slumped back into his chair. "Please accept my condolences... on your brother and his family. How is Lady Firebird?"

"She's quite sick of being pregnant."

"How long now?"

"Under three dekia, if she carries full term." He felt Tellai's spirits sink.

"I suppose you'll wait here for that."

"What do you mean?"

"That you won't go anywhere until the baby comes."

New information: Netaia didn't know Firebird carried twins. "That's right," Brennen answered. "Naturally. There will be other factors to consider, as well. Professional commitments." He drew a deep breath. "If I were to leave Thyrica, it would take time to decide how to move, and whom to leave with Firebird when she was vulnerable, with... a newborn. Others might assist you." *And what about those missing fighters?*

Tellai folded his elegant hands. "I'm sorry I must ask this, but I know nothing about Thyrica—can you find me a place to stay? I shall certainly repay your services."

This time Brennen ignored the subtle snub. "It's more to the point that you'll have to be guarded, and that I'll need to know where you are. But I don't want to have you locked up." As Brennen considered housing Tellai on base, down in Soldane, or inland at the college, he realized that this day's other news made him even more nervous about leaving Firebird alone in their apartment.

He eyed Tellai, startled by a new thought. The prince did have ears and eyes. And if he could be absolutely sure of the man... maybe put him under voice-command... "I'll make an offer with a price," he said cautiously.

"Offer away. I can probably afford it."

Then buy yourself a planet. The retort flitted across Brennen's mind. Instead of venting it, he eyed Tellai over folded hands. "The price is a deeper access, Your Highness. I want to know precisely how you stand in this intrigue with Phoena, and why."

Tellai's face lost all color.

"I wouldn't ask for deep access lightly. If you can convince me you're not a danger to us, that will alter our relationship—permanently. Prove that your concern is genuine, and I'll try to find an apartment in the complex where Firebird and I have taken a suite—if she approves. If she doesn't, or if I suspect you when I have finished, I can offer protective custody here on the base or send you hotel hunting. But I warn you, you might not be safe in public housing."

Tellai clenched a fist in his lap. "I can't waste days looking for secure rooms. I begrudge hours." He laid his head against the back of his chair and stared at the ceiling. "I need you," he admitted. "It would be more than I expected, if you would allow me that close. What do you prefer?"

Brennen walked to a chair beside the abashed young prince, then sat down. "I want the truth, Tellai. I know how to keep secrets, and a strict code of law controls my use of anything I learn. I don't abuse what I learn in deep access. But that is what I want."

Tel's eyebrows lifted again, pleadingly this time. "No brainsetting? No—what did you call it, 'lulling?'"

"None. And I give you my word that if I feel it's necessary to use voice-command, I will tell you in advance."

Tellai covered his face with his hands.

11

ULTIMATUM

con sordino
muted

"They've been in there for over an hour, Damalcon," said Ellet Kinsman.

She was taking her kass break in Air Master Dardy's office, hoping to get news from one of Brennen's closer friends. Ellet was a classical Thyrian beauty, tall and slender with a long face and a slim, slightly prominent nose, and she'd worked with Brennen at Special Operations on Tallis.

Air Master Damalcon Dardy had a small base office with room for a desk and two reasonably comfortable chairs, and a small cliffside window. He plunked one booted foot on his desktop and shrugged, smiling. "I saw His Highness arrive. Quite the little fop."

Leaning back in Dardy's extra chair, Ellet examined her fingers. "Of all the complications we don't need," she muttered. *Another Angelo,* she thought behind her static shields. *I would to the holy Word they'd all been smothered in their gilded cradles.*

She felt an answering sweep of comforting frequency, and she glanced back at the tall man behind the desk. Physically, Damalcon Dardy out-muscled Brennen Caldwell, but in rank and epsilon rating no one began to compare... and now a faithless outworlder had conceived the next heirs to the Carabohd prophecies. Personally, Ellet believed that Netaia, not the Shuhr, was responsible for Dr. Caldwell's murder.

I tried to save you, she reprimanded Brennen in a shielded corner of her mind, where his friend Dardy wouldn't sense it. Brennen was reaping a harvest he sowed back at Veroh, where he lost his affective control during an intelligence-class interrogation. Tellai's flight to Thyrica proved that

Brennen hadn't simply pair-bonded First Major Lady Firebird Angelo. He had wed into a turbulent, powerful dynasty.

Pair bonding might last until death, but Ellet guessed Firebird Angelo wasn't the kind of woman to enjoy a long life. She would take the wrong risk someday. Hopefully, someday soon.

Dardy levitated a stylus and passed it from one hand to the other. "They may have to run for Hesed House."

"Are they planning to go? What do you know about it?"

Dardy touched the stylus to his forehead. "If they were actually planning, and if I knew anything, it'd be confidential. But I'm not in on all Caldwell's confidences. There's deep water in that sea."

"I understand." *He feels too cordial,* she realized inside that quiet, shielded corner. Was Dardy building toward a connaturality probe, wondering if she might make a suitable mate? He was just enough older to have missed meeting her in college. He'd introduced himself only a few months ago.

Connatural with Dardy? Ellet shrank from the notion. For one man only, she was prepared to wait half a lifetime.

Not Damalcon Dardy.

• • •

Another Sentinel in the Base One complex also had Damalcon Dardy on his mind. Staff Officer Harcourt Terrell's office was on the first floor below ground. Though he lacked the status to get a cliff window, the designers had installed a real-time receiver on the top half of his inner wall. He could've watched surf lap the cliff while shrieking sea-gliders rode updrafts, diving now and again for helpless fish in the shoals.

Terrell wasn't watching the image. He had just checked Air Master Dardy's location with a subtle quest pulse.

Harcourt Terrell had been a restless youth, barely accepted into Sentinel College, slow to win promotions. Three years ago, a stranger had made him an incredible offer: youth-restoring cocktails and biennial injections of a substance that wouldn't just put off his waning, but—unbeknownst to his colleagues—increase his epsilon output. The stranger only asked him to provide a tissue sample and then stand ready for a further assignment.

Who could've refused?

Four dekia ago, they had contacted him again. They had given him a fresh ayin treatment, the strongest he'd ever had, and explained his assignments. Whether he succeeded or failed, they would then transport him to the Golden City. He looked forward to learning new skills at Three Zed. He'd started here with the watch-link that gave him an eerie, occasional sense that someone was looking over his shoulder. A team of them could see through his eyes, move his hands, even put ideas into his mind and read his uppermost thoughts, from considerable distance.

As assigned, he had switched off the college security grid for Emil Paxon's hijacking attempt. A bold effort, but in Terrell's opinion doomed to fail. Too public, too slow.

Since then, he'd maintained a mental list of Alert Forces by location. General Coordinator Caldwell posed the greatest danger and naturally took the top spot on that list—but even after Terrell defeated Caldwell's access probe, he knew better than to use quest pulses to track a Master Sentinel. That mistake cost Paxon his life, by Caldwell's own admission.

Last week, Micahel Shirak himself had reappeared. He'd admitted that he set up Paxon as a diversion and boasted that it worked. After Paxon's death in the crash, Soldane police had stopped looking for the new Caldwell assassin.

Now Micahel would hit Thyrica. He was timing the strike to follow Mistress Caldwell's impending childbirth. His new force waited a two-day slip outsystem. The moment Terrell heard she'd gone into labor, he would alert a particular messenger. Then, while Micahel distracted Caldwell and the home forces, Terrell would switch off the college grid once more and clean out the nest like an egg snake, mother bird and all.

Even before Caldwell had probed Terrell in the recent security sweep, he'd disliked the Master Sentinel. Years ago, Terrell's personality examiners had warned him to beware of jealousy. He'd fought it with a whole heart, until one day he realized he simply acknowledged a genuine injustice. Since the access, he'd deeply resented Caldwell. Terrell had seen the man's arrogant side—

He did pity Mistress Caldwell. By all accounts, she'd been an outcast. She'd lived with injustice too.

Still, for a chance at personal greatness—and he had never guessed that he would learn to beat access interrogation!—he would fulfill his orders.

The next step puzzled him, for Micahel had assured him that he would escape. They intended to destroy the college and Caldwell simultaneously. Terrell didn't understand the timing, or how he would get away. Sometimes, he suspected he'd been subliminally manipulated.

But they wouldn't do that to a loyal recruit.

• • •

In the apartment complex's downlevel lounge, a whistle interrupted Firebird's best session yet on a blazer-simulation game. This was one way she could still train... sitting down. Gripping a mock Federate-issue service blazer, she plodded across the empty lounge and keyed its com screen console onto "answer" mode. She didn't even count off the ID rhythm. The only person who called here was—

Brennen's face appeared. "Mari?"

She laid the sim blazer on a kass machine. "Brenn. What is it? Someone for dinner?"

Brennen looked slightly aside. "Maybe. Prince Tel is on Thyrica."

"Here?" She shoved hair back from her face. "On base?" Then she made a guess. "He's heard from Phoena."

"Yes. He came to ask my help."

Oh no. No, Brennen. Don't do it. "Any confirmation on where she is?"

"The good news is, she's alive. But she is with the Shuhr. She seems to have gone to them of her own accord."

Well done, dear sister. Firebird groaned. "Then Tel can't be serious."

"I took him under access, and he means us no harm. He loves that woman with a selflessness that borders on idolatry. He's in the waiting area. Would you be willing to let him take the spare living unit on our floor until I decide whether I can give him any assistance?"

"Say that again?"

He did.

She shook her head. "Do you mean to let him stay that close to us? Is that wise?"

"He actually seems rather devoted to you, Mari. But he's terrified for Phoena's sake."

"Of course." *Sweet-face Tellai.* Firebird snorted silently. *The noble who was fool enough to propose to my bloodsucking sister.* At least he had more sense than to charge off toward the Shuhr.

So did Brennen, didn't he?

"Are you all right, Mari?"

She glanced back up to the screen, glad that Brennen sat too far away to pick up her uneasy scorn. "You offered him a place?"

"I did, but it's contingent on your approval. He'd be company for you. And backup. But you don't have to agree. There are protective custody rooms on base." His lips twitched into a smile. "If you can endure that, he can."

That would only be fair. Still, Tel wasn't the guiltiest party. He hadn't gone to the Shuhr. And what would it be like, married to Phoena? She winced. "If you offered a place, I can't turn him away. I'm as much a Tellai as he is. His grandfather was my father's older brother. Look at Tel. Small boned and long-waisted. Just like me."

"We can reprogram the security alarms if he'd worry you."

Tel? That was a joke. "You said you accessed him."

"I did."

"Then I trust your judgment." Though it was hard to believe Brennen's generosity extended to that young idiot. "And your ability to command him, if necessary. Tell him he can come."

"Thank you, Mari."

"Brenn."

"Yes?"

"Don't do anything rash." She touched off the screen and rode the lift uplevel.

• • •

Firebird breakfasted with two men the next morning, and when she finally sent Brennen off to his Advisory Board briefing, it was with a touch of irritation. He'd never hovered before. Finally, she took him aside and showed him the shock pistol she'd belted beneath her skyff as well as the dagger up her sleeve.

Brennen also demonstrated the voice-activated auxiliary locks. He explained how Firebird could secure herself in the master room if necessary, and Tel seemed completely cooperative.

Then he stepped off down the hall. Firebird returned to the servo table and sat down across from her young second cousin, now also her brother-in-law—this heir of his house, who'd never associated with wastlings—and folded her hands. "All right, he's gone," she said severely. All wastlings hated and envied heirs, who had the power of life and death over them. "You have other questions, don't you?"

Tellai brushed a speck of dust from his blue sateen knickers. He'd come to them without a tailor or a dresser, poor thing, and he'd nearly fainted when he first saw the size of her. "Well, yes, I do. Especially about him."

His Netaian accent sounded so melodious, though. She wondered if she had started to speak like a Thyrian. "I probably asked the same questions," she admitted.

"Has he—has he twisted you, Firebird? Forced your mind—changed you? Would you even know if he had?"

She took a deep breath and stretched her weary back muscles. "He wouldn't. He waited for months while I settled my own mind about the Federacy. The Sentinels can't impose their convictions on other people. They face the death penalty if they're caught meddling." Now she'd taken that sobering vow too. She wrapped her hands around a steamy cup of cruinn and drew a long, grateful whiff. Tel had produced half a kilo of the spicy Netaian beverage from his luggage. "Brennen gave me reference materials, and he answered questions, but he never, never forced me."

"But he trapped you." Tellai's voice trembled. "We all know that. He met you, and *zzt*, he wanted you. That's not natural, Firebird."

How had Tel known that? She sighed. "They call it 'connaturality,' when two individuals' minds follow the same thought patterns, but their personalities balance each other's strengths and needs. They're trained to stay alert for connatural individuals simply because they can't marry anyone else. Only the highly connatural can pair bond, and Brennen's nature isn't like most of the starbred. He hadn't been able to find a mate near his own age among them."

"What did you think of all that?" Tel raised a narrow eyebrow.

"He frightened me. But he offered something tempting."

"Oh?"

"Life." Firebird stared between window slats at a red stone wall that constituted her outdoor view. It suggested one more visualization—if ever she returned to Netaia, the redjackets would bolt her to a wall like that one, and...

She steered the thought aside and gently hugged her twins. "Life with honor," she added, "and a cause that I found I could believe in. And now, an enemy to fight together."

Tellai pulled his hands into his lap at the mention of that enemy.

When his hands vanished, Firebird's crept toward her shock pistol. She didn't think he meant to attack, but she mustn't drop her guard. "These Shuhr," he said in a soft voice. "Who are they really?"

"Gene-altered Ehretans like Brennen," she answered, "with mental abilities like his, but who don't follow their laws." *And Singer, why don't you blast them out of existence?* "The little I know isn't pleasant. Are you sure you want to hear it from me?" She brushed the servo table's surface with one hand. "We can access the Federate Register from this terminal."

"Would you?"

She refilled their cruinn cups and then punched up the database. "All right," she said. "Shuhr."

• • •

A coded message headed Brennen's queue when he arrived. He reached for his touchboard and frowned. A familiar row of letters and numerals indicated its source—and Regional command, Tallis had little reason to contact him since forcing his resignation. Brennen touched up the decoding sequence. A golden consular crest flared on his screen.

He read the message that followed.

• • •

General Coordinator Caldwell, Greetings.

Regarding: The disappearance of Her Highness Princess Phoena Angelo of the Netaia Protectorate System.

The Veroh scout station has confirmed the passage of a subspace wake matching that of a missing craft posted to us by Governor Danton of Netaia, and its course toward the Zed system of the Shuhr.

If Her Highness has indeed been abducted by that people, or even if she went freely to them, repercussions among other Federate protectorate peoples could be disturbing. "Protectorate" status implies enforced safety for a people under our shield.

Because of your intimate knowledge of the Netaian aristocracy, the Regional council requests that you assist Special Operations in the matter of Princess Phoena, as an independent on-site operator. Our reciprocation would include your restoration to full Security I privileges, and also to eligibility for use of Federate facilities, even should you remain in Thyrian service.

Lady Firebird's own status remains dubious with the Netaian government. Measures have been proposed in some quarters to petition the Federacy again for revocation of her transnational citizenship. Technically she remains under our protective custody, as you know, as surety for her conduct.

Honorable Madam
Kudennou Kernoweg
On behalf, F.R.C.

• • •

Brennen resisted a sinking, angry sensation. *You can't mean this, Kernoweg.* That councilor had made a personal crusade of currying Netaian favor, and this wasn't the first time her policies threatened Firebird. Revoking Firebird's transnational citizenship would leave her wide open to the execution of that death sentence. Chilled despite his emotional control, Brennen reviewed the message.

"...as an independent, on-site operator."

The Council, not just Kernoweg, was asking him to go to Three Zed. But they couldn't give orders after asking him to resign. They could only hold Firebird's status over his head, and that tenuously.

Lee Danton carried a heavy burden. Brennen had found flaws in several Federate policies toward Netaia. Economic conciliation only encouraged the wealthy Netaian separatists.

He glanced back at the screen. So Phoena's whereabouts were public now. Her defection did point a finger at a real problem. No ordinary Netaian would believe she'd gone willingly to the Shuhr. They would think she had been kidnapped, or else brainwashed... which was not the seduction he suspected. A seduced individual was still responsible.

Regional, then, was scrambling to prove it could protect subjected citizens without causing conflict with the Shuhr.

Especially with those new fighters missing, he realized. Since Regional didn't want to provoke Three Zed, they hoped he would go on his own. He had established a precedent by going to Netaia.

Scanning the third full paragraph, he confirmed its unwritten ultimatum: If ever he hoped to return to Federate service, requisition a Federate ship, or use security channels, he must attempt this mission.

It was the last thing he wanted to try.

Alert Forces could possibly pull off a rescue, though. He'd already talked to Claggett and Dardy about the need to run a reconnaissance ship past Three Zed.

Even alone, he'd attempted clandestine missions before that trip to Hunter Height. Sometimes a lone agent could accomplish more than a large, visible force. To get back on track for the high command, his life goal, the risk might be worth taking—

No! This was insane. *Ambition,* he warned himself, *overconfidence. Be careful!*

If, and only if, AF would assist him? He could ask Dardy.

He eyed the message's coding sequence, hoping to find reply passage prepaid. It was not. They didn't want any reply extant in their file. If he failed in the effort, Mari would have only this message to prove that

Regional had requested his action. He'd seen Federate pensions granted on such evidence to widows and widowers with dependents.

He keyed for a hard copy and watched letters appear on a sheet cradled by his print unit, snatched up the page, and then hesitated. Pursing his lips, he watched another transport soar over his slice of the glasteel dome.

Actually, he had no intention of complying. The reward—his questionable chance at the high command—wasn't worth the risk with those babies due. Firebird, too, had been stung by Regional's request for his resignation. Why was he even considering pension issues? She would accept no pittance from Tallis, with that pride of hers.

Deeply relieved, he decided not to mention the message to Firebird or Dardy, unless further developments made it important to speak.

But he wouldn't answer Regional, either. If he told Madam Kernoweg he would not comply, the high command was gone for good. There must be some way to revive that hope without taking insane risks.

He shifted his hand over the touchboard and saved Regional's message. Then, turning to his schedule, he dropped the printout into his sonic shredder.

12

THE DARK

stringendo
pressing, becoming faster

Particles of shredded debris were settling in Brennen's waste bin when Firebird straightened and took a long, deep breath. Something like a strong hand gripped her taut belly and squeezed hard enough to hurt.

She set her third cup of cruinn on the servo table. She'd sent Tel back to his own apartment and settled in to her work. She had almost finished composing a final essay for her home course, on behalf of the imaginary Mari Tomma. Mari would soon have one more credit toward an upper-level degree in governmental analysis.

She stared out into a steady rain. *Is that you?* she asked the twins. *Can't you wait just two more weeks?* In case it might help, she choked down another dose of Spieth's vile syrup.

Before noon, she had no doubt. Syrup or no syrup, they were coming. She'd delayed this as long as she could. She touched the SEND button to submit her essay and then called Brennen.

• • •

Weeks ago, Master Spieth had warned Firebird that childbirth pains would start slowly and accelerate—and that Brennen wouldn't be allowed to block them, except at certain stages. Pacing a secluded walkway near the medical tower, gripping his arm, Firebird started to sense the acceleration. Rain drummed on the walkway's awning, a mezzo-soprano drone she found pleasantly hypnotic.

Before night fell, her labor established in earnest. A pattern emerged: Each contraction started like a jab in her lower back, then her muscles tightened around her sides, ending with the girdling stricture. Each grew just slightly harder and longer.

"All right, love?" he whispered, pausing near a tall kirka tree.

The pressure eased. "Still fine." He knew that, of course. But he also knew that it comforted her when he asked.

"It's almost too dark to see. Let's go in."

"One more. Please. It may be a while before I'm out in the fresh air again."

An hour later, he insisted. Then, she walked with him inside the medical tower's misty atrium, skirting a shallow reflecting pool edged with more moss-hung trees. Controlling sensation with focusing skills Master Spieth had taught her, she also concentrated on closing out a series of amazingly strong emotional surges. Brennen would need to shield himself from those. *Breathe,* she reminded herself. Focus—relax...

She clenched Brennen's arm and felt his concern. "That one almost got away from me," she admitted.

"You've done enough alone. I'll send for Spieth."

She rested her head on his shoulder. "I'll be all right a little longer. Let her sleep."

"Too late." He touched her hand. "She's awake now."

● ● ●

"The contractions begin... how?" White hair neatly combed as if she always rose just after midnight, Master Spieth laid a fluffy blanket across the second tiny cot in a white-walled birthing room.

"Here." Firebird sat astride a complicated, angle-adjustable chair. Brennen rubbed the small of her back as the precious minutes passed between contractions. *If this doesn't get too much worse,* she reflected, *I wouldn't mind.* At the edge of her vision, Brennen reached for his kass cup and stole a sip.

Spieth folded her wrinkled hands. "These little ones are both head-down," she said. "They should come easily."

"I wasn't supposed to have children at all." Firebird winced as tender muscles tightened again. She glanced at Brennen. To her surprise, the discomfort faded. Perversely, she tried to shake off his help. She ought to face the contraction, ride through it. Clutching the chair's back, she rocked back and forth. The pressure became pain as she lost control. "The redjackets execute wastlings who become pregnant—or force abortion on them—"

"Breathe—focus—breathe, Firebird!" Startled by Spieth's voice-command, Firebird obeyed.

"That's better," Spieth said when the contraction let go. She strode around Firebird to glance at numerals that glowed on the room's side wall.

"Be reasonable. He was only showing you how he can close out the worst of it, when it comes. –You're doing perfectly," she told him aside as she took a turn massaging Firebird's lower back.

"Has Tel been sent for?" Firebird gasped. Yes, she was being unreasonable. She didn't care. "Brenn, send for Tel. The Electorate will demand a witness to their parentage."

Brennen grasped her shoulder. "He's down a level from here, reading, under guard. Be quiet, now. Review the calming patterns you studied..."

Firebird shut her eyes and concentrated, as Spieth and Janesca had taught her, on that granite wall, stout and strong and impenetrable. That last part—the impenetrability—seemed real enough. Concentrating on the image did keep her out of pain's reach, forcing her to focus her mental effort elsewhere instead of fighting every contraction. She rode through one spasm without feeling truly uncomfortable. Opening her eyes at its end, she grinned her triumph at Brennen.

As hours passed, though, as morning-shift workers came on duty and then vanished for lunch, her exultation faded. Evidently the twins hadn't heard Spieth's prediction of a short, easy labor. Enough of this! *I want to see my babies.* Firebird knew she must maintain focus—not mindlessly, but with mindful attention—but her strength was fading, her concentration starting to wander. The contractions became more painful, though Brennen eased them whenever Spieth let him.

Night fell again, according to the wall chrono. Master Spieth helped Firebird back up to the kneeling position she found most comfortable. Firebird draped her arms across Brennen's shoulders, feeling vaguely disoriented.

"Transition phase," Spieth announced. "Thank you, Brennen. You must let her go on alone for a while."

At last! But this would be the hardest part, even harder than delivering. Now Firebird must concentrate her mind on the calming patterns, letting her body use these waves of physical power to speed delivery along.

Whether from stress or exhaustion, all her senses seemed to blur. Had she lapsed into a link with these frightened twins who would have Brennen's epsilon strength? Was that possible? If they were conscious, what were they going through?

Brennen's voice, though close against her ear, sounded faint. Spieth's lined face faded. Only this unbearable pressure seemed real. Again she envisioned the granite wall surrounding Hunter Height. In this variation, it separated her from pain.

A thought struck her. *How could both visualizations be valid?* If she wanted to turn, maybe she was doing this wrong, trying to break out to a new perspective. She actually needed to locate mental energy that already was close at hand. Her birthright.

She blinked. As Brennen stroked her back, she closed her eyes and envisioned the same wall, but from outside. Was this the right way after all? She pressed harder. *Mighty Singer... help me... push...*

Rough granite gave way. She plunged through and found... not Hunter Height, but terror.

So black that it absorbed all light, this darkness rippled and flamed in phantasmagorical patterns, an ebony void torn by hungry black energies. Like black flames, they nibbled and gnawed even at the abyssal darkness around them. They reached out to seize and consume her. One tongue blasted right through her,

Scalded, her very soul shuddered. What was this? She tried to flee outward but couldn't find the wall.

Another contraction mounted. Heat and pain drove her back into the darkness, one powerless presence in a vast, flaming emptiness.

An instant later, she recognized the imagery. For years of nights, lying alone in her palace suite, she'd forced herself to imagine the afterlife Netaians feared most: the purgatorial Dark that Cleanses, grim fate of the disobedient. She had imagined the Dark in vivid detail—searing heat, utter blackness—so that lesser terrors wouldn't frighten her when she must die bravely, sacrificing a brief life to win everlasting bliss. Months ago, she had thrown off all hope of achieving bliss that way ...and supposedly, all fear of the Dark... yet deep in her mind, this hideous vision remained.

What did this mean? Did the Dark exist after all, and the scorned Powers too? Were they showing her where justice awaited her? –Or was this only a phantasmal memory, a truer glimpse than ever of the old life she'd escaped?

Battling the pain of yet another contraction and pursued by a blast of black flame, she fled back toward where the wall must be... found it... and couldn't thrust through. Trapped in her own visualization, she spun and pressed her back to the wall. The flame licked like a beast eager to devour her.

She must have died and passed into the Darkness. Why else would she feel herself vanishing... fading... disintegrating...

She would never see her sons.

Help! she begged the Singer. *If you're real, if you're listening! Help me!*

Sudden anguish assured her that she was alive. Another contraction gripped her. Voices muttered. Brennen urged, close to her ear, "Mari! Firebird! *Breathe!*" He turned away. "Spieth! She's..."

She struggled to focus on reality and Brennen's cue. Master Spieth's voice approached. "...blood oxygen is dipping dangerously, and the upper twin is trying to go breech. Keep her awake, or we'll have a crisis... No! You must still stay out!"

Awake.

The word jogged Firebird's memory to a phrase from Janesca's instruction book: "The inward-chasing of the mind's natural pattern that will lead in sleep..."

Dear Singer, had she finally turned? Was this terrible Dark neither a hallucination nor a memory, but the inner energy she'd tried to find?

"No!" she shrieked. "Brennen!"

Another clench of pain began. Someone seized her hands. Clutching back, she moaned, unable to regain control.

When it passed, she saw Brennen's ear and Master Spieth's head and shoulders and Tel hanging back across the room. The time was close. Another pair of ashen-faced Sentinels stood against the far wall. Unfamiliar medical equipment had been moved into the room.

"Don't let that happen again." Spieth's cheeks looked pale. "You have only a few moments before the next contraction begins. Prepare yourself."

Brennen slipped a chip of ice into her mouth. "You can't lose control like that, Mari. I can keep you conscious if you stay in control."

She swallowed the precious drops of melted ice. She must've been panting for hours. "But, Brenn! During that last contraction, I—"

"No time!" He motioned toward a monitor that gleamed green on a smooth black wall panel. "Focus, Mari. Relax. They're moving."

Despairing, guessing one more would finish her, she closed her eyes and obeyed. Again her senses faded. Again, before her mind's eye, the wall arose. She hesitated.

But if this were some bizarre visualization of the epsilon turn, then beyond that wall, inside that blistering blackness, there must lie an epsilon carrier. Medical tests had confirmed its existence.

I will turn, she'd said, *or die trying*. She flung herself through.

A fresh tongue of black flame blinded her inner vision. Another shot around her, tightening, pinning her in place while a third threaded straight through that spiral and burned through her soul's very center.

She'd believed, all those wastling years, that imagining purgatory would help her die with such courage that the Powers wouldn't send her there. Shielding herself with thin, flammable rags of courage—and a new faith that was barely a hope—she broke free. She dove deeper into the darkness's heart.

Something flickered down there, a faint nebula of blue-white energy. Around it the darkness flamed hotter, licking and hissing as if it craved this too. Maybe this gleaming center anchored the Dark inside her subconscious. Maybe it kept the black flames from haunting her adult dreams, the way they had during her childhood. Could that flickering center be her epsilon carrier?

What else could it be?

Pain and exhaustion suffocated her now, within sight of fulfilling her quest. If she lost sight of the glimmering nebula, she might never see it again—but if she touched it, she might finally learn to turn, to access other minds... to be a Sentinel mother to a Sentinel's sons.

She pressed even deeper, farther from consciousness. A new flame roared to life. It seared into her lungs, burning her from the inside out. Coughing and choking, she closed her airways against it, certain that if she inhaled that fiery miasma once more, it would consume her.

From another dimension of existence, a blast of pain exploded in her face. Brennen's voice shouted, commanding her to do something she couldn't comprehend.

Flaming darkness ripped away one edge of the glowing nebula. She would fail—she was too late! Anguish tripled her strength. With lungs all but bursting, she groped through dark flames, stretching toward one faint blue-white line of illusory force.

She seized it. It pulsed under her touch, icy cool, growing and shrinking at the same time like something from some unimaginable dimension.

Again pain burned her face, then the pressure of the fires forced into her lungs. She choked and struggled not to breathe. Gripping that knotted line of force, she tried to wrench it free of the darkness, back toward the rugged wall. She must pull it through, outside, away from the horrors and into the outside light—or else the Dark would destroy it. Longer than she could've believed possible, she held her breath. Like a last, tickling touch of coolness and light, the thread energized her.

But her strength faded. Something stabbed deep down her airway.

A new pain came on, a tearing pain she'd never felt before. Like thousands of cruel hands, it seized her, squeezing, tearing her open...

Master Spieth's lined face focused in front of her eyes, over the clear lump of a breath mask. The keen otherness of the medical master's epsilon probe drove into her consciousness. All shreds of illusion fled. "Hold there, Firebird!" Spieth shouted. "Push! Brennen, now!"

Firebird tried to shake Brennen's arm off her shoulder. He mustn't see the imagined horror. She would die of shame—

He grasped her chin and turned her to face him. "Mari." He held her stare with full epsilon force. "You're in my strength now. Yours is gone. Hold on! Only a few minutes more..."

Pain! Firebird gave a last startled cry and then surrendered to Brennen, unable to move or struggle or even think. She saw only his eyes, blue and

unblinking, felt only the command that held her. Longer, longer... she was
turning inside out...

Without warning, he released her. She gave a little hiccupping gasp, saw
the startled look on his face—and then saw nothing.

• • •

Firebird awoke to see Spieth's iron gray eyes hovering where Brennen's had
been.

She lay on her back. She hadn't done that for weeks. She recoiled as
memory returned. What had she seen inside her soul?

"You fear me?" the master asked quietly. A delicate probe flicked the
fringes of memory.

Firebird choked. "Master, are the twins—"

"Be still." Spieth drove her epsilon probe deeper. Afraid to do anything
else, Firebird held down her defenses, though the deep touch brought up
waves of queasiness. She waited out the access open eyed.

Movement at the corner of her vision caught her glance. Spieth's blue-
skirted apprentice approached with both arms laden. The oblong mass on
the girl's left arm yelled vigorously, but Firebird couldn't focus on it. Spieth's
otherness felt too strong.

After a minute Spieth averted her stare and withdrew the probe. For several seconds she sat silent and erect at the edge of Firebird's bed while Firebird fought back tears of lingering embarrassment. "Please," she mumbled.
"Give me my babies."

"In a moment," Spieth said at last. "Now I see why you struggled so. I
wouldn't have thought such a thing was possible. If you'd been alone, we
would've lost you—and both your sons."

Both? An awful fear gripped Firebird. Apparently the master sensed it.
"They live," she answered before Firebird could ask. "Both are healthy, in the
nineties on their physical response tests."

She glanced at the student-apprentice sekiyr's squalling burden, then
whispered, "Where's Brennen?"

"Gone to rest. I put him down myself. He was distraught. You'll see him
soon." Spieth pressed a hand against Firebird's forehead. The touch felt cool
and satiny.

"Give me..."

Spieth beckoned and touched a control, raising the head of Firebird's bed.

Firebird turned to the sekiyr and reached for the source of the wailing
that'd gone on at the edge of her attention. The sekiyr laid an infant in Fire-

bird's crooked elbow. Firebird tugged back a fuzzy warming blanket and found a tiny sloped head, wrinkled from forehead to chin in fury. "This is the second-born," the girl whispered.

This is mine? "What's wrong?" Firebird clutched the tiny, shaking damp thing. It smelled of disinfectant. "Is it... is he all right?"

"Hungry, I'd guess."

Though the baby shrieked on, beneath Firebird's bewilderment surged a deep, awestruck joy. For once, she felt sure that she'd done something absolutely, inarguably right.

She peered at her firstborn, who lay quietly on the girl's other arm. The sekiyr fingered his blanket away from his face. This head wore a faint sheen of light brown hair. Glancing down to confirm a surprising comparison, Firebird ran a finger across the second-born's wispy curls. As they dried, they showed plainly auburn. "Kinnor," she murmured. "Little kicker. You have my hair, but it's curly."

"Kinnor—kinnora. That's lovely." Spieth stepped behind the sekiyr and reached onto a service cart for something Firebird couldn't see.

"And this one?" The sekiyr sat down on the bedside. Firebird couldn't look away from her firstborn's gently squared, fine-featured face.

"Kiel. Brennen and I chose the names months ago, to follow my family tradition. 'Kiel' is a Netaian hunting bird. Kiel Labbah, after Brennen's father, And Kinnor Irion, for mine." She felt her chin quiver. She still couldn't look away. "Oh, Master Spieth. Kiel looks so like..." She gulped. "*So* like..." She struggled to finish the sentence. "So much like Brennen."

Then she wept without hope of controlling herself, clutching Kinnor to her breast. *What is Brenn going to think of me?*

An hour later, after Firebird tried to feed both twins and then, exhausted, surrendered them to the sekiyr's care, Brennen came down. He stood motionless in the doorway for several seconds. She sensed his emotional state firing off in all directions, like his disheveled hair. Letting the door slide shut behind him, he came in and sat down beside her on a chair.

"Have you spoken with Spieth?" she asked.

He leaned toward her. "Briefly. I won't stay long. You're exhausted, physically and emotionally. But, Mari..." He leaned away. "She confirms..." He lifted his chin and looked into her eyes. "Mari."

"I turned."

"I felt it."

To her surprise, the door swung open. Spieth stepped in. Firebird felt Brennen's irritation rise, and then all foreign emotion cut off. Which Sentinel was shielding her perceptions?

Brennen gripped his knees with both hands and cleared his throat. "We'll have to speak to Shamarr Dickin," he said in a louder voice. "He needs to know what happened, and he'll want to see how your established alpha patterns are reorienting. It could drive you mad if you tried to continue. You must believe me. But, Aldana…"

Firebird opened her tired eyes wide. She'd never heard him call the medical master by her first name.

"Dickin could order… what happens to Mari?"

What was he talking about?

"No," Spieth said calmly. "Not yet. She's been weakened too badly. She can't face an evaluation access during maternal bonding. I'll approach Shamarr Dickin. Brennen, congratulate your wife." Spieth pointed at him. "She made her first turn under extremely difficult circumstances."

"I do," he said softly, and Firebird thought she saw sincerity in his gaze, though she couldn't feel it. "I knew she could do this. Mari is the strongest woman I've ever known."

Spieth gave Firebird a tiny, triumphant smile. "It's good to hear him say that, isn't it? Now, Firebird." Spieth's lips curved down again. "You *will* do nothing about turning again until we speak with the Shamarr. You haven't got the strength for it, and at any rate, Brennen is right. There is a significant risk of madness. You're suffering an intense upheaval in your alpha and epsilon matrices. You will not speak of what happened."

"Gladly." Firebird rubbed her fingers against her palms.

"I'm glad you consent, but you may as well know you didn't have a choice. I've put you under command for a full day. And Tellai, and the sekiyr Linna too, until I release them, Brennen. They won't tell anyone she turned—if they even realize it. For now, it is our secret." She took a step backward. "Keep it so, Brennen. You're the only one who is free to talk besides myself."

She hurried out. Once again, Firebird sensed Brennen's disquiet. He took her hand and threaded his fingers between hers. "Tell me what you saw," he said, "if you can. No one wants to access your memory for it, but we all felt your terror release when you fainted at the end. We thought it was only birthing pain, but it seemed exceptionally intense even to Spieth."

In a faltering voice, she told him about the nights she had spent, years ago, scalding her mind with a hellish fear, hoping it would empower her to face glorious death.

"Willfulness, impatience, pride," he murmured.

Firebird glowered. "That's not fair!"

He clung to her hand. "Mari, you thought that on your own you could face down your mightiest enemy, death itself. Isn't that pride? And," he pressed, "you insisted on willfully doing it yourself, long before you truly needed to do it, as if you couldn't even wait until they gave your geis orders..." His voice trailed away.

She couldn't argue. "I don't think I have much to be proud of in this."

Brennen kneaded her wrist and hand. "Oh, Mari. Mari, I am proud of you. Proud as I've ever been. But I'm afraid for you too."

"Is there really that great a risk of madness?"

It pained him to speak—she felt it—but he met her stare. He spoke softly, almost in a whisper. "All I know is this. With your epsilon carrier so firmly anchored inward, behind imagery like that... if you ever tried to use it, what would it do to you? How could anyone control it, even with training?" He shook his head. "Not even Janesca will know how to train you, because no one has ever... ever... experienced this kind of a turn before."

"Pray for me, then," she whispered. "Please. Right now. I'm too tired to even try."

He bowed his head over her hand, brushed her knuckles with his lips, and then squeezed his eyes shut, furrowing his forehead.

13

SECURITY BREACH

forte, marcato
loudly, stressing each note

Brennen tried to ignore a persistent shriek from the apartment's servo table, but the rhythm chirped on. After one day's rest in the medical center, they had moved back to the secured apartment. Firebird slept with the twins in the master room for the present, while he took the entry room lounger, on night guard. She seemed less emotionally brittle now, but her uncontrollable epsilon turn had plunged them both into postpartum depression.

What had she really seen behind that wall? Was it only a memory, or something more ominous? He prayed those questions again and again, listening intently for the Holy Voice. This time, the Speaker's first answer was silence.

Bleary-eyed, he sat up and paid attention to the rhythmic signal.

Five. Pause. Two. Longer pause.

Base One, Priority Two. No social call.

He stumbled to the small servo table, touched for a cup of kass, then hit the ACKNOWLEDGE key. The abominable shrieking, more discordant than Kinnor's cries to be fed, finally stopped. "Call-up, General Caldwell," said a synthesized voice.

He stared at the servo cubby where his kass cup would appear. Frowned at its glowing chrono. He'd slept less than six hours. He stabbed three digits with his index finger and got a human answer.

"General Caldwell," a mature voice clipped, "are you confirming your call-up?"

"Y-no. I'm sorry, but my wife delivered our twins yesterday. No, the day before. I should be on the med-leave list."

"You are," the voice agreed. "This is an AF call. We've got a three-flight of NF-316s coming in. They won't ID."

The stolen fighters! But where were the rest of them? "Point of origin?" Brennen gathered the rest of his wits.

"We've read an anomaly out near Shesta that could be a carrier. You'll be briefed when you arrive, sir." Shesta, one of Thyrica's companion planets, was at its closest orbital approach, almost in conjunction.

He left the kass cup steaming in the cubby.

• • •

Firebird woke with the uncanny feeling of being under surveillance. Not quite half an hour earlier, Brennen had checked in on his way to the base, apologizing for his AF call-up. Feeling too tired and defeated to tease about his poor timing, she'd dismissed his apology with all the false cheer she could summon and then fallen back asleep. The college was providing meals and housekeeping service, and with Brennen's help, she'd spent two days simply feeding, cleaning... caressing... trying to forge a mother-child bond that she'd never experienced and wasn't sure she would recognize. She felt dull with exhaustion, oddly distant from these precious children. They had awakened her seven times last night. Kiel slept through Kinnor's feedings, but every time Kiel woke first, Kin wriggled awake and squalled too.

Had she sensed another unfriendly sound? She sat up.

"Mistress?" a pleasant male voice called outside her bedroom door. She heard a soft rap-rap. "Med center."

"Just a minute." She glanced down into the cribs. Her sons, once only dreamlike images, now had faces—one so Brenn-like that he startled visitors, and the other an elfin intermingling of Brennen's fine cheekbones and firm mouth with her delicate nose and large eyes. Each boy had his own beauty.

She swung her legs over the bedside toward the security panel and wrapped her nightrobe over a belly that still looked too round and felt too soft. It hurt her to sit, even on the soft bedside. As she reached for the lock panel, programmed to confirm her index-finger print, something inside her woke up.

The main entry alarm hadn't sounded. No one should be inside the front room. Not even another Sentinel, whom locks rarely stopped. Not with this new security unit!

"I have medicine for Kinnor," came the smooth voice. Underlying the words she felt the powerful compulsion of voice-command: Let him in!

Firebird froze. College security had gone down again. An enemy had breached the net and even released their apartment's entry lock. If not for their layered auxiliary system, she would have wakened to find him beside her... if she'd wakened at all!

She rolled across her bed, away from the cribs and security unit. *Mighty Singer... help!*

"Lady Firebird," the voice said. "Unlock, please." Relaxing, she stretched toward the console again.

Then she yanked back her arm, resisting the kindly voice. Without epsilon shields, she couldn't withstand this subliminal urging for long.

But she must! If she touched that confirm panel and spoke to deactivate the voice lock, she'd die... and so would beautiful Kiel... and Kinnor, her red-haired reactionary.

"It's all right," urged the mellifluous voice. This time, she plainly heard the Ehretan modulation. It would be simple to hold down the tab, she realized. To speak just a word. Then all her struggles would end. She'd have real peace.

No! Sentinels never, never used their powers this way. She shoved a finger into each ear, fighting the impulse. Could Tel help her?

How? She'd locked him out. Anyway, his mind was as shieldless as hers against epsilon attack.

Keeping those fingers jammed in, she slipped off the bed's foot toward her dressing table. A gleaming shock pistol lay between her mira lily and the night black dagger.

Halfway there, her feet stopped as if tethered. She heard nothing this time. Evidently the intruder had altered his attack when she changed her resistance.

Perspiration beaded on her forehead. She had to take three more steps to reach that pistol. She couldn't.

A glance aside at Kinnor, serene in his sleep, gave her the will to step once. The invader didn't want just her. Someone meant to wipe out Brennen's family. Their hopes, their destiny. She couldn't let him win.

Her legs stiffened. The room seemed to rock. How was he doing this? If she fainted, would he take control of her body?

He's a friend. Let him in. The silent urging was almost irresistible. She fought anyway. "Tel!" she managed to shout at the wall between apartment units. Instantly, she regretted it. Tel could never get in through the entry, and her shout wakened Kinnor. A choking wail started in his crib.

"Be quiet," oozed the intruder. To Firebird's alarm, Kinnor's cry cut off. She sprang toward his crib. He lay on his back, wide-eyed and breathing shallowly.

She pulled a deep breath and shouted again, "Tel?"

"Are you all right?" Tel cried through the wall.

"No," she moaned.

The voice: "Be quiet."

She couldn't hold out much longer. And could the invader read her intentions as easily as he could voice-command?

A door rattled. Terrified, she eyed hers. It didn't move. That had been Tel, trying the entry... but it was fail-safed. Brenn had checked it.

So how had this man—

Tel shouted, "Let me in, Firebird!"

"I..." she squeaked.

"Be quiet." So calm, so reasonable. "Unlock your door."

No! Was this the same man who murdered Destia? Tarance, Asea, and those polite, spirited boys?

"...can't!" she squeaked again, stretching toward the dressing table, trying to reach her shock pistol.

"What is it?" Tel cried.

As she struggled in too many directions, her mental control slipped. She rounded the bed and strode past the cribs. Before she could stop it, her arm reached for the console. She watched her own finger press the confirm panel and hold it down.

"Now speak."

One word, one inarticulate grunt, would complete the voice-print circuit and open the door. She bit her tongue. She tried to wrench her finger away. It stuck as if cemented.

Tel's voice rose. "I'm coming," it called. *No!* she wanted to scream.

"Speak!"

She spotted an alarm key. Before the invader could sense her inspiration, she hit it with her thumb. Even if someone put down the college's entire security net, Brennen's personal-carry would alert him. But Base One was seventeen minutes away.

Was he there yet, or delayed en route?

Seventeen minutes. Almost forever.

"Speak!"

Tel pounded on the entry.

• • •

Recon satellites had picked up those intruders coming in at startling speed. By the time Brennen reached Base One, Thyrica knew that they didn't intend to decelerate. This was a suicide dive from beyond orbit. At all five major bases, surface-air defenses tracked the plummeting bogeys. Base One had already dispatched a messenger ship to Regional command. Orbiting ships were diverting to try an intercept.

But by the main computer's calculation, the hijacked ships would burn up at precisely ground zero. Brennen caught his first glimpse of the tactical display as he sprinted into the cliff-side com center.

Base Commander Moro bent over the tac board. "Sunton," he exclaimed. "Get shields up at Sunton!"

A synthesized voice confirmed Moro's pronouncement: "Impact at two three south, four six point two west. ETI two minutes." Simultaneously, a light flashed on the far coast of Thyrica's single continent. In two minutes, the ships would smash into the ground at that point.

"Negative, shields for Sunton," said the controller in front of Moro. The town supported no military presence, so it needed no shielding dome. "Evacuate outlying areas?"

"No," Moro shouted. "No time. Send them to shelters!"

Brennen stared, appalled. This attack was insane. Sunton was an arts and retirement center, one of the loveliest cities on this world, and utterly vulnerable.

Moro shouted into his collar mike again, evidently at a civilian defense commander, "Yes, I'm serious. We're going to lose Sunton. If they try a second hit, it'll be too late to confirm a second trajectory and evacuate. Get all population centers into shelters. Repeat, all! Evacuate outlying areas. Scatter whatever you can without killing people in the air or on the roads. Move, move!"

On screen, the flight plummeted. ETI forty-six seconds.

Brennen felt a hand seize his shoulder. He glanced up into Damalcon Dardy's grimace. "Sunton is almost as far from the college as you can get," Dardy said.

Suddenly a high tone sounded from Brennen's personal-carry com. "Firebird," he exclaimed. She wouldn't use that alarm lightly. Firebird... and their sons.

"Wait," Dardy exclaimed. "If the college is targeted, that's the last place we want you. I'll send college security."

Brennen gaped. How could Dardy say that? "Sir?" He whirled toward General Moro.

"Go," Moro barked.

Brennen spun on his heel. "Call security anyway," he ordered Dardy. Two minutes later, he yanked his little jet's hatch closed and fired its engines. "Caldwell," he snapped into its transceiver. "Takeoff clearance. Expedite."

Rapid engine check, control check. He'd do them no good if he crashed halfway home due to an equipment malfunction.

"Clearance granted, General Caldwell," the controller crooned.

He took the eastbound breakaway strip at max. After that, he could only set his controls for automatic. Below him, air and ground traffic scattered out of Soldane, north up the fjord and east into the Dracken Range. Everyone who could leave quickly was evacuating.

He touched up a secure channel. "Caldwell to Base One. Command Center." Even full particle and energy domes, even deep underground shelters, couldn't protect Sunton's population. The mass and speed of three ships gave them horrendous momentum. Outside Sunton's impact zone, though, there might be survivors in underground bunkers. *Holy One, help them!*

"Caldwell?" a voice on his interlink answered. "Dardy here."

"Sunton?" Brennen held his stick and throttle in a death grip.

He heard a moment's hesitation. Then, "No damage reports yet, Brenn. Just a fireball. Get her—get them out of Arown."

"Any more threats out there?"

"We've confirmed a carrier near Shesta. Moro's diverting *Lance* to intercept."

"Nothing inbound?" Brennen glanced down at his console chrono, out at landmarks. Twelve minutes to college. *Save her!* "Not yet—" Dardy's voice broke off, "Yes," he exclaimed. "Confirm launch from that carrier. It's time, Caldwell."

Weeks ago, they had created a plan. He'd hoped to try to trap the Shuhr attackers alone. But now, if he escaped college alone, that would mean... tragedy. He'd always been able to quest-pulse to Mari over surprising distances. He focused his strength and reached toward her, but felt nothing.

• • •

Firebird stood her ground, silently sweating. She thought she heard a familiar klaxon out in the hall and someone pounding on something.

Abruptly the voice changed again. "End this, then, Mistress." On the stranger's epsilon carrier came a self-destructive convulsion. Firebird's own hands rose to squeeze her windpipe. Ducking her chin and struggling for breath, she collapsed on the carpet.

"Firebird!" Tel pounded as he shouted. "Tell me what to do!"

"Quiet in there!"

Tel's pounding stopped. Firebird dug in her chin and gasped down a deep breath.

Then the invisible assailant flung back her head to expose her throat again. She had no epsilon shields yet, and her turn was a powerless agony—but it was all she could think to try.

Only in service to others... was this... Surely self-defense was allowed! She dove inward, imagined the wall, and swept through.

The intruder followed into her mind, a second presence that held on to hers like a limpet. Something else, something evil, seemed to be staring over his shoulder. She felt the intruder's surprise, his terror, then his determination to use the flaming agony that he saw through her mind's eye. He drove her deeper. Darkness licked up to welcome them both with a fatal embrace.

As her brain ran out of oxygen, Firebird stretched toward her distorted core of epsilon strength, that glimmering visualized nebula. Deeper— deeper—

With her last strength, she touched it.

The darkness exploded.

• • •

Brennen held two fingertips against Firebird's throat, tracking the faint pulse in her carotid artery. She lay unconscious on the bed, much too pale. Her hair looked like tangled dark flames over the pillow and her nightrobe. He'd arrived to find college security cutting down the bedroom door, stymied by his supplemental locks. Bursting through, he'd found Mari lying half dead on the floor, her nervous system failing.

Nothing he tried revived her. Tel couldn't explain, either. There'd been a voice. Firebird had panicked. There'd been a thump, as of someone falling... and then silence.

No silence now. Tellai had steered the warming cribs into the other bedroom while Brennen called for help, but Kinnor wailed on, and on...

Tel sat opposite him on the bed's other side. "Pulse still steady," Brennen told him.

"She's too tough to fade on us, Caldwell."

Brennen managed to smile.

The entry alarm chimed. He sprang up. "Stay with her," he ordered. Tel nodded.

Brennen dashed toward the entry. In the main room, two security men huddled over a blanket-covered form near the master room's door. From the media unit, a voice tolled the destruction at Sunton and repeated orders to evacuate all population centers.

Master Spieth burst through. With her came someone Brennen hadn't called, Shamarr Dickin. "Come in," Brennen exclaimed. "Tel's with her."

Dickin swept toward the master room, then paused to glance down at the shrouded corpse.

"Harcourt Terrell," Brennen explained. "Staff officer on base. Security tech." Mari had been right, suspecting Terrell. But how had Terrell defeated interrogation? He lay dead, with no mark on him except for his bulging, terrified eyes. Sprinting to Firebird's side, Brennen had almost tripped on him. Tel had covered him with the blanket.

Dickin frowned, then plunged into the master room.

Firebird still lay motionless. To Brennen's surprise, Tel stood and bowed to the Shamarr.

Dickin walked briskly to the bedside. "No brain activity at all," he murmured as he threw off his cloak. "Spieth. Caldwell. Assist me."

"Tel, see to Kinnor." Brennen sank onto the bed.

• • •

Blue.

Blue everywhere, a vast firmament, a wide sea. Could she be swimming underwater?

No, she felt solid warmth under her. She blinked hard. Blue again. Blue eyes. Brennen's eyes.

She lay on her back. Brennen held her in his stare. Her arms ached, stretched taut by his weight as he leaned over her and gripped both her wrists.

"There," he said, and she felt an intense inner tension release. "That's done it. Tel, get her a glass of water."

Firebird shivered, euphoric. She was alive!

Brennen let go of her arms and sat back, still staring from beneath lowered eyebrows. Her wrists hurt. She rubbed them. Had she been struggling to hurt Brennen, or herself? Memory rushed back like a nightmare. "Brenn, I—"

Master Spieth seized her right wrist and held a medical scanner against it. One second later, Firebird recognized the Shamarr. Not a large man, nor handsome by her world's standard, Thyrica's spiritual hierarch still had such a potent presence that Firebird knew she should stand and salute— or curtsy. His snowy hair and white tunic drew attention to the only ornament on his clothing, his Sentinel's star. Eight-pointed like Brennen's and Spieth's, it was set with a single large sapphire and circled in silver. Her next reaction was to try not to think about the darkness behind her turn, or the way her own hands had tried to strangle her. "Brenn?" Her voice still squeaked. "What happened?"

He stretched forward and touched her lips. "Lie still, Mari. Don't ask questions. We'll tell you what we can."

Tellai came back with the water. Barely rising on her pillow, Firebird took the glass left-handed and drank deeply. Tel walked to the foot of her bed and sat down with Brennen, pale cheeked but determined.

Firebird gave Spieth the empty glass and braced for a humiliation. Pride, impatience, willfulness—the Dark—a horror lived inside her.

Brennen hunched over the bedside, speaking gently. "Mari, your alpha matrix was just manipulated. We're not sure what else happened, but as of this moment, we must assume that everything you see, hear, or verbalize is telegraphed straight to the Shuhr. Shamarr Dickin brought you out of deep shock."

Telegraphed? To her attacker? She glanced up at the white-haired Shamarr. Dickin stared solemnly, as if examining her soul without needing mental access. "How could I be telegraphing?" she asked. "I don't feel anything."

"This isn't access," the Shamarr replied. "It's called a watch-link. We don't use it, but we know it can be done."

"It's not permanent," Brennen assured her, "but the range is considerable. Comparable to planetary fielding."

She shut her eyes and shook her head. Why did they ever leave Hesed? Why try to have sons if they'd only be murdered? At least Kinnor's cries meant that he too had survived. "Is Kinnor all right? Is Kiel?"

"Yes. We must assume you're watch-linked," Brennen said softly, "but it might not be so." He stroked her cheek. "Rest for a minute. It's all we can afford. I have to speak with Shamarr Dickin."

"All right, Brenn." Watch-link? The Shuhr had trapped her from inside her own mind, mocking her hopes that once the twins arrived, she would be her old, independent self again. *Singer, I'm grateful to be breathing… but I'm sick of helplessness!*

Brennen strode from the room, followed by the older man. Master Spieth dropped her monitor beside Firebird's pillow. "You're coming up," she said, "but not quickly enough to suit me." Frowning, she strode to the door and poked her head out. Firebird faintly heard a media voice out there. She guessed someone had turned on a newsnet station.

All right, Firebird thought, deliberately shaping angry words, *if anyone's listening.* She told the Shuhr what she thought of them, with a vicious string of vituperation she'd learned in the Planetary Naval Academy and never spoken aloud.

Spieth returned to the bedside. "Sit up if you can," she said. "Tel, help her."

Firebird let them pull her upright. Spieth pressed the monitor against Firebird's wrist again. "You have to be able to walk. We're evacuating college."

"What else is happening?"

"Sunton was just attacked." Spieth studied the monitor, then looked hard at Firebird's eyes. Evidently she didn't like what she saw. She reached back down into her kit bag.

"What do you mean, attacked?" Firebird asked.

"Shuhr. Suicide flight." The medical master rummaged in her kit. "Three fighters, probably with pilots under voice-command."

Firebird didn't like the way Spieth kept her hands hidden. "Anyone hurt?" she asked, stalling. What was Spieth doing in there…?

"Look away," Spieth ordered. "Tel, talk to her. Distract her." Out of the corner of her eye, Firebird saw Spieth moving in with a swab and a venous injector.

Tel nodded grimly. "Firebird, it's bad. They came in from space without really decelerating. A whole city was destroyed. To ground level, and deeper…"

To Firebird's shame, she couldn't concentrate on the tragedy, only on the foreign object that pierced skin and muscle, then injected cold, stinging fluid. She'd tried so hard to conquer this wretched phobia. She could barely breathe until Spieth let her go.

As she lay back on the pillow, Brennen stepped into the bedroom again. Firebird had never felt him so dismayed. Dickin didn't reappear.

Evacuation? Had she heard right?

She kneaded her arm as Brennen and Spieth exchanged a long glance that was probably full of information. "We have to leave. Now," Brennen said.

Already she felt stronger. Embarrassed, she turned to Spieth. "Thank you. I apologize. That was childish."

Spieth dropped the injector back into her kit. "Brennen, I want to check her again. Call as soon as you're back."

Brennen nodded once. Now Firebird realized that he carried a small, blanketed bundle. He handed it to Tel, who took the swathed infant as Spieth hurried out.

Firebird resisted the urge to grab her baby from Tel. "Tel," she said as she rocked to her feet, "thank you for trying to help. I never expected that."

"Oh. Ah." Tel's childish eyebrows arched. "Heavens around, Firebird, how could I have done any less? I won't forget looking down your gun sights at Hunter Height... and that you didn't fire."

She flushed, ashamed that she'd even considered touching the trigger. Tel couldn't have hurt her.

He hurried out. With Brenn's help, she pulled on the first clothes she could find, a rumpled red skyff and loose blue pants. "I'll get Kiel," he said. "Grab what you can. We may not be back."

Her dagger lay on the clothes chest. More determined than ever to protect Kiel and Kinnor, she strapped the sheath onto her left forearm and pulled down the skyff's loose sleeve to cover it. From now on, she would learn to sleep wearing it. She pocketed her precious pendant too, then hastily clipped the lily to the front of her skyff.

Brennen came back, carrying the other tightly swathed bundle. "You'll smother him," Firebird cried.

"I've put them in t-sleep."

"Oh. Good idea." Many Sentinels could induce tardema, a deep unconsciousness that was barely alive. Any Sentinel could waken them later, when they arrived... wherever on Thyrica they were going.

She didn't dare ask. Watch-link! Numb and silent, she stretched out her arms.

"I'll carry him," Brennen said.

"Please!"

Brennen gave her the bundle. She fingered white fabric away from its small end. Kiel's dark blond baby fuzz was only a shimmer against a birth-pointed skull. Tel laid her rain cloak over her shoulders. She pulled it forward and draped it over Kiel too.

"Hurry, Mari," Brennen said. Her clairsa case hung over his arm. Steadying her shoulder, he walked her out the entry.

The college was eerily deserted for this time of morning. As they strode between buildings, Firebird spotted activity in a security blockhouse. She glanced up. Something shimmered between ground and the gray sky, probably the college's particle shield. That would explain why it didn't seem to be raining. Not at ground level, anyway. The shimmer was probably water streaming down the shield's surface.

What had Tel said about an attack at Sunton? She was finally starting to wake up. "Brenn," she said as they hurried toward the small airstrip, "who just attacked me? Have they caught him?" As she spoke, she suddenly wondered if the Shuhr had shot that thought into her mind, using the watch-link to see how far afield the investigation had already gone.

Brennen kept one hand on her shoulder and practically pushed her forward. Tel came behind. "You honestly don't know." Brennen sounded concerned, but she could barely sense his feelings. He must have forced them down deep, under affective control.

"Know what?"

He shook his head. "Please. Don't ask questions. I'll tell you all I can."

What had she done? Her mind buzzed with questions she mustn't ask. To her surprise, Brennen bypassed their parking row at the dark breakaway strip. He gripped her arm. "I don't think it will surprise your Shuhr listeners to know," he said, still propelling her forward, "that we're going to take something that can shoot back."

14

FUGITIVES

tremolo
fast pulses on one tone

"AC-128." Brennen identified the craft, an armed courier with rounded lines. He stepped once around, running a hand across its surfaces. Tel steadied the stepstand as Firebird groped up it, cradling Kiel. Her cloak flapped at her ankles. Nearby, beneath an undulating rain screen, she spotted a single deeper shadow: one intercept fighter, the Federacy's primary front-line attack and defense craft. She had flown against those intercept fighters, in a Netaian tagwing.

She'd lost.

This courier had a significantly larger cockpit than either of those fighters. She ducked through its hatch and eased between its padded rear and front seats, then over-between-down onto the wonderfully padded first officer's chair, side by side with the pilot's seat. She found and touched the striplight control on the bulkhead beside the hatch, then carefully laid Kiel—so limp and quiet!—on her lap. Brennen secured the entry as Tel dropped onto the backseat behind her. A sucking whoosh thrust into her ears, and the sealed cockpit started to shimmer with blue light.

"The controls are set up just like on the sim we had at Trinn Hill," she observed, fervently wishing they could've stayed there. She suddenly envied people who lived dull, peaceful lives. "Except..." She waved a hand over one end of the silvery console that curled around both forward chairs, a dotted patchwork of screens, panels, and gauges.

"That's an advanced energy-layering system." Brennen reached for a cargo net between seats. By searching out mirror-image controls, she found the other. In half a minute, netted securely with a blue lily between them, Kiel and Kinnor slept unmindful of their strange bedroom.

Tellai peered over her shoulder at the display. Firebird wondered if they could trust him on board.

Yes, she realized, they could. He'd let Brennen perform a deep mind-access, just as deep as he took Firebird's memories at Veroh. Tel was no Shuhr agent. He was exactly what he seemed, a pitiable aristocrat. They couldn't leave him behind, and there was no time to send him elsewhere.

Brennen activated the generators. "The AC-128 is the best-shielded courier in the inventory."

"You should know." As she pulled off her cloak and folded it, she felt his emotional blocking slide away.

He lit the navigational computer screen and charged the ordnance banks, then put on a headset. "Two-Alpha coming up." She felt him poised and determined, precisely as if he were headed into battle.

Firebird straightened on her seat. For nine months she'd done practically nothing but eat and sleep and grow. "How can I help?" she demanded.

Six external sensor screens took up a pale blue-gray glow. "Just strap in and help Tel." Brennen glanced over his shoulder. "Tellai, how do you do with high speed?"

Tel netted the long clairsa's hard-sided travel case at his feet. His face looked pale beneath the blue striplights. "Poorly. Motion sickness."

"Then strap in tight," Brennen ordered. "Your helmet's in your sideboard. Keep your hands off the controls. I'm sorry, but this will be rough."

"But we have nothing with us!" Tellai clutched Brennen's seat back.

Firebird twisted around and helped Tel pull black harness webbing across his blue velvette shirt. "We have rations in the compartments and clothes on our backs," she declared. Though her eyes were adjusting to the odd light, he looked green inside his helmet. "Brenn, do we have any trisec?"

"Under your seat." He slipped into his own helmet, a close-fitting black cap. He slid a lever back. The ship rose smoothly and started to glide forward.

Bending double, which felt glorious, she stretched her arm to reach a little shelf between metal struts. She eased out several strips of wafers in clear cellopaper. "Here, Tel. Chew two of them." She sorted out a sheet of triangular green tabs and tossed it over her shoulder. "And the rest if you need them. They'll keep breakfast in you, if you got any." Her stomach growled at the thought. She peeled two trisec tabs off another sheet and chewed them.

"Thanks," Tel said weakly.

She tipped her head into her own helmet. "But if they're watch-linking with me—"

"This isn't what I wanted," Brennen said tightly. "No one at college or base even wants you on board. Or them," he added, glancing down at the twins. "I'd blindfold you, but I need you. The simplest infrared detector would spot a flight of this size, anyway."

Blindfold? She shivered, but she understood. The watch-link made her an unwilling Shuhr spy.

"They've brought a carrier behind Shesta. Maybe if we leave Thyrica they'll stop pounding it." She felt his fury, but he mastered it quickly. "They're probably waiting for us to do exactly this. They don't know our ships, though. Nor our pilots. We may surprise them."

This ship was taking forever to taxi! "But, Brenn—"

"They could be catching your *vocalized* thoughts." He touched another panel, and the engine's pitch rose. "Those uppermost in your mind, the ones you slow down and think in words, are all they can track. Try to stay calm. Try to just react."

"All right," she mumbled, adjusting the webbing on her seat.

"Mari," Brennen added softly, "this is an order. Pray."

She shot off a request without hesitating. *Mighty Singer, don't punish Brenn or the twins for my willfulness. Protect Tel, even. Help us, and save the college. Show your huge mercy—*

The interlink interrupted. "Flight Two, stand by. We're on approach. You're covered."

Brennen flicked a switch. "Two-Alpha, on taxi." Other voices echoed from the transceiver. "I'd hoped we five could go alone if we had to escape, but they're watching for us. And now they sense your location, because of the watch-link."

She nodded and eyed the readouts in front of her, then wondered if she ought to even look at the board. She'd spent hours in a simulator at Trinn Hill, reprogramming her reactions from familiar Netaian fightercraft to standard Federate controls. Maybe she could help Brenn with her eyes closed.

Movement on the sensor display over their weapons board caught her attention. Their ship had skimmed to one end of the breakaway strip, but she hadn't realized they were being followed. Now she saw five heavy fighters arrayed behind them in a long, narrow wedge with Brennen's armed courier flying lead. She was glad she hadn't known Brennen had an escape plan. She would've revealed it to the enemy.

Brennen diverted full generator power into propulsion. All across the board, lights came on. The engines roared. "Go limp, Tel," he warned.

Suddenly the sensor screens flooded with blips. A mass of ships swept in from behind, perfectly aligned to destroy them. Firebird choked back a cry.

Acceleration smashed her into her seat. The pursuers appeared on the curving visual screen overhead, and as the ship went airborne, she realized they were Thyrian too... a larger group of gray heavy fighters, flying escort in mass delta formation. The rumbling shock wave passed over. She flexed her hands in relief.

Brennen pulled in below and behind the upper group's second echelon. The flight shifted, going three-dimensional as it swept high over the sea and eased into a thick cloud bank. Above her, the curving visual screen glowed eerily, a ghost cloud illuminated by other crafts' lights. Like a flock of kiel hunting along Netaian cliffs, the flight banked again, broke through the storm, and soared over atmospheric blueline.

Brennen frowned. Finally he explained, "We think the strike at Sunton was either a feint or a test run. I'm sure we were their real target. The college's governor asked us to leave."

That was no surprise. "What happened at Sunton?"

"Three ships they stole from the Federacy were piloted from space down to the ground. No deceleration. The city's a crater. In a small way, that could work to our advantage. The Shuhr commander just sent three of their pilots, probably voice-commanded, to their deaths. I doubt they trust him at the moment."

Firebird seized the thought and repeated it silently, aiming it in fury at those unseen listeners. Surely they didn't prepare from early childhood to commit noble suicide.

She pressed a resolution panel and extended her beyond-visual sensors' range a hundredfold. On BV, the Thyrian squadron shrank from a majestic flight to a small blunted cone, dashing into a wide exposed field of space.

Her conscience raised a protest. Those other pilots were flying with them straight into a trap, offering more lives to save her family.

"They're all Sentinels in the other ships," Brennen answered before she spoke. "AF chose them out of the Home Forces because they could keep this plan shielded away secret and defend themselves against Shuhr. All had the option of staying back. It's prophecy they're defending, not us."

Did the Shuhr believe, after all, that Brenn—or Kiel or Kinnor, someday—might destroy their headquarters? And if that was a minor part of that prophecy, what was the rest of it?

She'd come so close to finding out!

Her seat vibrated. A ventilator hissed. She looked down at the little passengers webbed snugly into cargo cradles. *Tardema-sleep.* She shook her head. He'd planned well.

But how soon could he wake them? Her body wasn't feeding them well, but... hours? Days?

No time to worry about discomfort. Breathing deeply to control her adrenaline, she glanced at the sensor display. A Thyrian cruiser and six support ships hung in high orbit, already deployed to prevent another suicide attack.

Wait... should she be looking?

"I'm going to need you," Brennen said tightly, and she guessed he'd struggled with the same thought. "Cover the ordnance board, but if you find yourself acting irrationally, stop shooting. Instantly."

She examined the orange weapons console near centerline. Controls protruded for six energy guns, twenty heatseekers, and two Nova-class drones. More adrenaline gusted into her bloodstream, focusing her concentration and shortening her breath. Shutting her eyes, she flicked the guns' tuning slides randomly to cover several slip-shield wavelengths.

"There they are!" Tellai cried.

She opened her eyes. An ominous, threat-red oval shape and an insect-like flurry of fighter speckles emerged on the port BV screen from behind rocky Shesta. The bogeys fanned out in all directions. "Trying to trap us inside a globe formation," Firebird muttered. "Classic strategy." *Because it tends to work,* she remembered Marshal Burkenhamn's explanation.

Brennen called a series of numbers. Firebird eyed the screens. Their own formation didn't seem to change. "Laying in a slip course will be tricky," she said. To escape this horde, they must clear Thyrica's magnetic field, then jump into slip space beyond light speed.

"That's why they're close." Brennen nodded. "They want to take us before we can slip."

Firebird bit a fingernail. It split, leaving a ragged edge. They'd reached only point-one *c.* The heavy courier accelerated far slower than the little Federate messenger ship she'd ridden before.

"Brenn!" she cried. Three enemy ships appeared high on the starboard screen, diving into that half-globe net. An instant later, she spotted another enemy attack wedge on port ventral.

"Target vector one, one-two-zero, mark," Brennen called. "Vector two, six-zero, mark."

And another wedge! Firebird rubbed the ragged fingernail against her seat cover and stared. Besides englobing, the Shuhr were threatening from three points of an equilateral triangle. The globe would prevent their escape while the wedge-formation pilots attacked.

This is what you wanted, she reminded herself as she steadied shaking hands against the ordnance board. *You're out of the apartment, fighting at his side in a Federate ship!*

• • •

Ellet Kinsman sat twelve levels below ground in Base One's command complex, playing and replaying a satellite image. The Shuhr suicide flight plummeted almost wing tip to wing tip, overheating as it decelerated, holding together until less than a kilometer over Sunton.

Then for a second, the flight turned into a small sun. Ellet keyed for slow motion and stared. For two images, the beautiful vacation community remained as she remembered it, lit dazzlingly from above.

Then every flammable object—green trees, grassy lawn, wooden buildings—burst into flame. A shock wave blasted two kilometers into bedrock. The satellite image vanished, obscured by flying debris.

Ellet decreased the image's resolution. Even at orbital distance, by daylight, the flash showed plainly. This was a terrible blow to the Federacy. It could happen again. Anywhere. The fleet must strike back, she vowed. Three Zed must not get away with this.

A message alarm whistled from one corner of this small data desk. Ellet slapped the blinking light that appeared with it, then read her message.

• • •

SENTINEL EYES ONLY, FROM SHAMARR DICKIN. ANOTHER ATTACK HAS TAKEN PLACE ON THE CALDWELL FAMILY. MISTRESS FIREBIRD CALDWELL IS NOW ON *AVOID* STATUS. DO NOT APPROACH. MAINTAIN EPSILON SHIELDING IN HER VICINITY.

• • •

A-status? What in Six-alpha had happened? Ellet stared at the message for a full minute, trying to reconcile those sentences. Who attacked whom? Had Firebird proven to be a Shuhr spy? What else could make her a deadly threat and put her on A-status?

And what about Brennen's new twin sons? Ellet would defend them with her life, if allowed. It was even possible he'd named one for her. Kinnor might be a fanciful nickname for Kinsman.

Dardy! She snapped her long fingers. Damalcon Dardy would know what had happened. Leaning over the touchboard, she punched up his call code. *Not only would he know*, she reflected while waiting for relay, *but he'd want me to know quickly*.

Two minutes crept by. Ellet glanced around the emergency center. The scurrying and shouting died away, leaving a stunned calm. Dardy didn't answer. *He's involved, then.* Sudden memory swept her back...

...to his office. Tellai had just arrived. She'd asked if the Caldwells might leave Thyrica. Dardy had touched a stylus to his forehead. "If I know anything, it's confidential, Ellet." She felt again the tingle of his epsilon static, something he didn't normally use in her presence.

Dardy. He was involved. He was gone.

He was closer to Brennen than she'd realized.

Surely they were fleeing to Hesed House, the Sentinel sanctuary. *How can I get to the Procyel system?* she wondered.

And if Firebird had been placed on avoid-status, what was Brennen going through? Was there a chance of... freeing him from that woman, now that she was on A-status?

The alarm pulse rang again. Quickly, she touched a key.

• • •

OUTSYSTEM MESSAGE RECEIVED AND PROCESSED FOR CAPTAIN ELLET KINSMAN.

• • •

She touched in her code sequence. One more line appeared.

• • •

REPORT MAXSEC, TALLIS.

• • •

No explanation followed, no further order: Regional command had called for her days before this attack force arrived.

Ellet grimaced. She wanted to go to the Procyel system, not Tallis! But at Tallis, she might help steer a Federate response to this strike. She might be the first Thyrian witness reporting to the Regional council.

If she hurried.

• • •

Firebird glanced from screen to screen. Like heatseekers locked on a target, those three attack flights closed on the Thyrian heavy fighters. Beyond them, the incoming net kept closing, catchfield ranges overlapping, cannon lighting even from beyond ranging distance. Didn't they know their own weapons? Firebird slid into the familiar, almost hypnotic accord with her sensor screens, translating two-dimensional readouts into a three-dimensional battle. She poised both hands over her orange weapons board.

"Ready, Tellai?" Brennen accelerated. Tel groaned.

"Ree-a," Brennen ordered into his headset. "Six-zero. At will."

"Confirm." That was Dardy's voice. Firebird was glad to realize she had another friend out there.

Three Thyrian ships broke formation. They veered to high starboard and charged one attacking wedge. Stars shifted on the visual monitor as Brennen vectored low, port, toward the slightest gap in the net.

He kept calling orders that were so much gibberish to Firebird... to her relief.

Could the Shuhr read strategy from her mind anyway? No time to worry about it. They swooped into targeting range. Firebird raised slip-shields. Brennen steered toward that slight gap.

Scarcely aware of the familiar quivering in her body as their slip-shield took hold, Firebird felt the ship reel with unevenly absorbed energies. Brennen fought the armed courier stable to give her a clear shot. She targeted the closest enemy with her port gun, fired twice, then sent a heatseeker down the beams.

Brennen glanced from fore to visual screens as he pushed the ship toward escape velocity.

"Blast," Firebird muttered. The enemy had caught her heatseeker in midflight and sent a missile flurry in return. She clipped one an instant before it passed on her starboard wingman's side.

"Thanks, Alpha," came a deep male voice on the interlink.

"Anytime." Enthusiastically, she picked away the rest of the missile swarm with the port laser cannon. They could've been deflected with particle shields, but that would drain the generators. Brennen needed their output for speed.

The ship lurched sideways. Firebird glanced at the screen and saw only empty space where that wingman had been. Her insides sank.

"What was that?" Tellai's voice quivered.

"They got Gamma from the other side," Brennen said tightly. He rotated upper-starboard and gave Firebird a clear shot at the ship that had destroyed their wingman. Betting that the enemy pilot would also avoid using particle shielding, she sent him a missile and counted three. One bogey on the screen vanished.

As the metal hail swept by, she doubled her particle shields, which briefly arrested their acceleration. A brilliant light charge passed before their noses, atomizing a candescent trail through debris and momentarily blinding her through the visual screen. Firebird bit the tip of her tongue. If they'd been just quicker, just farther along, they would've been overloaded—and dead.

Which we still could be at any moment. We lost shield overlap! She glanced down at Kinnor and Kiel. Surely the Singer would spare them. Surely!

Stars spun on the visual monitor. To her dismay, Brennen pulled away from the net, unable to pierce it here.

They dove back toward its empty center. Firebird searched her screens. One Shuhr attack flight was engaged, but the other two closed rapidly.

"Max shields," Brennen ordered. "We're outgunned."

15

OUTFLANKED

martellato
with "hammered" strokes of the bow

As the ship decelerated, Brennen spoke again. "Flight One, maneuver echo. Course two-three-zero."

Firebird engaged every shield on the board. On screen, half the friendly pips peeled away. She gasped. What did Brenn think he was doing, splitting this flight, with three enemy fighters dead ahead?

"Hold fire, Mari. I need power."

She clenched her hands. Her shield board flashed as slip and particle protection deflected fire. This moment was meant for a massacre. Yet stars spun and slipped sideways as Brennen jerked his throttle and stick. The pips that were his remaining wingmen followed through every maneuver. She stared, awed. Maybe they were outgunned, but they weren't out-trained.

Abruptly, a wave of hostility washed into Firebird from nowhere she could see. "Brenn!" she cried.

"I felt it. Sit back," he snapped. "They could make you shoot our own ships."

The ventral screen flashed. The enemy's attack wedge passed so close she could count its guns.

"Mari!" Brennen shouted.

Startled, Firebird pulled away from the console... and the ordnance board.

"Sit on your hands. I can't help you."

"But can't I—"

A massive firebolt grazed their shields. The ship lurched. Brennen's anger flooded the bonding resonance for the first time in Firebird's experience. "Tel" he shouted, "grab her hands. Mari, give them."

Abashed, she stretched her arms to both sides and bent her elbows.

Clammy hands seized her wrists. "I could do some shooting for you, Caldwell," Tel offered. Firebird heard an edge of determination in his voice.

"Only if you hold her too."

Tel's grip shifted as he tried to grapple both her hands in one of his own. She'd seen a side-hand ordnance board back there.

"Can't do it," said Tellai. "Sorry."

"Then hold her."

Pinned to her seat, Firebird watched the screens. The net closed inexorably. Slowly, the Shuhr attack wedge that had passed them decelerated and turned about. Within minutes, it came back, accelerating. Ships out in the net started to spew missiles again.

"Arm Nova One." Brennen reached for the orange ordnance panel and touched a prominent button. It turned brilliant red. "Fire!" He punched it flat against the board.

The ship gave a coughing groan.

Brennen followed the huge missile for a few seconds. "Tighten up," he called, then he banked hard to port.

The drones Brennen and his pilots had launched sped forward. The fighters banked aside. On enemy screens, the clusters of blips would look alike until targeting computers reprogrammed. That would take less than a minute.

A Shuhr attack flight split. Two ships closed in on the Novas. One followed Brennen.

Seconds later, the drones and attackers connected. The visual panel splashed with white light. Attuned to six pale screens, Firebird felt the flight ride broadside along a wave of debris that had been two top-line Federate ships—now Shuhr contraband—and several Nova missiles. Brennen accelerated toward the net again, gripping his stick while he checked his navigational computer. "I'm afraid it'll be worse than this trying to get down at Hesed. If they could send DeepScan signals over that range, we'd never make it."

Hesed, of course. They'd be safe at the sanctuary! "Can we jump for Hesed on this heading?"

"No. Have to make an intermediate jump."

Her eye caught movement on the ventral screen. The second attack wedge, reduced by one, left the other Thyrian flight behind and accelerated toward Brennen. The other Thyrians pursued.

Suddenly Firebird had an idea, so crazy she almost dismissed it—or was it a plant? She decided to speak anyway. "Brenn, do we have power and life support enough to hit their base at Three Zed and still get to Procyel, or could that be a trap?"

"What?" He lifted one hand off the sideboard.

"You're afraid they've got ships at Hesed waiting for us. Could we draw some off by hitting their home base? At least these ships would follow us there instead of attacking the sanctuary. At best, we could do some serious damage." The prophecy...

He scarcely moved. "Yes!—but... yes, that may be one thing they wouldn't expect us to try. They've probably pulled their defense force to gather this fleet." He bent back to the computer. "We can do it," he said, "and it's in this slip quadrant. If we can get clear to jump."

She hadn't missed that pause. "But" what? Chilled, she squelched the thought. Who else was listening?

Brennen jinked wildly, closing the distance to the remaining hostile ship. Obviously he meant to take it before two others joined it. "Gemina maneuver," he called suddenly. A signal?

Yes! He'd been decorated—and rebuked—for that battle at nonaligned Gemina.

Tel released Firebird's hands, probably to wipe his forehead. Immediately she found herself reaching for the ordnance board. Disgusted, she twined her fingers into a double fist and clenched it between her knees, then crossed her legs. In her tagwing, that wouldn't have been possible. *Got you!*

Brennen accelerated the armed courier, then pulled straight back on the stick, looping vertically. Firebird pressed deeper into her seat. She tightened her legs on her weirdly rebellious hands. The attacking pair shot off low, to port.

"Arm Nova Two." He touched the second button. "Fire! ...and... mark one."

To Firebird's disbelief, he retrofired, plunging her forward against her harness straps. He would be rammed by his own pilots!

No, they braked too. The drones sped toward the net.

"Mark two." He shoved the stick forward. The ship accelerated again, chasing his own drone.

Firebird held her breath. Chasing missiles to targets was suicide... or was it, if this ship had the best shields in Thyrica's courier inventory?

Again Brennen maxed the particle shields. "Hang on, Tel." The fore screen flashed. "Pull in," Brennen ordered.

The ship tossed wildly, thrusting into waves of debris that expanded in concentric globes. Firebird clenched her hands as turbulence buffeted them from all directions. An alarm light pulsed on the shielding monitor. "Doubling's down," she cried.

Brennen stared straight ahead, pushing the stick left, down, up, right. On the visual screen, along the outer shock wave of destroyed Shuhr ships, their less massive fighters—whose shields couldn't turn the metal storm—came apart to form waves of brilliant chaos.

Suddenly the fore screen blanked. That was deep space. They were through! Brennen swatted off the particle shields. Acceleration mashed Firebird against her seat. "Three Zed heading," he ordered. "Jump in fifteen seconds. Who else is clear?"

Ten pilots responded. He touched ten panels in rapid succession, then hit a bar to cross-program the other navigating computers.

The jump light pulsed. One kick and they'd be free.

"Be ready for anything when we break at Three Zed," he called to his escort.

It didn't matter if the enemy heard him. Clearly that was his intention. Firebird whooped. "Hang on, Tel!"

Brennen poised both hands over the board. "Mari! Shut your eyes!"

Startled, she obeyed. She felt the ship buck as she faded into her seat, and then a scarcely tangible touch slipping away, as if she'd stepped out of polluted water. She was finally free of the watch-link.

All six external screens shimmered with the blue chaos of quasi-orthogonal space. Firebird yanked off her helmet and let out the breath she'd been holding.

Brennen too set his helmet aside. He presented his right hand, smiling faintly. "Very professional, Major."

She pushed her back deep into the seat. "Where are we really headed?" Her heart still pounded.

He brushed sweat-soaked hair from his forehead. "Hesed," he said. "They wanted to lure us to Three Zed. That told us they couldn't be blockading Hesed."

"Why not?"

"Numbers. There just aren't that many Shuhr. Actually, you saved us twice. That 'Gemina' command was a decoy signal too."

She pulled him close and kissed him so hard her teeth hurt. It hadn't gone anything like she'd planned, but they'd fought together at last. She must thank...

Mighty Singer, you showed yourself. Thank you. For their sake. She glanced down at their infant passengers.

Finally she remembered Tellai. Massaging her scalp, she twisted around. His eyes shone as big and round as Triona's twin moons. Focused as though hypnotized on the sensor display, they glimmered with tears and the reflection of sensor lights.

"Are you hurt?" she asked, pressing a control to recline her high-backed seat.

"I guess not." He cleared the gravel from his voice. "I was... thinking about Phoena. Those are the people who have her. Was that a major battle? That is, compared with... you've both done that sort of thing before."

Brennen rubbed his palms on his thighs. "If our shields had gone we'd be dead, just as if it'd been a full-scale war. Actually," he said soberly, "this might be exactly that. War."

Tellai groaned. "I'll never make a soldier."

Firebird dried her own palms, and the ragged fingernail scraped her skyff. "Will you have to go back to Thyrica?" she asked Brennen. He wouldn't take them to Hesed and leave them there, would he?

"Not for the moment. General Moro ordered me to Hesed. Once there, I'm under Master Dabarrah." He pulled a packet of gray concentrate cubes from below the console and shared them around. Firebird crunched and swallowed, stretched, and pushed her seat back farther down. She ached with exhaustion, but her blood was so full of adrenaline that her hands shook. Not to mention Master Spieth's injection. Surely it wasn't normal for a new mother to do what she'd just done, without medical assistance.

"You should sleep, Mari."

"You're right." She glanced down. This time, the babies wouldn't wake her up. And she felt too comfortable. Maybe she wouldn't be able to nurse them after today. "But I won't sleep without your help."

Brennen reached over and touched her forehead. Instantly, drowsiness wrapped her like a thick bedcover.

• • •

"Whatever she is now, she was born an Angelo."

Carradee Second stressed that last word. On the hand-woven carpet of her sitting room, erect in a row of gilt chairs, sat three members of her Electorate: the Aquaculture Minister Count Wellan Bowman, Baroness Kierann Parkai of the Judiciary, and His Grace the Duke of Claighbro—and Trade Minister—Muirnen Rogonin. As she reached his end of her course, Rogonin shifted on his slender-legged chair and lowered his manicured brows. Carradee ignored the implied criticism. She needn't be cowed by Rogonin. She might not be a strong queen, she might be drifting away from the Powers' ways of ruling, but she was queen.

"Born an Angelo," she repeated. "We will not move that she be restored to the succession, nor the Electorate, but that she be given back her citizenship, noble electors. The Assembly's review of her conduct at Hunter Height was conclusive and final." If only the Assembly had acted sooner, before that terrible trial! "Lady Firebird took no unnecessary action, spared life when possible—from the standpoint of self-protection, and her mission objectives—in short, she defended herself and her..." It still felt strange to say this, glad though she was for Firebird's happiness: "... and her husband, from harm. Whatever our views regarding the Federate presence, Princess Phoena's motives and actions at Hunter Height must be called dubious at best."

Carradee eyed Muirnen Rogonin as sternly as she could, with the steely glance she had inherited from Queen Siwann and practiced in front of her boudoir mirror. She had been furious—furious!—to learn that Phoena had established an illegal weaponry lab at the family's lovely old vacation home, and now she knew Rogonin had been another prime instigator. She had stood back and let Occupation Governor Danton levy a stiff fine against Rogonin's estate. Not that Rogonin missed several million Federate gilds... and with Carradee's approval, that money had gone straight into Federate programs to repair selected war damages.

Phoena's secessionist movement had not died at Hunter Height. Nor did Carradee imagine Phoena had left it leaderless when she went... wherever she was in hiding. Surely its new leader sat here, opening a tin of after-dinner mints, with his sateen-swathed bulk resting uneasily on a delicate chair. Carradee didn't entirely disapprove of the movement. She too wanted Netaia to be independent again, but some of Danton's reforms were clearly benefiting her most impoverished subjects. If Netaia joined the Federacy as a full covenanting member, the general good might outweigh the loss of full independence.

"She took Federate transnationality, Majesty." Rogonin flicked a mint under his tongue, pocketed the tin, and then folded both hands across his middle. "Renounced her citizenship, the Powers, and all hope of eternal bliss. You would rewrite her name on the rolls of the righteous?"

"Who knows how deeply her conscience is aching?" Though her Electorate daily took back more of its dominance over planetary affairs, Carradee vowed she wouldn't back down on this issue. Firebird plainly had been determined to fulfill her martyrdom and earn glory in Netaia's electoral pantheon at Veroh. Carradee couldn't imagine that Firebird was comfortable or content out in the Federacy.

She pulled a white notum blossom from a bouquet on the end table beside Rogonin and rolled its stem between her fingers. Personally, she held nothing against Governor Danton anymore. He was a better administrator than she'd been led to believe, ordered to believe, at Siwann's deathbed. To appease the Powers, though, and their other noble representatives, she would keep challenging Federate reforms. She still needed Strength, Valor, and Excellence... and the other Powers... to help her rule.

"Madam." Count Wellan Bowman tapped his brass-tipped walking stick against the leg of his chair. Bowman was a tall man, with the full but softening shoulders of a former athlete. Frowning, Carradee held the notum bloom to her nose and peered at the nobleman over its petals. "Madam, if Lady Firebird's survival confuses the succession, how much worse now that she carries the heir of an offworlder? A Federate, a—a Sentinel? She may have already given birth. What status must we grant her children? Will they be noble wastlings? Or common, like their father?"

"We have considered that, Bowman. If the Electorate and the Assembly chose to restore Lady Firebird to the succession, then we would consider her offspring. But for what circumstance would she be restored to the succession?" She lowered her voice. "There is no need. Our elder princess is nearly of an age to be confirmed." Four-year-old Iarlet could be ceremonially declared an heiress to the throne as soon as she memorized a short electoral litany, and Iarlet was a brilliant child. For that matter, Iarlet could be crowned if Carradee died before naming an heiress.

Carradee strode up the center of the long, high-curtained sitting room. At the end of the chamber nearest the dark fayya-wood door, she laid the blossom on a butler's tray. "Noble electors, we shall make the motion tomorrow. We would be pleased to count on your support." *Not that I expect it from any of you,* she thought, but she would not say that aloud. "I'll ask only for her citizenship—as a token, my friends. If she had meant to harm us, to damage Hunter Height—" Carradee collected their stares and held them a moment. "Escaping in a tagwing fightercraft, she could have done serious damage. She is a fine pilot and a skilled markswoman."

She tapped the door twice. A servitor opened it from outside. Parkai and Bowman left silently.

Carradee paced to the near window and gazed out. This room faced the palace's public gardens. Beyond those, a bluff fell south toward the serene Tiggaree River. Two long white groundcars pulled slowly toward the curb to receive Baroness Parkai and Count Bowman.

She frowned. Only the four commoners she had personally appointed supported her in the Electorate. Phoena's poor, lonely husband, Prince

Tel, would vote with Rogonin when he returned. The other young nobles followed similar patterns, shadowing their elders.

That wasn't the way Mother's Electorate voted. The Crown was a figurehead once again, ruling on behalf of mighty Authority.

Did she really believe her coronation made her a priestess, even a demigoddess?

Fingering a yellow curtain—she despised jeweled window-filters and had replaced them all with antique sheers—Carradee sighed, then turned.

Rogonin still sat.

"Majesty." His eyes narrowed beneath plucked brows. "What do you intend to do if she turns on us again?"

"She won't." Carradee stopped in a warm shaft of lamplight. "She never did, Rogonin. She protected herself and exposed an illegal operation."

The Duke sniffed and strode out.

Carradee waved off her servitors and retreated through the chamber's east door into her private apartments. Prince Daithi sat in his own room, propped against several pillows, reading a scan cartridge on a viewer that made his face glow. "Daithi?" she asked softly.

His eyes were soft and dark like a brownbuck's, and brown curls formed a cap on his head. Though eight years her senior, he looked up to her. Sometimes he seemed like the younger brother she never had—the brother no Angelo had had in over a century.

"Would you sleep in my room tonight?" she asked.

He laid the viewer on his brown velvette coverlet. "Of course, Dee." She rested one hand on his shoulder and touched his smooth throat, and he reached up to grasp her hand. She smelled leta-wood soap. He'd bathed a second time today, as usual, in case she made that very request.

She walked through his room into the adjoining double boudoir and changed into her nightgown. A chambermaid followed Daithi through, carrying cool drinks on a tray. Carradee sighed contentment. Daithi would help her relegate Rogonin to the zone of forgetfulness.

Hours later, she woke perspiring. Muirnen Rogonin had stalked her dreams, challenging and belittling her. Rogonin wasn't really like that. She stumbled out to the boudoir. Examining her scalp, she thought it looked oily. A hundred strokes would do it good and wake her out of this daze.

She found her pulse brush and set it for low speed, held its vibrating bristles to the crown of her head, and shut her eyes. Then she set to brushing.

At the ninetieth stroke, terror seized her. She dropped her brush.

The powerful, irrational sensation almost paralyzed her— *It's coming from another mind.* The thought flashed into her consciousness.

Sentinel? she answered with a thought of her own. She thought she felt distant, scornful laughter.

Shuhr? Firebird had sent warnings. Now the thought rang so loudly in her mind that her lips formed the word.

A sharp crack echoed behind her. Walls groaned. The world flew to pieces. Screaming, she flung up her arms to protect her face. Something struck her from behind. She tumbled off her stool, clutching long tufts of carpet. The floor heaved. Rattling noises trailed off into silence and absolute darkness.

She tried to get up and run. Something pinned her down, making her shoulders and legs throb with pain. "Daithi?" she cried. The explosion had come from behind her, where Daithi lay sleeping!

16

SANCTUARY

lucernarium
song for vespers, evening worship; its texts often refer to light

Carradee thrust down harder with her arms and pushed up with both shoulders. Her head smacked something.

"Daithi," she moaned. "Are you there?"

For some time, she drifted in and out of a faint. Crashing and crunching sounds roused her. Perhaps someone called her name, perhaps not. *Shuhr? No,* she thought. *Sentinels?*

What if they're in league?

Holy Powers, she pleaded, *help us!*

The weight shifted, slicing into her legs. "Hello," she gasped. "Hello, I'm here."

"Majesty." It was a male voice, breathy as if he were frantic. "Majesty, keep talking."

"I'm at the dresser," she shouted. "It's dark. I think my legs are hurt, and maybe my back—"

Light flashed on a slab of rubble above her. "You can stop, Majesty."

She saw two faces, one familiar and comfortable. "Doctor Zoagrem," she cried. The weight on her legs lifted. She grappled forward, trying to crawl out of the debris. "Daithi was in my bed. Find Daithi."

The doctor pressed something cold against her arm. "We will, madam. Lie still."

• • •

It was good of Governor Dantonto come to her hospital room. Carradee shifted on the bed, and its contours shifted underneath her. Doctor Zoagrem had assured her that the fractures would heal, and with regen therapy she would soon walk without limping. But Daithi...

He'll live, she reminded herself. *Be grateful for that, and wait to see what else the doctors can do.* She had sent her servitors away. She gulped back an urge to weep on the shoulder of this professional Federate diplomat who'd always been kind; with whom she never had to fight, the way she constantly battled her electors. But she mustn't weep with him. She was queen, though every instinct screamed her anguish.

"If," she said steadily, "you can get Iarla and Kessaree to a safe locale, do it. Please. Do it quickly." Then her reserve crumbled. The electors would not approve, and she had to make someone understand. "Up until now, Lee, whenever we've talked I have spoken as queen. Now I'm only a mother. I cannot explain these instincts, only obey them. I'll answer for my own safety, but I could never live with myself if there were anything I could've done for my daughters, and through my not having done it, they were harmed. Do you understand?"

He nodded. Fading afternoon light gleamed in his blond hair. "I do, Majesty. I had three children of my own. Lost one. Only between us, madam, I dream of her—monthly, sometimes. I do understand. Now, there are several possib—"

"No." Shutting her eyes, Carradee pressed her head into the pillow. Her mouth tasted queer from some medicine they'd given her. "I don't want to know where, Governor. If your suspicions are correct—if what I felt before the explosion was some sort of psychic taunt, meant to trumpet my killers' identity—if they come here again, and they can read my mind—I want no knowledge of where my daughters are sent into hiding." Grief tugged at her. "At least, not yet. You can tell me later, but you cannot unsay anything you say now."

She opened her eyes and saw Danton nodding.

"Do they want us all dead?" she whispered.

The governor swung one leg over the other. "You are well watched, madam. We've enlarged a special guard for you and your daughters from the Special Operations branch of Federate forces, including five Sentinels to cover all watches. Any Shuhr agents on Netaia will have to be very careful. I don't think they'll try anything against you for some time."

"But you'll see to the other matter?" she asked. "Please?"

"I will, madam."

• • •

Muirnen Rogonin took two steps along the north colonnade and stopped to run a fleshy hand up and down the smooth white marble of a supportive pillar. Fortunate that the ancient palace still stood. Only one wall had collapsed. Danton was wrong to credit precision explosives: The virtue lay in Netaian architects, who designed for strength. They had built a strong palace, a strong Electorate... a strong Crown, backed by Powers the Federacy could not call on.

Fortunate too, in a way, that Carradee had been brought down before she could press for the wastling's citizenship. Carradee Second tended to forget that her sister Firebird still stood under a well-earned death sentence for treason, sedition, and heresy.

"She will be disabled for some time," he told Count Wellan Bowman. A breeze fluttered his collar. Irked, he smoothed it. "Emotionally, she'll be unable to govern for several weeks at the inside."

"According to...?" Bowman asked.

"Her own physician. Zoagrem."

"She is distraught over the prince's injuries," Bowman suggested. "She mustn't be given authority until his condition stabilizes."

Rogonin shook his head. "The Electorate is authorized to designate an interim regent, with Crown authority to act at electoral meetings. Emergency powers only, of course," he added, "but there is no need to set a limit on his term of service."

Wellan Bowman rapped the column with his walking stick. "'Iarla's accession, at her majority' would make a logical phrase, should any of the new faction press for a limitation," he said smoothly.

That would give him fourteen years or more. In fourteen years, a regent might throw off the outworlders. He could assemble his own Electorate and establish his own family in the palace. "Yes." Calmly, Muirnen Rogonin drew out his tin of mints. "Yes, it would."

• • •

When hunger woke Firebird, the autopilot chronometer read eighty hours, and both men slept. Tel curled toward the aft bulkhead. Asleep, he looked even more childlike. Brennen lay beside her, resting his head lightly against the back of his seat, as if the slightest change in attitude would wake him.

Firebird crossed her arms, pressed hard against her chest, then exhaled heavily. One more small defeat. For better or worse, she would not be nursing those infants. She located her cache of flavorless gray concentrates and washed down a double handful with a packet of vaguely tart electrolyte drink, wondering if she should awaken either of the men. The break indicator showed over two days remaining on their jump to sanctuary. She glanced down at Kiel and Kinnor, who still lay like small duffels stowed between seats.

They were safe. Nothing else mattered, not even the blue mira lily that had slid loose. Two of its long, curved petals hung limp, crushed and mangled.

Brennen had been so happy to give her that blossom. *If that's our only casualty, I have to be grateful.* Sighing, she loosened her harness, pulled up her cape, and tucked it around her, for comfort more than warmth. Her thoughts wandered...

This retreat would end her college training, probably for good. The thought struck hard, and then a humbling response: She would miss Janesca, but what little she had accomplished at college had been a disaster.

That raised another disquieting thought. The Shuhr had unilaterally attacked Thyrica. How could the renegades hope to survive with the Federacy's might turned against them? ...Unless, she reflected, the Federates balked, more afraid of the Shuhr than they were of the Sentinels who served them.

But why, if Three Zed meant to kill Sentinels, did they attack Sunton instead of Arown? A feint, as Brennen suggested, or a test run? To her, it sounded like incompetent leadership. Or maybe they meant to turn Thyrica against its small starbred communities. Thyrian mobs might do Three Zed's dirty work, sending Sentinel families fleeing to Hesed House.

Hesed, in the Procyel system, lay off the trade routes. Procyel II had been marginally developed during the first human expansion, then abandoned during the Six-alpha catastrophe. Four centuries ago, Sabba Six-alpha—a star near the Whorl's midpoint—had started to spurt ionized particles and deadly radiation in unpredictable, decades-long bursts. Intersystem travel had ended and civilizations declined all over the Whorl. That storm lasted two hundred years.

Between its last bursts, Brennen's people had made a high mountain valley on Procyel II their refuge. They dug out an underground complex.

Firebird would never forget her first glimpse of the sanctuary's central commons, almost a year ago—

• • •

She'd stepped through golden double doors, and a vast white hall opened ahead of her. Ahead shimmered a shallow artificial lake surrounded by a latticed rail. Paths of square stepping stones connected islands of greenery, and sunlight streamed down from countless skylights, dancing and reflecting on the water. From somewhere she could hear more water rushing and splashing.

The Master Sentinel that Brennen had introduced as Jenner Dabarrah stepped around from behind them, tall and thin, with blue-gray eyes as pale as his golden hair. Dressed all in white with an eight-rayed star, he wore his age well: forty, perhaps? Or fifty?

"Have you eaten?" He touched a bell.

"Enough." Brennen squeezed Firebird's hand as she stood in motionless wonder. Escaping Phoena's forces at Hunter Height only days before, they'd exchanged their Netaian fightercraft for a Federate shuttle—with Governor Danton's help—and then at last, Brennen had asked the question she longed but dreaded to hear. Somehow, she summoned the courage to accept a telepath's marriage proposal.

Later on the night of their arrival, she'd walked with Master Dabarrah and Brennen—who looked like a lord in his Federate dress whites—out onto the stepping stones. Skylights dimmed. A band of pale light gleamed around the edge of the waters, reflecting blue and green off the stone walls and ceiling and Brennen's white tunic. Firebird wore a pale blue gown lent by a student-apprentice sekiyr.

They halted on a paved island beneath a spreading evergreen tree. Firebird faced Dabarrah, and Brennen drew close beside her.

"You have no doubts?" Dabarrah asked softly. "You will hold this bond before all other loyalties, Firebird. And you, Brennen? Your path may not be easy." He must've known their life together would never be simple.

Brennen nodded slightly. She did the same.

Master Dabarrah placed his hands on their shoulders, speaking softly and musically in a tongue she heard then for the first time, the Ehretans' ceremonial language. A blessing, she guessed, or an invocation. Brennen answered briefly in the same language.

Then Dabarrah dropped his right hand, leaving one on her left shoulder. "Firebird Mari," he said gently, "you have chosen a Sentinel. Your culture has done nothing to prepare you for this."

Firebird met the steady gaze of those pale blue eyes. "That's true, Master, but Brennen has explained pair bonding. I've accepted it—and him."

"Then I ask to touch your spirits."

She felt Brennen step close behind her. He circled her waist with one arm and pressed into her mind, far deeper than he'd ever gone before. For a sweet moment she held steady, but the inrush to union became a hurricane inside her, tearing her from her moorings even as it filled her with the presence she'd come to love more than flight, more than freedom, more than life.

She remembered little of the next few days. They'd spent most of it inside a skylit stone room, with one wall veiled from end to end by falling water. Here and there, a meal stuck out in her memory, homegrown foods like she'd never tasted... and one morning Brennen had taken her swimming in a river draped with fragrant trees.

In less than a day, she would see Hesed again.

Curling toward the starboard hull, she let the superlight engine's thrum and the slip vibration lull her into a deep, contented sleep.

● ● ●

No Shuhr ships challenged as they entered the Procyel system. Under falling darkness, ten heavy fighters and an armed courier settled on Hesed's grassy landing strip.

Firebird stepped out, feeling grimy and salty, clutching Kiel against her shoulder. She couldn't wait to see him awake again. She felt vaguely guilty for letting them bring him so far in tardema-sleep.

Near a boarding ladder that hung from the lead craft, two familiar figures stood waiting. Jenner Dabarrah, Sanctuary Master, was as tall, lean, and poised as she remembered, with pale yellow hair and a white tunic that almost shone in fading daylight. His wife, Mistress Anna, wore her dark hair long enough to touch her green belt. She smiled warmly, holding out both arms. Abruptly Firebird remembered that Anna was childless.

Feeling a new kind of pity, Firebird carefully gave Kiel to her. "He's in tardema," she said, then wondered if she needed to explain that to the Sentinel woman.

Cradling him tenderly, Anna pushed the blanket away from his face. "He's beautiful," she said, and Firebird felt warmer despite a chill sunset breeze. She glanced up at the mountains that surrounded Hesed House.

Tellai followed down the stepstand, carrying her clairsa case, and then came Brennen with Kinnor. Tel strode forward, "Tel Tellai, sir." He bowed to Master Dabarrah. "Actually, it's Tellai-Angelo, Your Honor."

"You are welcome at Hesed House, Your Highness," Master Dabarrah said, "as a member of Mistress Caldwell's family." He extended an arm and presented "My wife, Mistress Anna."

Anna Dabarrah inclined her head toward Tellai. Deep brown hair touched with silver slipped over her shoulder, covering Kiel. She swept it back.

"Master Dabarrah?" Firebird caught his eye and mouthed a thank you for allowing Tel to pass the security perimeter at Procyel II. Under other circumstances, he would've been turned away like any other non-Sentinel.

"Mistress Firebird." Anna Dabarrah rocked Kiel from side to side. "Are you and the children well?"

"Yes." Firebird inhaled free air as several other pilots passed by on their way indoors. This evergreen scent brought back a whirl of tender memories, with one image of Brennen, all in white, shining at its center. "But I could still sleep away a dekia."

"Come in." Dabarrah gestured toward the House's main groundside lift. "Please."

"Let me take the children while you bathe and eat," Anna offered. "Firebird, you surely remember the way to the privacy suite. Brennen and Prince Tel, why don't you freshen in our suite?"

They rode the lift downlevel to the vast underground chamber. As before, Firebird followed a young student-apprentice sekiyr. Beyond the white latticework railing, the huge reflecting pool's blue-green underwater lights still reflected asymmetric patterns off a high ceiling and dozens of darkening skylights. Paths of stepping stones dotted the bright water like floating square shadows.

She sighed. Breathing room!

In the skylit bedchamber where she'd spent most of her previous stay, she gladly peeled off her musty red skyff and blue trousers. She bathed without hurrying and almost fell asleep in a warm, deep pool in the freshing room. Then she slipped into a blue gown she found laid out on the bed—just as before—near the watery wall that cascaded down the room's south side. She studied its outflow, below floor level at the bottom of a finger-deep pool. Someday, she decided, she would simply stand in the flow and bathe here. Water flowed almost everywhere at Hesed. *Of course,* she mused as she smoothed the long, damp waves of her hair. *People from watery Thyrica built this sanctuary.* Had Ehret been a wet world too?

As her thirsty ears drank the sounds, she caught a whiff of the Trinn Hill woods. *So those are kirka trees on the island,* she reflected. The depth of her relief to have reached sanctuary awed her. Had the hormones of pregnancy and motherhood done this? Had she lost her hunger for adventure, or had her brief honeymoon in this place so enthralled her that she would never be a callow warrior again?

Her children were safe. For now, that was enough.

Brennen waited on the walkway with Tel, who wore a plain gray jumpsuit that lent him a new air of understated maturity. "You look more comfortable," Brennen said, extending an arm.

"I feel a world better." Deeply relaxed, she took his arm. Then she sensed his reserved mood. "Where are the babies?"

He stepped out down the walkway. "We're expected in Dabarrah's office."

The Sanctuary Master waited inside like a white-and-gold statue, but she saw no sign of Kiel or Kinnor. "Prince Tel," Master Dabarrah said, "forgive me a moment's necessary rudeness. May I speak alone with the Caldwells for ten minutes? Then please rejoin us."

"Certainly. I would enjoy a closer look at your island landscaping." Tel retreated out the arch toward the pool.

Dabarrah nodded to Brennen, who looked serious and now felt troubled. "You have to know, Mari. This won't wait."

As she sat down on a white stone bench, she had the odd sensation that a shadow was blowing toward Hesed House's rippling serenity.

"Before we left college," Brennen said, "Shamarr Dickin put two prohibitions on us. First, I'm not to touch your mind. No Sentinel can. I cannot now, nor... when I come to bed."

"Brenn!" she whispered, aghast. Not in loving her? Clearly that was the gist of Dickin's prohibition. Not to touch Brennen's depths... she would wither, starve, after months of feasting on intimate pleasure.

Had the Shamarr somehow discovered the darkness behind her turn? Had Spieth told him?

She glanced aside. Master Dabarrah sat across the room on another white bench, casually drawing one long leg up beside him. His sad eyes and open palms suggested compassion.

"Why?" she demanded.

Brennen cleared his throat. He sat down beside her and took her hand. "Mari, somehow—and this is the danger, we're not sure how—you apparently killed Harcourt Terrell."

Firebird blinked. "Terrell, the security tech?"

Brennen nodded, frowning. "He's the one who attacked you at college. He put you under the watch-link."

"I killed him? I didn't even see him."

He held her hand tighter. "We found his body outside the master room door, inside the apartment. No injury, no sign of suicide drugs. No other explanation."

Firebird looked at Dabarrah again. The elder Master Sentinel pressed his palms together and stared down.

She'd killed before. In memory, she dragged Baron Parkai's corpse into a wardrobe. She had meant to stun him.

"Do you remember what you did to Terrell?" Brennen asked.

"I didn't do anyth—wait. The last I remember, I tried to turn." She frowned, remembering. "You don't think I scared him to death?"

Brennen didn't answer directly. "When I arrived, your mental strength was completely spent. You were dying. I had to strengthen your beta energies to keep your autonomic nervous system functioning while your strength built again. It's called psychic shock." Shifting his feet, he fingered his cuff tab. "Tell Master Dabarrah about the dark images. I explained as well as I could, but he should hear this from you."

Though it brought back all her misery, she carefully described the flaming darkness and its precedent in Netaian mythology.

Master Dabarrah inclined his head when she finished. "Thank you. I see you dislike speaking of this."

Brennen touched her hand. "If your carrier is bound to that imagery, then maybe your epsilon strength is unalterably joined to the images. Maybe, just by turning, you did somehow kill him—and his death at such proximity sent you into shock. But we don't know, and even Shamarr Dickin doesn't know what to do, except to protect others from you. He put you on what's called avoid-status."

She stared.

"You only turned?"

"That's all I remember."

Brennen frowned. "Any trained Sentinel has substantial control over his own beta centers. It's possible Terrell shut them down involuntarily in response to your imagery and epsilon turn. If that's the case," he said, furrowing his forehead, "you could only harm the starbred. Especially those of higher potential. It would take the mental strength of two, at least, to kill this way. Yours, plus the attacker's—"

"Or so we believe," Dabarrah interjected.

"No Sentinel has ever been able to do this," Brennen went on. "You have no control, no training. I'm sure you see the potential danger—"

"To you! And..." Firebird paused, silenced by a horrible new thought. "The babies?" she whispered, turning to Dabarrah. "Could they be strong enough to—no, Master, Brennen wouldn't attack me, and neither would an infant. I was only trying to protect myself, and that nearly killed me. I can't turn accidentally. It's a battle to turn at all."

"That is all true," said Dabarrah, "but there are psychic reflexes no one can control. You did not counterattack. You merely turned. Under Shamarr Dickin's order, you must be kept from your children until we are absolutely certain you won't harm them... merely by turning."

Firebird gulped air. Heat rose to her cheeks. "You're not listening. I would never go after them. They wouldn't try to hurt me. Give me my boys."

"You did not kill Harcourt Terrell deliberately," Dabarrah murmured.

Nor Baron Parkai, but— "This isn't right!" she cried. "Brennen, tell him not to do this!"

Brennen seized her hand and held tightly.

"He is as angry and confused as you are." Dabarrah shifted on the white bench. "Still, the injunction is temporary. My degrees are in psi medicine, Firebird. I may approach you safely. I have developed special defenses. The infants' minds are unformed," he stressed. "They're utterly at the mercy of others."

Firebird clenched her free hand behind her back. *Blessed Singer, did Brennen put Kiel and Kinnor in tardema-sleep, clear back at the college, to protect them from me?* Had Brenn known about this status? She tried to pull back her other hand. Brennen held on.

Footsteps approached on the waterside walkway. A young sekiyr entered, followed by a gliding cart crowded with earthenware dishes. The sekiyr extended the cart's legs and carefully set out dinner. Master Dabarrah slid four stools to a wooden sideboard.

Tellai stepped into the arch. "May I join you?"

Brennen and Dabarrah turned to Firebird. "Come," she said numbly.

Firebird accepted the thick stew Brennen served her, filled with chunks of vegetables so bright they must've been carried on the run from garden to kettle, coarse brown bread with a seductive aroma, and plump berries—colored and faceted like garnets, they were the size of eggs but smelled like melons.

They tasted like dust.

She'd killed a man. Again. Again, it was self-defense... but this time, she'd used only the darkness inside her. What if she did harm Kiel or

Kinnor—or Brennen? Had a miraculous string of failures kept her from killing Janesca?

But if her turn killed people, then why was Medical Master Spieth alive? Spieth was there when she turned the first time... and Brennen, and Tel... and at least one sekiyr...

Brennen and Tel ate quickly, relating the battle at Thyrica to Dabarrah, though Firebird saw and sensed several inquiring, empathizing glances from Brennen. She did feel his hurt now, and his anger with Dickin. No wonder he'd shielded his feelings as they left the medical complex. He had known that the avoid-status barred her from contact with Kiel and Kinnor.

Once, only once, she'd tried desperately to stop Kinnor's wailing.

But never by harming him! She couldn't hurt a vulnerable child, the union of her very life with Brennen's.

"There's a chance we may be blockaded," Dabarrah was saying, "since they can't hope to attack through our fielding net. So we've run messengers everywhere our people live in numbers. Tallis will pass news to the high council at Elysia. No action is being taken yet, and we're fully self-sufficient, but plans of several sorts are being discussed—as is your RIA work, although only among ourselves."

Numbly shredding a chunk of brown bread, Firebird glanced up. What was RIA work? Immediately she felt a cautionary surge from Brennen. Tel, examining a four-bite garnetberry, seemed not to hear.

She dropped the bread chunk. Suddenly she wanted to be alone. Brennen rose. "I'll see you back to the room, Mari. Then I want to talk to Tel a little longer."

Her anger had faded. The numbness was passing, and tears would come next... and then, maybe, a plan. She pushed back her stool. "Thank you, Brenn, but I can find my way." She caught his glance and thought hard at him, *Leave me alone for a while. Please.* "Good night, gentlemen." She slipped out.

Halfway to her room, she broke into a run.

17

CALLED

appassionato
impassioned

After they finished eating, Brennen led Tel onto the waterside pavement. Overhead, the turquoise ceiling rippled with dusky blue shadows.

He'd returned, but neither at peace nor in triumph. He had known what Jenner must tell Firebird about Kinnor and Kiel. Shamarr Dickin had forbidden him to tell her himself. *She must see you stand with her,* Dickin explained.

You tell her, he wanted to retort. Sometimes, years ago, he'd resented his father. Now he knew Dickin too could be peremptory.

But Dickin was right. Until Dabarrah finished evaluating her, he could only comfort her. "I've loved and trusted Master Dabarrah," he told Tel, "since I served as a sekiyr under him. He shows the power of gentleness clearly." He stopped at the water's edge and rested both forearms on the lattice railing. An hour ago, he'd wakened Kinnor and Kiel while Firebird bathed. He'd held them tightly before relinquishing them to Mistress Anna.

"I see what you mean." Tel stepped up beside him. "It's not Dabarrah's authority that gives him such strength of spirit, but the other way around."

Brennen nodded, surprised. "You're stronger yourself than anyone realized. Until you came up against real adversity, you had no chance to show it."

"Thank you." Tel raised his head and stared out over the bright pool. "This is an impressive place, Caldwell."

"It's a far cry from the Angelo palace."

"It's quieter. But there's a deeper power at work. Even I can feel it."

"Hesed is probably the most heavily protected enclave in this region of the Whorl."

"Then Firebird and the babies finally are out of danger," Tel observed.

Yes. Out of danger, he thought, surprised to recognize another source of bitterness. *From the Shuhr and the Federacy's threats.*

Holy One, help us to take these separations as kindly as Shamarr Dickin surely means them. He'd never felt less kindly toward Shamarr Lo Dickin.

And how would the Sunton attack affect his people's standing with the Federacy? He stirred, unable to shake a heavy new dread. "I almost wish we hadn't left this place," he murmured, bowing his head. Would the Shuhr have blasted Sunton if he'd stayed here? What was the final death toll?

"If you hadn't gone to Thyrica," Tel asked, "would I have been able to contact you?"

"No."

"Then I'm glad you did."

And Kinnor and Kiel had been conceived because he and Mari went to the college for her diagnosis and treatment. He mustn't blame himself for the devastation on Thyrica. Others would do that for him.

Water lapped at the pool's edge near Brennen's feet. After a time, he spoke again. "We live close to the soil here. We do without weather control, we grow food the old ways, and keep animals—to refresh the spirit, and remind us of our kinship with the rest of creation."

"Then this is your... monastery?"

Brennen shifted his elbows onto the lattice and rested his chin on his hands. "Not quite. Everyone at college spends a rotation here, studying the commandments and our duty to carry them wherever we serve. And how to add beauty where necessity has been satisfied." He gestured toward the stepping-stone islands. Far out on the water the trees seemed to ripple with waving reflections. "Many of our elderly come back when their epsilon abilities wane. They spend their last active years in defensive fielding service, protecting the Procyel system. The sekiyrra do most of our manual labor, but everyone must work to maintain the retreat." There'd soon be an influx, he guessed: Sentinels with small children, fleeing before the Shuhr struck Thyrica again. Dabarrah was ready. For decades, they'd known Hesed would be their last haven. "Firebird will probably be excused from the heaviest labor because she's still recovering from childbirth," he went on, "but we'll join the task rotation tomorrow morning, you and I."

Tel flexed his slender arms, almost smiling. "That's where you built the shoulders, Caldwell?"

"It's a good life," Brennen admitted. "It serves a profound need in the Ehretan starbred. On Thyrica we've always been a people apart. You'll be content here."

Tel straightened his back. "No," he said. "Never content. Phoena is a prisoner." He drummed long fingers on the railing. "I came for your help. I don't know that I'd have the audacity to ask again, now that I understand your situation. But every day she's there, I can't help thinking she will be in more danger."

Brennen sensed Tellai's fear and hope. He glanced toward his own door and guessed Firebird would want a few more minutes alone. "If I stay here for Firebird's sake, will you try to go to Three Zed yourself?"

The dark eyes caught his glance, welcoming scrutiny. "Yes."

Brennen tried to relax his taut jaw muscles. "You haven't a chance against those people."

"I know."

Numbly he rubbed his face. Phoena had become a focal point, regardless of her personality. The Federate summons rose in his memory, and Regional's offer, and the veiled threat against Firebird.

Would that summons change? His mind worked backward, counting days, wondering...

Yes. The attack on Thyrica could've been launched after Phoena arrived at Three Zed. What had she shown them that helped precipitate it?

And what were the Shuhr doing to her? Questioning her, tormenting her? Altering her mind?

He cringed to remember that he had personally cleared Harcourt Terrell of suspicion. For decades, the Sentinels had thought they held back the Shuhr threat. Maybe the Shuhr had just been marking time.

Hesed, at least, could not be attacked the way they'd struck Sunton. It was fully protected from any piloted strike or unpiloted drone.

"The two of us might succeed. She'd come away for me." Tellai broke into Brennen's thoughts, then faltered. "I think."

"I don't mean to be unkind," Brennen said, "but for the moment, no one's going anywhere. Even if you tried, they have powers you can't resist. If I had to protect you, I wouldn't be able to work against their surveillance."

Tel tilted his chin up, though his eyes looked thick. "I understand."

"I'll contact the Alert Forces from here," Brennen said gruffly. "I'll help if I can, but first we need to see how they respond to the strike at Sunton."

"That could take weeks."

"I'm sorry, Tel. That's the way it has to be." Brennen glanced at the door again. *Now,* he guessed. *She needs me now.*

• • •

He slept badly that night. Well after midnight, he slipped into a familiar dream.

He gripped the controls of his intercept fighter, patrolling an unfamiliar world, with no idea why he'd been sent there. No objective glowed on his onboard computer, no route/risk data on his display. The console seemed realistic, but below him, landforms varied from the normal to the bizarre. He flew over a river that flowed preposterously up and down a line of rolling blue hills, then a city that looked like a two-dimensional grid map, with human icons traveling dashed-line streets. A huge golden cube stood at the grid's center, seemingly dropped from the sky.

He banked north toward a line of purple mountains. His atmospheric sensor showed well within the green range, so there must be breathable air outside. Still, his cockpit smelled stuffy. He couldn't stay airborne much longer.

"Brennen," a voice said in his headset.

This was new. So was the mountain that stood alone, surrounded by cloud wisps and dusted with snow. A wreath of broad white waterfalls obscured its feet. "Caldwell here," he answered.

Landing data appeared on his display. "Come. We will speak."

He activated an automatic landing cycle. A duracrete breakway strip appeared halfway up one waterfall, on a ledge that broadened as he approached. The strip had no support buildings, no hangar or parking area, no refueling dock. He circled once and touched down. His craft rolled to a stop at the waterfall's edge. He popped the canopy, then pulled off his helmet.

"Brennen," the voice said again.

He looked around. He saw no one. Disquieted, he reached for his blazer—

And then realized he knew that Voice. Sometimes it whispered at the back of his mind. He sprang out of the cockpit and dropped to his knees on the duracrete. "I am here, Holy One."

Cool air flowed down from snowfields high on the mountain. On both sides of the breakway strip, blue flowers nodded on long, leafy stems. The voice seemed to flow from that near waterfall, in a deep, mellow timbre without accent. "Your enemy plans to destroy Hesed," it said, "and most of your brethren. Stop him."

How could he feel so calm, conversing with the King of the Universe? Yet he knew how to answer, as if he'd been given a protocol briefing. "Thank you," he murmured. "This is the highest honor I can imagine."

"Go to Three Zed, for Phoena. Leave in two days."

"Three Zed? Alone, Holy One?"

"You are never alone." The voice didn't shame him for asking, but reassured him heart-deep. If he were ordered to go there, he would be empowered. Equipped.

He looked up at the waterfall, half expecting to see an ancient face in the spray.

He saw a faint rainbow instead, with water drops flowing through it like diamonds. "Thank you," he repeated. He bowed his head...

And found himself sitting upright in bed. Mari lay at his side, breathing peacefully. At the other side of his bed, the watery wall cascaded on.

· · ·

The next morning broke fresh. Bursts of autumn wind cooled sekiyrra who labored in Hesed's gardens, east of the hillside.

Firebird picked her way down a gentle slope. She and Brennen had walked up here after morning prayer service. Her pale blue gown trailed the last summer flowers, and tears chilled her cheeks. Last night, she'd cried bitterly in his arms over Shamarr Dickin's isolation order. And now, he'd had a dream. A mountain, a waterfall... a voice...

"But it makes no sense." Firebird pushed out the words as evenly as she could. "You can't—"

"Mari," he interrupted. His eyes seemed to focus on something infinitely remote, and his voice sounded distant. "I'm the oldest heir to the promises. Sometimes, at critical moments, the eldest is given a vision. Like the Shamarr. I never doubted, but I never imagined it could be so vivid. So plain."

He couldn't mean this. Only last night, he promised to stay here unless Alert Forces backed him up.

But she felt his utter confidence, his serenity, even a new strength. When they first met at Veroh, he'd seemed this remote and full of power.

Now he claimed that if he stayed here, the Shuhr would destroy Hesed. "Think it through," she urged. "At least wait until Master Dabarrah finds out if Terrell did further damage. Dabarrah might want help with my dark visions too. And Kiel and Kinnor need us, not Mistress Anna."

"Dabarrah estimates several weeks to help you. I must go in two days, Mari. Supposedly, Hesed's fielding will turn back any attack, but can we be sure now?"

"Nothing has changed," she insisted. Halting, she reached toward him.

He stepped into her arms. "I've made a career of military intelligence," he reminded her. "I've been prepared for this. I don't want to do it, but I must."

Stunned, she pressed her cheek to his shoulder. One week ago, she'd had a family. She'd been a mother, a wife.

She still was both! "You're not being overconfident?"

"He wouldn't send me," Brennen answered, "if He didn't know I was capable, with His help." He curled one hand around the back of her head. "Dabarrah is equipped for his work too. The children have him, and Mistress Anna, and every teacher and sekiyr and elder here to care for them, until Dabarrah feels certain you can... control that wild talent."

"But it's a trap, Brenn! It's not Phoena the Shuhr want, it's you! Listen." She pulled away. "The Federacy won the Veroh War quickly because you took two prisoners. Me, and then Dorning Stele. What would the Shuhr do with all you know? They opened a war against the Federacy. You could betray it." She remembered that guilt and shame too well.

"No," he said. They walked on down the grassy hill. "My situation is different from yours. Special Operations trains its agents in selective amnesia techniques. Those cannot be broken. I'm not just equipped to resist mind-access. I can defeat any interrogation."

She sensed, though, that the thought finally broke his serenity. She felt him cringe.

"If you don't find Phoena there, they'll kill you. And for what?"

"For the Sanctuary. This call is an honor, an expression of the Speaker's trust in me."

Firebird lengthened her steps in pursuit. "But not even Danton wants Phoena around!"

"No." He turned his head so she could hear his answer. "There, you're wrong. The Federacy contacted me shortly after she disappeared."

"And?" Shocked, she halted in midstride.

"For them, it's political. Apparently they realized how badly they want Netaia as part of the Federacy. Madam Kernoweg herself asked me to consider going to Three Zed."

Firebird gaped. She'd squared off against Councilor Kernoweg's greed... and seen recent stats. Even after demilitarization, Netaia's resources were estimated at almost a quarter of the Federacy's.

"They urgently want to show Netaia they can protect their own. Even though she probably went to them, Mari."

"But—"

"I know, Kernoweg only makes marginal sense to me too. But the Council has declared that trying to save your sister is a security matter. That frees me to use all my abilities without breaking the Codes, even if I have to take her against her will. And if I succeed, the Federacy wants me back. Probably at Tallis."

"They need you now," she muttered. "More than ever, after Sunton. They're idiots to risk you like this." She stared out over the river into a red stone valley. At the corner of her eye she saw him take several more steps down the meadow, then turn back.

"All right." She balled a fist on one hip. "Then I'm going with you."

"You mustn't. The dream was clear about that too. The Speaker wants you here, for the moment."

He wouldn't thwart her that easily. "Is Phoena worth it, Brenn? Is... is the Federacy?"

He looked up at her, and she devoured the sight of him standing square-shouldered with the wind in his hair. "I would never leave you for Phoena, nor for the Federacy. Only for one Person anywhere." He shook his head, and his eyes wandered again. "I never thought to be called like this." She felt his heart deeply at peace. Not even terrible danger could turn him from this resolve.

Nor could she! *Your fame's assured,* she wanted to cry. *Do you have to be a hero ten times over?*

He reached out and closed his fingers around her hand, and they walked down toward the house. "Remember why Tel came to us, and what I promised him. It's been as hard for him to change his thinking as it was for you."

"Harder, probably." She stepped over the burrow of some small creature and lengthened her stride to match Brennen's. On the ground, leaves were reddening on red stones. "Tel has a secure position on Netaia. He could still go back. I had nothing left to live for."

"I'm glad you see that." He stopped again. "Now that your sister has seen the enemy, maybe she's even found enough wisdom to realize what they are."

"Brennen." Her eyes filled with stinging tears.

He drew her into his arms. It was on the tip of her tongue to beg him: not to go alone to Three Zed, not to risk himself when she needed his support. Or at least to bring her along, now that she could move and act and fight without endangering Kiel and Kinnor.

But they had agreed that a person needed one highest priority, something to serve above everything else. He was called. Firebird had been ready to die for much less over the red sands of Veroh. *But how can you do this now, Mighty Singer?*

"Please," Brennen said softly, "send me with your blessing. I've never saved my life by sheltering it. If I don't go, Hesed will fall, and we all could die. You, me... most of the kindred. It was clear, Mari. There was nothing eerie or questionable about it."

And now she knew how it might happen. "But it's the wrong time. And Phoena's the wrong reason." And he would not go alone. Maybe he'd feel less responsible if she stowed away. She could do it...

But could she hide her intention? He could sense even a stranger's dishonesty, unless that stranger were a powerful impostor like Harcourt Terrell. Her chin drooped.

His arms tightened their circle. He didn't answer, but she read a new emotion in him. He ached beneath his confidence, for her and for the timing. She also felt his growing paternal pride.

And did he fear her mysterious killing ability?

Surely he must. She did. "I can't bless you," she said at last. "I don't know how. But you know I won't forbid you. Don't ever diminish yourself for me."

He nearly crushed her against himself. "Your strength," he whispered beside her ear, "has always been greater than your fear. Be strong for Tel when I'm gone."

Gone. It sounded so final.

She drew on his calmness to gather herself. When she'd mastered her grief, she tangled her fingers with his. They walked on down.

He led her to a musty underground hangar. At the hilltop fielding station, he'd shown her a defense system that protected Hesed. A fielding team of Sentinels could project subtronically coordinated mental energies over a distance, just as a Shuhr team had kept her under watch-link during the Thyrica battle.

In the hangar, she saw that most of their escorts had shipped out, leaving one heavy fighter. It lay partially gutted. Busy crewers transferred portions of its electronic heart onto a smaller craft. She watched a thin sekiyr walk across the hangar, carrying a large cylindrical object several inches above his outspread hands, practicing epsilon skills as he helped.

Brennen beckoned her outside. On the grassy breakway strip, new growth glistened in the scars of recent landings. "Back at Thyrica," he said, "several of us were working on a device that would let one Sentinel extend his or her skills much farther than across a room. Ship to ship, actually."

She thought that through. "Was that what got us past the englobement?"

"Yes. Dardy tested it there. We call it Ree-a, Remote Individual Amplification."

She formed a small "o" with her lips.

"We progressed with it far enough to mount two systems into HF-108s before the emergency arose, and we brought one along," Brennen said as he walked. "The power's still low, but it should give a Sentinel the remote capability to pass through a fielding net undetected. We know the Shuhr use fielding technology to defend Three Zed."

She sighed. "So you'll take that smaller ship. The one they're modifying now."

"Exactly. Mari, I know what you want. I'd bring you if I could. Your skills would be invaluable. But you must stay and work with Jenner. It's urgent to get our children back."

She didn't look up. "You can't wait? You're certain?"

He shook his head. "The Shuhr are as unbalanced as they've ever been. We've disabled their fleet. Now is the time to go, before they recover."

"Brenn." She halted at one end of the landing strip. "If you have one day here, could I be consecrated? Will they still have me?" she added, feeling dubious. "On avoid-status?"

His grip tightened on her hand. "I was just trying to decide how to ask if you might want that. Yes. Master Jenner is a psi healer. Even with A-status, he can access you to give you the ritual memories."

Had he thought of it for the same reason? she wondered. If he didn't come back, then she wanted to remember standing beside him, fully accepted as one of his community. If it was the last gift they gave each other, she would hear those mysterious prophecies explained in his own tenor voice.

"I only wish," she muttered, "you weren't doing this for Phoena."

"Not Phoena, Mari. This is for you. For Kinnor and Kiel, and for Hesed."

• • •

"Two hundred ships!" thundered the Eldest, Eshdeth Shirak. "Nearly all that we had!"

Phoena covered her ears.

Eldest Shirak wore black, as did forty other men and women who stood between his Kellian tapestry and that misty battle curtain. He'd declared a day of mourning. Before him, side by side under scrutiny, stood his grandson Micahel and a smaller man with arrogant pale green eyes.

"And Caldwell had how many?" purred Dru Polar. He sat near Phoena on one end of Shirak's obsidian desk top. Polar's satiny orange sash was the brightest flash of color in the room, outshining the star tank's tiny jewels. Phoena liked Polar's sash belts, though she distrusted his lingering glances at Cassia Talumah, who looked ripe and supple in black ship-boards.

"Thirty-two, mine Eldest," said the smaller man.

"Shef'th," Polar swore.

Lumpy little Juddis Adiyn sat near a gold-sprayed wall. Mockingly, he touched one ear. "What was that, Arac? I couldn't have heard correctly."

Micahel glared at his comrade, his fury obvious even to Phoena. The other's—Arac's—pale green eyes hardened, as if he foresaw his fate. He had failed the Shirak family. He would pay with nothing less than his life. "Thirty-two ships," he repeated distinctly. "They rendezvoused at the Sentinel College and took off from that point. Heavy-fighter class, trained to fight as a unit, and solidly led. And something else too, some disruptor field we've never encountered before. We had more guns, Eldest, it's true, but many of our pilots hadn't flown warships before last month."

"We still would've taken that one vital ship," Micahel growled, "if you'd paid closer attention."

"How so?" Eldest Shirak rose from his chair. He strolled around the projection tank.

"Before we lost touch with Harcourt Terrell," Micahel snapped, "he brought the Caldwell woman inside his watch-link. Arac supervised. We should've been able to anticipate their every maneuver. We should be celebrating an overdue victory."

Shirak turned on his grandson. "And if you had attacked the college first, instead of testing your equipment somewhere else, they wouldn't have had time to run. If you were any kind of commander, you would have hit the target we wanted. You could've taken out a hundred Sentinels with one strike. Half of them, Micahel. Half!"

"But the Federacy would've defended the rest of them." Micahel set his chin. "This way, Thyrica lost more nonaltered than starbred. They're the ones we need to frighten."

Phoena only understood this much: Caldwell's squadron had delayed Micahel's force long enough for Thyrica's Home Forces to launch more ships. The Thyrian force smashed Micahel's battle group, taking revenge for that cratered town. His fifty-ship command flight had fled back here. Other pilots—settlement recruits, voice-commanded to fight to the last missile—covered his retreat.

The Federacy wouldn't dare to try striking back here. A fielding team could disrupt and destroy the attackers' minds as they approached. It could divert falling objects. Three Zed was impregnable.

"Do you have any idea," Micahel's grandfather said, "how much work went into collecting that fleet?"

Phoena compressed her lips as the graying Eldest paced before the two young men. The idiots. She couldn't believe it herself. First, the Netaian strike team missed Carradee. Now all those young Shuhr had died, while Firebird eluded them again. They might've eliminated not only her but two illegally conceived male—male!—by-blows of the Netaian nobility.

She lowered her eyebrows at Arac. It seemed clear that he, at least, would pay.

"I do know, Eldest," Arac said quietly. "I went on the Narkin raid."

"Do you think that excuses you?" Shirak's pacing brought him close to Phoena and Dru Polar, where he turned again. "We can live two hundred years. If we risk ourselves in battle, we expect to return safely. Your surveillance team was our guarantee. You betrayed us."

Phoena glanced sidelong at Dru Polar. Dru stood with his arms crossed low, over his sash.

"Eldest," Micahel said, "this is no defeat. We know exactly where the Carabohds are now. All of them. We can take them out. Let me try this again, at Procyel."

"Hesed has epsilon fielding! How many ships do you think we can throw away?" Shirak lowered himself into his desk chair. "Adiyn, have you seen my grandson die in this room?"

Juddis Adiyn stood close to the tapestry. He looked hard at Phoena. "Not Micahel," he said, "but Arac." The green-eyed man flinched. "I have foreseen a lost Ehretan family stretching out a hand of execution. Casvah, the vessel, a cup full of death."

Phoena frowned. She was no Ehretan half-breed! Dru accused her of carrying Sentinel genes, though. She'd given up arguing. He was a titillating companion. Fascinating, frightening. Thrilling.

"Good," Shirak said. "Polar, show Her Highness how to operate the striker."

Polar slid a weapon from his sash. Arac raised his head, and his green eyes widened.

Phoena leaned closer, examining the weapon as Polar rolled it between his strong hands. It had the look of a baron's baton of office, a silver rod with several buttons within finger's reach of its knurled handle. Dru touched one. A needlelike probe sprang from its far end.

She reached out a hand.

"If you'd like to see what it can do, use a low charge and avoid the nervous system. You'll have to be careful if you don't want to kill him." Dru slid a black stud toward the pommel. "The farther up the shaft you set this, the more power to the probe. Activate here." He stroked an orange button below the thumb cradle.

Phoena snatched the baton. She'd never personally killed anyone, not even a wastling, and she didn't want Polar or the others to know that. If one counted the hundreds of cloned embryos whose brains they'd pulverized, she was the only person in this room without that distinction.

For a minute she merely retracted and extended the probe, getting the feel of holding it. Then she stepped out beside the desk, faced Adiyn, and inclined her head. "Sir, I am no Casvah, but the house of Angelo honors those who assist it. Shall I demonstrate the consequences of failing us?"

Adiyn smiled benignly. "Please."

Phoena considered Arac, who outweighed her by half. "You. And you." She flicked a graceful finger at two of Shirak's staff. "Hold him for me."

Arac flinched but didn't cry out when she touched the probe to his elbow at very low power. She crossed behind him, considering, then pierced the back of his knee. When again she pressed the orange stud, his weight shifted. His involuntary back kick missed her by centimeters, and then his leg hung twitching.

Intrigued, Phoena started to experiment in earnest.

• • •

Later, Dru escorted her to her rooms. "What was your hurry?" he asked. Arm in arm, they rounded a corner of the steely inner corridor. "We were enjoying ourselves."

"I didn't expect the highest power level to kill him from a finger touch. That's a long way from the brain."

"Effective use is complex," he confessed. "At that power, if you even approached a major nerve, he'd have gone almost instantly. As it was, he took several minutes to die."

"He did." Phoena stepped regally, savoring the sensation of having ended a life. She felt almost omnipotent. Later, she would look up "Arac's" life story and find out whom she'd executed.

This striker would make a fine deterrent for Netaian criminals. She would order a production plant built to furnish her Enforcement Corps.

At her door, they stopped. She turned toward Dru, though not too close, and lowered her eyes seductively. "If I ever get a chance at Firebird, Dru, will you lend that to me again?"

"If it can be arranged."

"What's the absolute worst you could do with it? I'd want to know I was giving her the very hardest way out."

"Lowest power, throat pressure point." His eyes seemed to crackle as he reached for the side of her neck. He caressed the smooth skin over her jaw, below her ear. "Here," he breathed. "Not as slow, but excruciating."

She pulled away in fright. "No," she said firmly. "Not me."

"You deserve no better, Phoena Angelo. You're a traitor to your own kind. Your own sisters."

Phoena tried to struggle out of his arms. She'd wondered, she even suspected that the Shuhr never meant to make her queen. She had one moment of ghastly lucidity—

Blank.

Fully relaxed, she pressed against his hard, muscular body. No man had ever drawn her as intensely as Testing Commander Dru Polar.

"Will you come in?" she whispered.

Dru dropped his arms and stepped away. "I'm tired. I've had enough pleasure for one day."

Phoena pressed an open palm against her door's lock panel, then slipped inside, giving Polar a kittenish farewell smile. Content again in her lovely little gray rooms, she sealed the door she could open so easily from the passway—but not from inside.

18

CONSECRATED

moderato
moderately

Firebird stood in the broad entry to Hesed's chapter room, shifting from one bare foot to the other. The flagstones felt cool underfoot. Inside, voices sang softly.

Finally, she could put this behind her. No more covert looks or whispers, no regretful subvocalizations on Brennen's behalf.

She flexed one foot and toed a crack in the stone.

Years ago on Ehret, Brennen's ancestors had welcomed each new consecrant with a blood sacrifice, to illustrate the Speaker's covering for his or her transgressions. With Ehret desolate, those temple sacrifices could no longer be practiced, but the faith community still insisted that every child inherited the taint of evil... and that until the Speaker himself made perfect atonement, a believer should confirm true faith by attending a sacrifice. Now, instead of bloodying their hands, they passed down an excruciatingly vivid memory.

Brennen stood close by, waiting with her for the door to swing open. He wore military dress whites again. She'd borrowed another simple sekiyr's gown—white this time. Traditionally, a consecrant came unshod. "You're all right barefoot?" Brennen had asked, washing up after his morning's fieldwork. He'd taken his place on the task rotation, no matter how briefly he would be staying here.

"I don't mind." She liked her toes free, especially now that her feet weren't swollen. Still, she felt uneasy. Remembering her catechismal answers didn't worry her, but she didn't look forward to what would come after, when Master Dabarrah transferred that last sacrifice into her memory. From Path instruction, she mostly understood the concept of substitutionary sacrifice, but she still didn't like it. Even after finding that Darkness inside her, she didn't feel evil… and the Singer had already brought her to himself, accepting her despite all her flaws.

Still, the faith community felt it necessary to prove how seriously the One took a believer's shortcomings. The memory transfer was considered a teaching tool, to stress that even now, covering was only bought with a death.

"In that case," she'd demanded, "how could the deathless Singer ever finish a perfect atonement?"

"A mystery, as yet unrevealed," her Path instructor had said.

"We aren't told exactly," Brennen had explained later, but she felt a suppressed tingling in him. He had a guess, or at least a suspicion.

Fine, she reflected, toeing another rough spot. *I'll do this, but they still won't convince me I'm tainted. I know what evil is. Phoena is mostly evil. Shuhr are totally evil—aren't they?*

What about Shuhr children? she wondered. The soft singing stopped. She glanced up.

Brennen took her hand and kissed it, and she felt his assurance. "Just don't try to turn," he reminded her.

"Not a chance." She didn't want that flaming darkness to ruin this occasion. From all she'd heard, the sacrifice was awful enough.

But she'd seen death. She was as well prepared as anyone. Better than most.

One door swung open, held by a smiling young sekiyr gowned, like Firebird, in white. "We're ready," she said.

Firebird stepped into the long room. On benches at both sides of its carpeted aisle, about fifty Sentinels and sekiyrra stared back. She hesitated on the threshold and glanced around. Most of Hesed's transient population must have gathered. This would be no private rite, the way she'd originally planned it. Holding Brennen's hand, she paced forward.

Master Dabarrah waited under a skylight, near the center of a curved platform. Behind him stood an altar like the ones in other chapter rooms, its length draped with brocade cloths of pure red, blue, and green. An oil lamp burned on the green cloth between open copies of *Dabar* and *Mattah*. Behind, on a wall built of red stone, a large gold Sentinel's star hung seemingly suspended in space. Faint light also came from tall candles burning on gold sconces along both walls. On the altar's right side, a tall youth sat on a chair, playing a kinnora like Janesca's. The congregation sang with him in that strange, throaty Ehretan language.

A kneeling bench, cushioned in red with a smooth wooden rail, had been moved to the center of the dais, in front of the altar.

She approached it.

• • •

Brennen gripped her hand. He'd longed for this day, never guessing it would come here, but the Speaker's timing was always perfect.

He glanced at the young kinnora player and smiled. Someday—probably soon, since Mari would be anxious to meet him—she would find out that this solemn sekiyr was Ellet Kinsman's brother.

Fill her heart, Holy One. Her eternal standing was already assured, but this rite never left a consecrant unchanged. Besides, ceremony meant the world to Netaians, especially to Mari.

And so Master Dabarrah had made him a special promise, for afterward.

• • •

Firebird looked up as they reached the aisle's end. Master Dabarrah's eyes shone with the solemn joy she'd seen in Brennen on other holy occasions.

"Come," he said, beckoning them up the three steps. As they stepped onto the dais, he said, "Brennen, take off your shoes, for this is now holy ground."

Brennen left them on the steps. Firebird peered forward. Sure enough, Master Jenner and the musician also stood barefoot.

She smiled slightly. They probably didn't kick off their shoes as often as she did.

Standing before the small bench, she reviewed all she had studied with her Path instructor. Fortunately, Master Dabarrah would ask, and she could answer, in familiar Old Colonial. Brennen's consecration had been done in the high mode, entirely in Ehretan.

Not long ago, she had sat on a chapter-room bench on Thyrica, listening while Destia Caldwell answered the same questions. She would never forget patting a handful of tear-dampened soil onto Destia's grave. She blinked and swallowed. Surely Destia was safe in the Singer's strong arms.

Master Dabarrah led her through the main tenets of her new faith: the Singer's oneness, His infinite holiness, wisdom, and power, His sovereignty over history. And His merciful love, so different from the unfeeling Powers.

She'd made the right choice.

She made it through her questions without major stumbles. Finally, Dabarrah looked deep into her eyes and her mind and asked, "For what purpose have you come, Firebird Mari Caldwell?"

She answered firmly, as she'd memorized, "To see the sacrifice for my covering."

"Then come and see." Dabarrah laid his hands on the kneeling bench's raised rail.

She stepped away from Brennen, rested her hands between Master Dabarrah's, and sank onto her knees. "Take a few seconds to get comfortable," Brennen had warned her. "You'll be there for a while. You don't want your legs to fall asleep."

The soft harp music started again. She braced herself, then looked up at Dabarrah's gray-blue eyes. *Do your worst,* she thought at him.

He half smiled. "What you will experience," he said, "actually happened to Timarah Gall, a young person of Modabah city, on a morning 190 years ago." The Sentinels sang on, but as Dabarrah's epsilon presence entered her mind, her vision shifted. The chapter room darkened. It grew, stretching into a huge arena... no, an auditorium... a temple, six-sided, almost totally blacked out. Timarah Gall wore loose, lightweight clothing, as if for a warm summer morning.

Firebird could barely see Dabarrah or the altar. She shut her eyes.

Timarah seemed to be tiptoeing behind two men in their twenties, one of whom waved her abruptly to halt.

She listened hard with her epsilon sense... and Firebird plunged willingly into the vision. *So this is how turning should feel!* she realized just before she lost all sense of separation from young Timarah.

She pulled hard on a rope wrapped around her left hand. Gently she curled her right fingers around the soft muzzle of a knee-high animal, black-headed with tall, hairless ears, but otherwise covered with an exquisitely soft, curling beige pelt.

It was a kipret, a sacrificial yearling. After searching for a week, she'd found this one wandering the hills, driven from its pen by raiders.

Ehret lay bleeding, gripped by a war between generations. Her own father had murdered her brother in his bed. He'd been reaching for her when she'd leaped out a window. Her friends had all died. She'd found these two young men, former temple acolytes, by accident—or divine help. The newest peril was plague, a hideous disease created by *her* side.

The young Altereds had sacked the Elders' temple, slaughtering kipreta out of scorn for the ancient faith. Only a few of the new Altereds still bowed to the Speaker, as she did. If Elder forces caught this trio today, they would die gruesomely, with special measures taken to destroy the brain centers the Elders had bred into them.

She listened again, questing cautiously outside each door as she stroked the kipret's furry head. It licked her forearm, then butted her leg. Unfortunately, she'd grown fond of the moronic creature. They came here in the pre-dawn, hoping to finish and escape undetected.

She'd put off this appointment for too many months. Then the war had erupted. Surprisingly, she found herself clinging to faith as friends died around her. The Speaker couldn't look on imperfection, though, and she was full of old lies, selfishness... and now hatred too. She stood condemned by her conscience and by the repentant but deadly determined Elders who once worshiped here. Coming here might cost her life, but if she made it down these steps, she could die with every possible assurance.

The others crept forward. *Hurry,* one urged subvocally.

Releasing the kipret's muzzle and tugging its rope, she followed. *This won't hurt,* she tried to assure it. *They'll be quick.* Still, she wanted to drop the rope, slap its rump, and drive it away—to rescue it, save its life.

Instead, she led it down, down the long stair-stepped aisle to the platform at center. Two high altars shared that platform. She hurried the stiff-legged beast up three steps. A cold breeze blew through shattered black windows.

The men pushed her into position between the altars. She knelt with her arms around the furry kipret's neck, repelled by what she had to do, comforted only by the sweet, blank-faced idiocy that had been bred into kipreta. "I've come," she murmured. "I'm here, Eternal Speaker, to see the sacrifice for my covering. Thank you for purifying my heart, for joining me with you in eternal communion. When my death comes," she added, glancing up at one of the six huge doors, praying no Elder forces waited outside, "take me to yourself. Accept my faith, small though it is. So let it be."

One of the men brought up a large wooden bowl. He set it on the rubble-strewn floor in front of the kipret, who started to nibble a ripped curl of carpet.

The other moved close, gripping a gleaming knife. Bone handled, that blade was almost as long as her forearm. "Hold its head up," he ordered.

She swallowed hard and tugged on the rope. Bile rose in her own throat. She squeezed her eyes shut.

She heard one gargling bleat, and then the rope wrenched her arm straight. She let go.

The kipret had collapsed over the bowl. The older man dropped his knife, wiped his hands on the twitching creature's back, and curled his fingers around her head, reciting the scriptures that promised her full acceptance.

Moving quickly, they worked as a team to haul the kipret by its legs onto the higher altar. Tears thickened her eyes as she carefully bent its still-warm limbs. Blood stained its chest and back.

The younger man knelt beside the bowl. Shuddering, she crouched beside him. The creature's blood smelled more like metal than meat.

Now she must identify, symbolically, with the kipret's death. She could finish her part with a drop... or by immersion. Considering the price she might pay for it, she wanted the full experience. She pulled a deep breath, eyeing the bowl that now looked in dim light to be full of blackness. *That's the kipret's very life,* she thought, staring at it. *Now its death... a bowl full of death... because I needed covering.* Everyone who ever lived had fallen into disobedience...

Blackness flamed at the depth of that bowl. Suddenly Firebird felt herself flung out of the ritual. The blackness licked up as it had done at the depth of her mind, luring her down, drawing her in. It called to her, singing of power and mastery and death. Consecration? A ludicrous hope. Eternal music? Only the black silence was real. *Turn,* it sang. *Turn, turn to me instead...*

Master Jenner, she thought frantically. *Help!*

Dabarrah's epsilon presence folded around her. The vision refocused. No more flames roiled in the bloody bowl—symbol of life and then death, and finally of the most sacred atonement promised for all her transgressions. She only needed to take a drop on one finger and touch the skin over her heart.

She hesitated, appalled by its gruesome, sticky-looking reality and feeling—for once—completely separate from every offense she'd ever committed.

Firebird identified utterly with Timarah. She'd hated, she'd lied, she'd broken her own promises. She still served Excellence and Pride instead of the Speaker's will. *I've bloodied my hands, even though they look clean.*

She made it her confession and plunged both hands to the bottom of the bowl.

The elder acolyte pushed a soft cloth at Timarah. She wiped her hands and wrists, pausing to touch one finger to her chest, knowing that it would stain her best pleated tunic. Now she was marked. If they caught her before she could bathe and change, they would know why she had come and would punish her for desecrating the altar. Altereds were no longer eligible to offer sacrifice. Elders decapitated her kind for a bounty.

One man raised the bowl to the high altar and draped the cloth over it. The poor kipret lay with its eyes and mouth open, its thick pink tongue clearly visible. Firebird shuddered at the contrast between the living beast and this stiffening corpse. She hated herself for luring it into her arms with honey flowers, when it could've gone on grazing wild in the hills.

Her offenses had turned its life into death. Only One could restore life...

The other man hurried to the low altar. He fingered open a hidden panel and reached for a control. *Ready?* he subvocalized.

As her hands dried, they tingled and itched. She dropped to a runner's crouch and faced one aisle. The other acolyte's footsteps pounded off in another direction.

Ready, she sent back. She must stand on the dais as he fired the altar...

A whoosh filled the temple. Orange light illuminated all six walls as flames consumed corpse, bowl, and blood, and she ran for her life...

• • •

Disoriented, Firebird clutched the kneeling rail. Master Dabarrah was speaking again, but she didn't understand him. Her hands felt wet. Cringing, she opened her eyes and looked down at them.

Not blood, but her own tears glistened there. Relieved, but more repelled than ever, she wiped her eyes, mortified that the Ehretans had been told animal sacrifice was necessary. And yet... yet, as a teaching tool, it worked. Her insides roiled, whipped by revulsion, both of the ritual killing and of the darkness in her own heart and mind. Darkness like a deep, black bowl full of blood, like consuming dark flames. She had never despised evil so deeply before.

She'd just recited to Dabarrah that the Speaker could not be approached by uncovered imperfection. Now she felt it at gut level. Before giving her life to the Mighty Singer, she was repulsive to His holiness, every bit as offensive as a bloody-handed killer, despite all the goodness she could claim. Somehow He placed her under His own protection, loving her because she reflected His image—not for her accomplishments. The Adversary could not snatch her away.

A large hand pressed down on her head. Still struggling for self-control, she took several breaths. She'd sensed, she'd shared, Timarah Gall's sympathy for the innocent kipret. She'd never had a pet of her own, but she'd adored the small animals Carradee brought home. *Was this truly necessary?* she begged the Singer.

"Draw comfort from this assurance," Master Jenner announced to her and the congregation. He lifted his hand from her head and touched the underside of her chin. She looked up. In his other hand, he cradled a copy of *Dabar*. He read several sentences in Ehretan.

Close behind her, just as he promised he'd be, Brennen translated.

"You are my beloved; you are mine. Your transgressions lie beyond the sacrifice, separated from you as far as the galaxy's hub from the outermost worlds. Be not afraid, but comforted."

The congregation kept singing. Firebird realized she'd heard music continue throughout the grim vision, beneath her consciousness... amplifying her emotions, making her even more solemn and sad.

She blinked, still slightly nauseated. She reminded herself that she knelt at Hesed. No one waited outside those double doors to lop off her loathsome head. She wouldn't have to pick out a herd beast to die on this altar. She checked her fingernails anyway, making sure they weren't crusted with blood.

The sekiyr who'd opened the door walked forward, carrying a circlet of white ribbons and flowers, and she gave it to Brennen. He laid it over Firebird's hair like a crown. She tried to smile back at him, but she still felt more stunned than satisfied. Now she knew why Destia had risen white-faced from that kneeling bench.

Brennen steadied her as she stood, then took both her hands and faced her, keeping his back to the altar, so that she looked up over his shoulder at the beveled star that seemed to float over the altar flame. She would never see that flame again without remembering one poor beast whose body burned on a much older altar.

Master Jenner still held the book. "We depart now from the usual rite, Firebird Mari." He raised a hand and spoke in a strong baritone, using the unintelligible Ehretan.

Weren't they finished? Firebird wanted only to relax, to rest, to think about what she'd just seen.

"Hear the words of the prophet Melauk." Brennen translated Dabarrah's quotation, but she paid little attention. She could almost feel the planet spinning under her soles, but she couldn't focus on Brennen's voice until he nearly finished speaking. She caught only the last few words, "'...who shall rule over all worlds and peoples.'"

She raised her head, wanting to ask him to repeat what he said. Dabarrah reached up and spoke again.

Brennen's hands tightened momentarily on hers. He must've felt her senses start to return. "Hear the words of the prophet Renonna," he said, looking into her eyes. "'From you shall spring the Mighty One, Word to Come, king of all nations and tongues, eternal and merciful.'"

Suddenly she realized what she was hearing. These were the prophecies she had wanted to hear, and he longed to explain.

Dabarrah spoke again.

Then Brennen, solemn-faced: "Hear the words of the prophet Amar. 'You are few but precious, and My hand shall be on you forever...'"

"'...In Him shall perfect peace, true atonement, be fully accomplished. In Him is your covering swept away, made unnecessary, and drowned with your offenses in the depths of forgiveness...'"

"'Out of you, Carabohd, shall come this mighty One, and all the worlds shall worship...'"

"'...and in His hand shall be power to unmake all that His hand once made; unmake the universe and form it again, perfectly, as in the beginning. A new song you shall sing...'"

Brennen spoke firmly, without hesitating on any of the Scriptures, and she realized he wasn't even translating. He'd committed these verses to memory.

Her eyes dried as she stared, stunned a second time. *Our child?* she thought at him. *This could be our child?*

Still reciting, he finally smiled. He laid his hand on her arm and turned back toward the holy flame.

The Sanctuary Master rested a hand on her forehead. She heard the Ehretan voice modulation as he solemnly commanded her never to speak thoughtlessly of what she'd just heard, and not to reveal it at all to a non-consecrant.

Brennen had been under this very command all along. Now she joined him in this too.

Our child? No wonder the Alert Forces defended Kiel and Kinnor! The musician steadied his harp again. The congregation started a hymn. Firebird recognized it, but she couldn't find her voice. Dabarrah laid his book on the altar, then gripped her shoulder and Brennen's, murmuring, "May He bless you both." Then he stepped away.

He could have formed inside my body?

Brennen looked deeply into her eyes, and she felt another steadying caress before he turned his head toward the door. Feeling deeply self-conscious, Firebird faced a hundred eager eyes. The other Sentinels kept singing, but now she knew why Brennen and Dabarrah had conspired to tell her these things here. The faith community was seeing and sensing the awe she felt as she finally learned what was promised to Brennen's lineage—and now hers. They would pass down this memory, honoring her as one of themselves, sharing and remembering her awe.

She wanted to smile at them, but she seemed to have lost control of her face, as well as her voice. Walking in step with Brennen, she hurried toward the double door. As she stepped off carpet onto flagstones, she exclaimed, "Your shoes!"

Brennen laughed, and the strong set of his shoulders softened. "I'll go back for them another time." He steered her along the stone wall, out of sight of anyone inside. Then he seized her and held her close, murmuring against her ear, "Yes, Mari. Our child. Or one of our descendants. Word to Come, Holy Messenger, King of the New Universe. All the might of the Speaker, in human form."

She held tightly, still trying to imagine such a person even existing, let alone calling her one of His ancestors.

And she'd grown up forbidden to even consider having children! "Brenn," she mumbled, "could we be alone for a while?" She still had a head full of glistening fog.

Brennen nodded. "We don't have to stay."

They hurried back to their room, found shoes, and then walked up the stony hillside once more. At a large flat rock, they sat in the mountain valley's vast silence, staring up at snowy peaks and speaking in whispers.

At one point, it occurred to her, *Now I know why Ellet wanted him.*

Irked with herself for even thinking such a thing, she thrust it away. *Kiel?* she wondered. *Could He be… my Kiel?* Or did Kinnor's struggle for comfort with physical life mean that he came from a better existence?

Undoubtedly, Brennen's mother had wondered this about him and Tarance.

Brennen's deep peace eventually brought her back to the valley, comforting her even as he remembered—vividly, she knew—being given that ritual memory. "It's said," he told her, "that everyone sees something different, deep in that bowl. Don't worry," he added quickly. "I won't ask. That's between you and the Holy One."

She nodded. "I won't ask, either." White ribbons fluttered around her face as she curled forward, closing her eyes. *Thank you, Holy Singer,* she prayed, *that Kiel and Kinnor are safe here. Give them back to me soon.*

And while she was at it…

Singer, there isn't much time, but you're so good at mercy. Change Brennen's mind. Hurry, she begged as she clutched both hands into fists. *Give him another dream tonight, a better one. Keep him here, if you love him as much as I do.* What renegade would love to bloody his evil hands by taking Brennen's life?

No, she begged, doubling over. Brennen seized her shoulders and tried to flood her with comfort, but nothing could touch this grief, because she hadn't yet suffered the loss.

19

FOR HESED

offertorium
presentation of the offering

Carradee limped into her dusky sitting room. Regeneration treatments and three lightweight braces had her back on her feet, but a servitor waited just outside with a mobility chair.

Sandy-haired Governor Danton rose to greet her. She extended a hand. "Excellency," she said in a soft voice. "You wished to bring news personally and not through our acting Regent. Are our girls safely hidden away?" She seated herself beneath a dark window.

He took his own wing-back chair again. "Madam, we could not hear of their safe arrival for several days yet. There is a long communication lag. But official news has arrived from Thyrica regarding Lady Firebird."

"Ah! Do we have a niece?"

Danton's lips twitched as if he wanted to smile. "Your sister delivered twins, Madam."

"Twins!" Carradee laced her fingers. "There's no twinning in *our* family."

"Fraternal brothers." Danton crossed his legs and leaned back. "Kiel Labbah and Kinnor Irion."

Carradee's hands fell limp on her lap. Brothers?

He beamed. "She sent us messages some months ago that her medical practitioner had discovered a distinctly Ehretan syndrome. Do you remember?"

Carradee rose off her chair. Scarcely noticing that Danton stood too, out of protocol, she took a few tentative steps down the patterned carpet.

"She was treated. I do remember. We discussed that. Phoena nearly died of rage at the suggestion."

"Yes, Madam." He stepped to her side and offered his arm.

"When Daithi is... better," she said, remembering her beloved lying paralyzed on his bed, "perhaps I too should be... treated. Quietly." She faced him. "Can your medics hold their tongues?"

"Of course, Majesty."

"I cannot decide now. Later. Thank you for coming, Governor. Is there any other message you wish to give me?"

"No, Majesty."

"Is there no..." She would prefer to sound queenly, but she was deeply afraid. "No more sign of Shuhr activity here?"

"None," he answered.

"I—we hear you won a great victory yesterday." She limped to a chair and sat down. She'd been warned not to walk too much yet. "In the Assembly."

"That was not my victory. It belongs to your people. The first three ministerial monopolies have fallen."

The Ministries of Agriculture and Aquaculture had been under pressure from the low-common class for decades. And Science had lost all real power when information started to flow from the Federacy. "So the door has cracked open." She frowned up at him. "Where will it end, Danton? Will you destroy the noble class?"

He crossed his arms high on his chest. "No! Its grandeur, and much of its wealth, can be maintained even if some riches are reinvested to benefit more people."

"Reinvested?" she asked wryly. "Sir, your new taxes will wipe us out."

"No," he exclaimed again. "Majesty, the Federacy cannot bear the whole cost of upgrading your world's defenses—"

"Though your battle group destroyed them?"

He spread his hands. "Madam, your pre-demilitarization defenses wouldn't have turned an attack like the one at Sunton. Your class is now truly fulfilling a role it always claimed—that of protectors. You wouldn't run to the countryside while the Shuhr attacked Citangelo. The Powers honor charity," he reminded her.

"And Discipline." Sunton images from the newsnets had haunted her. "You've made no move toward reforming our penal system. We have watched closely."

"Why, madam?"

Her cheek twitched. "Lee, I don't want to watch Firebird die by milli-meters. I think I know something, now, of what other Netaians suffered when their loved ones were sentenced to execution. My class shows little sympathy for the commoner or the servitor. Yet they too love their chil-dren," she said, faltering. Where were Iarlet and Kessie bound, and how soon would she see them again? Gathering her poise, she folded her hands. "Daithi's condition is showing me something that disturbs me, Governor."

"Majesty?"

She shook her head. "Swear silence, Danton."

He raised both eyebrows. "I do."

She glanced all around. Her most loyal servitors kept this sitting room secure, but that naturally made it a target for Rogonin and the electoral police. The Electorate, not the Crown, was Netaia's highest governing body. Breaking protocol, she beckoned Danton closer. He bent toward her. "That penal system is founded in our worship of the Powers, Governor."

His eyes widened. "Majesty?" he whispered.

Carradee bit her lip. She'd said too much, hinted too plainly at her painful doubts. Since her accession, she'd signed twenty execution orders, including Firebird's... and twice that many reductions to servitor status. Although the holy Powers required their priestly electoral representatives to practice charity, their laws—their penal system—offered none. Each time Carradee had signed one of those orders, her heart had cried, *This is wrong! Electors aren't omniscient. We've made mistakes, but we're never allowed to for-give...*

Straightening, she extended a hand in dismissal. He touched his lips to it and stood, then left the chamber with one glance over his shoulder.

Carradee rang for her servitor. A middle-aged woman hurried into the chamber, steering the sleek mobility chair. Carradee sank into it gratefully.

My children... She'd made it a point to spend time with Iarlet and Kessie, far more than she'd been given by Queen Siwann. She missed their adoring faces, their soul-tickling laughter.

And her husband...

She guided the chair toward a slender pole lamp. Danton didn't know—couldn't be told—that the finest medics on Netaia barely kept Daithi alive. He lay in their temporary apartment, a wastling's suite, sedated as heavily as they dared keep him. Quietly, with Rogonin—whose work as her tem-porary Regent, until she could settle her familial concerns, had been irre-proachable—she had finally agreed that they must try to conceive another child, a wastling. The electors demanded that assurance that a noble line would continue if anything unforeseen happened. She hated the idea, but for the sake of stability in unstable times, she must make the sacrifice.

But the act proved impossible, and electoral law would automatically disbar any heir medically conceived.

Daithi did have moments of painful lucidity, granted by the doctors who felt even the safest sedatives couldn't be administered continually. Daithi understood the situation. If anything happened to Iarlet and Kessie, he would feel it his duty…

No. He mustn't, she wailed to herself.

…to suicide, leaving her free to marry again as her own proper service to the Electorate.

Phoena too was an heiress of this house. Appalled by Phoena's defection, Carradee intended to quietly and privately eliminate Phoena from her list of personal heirs. Officially, she couldn't afford to do so (*not in front of Rogonin!*). That would leave only—

Carradee sat upright. Did Firebird truly have sons? If they were confirmed as heirs… even only one… that might buy Daithi time. By Netaian tradition, the second-born was considered to be first conceived and was therefore the true elder. That would be… Kinnor Irion?

Her servitor hung back by the door. A huge, glowering portrait hung between two high windows, and Carradee raised her hand to touch its ornate frame. *Could I have Kinnor Irion named a reserve heir?*

Rogonin would oppose it, of course. But what about the others?

There were more male than female electors. They might support the possibility of naming a prince. If they could be made to understand that the Angelo line was part… Ehretan… already and had served Netaia for three centuries, then maybe the electors wouldn't consider Brennen Caldwell's heritage alien.

Glancing up at the glaring, long-dead grand duke, she snatched her hand away from the portrait's frame. *Yes they would!* They could even strip the throne from the Angelo dynasty. The Electorate had that right.

Her sense of heritage rebelled. She gazed out over the lights of Citangelo, broken only by the Tiggaree River's sluggish swath. Even the city carried her name. There would be no new taxation, no costly particle-shield generators under construction, if Netaia weren't now a Federate protectorate—if Siwann hadn't attacked Veroh.

Painfully she recalled her mother's masterful way with her electors. The queen was a legal figurehead, but Siwann had been a real ruler, adored by her electors. Only once in Carradee's memory had an elector dared to countervote Siwann on a unanimity order. That stubborn young honorary elector had been Firebird, on the occasion of initiating the tragic Veroh War.

Firebird had been right to oppose that conflict. It had changed Netaian history forever.

Carradee drew herself erect. *I'll be strong. I must.*

• • •

Brennen let no one but Firebird see him leave.

They stood on the scarred, grassy breakaway strip beside his RIA modified craft, clinging to each other.

"No regrets." He kissed her cheek. "This is my calling. You knew my work when you married me. I'd take you again if you'd have me."

She felt one of his legs press against her own, smelled his warm breath, gripped his fingers. "You'd do it again, knowing that in bonding with me, you got a willful, proud woman who had to learn to turn—and Phoena in the bargain?"

"Yes." Tenderly he pressed his lips to her other cheek. "Be patient. Grow in faith."

"I love you," she answered. "I'll always love you. Go and fulfill your part of the prophecies."

His surge of love and gratitude burned as he covered her lips with his own, held tight, then pulled reluctantly away. From the pocket of his belt he drew his bird-of-prey medallion on its gold chain. "Keep this." Her hand closed on the memento of his childhood. "Stay close to Dabarrah until you're healed. I'd serve Shamarr Dickin by living or dying, but Master Jenner I trust out of love. He and Mistress Anna will do everything for you that can be done."

"You'll be back," she insisted. "And on track for the high command."

Smiling gently, he swung up into the cockpit with the briefest glance over his shoulder. Firebird clutched the golden bird and backed away. The dawn sky was thickening to rain, as on the spring morning when they had lain in a stone shelter just upriver from here, with all the worlds and the future in their hands.

The hatch swung shut. Firebird felt his anguish, tangibly distinguishable from her own, gradually disappear under attention to procedure as the generators' howl modulated into purring sublight engines. She knew she should cover her ears, but she couldn't. That roar meant Brennen was still here. The silvery craft rose, seemed to hover a moment, and then streaked skyward. She clung to the awareness of his presence as it slipped from her. Farther... fainter...

It flickered and went out. The roar faded.

• • •

Incredibly, the sun rose over the Hesed Valley, even though Brennen had left it. Firebird sat through a lengthy *Dabar* reading in the commons, then went at Master Jenner's request to his private study. Motioning her to take a wooden chair near his desk, the lanky blond master seated himself. "Are you all right, Mistress Firebird?"

Firebird crossed her ankles under her chair. "Not really," she muttered. Her chest ached as if someone had kicked her. She wanted to lie down and sleep until Brennen came back.

Dabarrah extended a hand across the desk. "It's normal for the pair bonded to grieve when separated. We learn to deal with the depression. Unquestionably, Brennen is feeling the same."

You're trained, she protested silently. *And so is he.*

"He warned you to expect this?"

She clenched her fingers. "Master, everything that matters–except my faith–has been taken away from me. How would you react?"

He drew back his hand, but the compassionate arch of his eyebrows didn't relax. "Then are you prepared to see what can be done? It's possible that you had less to do with Harcourt Terrell's death than we've had to assume."

"For Kiel and Kinnor's safety. That's the only reason I can stand this isolation."

"I'd like you to turn again now. I'll observe from a distance, well shielded."

"I'll try." Could she even do it, feeling this way? If she succeeded, she wondered how he would react. To rally for the effort, she would have to forget the Dark's fiery, seductive pain.

"I'm here for you, my lady."

She steeled herself and pressed inward. No sense of a probe followed, so Dabarrah had to be shielding heavily. Twice she called up her vision of the stone wall and recoiled. Forcing herself to focus, she pressed through.

The searing darkness engulfed her. Burning in every nerve, she groped toward the glimmering cords of energy. She took a deep breath, dove toward one cord, and grabbed it. It stabbed, it strangled, it scalded, its energy steeped in the anguish that had surrounded it so long. Humbled by this scar of her wastling years, she let go of the turn and opened her eyes.

Dabarrah paced rapidly from wall to wall, clear across the room. It was so unlike him—unlike any Sentinel—to show such agitation, that Firebird stared speechless. Had she done something peculiar to him too?

At last he sank back into his desk chair, furrowing his forehead. "Now," he said, "now I understand." Firebird wondered if he realized how rapidly he was speaking. "I must think this through. How—I'm sorry, Firebird, I'm not feeling myself. Let me think... Thank you. Oh," he added as she stood, embarrassed and frustrated. "Well done. Your turn. A remarkable feat for one of your age and background."

"Thank you," Firebird mumbled. She started to hurry away, but paused just short of the archway. "Master? What is that, inside my mind?"

He raised his head and drew a deep breath. "Come back in, Lady Firebird. I didn't mean to send you away."

She dragged back to her chair and sat down. "Please," she said. "Tell me what you think it is."

He moved his chair closer. "Hear me through. Don't take offense before I finish."

Not an auspicious beginning. "All right," she said slowly.

"I believe you've been given a terrible gift. You've been shown the evil, the Adversary's own foothold, inside your heart. We're all touched by darkness, but few truly know it."

Firebird's head came up. She'd entertained that thought, but only under the duress of childbirth. Since then she'd had time to reconsider. "But I'm accepted now. I'm covered."

"Let me finish," Dabarrah insisted. "I'm not singling you out."

She nodded cautiously. *We deserve death,* she heard in her mind. *We're not holy enough to survive in the Holy One's presence.*

"You admitted before the altar that He can't tolerate imperfection, and that you aren't perfect. Firebird, when we merely say that we're flawed, the necessity of atonement seems barbaric."

"Yes," she murmured, still sorry that poor beast had been slaughtered.

"But if we feel the reality behind those words, we'll do anything He asks, anything, for His assurance that we can be freed from evil."

Firebird frowned. Her motive for seeking consecration hadn't been that pure. She'd also wanted to hear Brennen explain the prophecies. "Those aren't my shortcomings behind that wall. Master, I'm willing to fight evil to the death, but... that Darkness isn't my character."–Despite the Electorate's death sentence! Incongruously, her one unconfessed crime sprang to mind. Alef Drake, Prince Daithi's younger brother, would have been executed for geis refusal if she hadn't helped fake his death while he had escaped Netaian space.

She shoved the memory aside. It was irrelevant here.

Dabarrah rested his chin on one hand. "We are exalted creatures, made in an immaculate image and likeness, but born with tainted souls. Our very nature is a paradox. Even at our best, our thoughts and our actions are... less than perfect."

Firebird straightened her pale blue skirt. "If everyone's evil inside, then how can you explain the fact that others—outside this community—have been loving and serving each other, even dying for people they never met, for hundreds and thousands of years?"

"That is the original image. The way we were sung into existence," he said. She'd shown him her beautiful vision, opening her memory to him, shortly after they met. "In the end," he added, "it isn't a sacrifice that makes us His willing servants. It is our own dying to personal ambition and fully accepting His life in us."

Dying? Firebird snorted. "Master, I sacrificed myself once for a religion. I'll really die, eventually, but I'm not in a hurry anymore."

"I'm not speaking of physical death. Dying to willfulness would release you from your final bondage to self. It would let you serve a higher purpose—and be at peace."

Willfulness. Wouldn't they ever let her forget that wretched character screening? She crossed her arms and steered the conversation aside. "I know what I see when I try to turn. When I was little, I believed that the Powers punish disobedience after our death. I created a mental image to scare myself into submission. That image is exactly what I see. It's only an image, a memory—not evil itself."

"It was not memory I just accessed. I know how to identify memories on an alpha matrix."

She stared straight ahead. "Master, why has the Singer let evil exist? Real evil, like Brennen has gone into?"–Although she couldn't dwell on that if she hoped to carry on a rational conversation.

"That," Dabarrah said, "is the strangest and deepest miracle. He made us independent from His infinitude. Think of it. We're even capable of acting against Him and deliberately working evil."

Independent from infinitude, which was everywhere... For an instant, she grasped the incomprehensible. "Yes!" Then she wilted. "But it isn't turn-darkness that's keeping me away from Kiel and Kinnor," she reminded him.

He shook his head slowly. "No. It's the fear that you would harm them accidentally."

If she had killed a grown man, what could she do to an infant? "I'm willing to cooperate, Master. Tell me what to do."

Dabarrah smiled gently. "Give me two or three days to create a strategy. I promise, we won't rest until those children are back in your arms."

Two or three days? How would she fill all those empty hours? "Master," she said suddenly, "I started a degree through Soldane University. Could I do course work here?"

"Excellent idea. Tomorrow, I'll set you up with one of the sekiyrra's tutorials."

She spent the rest of that day working outdoors with two sekiyrra, pulling spent garnetberry canes. Fine brown thorns dug through her gloves and pierced her hands, but she hardly noticed. *Singer, how could you do this to Brennen and me? Don't you love him like I do?*

Startled by the thought, she dropped a handful of spent canes. Was this heart-aching flicker jealousy? How could she be jealous of the Eternal Singer?

But surely, even He couldn't love Brennen as deeply as she did.

Ashamed, she blanked the notion. Only Phoena could be that petty. Yet why should it surprise her if sometimes she could act very much like both of her sisters? *Be with Carradee,* she prayed. *Strengthen and guide her. And... and Phoena...*

Her hesitation stretched into a numb silence. She couldn't pray for Phoena, not even now. For Phoena, Brennen was preparing to offer himself like a kipret led unknowing to the high altar.

But unlike a kipret, Brennen knew what could happen there.

● ● ●

Ellet Kinsman flung down a pile of hard copies and addressed the ceiling of her close little cubicle. "Any deadbrain with the Second Division could've done this!" Brennen had taken his sons to Hesed, and here she sat, on the Special Operations floor of the MaxSec Tower, at Regional headquarters on Tallis. Stuck in a dimwit's job. She'd expected important liaison work.

Sighing, she sent a flicker of epsilon energy at her desktop to sweep papers together. Daylight streamed through the window on her left. Through her open door drifted other workers' voices.

Regional command had just sent a full military division and a fact-finding team to Thyrica. To Three Zed went a strenuous warning to expect retaliation... not nearly enough, in Ellet's opinion. Retaliation should be swift, unannounced, and irresistible. Regional command didn't have the technology to break Three Zed's fielding, though. The Shuhr were as invulnerable as Hesed itself, behind the same kind of fielding-satellite web.

Except that now, Thyrica's Alert Forces were developing RIA. She wondered how long that secret would last if the Shuhr struck again. She'd filed a supplemental report with the SO office, recommending a general security upgrade on all Federate worlds.

Meanwhile, she found another compensation in being on Tallis. She undoubtedly knew more than Firebird herself about the current Netaian situation, about the secessionist element's attempt to set up a long-term regency, and the underlying movement to dethrone Carradee. Carradee's weakness and "alien blood" were both factors. Losing her royal connections would cure Firebird's pride.

Ellet scanned the top page of her official business again. It was a policy review, regarding the status of the Carolinian mining colony, Veroh. Brennen had watched the Netaian invasion of Veroh, witnessed the horror of weapons that sterilized air and ground for centuries. Apparently, the last colonists were struggling to keep Veroh's basium mines open—a skeleton crew, men without families, only enough of them to maintain the mining robots. But the Netaian attack had left deadly radiation in the atmosphere. Regional was drafting a recommendation that Caroli evacuate Veroh permanently. No dome, no matter how well shielded, would block all radiation. No wonder the use of flash weapons was forbidden by so many treaties.

Scorch those Netaians! All of them!

Ellet pulled the review board hardcopy from its slot, reconsidered it, then dropped it in again. She wanted lunch. Another day, and she'd be sent back to Soldane.

She rested her head and arms on her desktop. Could she get to Hesed instead?—and once there, could she convince Firebird to go to Three Zed and try to rescue her sister? She'd conceived a plan, playing on Firebird's pride, impatience, and willfulness, but she would have to set it in motion herself, there at sanctuary.

Ellet wasn't due for fielding rotation for years, though. She wasn't sick, needing treatment in isolation. The only legitimate excuse that would justify a trip to sanctuary would be pair bonding, and despite Damalcon Dardy's hints and meaningful epsilon touches, she was not a candidate for that state.

Not while Mistress Firebird lived.

Ellet pressed a control surface on her desk top, darkening her window glass. Then she shut her eyes to think.

20

THREE ZED

pianissimo
extremely softly

The Shuhr had settled a planetary system deep inside the Whorl, above the galactic plane. Its single temperate planet lay just outside a dense asteroid belt. Over decades, to supplement their fielding net, they had dragged many of those asteroids into orbits so skewed from their world's that no pilot could carelessly approach the inner system. Common sense suggested leaving slip-state in its outer reach.

Brennen ignored common sense, trusted his call, and used full particle shields at drop point. He reentered normal space to find himself thousands of kilometers from any danger.

His long-range heavy fighter had two narrow seats that could generously be said to "recline for sleep," a cache of emergency rations, and onboard water recycling. It had been a comfortless trip.

Just outside Three Zed's fielding net, he eased into a long orbit matching the planet's and activated the new RIA unit. He relaxed in his chair and tentatively extended his awareness forward. As in practice on Base One, the sensations that reached him through the experimental RIA relays became slightly blurred. He sifted space above the planet's surface for satellites and orbiting ships. That took several hours.

En route, he'd called up in mnemonic sequence all his dealings with Phoena and searched each encounter for a clue that might win her trust. Unfortunately, he'd never needed to access her thoughts. The puzzle plagued him. If he hadn't already solved it, it might have no answer.

Finally, satisfied that he'd located each fielding satellite, he asked his computer to correlate data. A pattern sprang up on the six screens. Portions of the local fielding net double-covered the planet, but over some areas only a single satellite projected his enemies' epsilon energy. He chose the single-covered area nearest the major colony and turned RIA toward its satellite, shielding himself from a barrage of destructive energies. Against that outwelling he felt inward, into the physical form of the satellite itself. Tracing its circuitry, he found similarities with the sanctuary's fielding design: resonal circuits, a toroidal juncture. Once he understood the differences, he nudged the energy in one line across a gap to another line, simulating a disruptive meteor pass. The satellite's main power shorted dead.

Quickly, knowing the groundside fielding team's checks could reset the malfunctioning circuit at any moment, he pulled off the RIA headset, engaged steering thrusters, and slid a throttle rod forward, alert for any challenge.

He could've used Firebird's help. She should be in that empty seat, with her alert eyes and keen intuition. She'd been more help than she knew against the Shuhr trap at Thyrica, even despite her watch-link. And he already missed Kinnor and Kiel—with a burst of epsilon static, he cut off his longing to rejoin them. He'd come here because of that family, his love sprouting into the future.

I will be back, he promised them all. *As soon as I finish here*—if the Holy One brought him through the attempt.

And he needed that seat for Phoena,

He dropped through the breach, slipped again into the RIA system, and probed ahead for Three Zed's mass detector. He was still untracked. He set an autopilot course, then again took up the RIA accord. With finely focused attention, he brought the ship closer. He sensed the mass detector's outer field as it started to echo with his craft's presence. His extended consciousness rode a wave down to the main complex. The part of his mind that remained free of RIA directed his left hand to slip-shields. Power to the mass detector dipped as groundside energy guns fired automatically on the threatening object. He might still be unnoticed, though, since bits of meteor debris occasionally passed any fielding satellite, and this system was rich with debris. At the moment that his slip-shields deflected energy, he nudged the mass detector's circuits. On the ground display, his blip vanished.

Once again he turned his attention to guiding the ship toward a tooth-like volcanic crag near the major settlement his sensors had confirmed. On minimal power, with occasional checks through the RIA unit to see if his presence was being monitored, he glided between black boulders to a small clear space, fired braking rockets to set down, then secured the ship. He wished he could camouflage it. On this black surface, its silver hull wouldn't go undetected for long.

He checked his uniform and belt pockets. From a hollow in the RIA bank he slid a small metal ring that was actually two rings joined around their circumference. This was a detonator mechanism for the ship's inbuilt explosive system, easier to conceal than a touch card. Now that RIA had proved it could penetrate a fielding net, its value to each side tripled. The Shuhr must not capture the RIA secrets, either from the ship or from him. If they took him, he must destroy the RIA craft... and take another step he dreaded. Special Ops memory blocks left an agent functional but mentally injured. A psi healer could release the block, but this left scars—memory gaps, personality shifts.

The ring felt cold on his finger and a little too large. He wriggled into an emergency vacuum suit and helmet, sealed and pressurized them, and then activated another security cycle. This one would stun anyone else who tried to gain entry. On his left side, opposite his blazer, he hooked a shock pistol. He wanted both options, the humane and the deadly.

He breathed a prayer as he swung off the ship onto a volcanic landscape. *I am here, as you called. Guide me now.*

A short dash took him to the entry, a panel four meters tall and five wide. It slid open as he approached, designed to admit small craft. He stepped softly through a pitch dark pressurization chamber toward a faint, pulsating blue luma.

Interesting. The outer door might open automatically, but this little side hatch had an epsilon lock, hardened against mental tampering. Fortunately, it wasn't activated. Brennen wanted to study it, but he couldn't take the time. He unsuited, hiding his gear behind bulky machinery. Then he crept out into the lava-tube corridor, surrounding his very presence with a shielding cloud of epsilon static. He remembered Phoena's aura vividly, but he didn't dare extend a quest pulse through any door.

He now walked where no Sentinel had gone and returned alive. He found a lift shaft and plunged to a lower level, looking for an unattended life-support relay, where he might access the complex's main database and find out where Phoena was being kept.

Catching a whiff of greenery, he followed its scent to an unlocked door arch and slipped inside. A vast lava chamber opened in front of him. Meter-wide shelves rose toward its ceiling, each shelf thick with plant growth. Water dripped between planted levels. Dazzling lights glared off the chamber's whitened ceiling and walls.

He stepped to one shelf, intrigued despite his hurry. Something grew on it, plantlike but fleshy and brown.

They cloned edible plant parts. Many Federate worlds used the technology. It seemed so ordinary that he felt encouraged.

He turned a full circle to make sure he was alone, then found a terminal close to the arch, against the fused stone wall. Its main display showed that this was the deepest part of the colony's night cycle—and he saw something else that made his neck hairs stand up. The touchboard's guide keys were labeled in the holy Ehretan language.

These were his kinsmen.

Several minutes of guessing and fiddling with the touchboard finally brought up a record of recent in-out traffic. He keyed cautiously, watching its circuits with care, alert for any alarm mechanism. Finally he found a power-use map. Here and there on the grid, active circuits showed that some residents of this colony had not gone to sleep.

Then he spotted what he wanted. In a cluster of temporary quarters close to this entry, only one air-circulation system drew power.

Phoena. As the Voice had said in his dream, he was never alone.

He tried to access security next, to plan a route that wouldn't take him past checkpoints. Just as his finger hovered over the final key to break into the security net, he sensed an alarm he'd primed with his previous touch.

He canceled the query, drew his blazer, and edged back out into the corridor.

He heard nothing.

Steel corridors connected the round-roofed lava tubes in this part of the complex. He crept along, wondering if–against all expectations–he might reach Phoena and escape without a fight. At one point he heard footsteps and sensed a human presence. He back-stepped up the corridor and waited until the sound faded away.

He found the door he wanted at the midpoint of another long passway. Carefully he evaluated the palm lock. It seemed unalarmed. He touched it experimentally. A door slid open.

Behind it he found a stark room, furnished with two chairs and a lounger, dimly lit by a freshing-room luma. He started to wave the door shut, then changed his mind. He couldn't cut off his escape route. He must do this quietly.

He tiptoed deeper inside, fully alert but fully shielded, and still holding his blazer ready. This could be someone else's quarters.

But he found Phoena lying on a narrow bed. She wore yellow, a gown of more color than substance. In her sleep she looked helpless, even frightened, and her resemblance to Firebird stirred his pity. He holstered his blazer, stepped to her bedside, and touched her shoulder almost tenderly. If only he could convince her to come away without fighting him...

She rolled over and murmured, "Dru?"

Then her eyes focused. She sprang off the bed like a cat, headed toward the outer room.

Brennen caught her in voice-command just short of the arch. Watching her dark eyes, he touched her alpha matrix, barely stroking, gently reassuring her. "Phoena," he whispered, using his voice to send calming overtones. "Don't fear me." Her will resisted his as powerfully as Firebird's once had done, but Firebird had meant to sacrifice herself, and Phoena's will was unswervingly selfish. He counted to ten slowly before dropping his hand.

"I'm sorry, Your Highness. I'd rather not have done that."

Phoena turned fully around to face him, clenching both hands at her sides, her hot brown eyes narrow and defiant. "Brennen Caldwell," she seethed, fighting the voice-command that kept her whispering. "This time, you two have gone too far." She glared around the bedroom. "Where is she?"

"'She,' Phoena?"

"Firebird." Phoena took a step backward. "Do you think you can destroy Three Zed the way you took Hunter Height? Are you letting her lay the explosives this time? Only this time it won't work. You'll never leave this place alive, either of you."

"She's not here, Phoena," he answered levelly, stroking again to calm her. "I've come alone. But not to destroy this facility, Your Highness. I've come for you."

"To do what, Caldwell?"

"To save you from the Shuhr before they murder you."

Her body relaxed, and she wheezed out a laugh. "Me? Sentinel, you've created a flattering little fantasy. I am the personal guest of Testing Director Dru Polar—whom, I assure you, is ten times your equal. I have been accepted among these people. I will leave their colony as Queen of Netaia."

As she boasted, he probed. He found an emotional discontinuity at her mind's surface, a scar that could only be caused by repeated, careless breaching and manipulation. Just as he feared, she was not herself—hadn't been for weeks.

He projected more understanding and respect into her subconscious, focusing his energies in a narrow pattern. "I came on behalf of your husband, Phoena. Prince Tel asked for my help. He had hoped to rescue you himself. I wouldn't let him try."

"For your information," she snarled, "I only married Tel to get Carradee off my elbow." She sat down on the other side of the narrow bed. "Carradee is a simpering idiot with no feel for the dignity of the throne. And Tel—"

"The Shuhr have lulled your defenses," he interrupted. "I would show you what they've done to your mind, but there's no time. You're in terrible danger. They're not letting you see it."

She met his stare, resisting him with unembarrassed hatred. "You were stupid to come," she whispered. "I'm not leaving. And the second you're gone, I intend to call Dru. And Micahel," she added cheerfully.

He didn't see an interlink in either of these rooms. The poor, deluded fool couldn't call anyone. "Then for the sake of your family, I must take you unwilling." He angled one hand slightly and modulated his voice to command again. "Come with me. Keep silent."

She opened her mouth to protest, but now no sound came at all.

He slowly lowered the hand. Still she didn't move. Satisfied with his hold on her, he stepped toward the outer door.

"Come," he ordered.

Her fury flamed beneath the compliant exterior, and for an instant he wondered how in the Whorl Tellai would win her back.

That, he told himself, was Tel's problem. *Mine is to get her to the ship.* "Your Highness, if we're caught they'll destroy us both. You must believe me. Even Testing Director Dru Polar has no affection for you. Give me your help." He searched her eyes for warmth but found none. Even after all his subtle stroking, he expected none.

He stole out the door and sensed Phoena's surprise. Couldn't she have opened it? He amplified her sudden fear. A chance—maybe a last chance to win her. "Yes, Phoena," he whispered. "You came on your own, but they made you a prisoner. I want to free you."

The escape route he planned took them down one more level, through a darkened maintenance area, toward the hatchway where he'd entered.

The inner door had been shut.

He pressed the palm panel, then probed the locking circuits. Nothing happened.

They have to keep their children indoors, he told himself firmly. *Particularly if they breed for talent.* "Where did you enter the colony?" he asked Phoena, then he forced the knowledge from her memory. There was a magnificent chamber, a golden-walled tube. Impressed, he nudged her. "Show me." He turned her toward a corridor that bypassed the heart of the facility and made her run.

Shuhr. Ahead. He felt the flickering energy of their epsilon matrices, heard audible voices. He shielded himself.

The muttering stopped. Brennen edged closer to Phoena, drew his blazer, and modulated his carrier for access, to command a breach deep into her alpha matrix. He could hide her if he acted quickly.

Leaning against a sparkling wall, gasping and panting, she shook her head and squeezed her eyes shut.

He pulled out his shock pistol left-handed, backed out of the deadly point-blank range, and fired. Phoena crumpled to the floor, unconscious and undetectable—now. As he hoisted her onto his shoulders, measured footsteps drew closer. They halted, then retreated again.

Maybe they hadn't felt her presence. They might know of some poorly guarded exit. If he quested skillfully, they might not sense him—

A foreign quest pulse brushed past him. Instantly he withdrew his own. Balancing Phoena over one shoulder to keep his shooting arm free, he ran back toward the rim of the colony, down a long duracrete ramp. From his trained memory he called up the map he'd seen at that terminal. He could try several ways out. Surely not all routes were guarded. He paused and risked another probe.

The counterblow nearly stunned him.

Down another side tunnel he pelted at a dead run. At every corner he raised his arm to fire, then let it fall and pump. Phoena wasn't light. How long would it take them to seal the complex?

Abruptly he felt a powerful presence close behind. He shielded himself with all the static he could raise.

It wasn't enough. He'd never felt such energy. It drew closer, suffused with the assurance that he could not escape. He blocked fatigue from his awareness and ran on with Phoena bumping on his shoulder. The presence followed without tiring. He passed a dozen doors, all closed. Around one bend farther, out of sight, he sensed other Shuhr in front of him.

Trapped! Breathing heavily, he dropped Phoena into a doorway, then pressed in to stand over her.

Footsteps echoed off to his right. He felt it again: the pursuer, the power. One figure rounded the bend on the left, then another. Which was it? —or were all Shuhr this strong? He stepped without hesitation across the hall and fired. An epsilon howl ripped through his subconscious. More figures appeared ahead.

He fired left, then right, trying to keep the Shuhr at each end of the straightaway. He didn't have time to draw his crystace.

Something lashed his left shoulder. Shock waves whipped through him. He fell senseless.

21

WELL REWARDED

straziante
anguished

Brennen woke curled on a glassy floor. His left shoulder ached where the shock pistol had connected, and his left cheek stung. He blocked the sensations. Multiple presences, foreign and strong, pulsed nearby. He shielded himself from their probing as he ran his right hand down his numb left forearm. They'd already taken his crystace, but his ring remained. Could he still get to the ship?

He stood—slowly, searching the tapestried office with his inner eye for weak spots in the strength that surrounded him, hoping to find one mind open enough to voice-command.

He found only Phoena. She glowed with triumph. Beside a massive black desk, she stood between two men with tangible darkness in their eyes. *Dru Polar and Eshdeth Shirak,* he understood without spoken word.

Dru. Her personal host, the man whose name she murmured as she awoke. Brennen saw confidence in that dark-browed face and magnetism in his lashless eyes. Beside Polar, Eshdeth Shirak seemed shadowy, though Shirak wore his authority like a broadsword. Subdued resentment sparked between them. If the circle had any weakness, it was that rivalry.

Brennen pulled his heels together and straightened his back.

Phoena sidled closer to Dru Polar. "Oh no," she exclaimed in a theatrical soprano. "The Federate revenge for our strike at Sunton. What shall we do?"

"Phoena," Brennen said sternly.

"Brennen," she mocked, warbling his name. She extended an arm with a twisting motion, as if flinging away dirt. "You'll never kidnap me again.

Do you believe me now?" She pressed her palms together and struck a graceful pose. "Gentlemen? I would love to see him crawl."

"Naturally." Polar slowly raised a hand. Brennen felt another quest pulse, a foreign mind savoring his dread. As Brennen waited under absolute affective control, the epsilon entity that had chased him down Three Zed's halls condensed before him.

Dru Polar's epsilon presence staggered him.

Command pressure fell on him like invisible wires that circled his limbs and then possessed them, slithering into his bones to move them at another's will. "Crawl to her, Caldwell," Polar sneered.

Brennen didn't waste energy resisting. His body buckled to the glassy floor, and then his arms dragged him to Phoena's feet. She wore shoes now, with small sparkling decorations. As he edged toward them, he realized what he must do. He twisted the halves of his ring, joining the contacts that would blast his escape ship apart. Then he focused deep inside himself. Using a skill that required epsilon power but no turning ability, he cued the Special Operations amnesia block. As it fell like a curtain over his military past, his arms trembled. Bile rose in his throat.

The world blurred for an instant. Then Phoena kicked him full in the face, knocking him over. He sprawled at the circle's center, automatically blocking excruciating pain in his cheek, counting rapidly to clear the haze from his mind. Eleven of them stood there. He remembered who they were, focusing probes and shields against him and waiting—for something specific, but he couldn't catch it. Should he have known?

He knew who he was, where he lay, and that he had hoped to take Phoena Angelo away from this place. He also remembered how to use his abilities, so he kept his static shield dispersed. He recognized one man, but didn't recall why.

And Dru Polar. He'd just learned that name. He rolled onto his stomach, scrutinizing the long-faced Shuhr with silky black hair. How could he resist Dru Polar? If Brennen were the strongest Master Sentinel of his generation, what chance did any of his people have against adversaries like these? Why didn't the Shuhr already own the Whorl?

His left shoulder throbbed as the shock pistol's pulse wore off. Pressing to his feet, he wiped warm blood from his cheek. Steadily he walked back toward the desk, halting three meters from Phoena. She stood like a queen, flushed with satisfaction and the pride that was her heritage.

Eshdeth Shirak grasped her hand. She smiled coyly as Shirak raised her fingers to his lips. "Highness, you have served us well."

She curtsied.

Brennen felt the circle of minds tighten with expectancy. He wiped his cheek again.

Shirak dropped Phoena's hand and bowed. "You may take that knowledge with you," he said, "to the bliss you so righteously expect. Or maybe into the Dark that Cleanses. Polar?"

Dru Polar reached into the folds of his sash and drew out an arm-length rod, its glossy silver surface momentarily reflecting orange fabric. A thumb cradle and several control buttons interrupted the length between its pommel and distal end.

Phoena saw it a second later. "Dru!" Outrage heated her voice, but she stared at Polar's hand, the whites of her eyes showing all around her brown irises. "He doesn't mean it! Dru...!"

Brennen guessed he should recognize the weapon. Obviously Phoena did, with her body stiff, her alpha matrix humming with terror.

"Don't toy with her." Stepping toward a holo tank full of stars, Shirak wiped one corner of his mouth. "It's too early in the morning. Just file her away."

Phoena took a mincing step backward. Her chestnut hair glistened under warm office lights.

"Ordinarily, I'd agree. She has been helpful, Eldest." Polar seized Phoena's hand. As she shrank toward the tapestry, he coiled his fingers around her wrist. "But she wanted to know about this. For her sister's sake, Caldwell. What were your words, little Phoena? Tell Master Brennen." His dark brows barely lowered. Brennen sensed a controlling thrust of epsilon energy travel from Polar to Phoena.

"If I—" Phoena squeaked to a halt. Polar barely strengthened his effort, and her voice dropped a sultry half-octave. "If I ever get a chance at Firebird, Dru, will you lend that to me again?"

Polar's hand slid up Phoena's arm. His control over her never flickered. "If it can be arranged," he said quietly, as if repeating old lines of his own.

Phoena blinked in lazy contentment. "What's the absolute worst you could do with it?" she murmured, oblivious to her leering audience. "I'd want to know I was giving her the very hardest way out."

Brennen pressed his lips together and calculated the distance to Phoena and Polar.

"Lowest power." Polar slid a control all the way into his palm. "Throat pressure point." He stroked the angle of Phoena's jaw with the weapon's needlelike probe, and slowly, he relinquished control. "Here. Not as slow, but excruciating."

He jabbed the contact into the side of her neck.

Phoena croaked a tiny protest. Her hands crept up toward the silvery rod. Polar shook his head sharply. "Put them down."

Phoena obeyed, drawing a long, husky breath. "I am, Dru. I did."

Brennen's trained instinct urged him to jump before Polar could trigger the weapon. He could beat most of these enemies to Phoena's side. But before he did, Polar would finish her.

He cautiously modulated his carrier. Maybe, even through those monstrous shields, Polar could be commanded.

Polar slid his hand around her shoulder, pressing his body against hers. "Poor little Phoena. I haven't done a thing, though. Maybe I won't. You know how we play."

His thumb shifted to poise over the orange stud.

"You don't need to do this, Dru. I—" Her voice took a new note, one Brennen never thought to hear. She begged. "Please, Dru... please? Don't kill me." She glanced toward Brennen. From her stricken eyes, all hope vanished—but though her dignity disappeared, those eyes glittered defiance.

He saw Firebird in those eyes. Infuriated by Polar's hands on that vision, he flung a disruptive burst of epsilon energy at Polar.

Polar flung it back. "Down!" cracked his voice.

Again Brennen tumbled to the floor. He lay still, dazed again, while his carrier rebuilt. Polar caressed the small of Phoena's back.

"Even now Caldwell would save you if he could." Shirak leaned against the glossy surface of the holo tank. "Isn't that touching, considering what you really are... our lovely traitor?"

Polar's epsilon aura flickered, and he eased a lulling, deep-level discontinuity off Phoena's consciousness. Brennen felt it happen. He sensed her moment of confusion—of hesitancy—and then her mental shriek as finally, she fully understood that she had never used Dru Polar. Polar had used her from beginning to end, letting her live only long enough to trap Brennen, and he was about to use her for the last time. Brennen also guessed Polar's reason for removing all of his anesthetic tampering: to let her recall all their abuses, feeding her terror so he and his comrades could enjoy it.

Brennen struggled to his feet. "Phoena," he whispered as he stepped toward the desk. He knew now that he couldn't save her life. He sent calm instead, peace for the Crossing. As to what awaited her on the other side... that was not his responsibility.

Phoena turned ferocious, like a cornered animal done with cowering. "You were going to make me queen!" she shrieked. She flexed her hand into a claw, pulled it back to strike Polar's face—

And Polar's hand tightened on the silver rod.

Phoena shuddered as if she were jolted... and then collapsed, wailing in a voice that sounded only half human. Polar followed her down, holding the rod at her jaw's angle until her head thumped the carpeted floor. A wave of neural overload spread down her arms, her writhing torso, her legs... upward, across her face... until in Brennen's epsilon sense there burned an explosion of pain, a glimpse at one of the damned.

He shifted his weight to spring.

"Hold him!" Shirak stepped away from the tank. Four Shuhr seized Brennen by his shoulders and arms, too engrossed in the spectacle of Phoena's agony to divert epsilon energy into commanding him. Polar stood motionless, hands pressed together around his weapon, eyes fixed and unseeing, mouth barely open, his tongue touched to his upper lip.

Revolted, Brennen leaned hard forward. His captors held on. Phoena's limbs flailed on the dark carpet.

Could he at least shorten this?

Another Shuhr, standing close to Brennen, sent laughter into his awareness. *Put her out of her misery? No, Caldwell. By your standards, her misery's only beginning.*

Brennen thickened his shields. Phoena moaned, gasped, and then moaned again. A third wave built, rippling back down her body, but this time no flailing went with it.

His hands tightened to fists. He glanced from the black-haired young Shuhr beside him to Polar and then away, repelled by Polar's rapture.

Phoena pulled into a fetal curl. A slow minute later, she gave a single gasp. Like claws, her twitching fingers reached toward Polar. A trickle of blood stained her cheek where she'd bitten her lip. She could no longer move, but Brennen felt her agony. Fully conscious, she had no doubt she was dying. She fought for another breath.

He dropped both his epsilon cloud and his inner shielding. If he could do nothing for Phoena, at least he could force the engrossed Shuhr to feel how deeply he pitied her. It might be the only compassion any of them ever experienced. *Mercy, Holy One! Show her your eternal lovingkindness. None of us deserve that.*

Polar's lashless eyes lost their glazed look. They focused on Brennen. "Release him," he rasped.

The gripping hands dropped his arms and shoulders. Brennen sprang forward and gathered Phoena into his arms, questing with a last pitying, calming touch for her awareness. But as he held her, it ebbed. One drop of blood from his stinging cheek fell like a tear onto her face. Her eyelids fluttered. Then the echoes of her agony faded with the pulse in her wrist.

Brennen knelt helplessly, cradling her yellow-gowned body against his own. What incredible irony. He was her only mourner.

At least Tel hadn't seen this.

Shirak flicked a finger. Brennen's captors stepped forward again.

Before they took Phoena from him, he gently closed her eyes and uncurled her clenched fingers.

Then he wiped his cheek, stood, and turned to face the colony's Eldest. Four young Shuhr carried Phoena out of the chamber.

Very chivalrous. Shirak folded his hands across his middle. His subvoice rumbled through Brennen's alpha matrix, using the ancient language Brennen's kindred reserved for worship. *But you're a fool. You face a similar fate.*

That's not in my hands, Brennen answered in the same way. He had been called. He had come. But what would happen to Kiel and Kinnor if he did not come back?

True, Polar projected, walking closer. A sated smile gave his eyes a sleepy gleam. *It's in our hands. We've had time to plan for your arrival. Read me and see.* He dropped all shields.

Instead of probing as invited, Brennen shielded himself and took two steps backward.

Polar laughed. *Coward.* He adjusted a power control on the silvery rod. Then he raised his left hand and said aloud, "Come here."

This time, Brennen planted his feet. The compulsion to move battered him, growing steadily as other Shuhr joined Polar to pound his resistance. Step by slow step he approached the Testing Director.

The contact bit his forearm. Agony lashed his body and crippled his senses. He felt eager probes lick forward, wanting information that he couldn't remember. Too distracted by pain to shield himself, he turned to his last defense. He disrupted his own beta centers, willed himself unconscious, and crumpled to the glassy floor.

• • •

He came to his senses lying in a cell that made no pretense of being a guest suite. The black ceiling rose far over his cot, which was a narrow slab without padding. A bare luminescent strip near his head shed little light, but he saw rough black walls. Ghost echoes of neural pain flickered through his body. His shoulder throbbed, his cheek burned. Gingerly he touched it, and his hand came away blood-streaked.

He hadn't been unconscious long, if that wound hadn't scabbed. Over him stood Dru Polar, with Shirak, and a buxom young woman with grotesquely striped hair. *Cassia Talumah,* she silently told him, and how she would love to rip him apart for destroying some of her brothers at a place called Mazar.

He no longer had any memory of that place, or any mission there. But as he dropped his feet over the cot's edge to sit up, he glanced at her hands. With those nails, she could do it.

Then he started. When she stopped sending he no longer felt her presence, nor the others, only pain that did not fade when he tried to will it away.

Turning with deliberate care to link with his carrier, he felt nothing. They'd dosed him with blocking drugs. For eight days at least, he would have no epsilon abilities at all. He was helpless.

"As I was saying," Polar began aloud as though the conversation had barely been interrupted, "we've made our plans. They're half fulfilled, Caldwell. We have already sampled your genes. That precious bloodline of yours will mingle with ours now. We'll be the Kings of the Universe," he said, leering. "And here's a generous promise. We won't kill you. At least—not until we've taken at least one other victim. Your wife, and hopefully your freeborn children."

Then they did know the prophecies. *You cannot break the perimeter at sanctuary,* Brennen subvocalized, then realized he couldn't send, couldn't even turn. He glanced around again and concentrated on the single factor working in his favor: They meant to hold him alive, conscious, and out of medical stasis. "You cannot break the perimeter at Hesed," he said aloud. They could have taken the sanctuary only if he'd refused this call. He clung to that knowledge.

"That's true." Shirak's head bobbed. "We can't, any more than your Special Operations agents can break ours. But we won't need to attack Hesed to take Lady Firebird. She'll come to us."

"No."

"You know she will, Caldwell. We know her too, you're forgetting. We know her... like a sister."

Phoena. They'd taken that knowledge from Phoena. And Mari would try. Would Jenner hold her back, out of mercy? Or would he—in mercy—let her make the attempt?

"When she dies here," said Shirak, "your bereavement shock will weaken you to the point where we can break you."

Infuriated by his shieldless transparency, Brennen tried not to think, to only feel. But his mind plunged ahead. He had to believe Mari would be protected. Even if the Shuhr killed them both, the children would be safe.

"Those children won't be able to threaten us for years, Caldwell. By then... oh, but you didn't know. By then, we'll have taken the Federacy. With your help."

Alert Forces had always suspected that intent, but this was a plain confession. It made escaping even more critical. Meanwhile, he must find out how they meant to do it.

"One more thing," Shirak went on. "We'll not actually kill your Netaian lady."

Brennen resisted Shirak's baiting until an image sprang into his mind, projected by one of the Shuhr. He shrank against the coarse wall. The image showed him with Firebird, and...

Cassia Talumah threw back her head and laughed enthusiastically. "Oh, that was classic!" Then, apparently catching an undercurrent Brennen could no longer touch, she stepped away from Polar. She looked fearful—and if Polar fed on fear, what did Cassia expect from him?

Polar reached into his sash. "That's right, Sentinel. The Eldest believes that the best use of her is putting you in bereavement shock. So you'll kill her yourself."

He flourished his weapon. "Phoena's way."

22

DEPOSED

ritenuto
holding back

Carradee gripped both arms of her ceremonial chair and stared down the right and left branches of her U-shaped electoral table, unable to internalize the debate going on around her, only sure that the Powers were about to deliver a blow even crueler than the blast that had injured her and Daithi.

Close on her left, Wellan Bowman stood. Formerly the Minister of Aquaculture, he cut a fine figure in black, tall and white faced, leaning on a diamond-crusted walking stick. "...but with Danton feeding this legislation to the Assembly," he continued, "it is seizing more power. Before the Electorate loses all authority, before these new taxes beggar us all, we must consolidate behind a strong ruler. I do support the Duke of Claighbro's motion."

Carradee kept her eyes open, her back straight. That made seven of them. Seven of her highest-ranking nobles, asking with a single voice that she leave the throne. Seven electors out of twenty-six. Not a majority, but enough to tear the Electorate apart and maybe destroy its ability to govern, if she resisted. Queens suicided for less.

Beside her, Rogonin shuffled his legs under his bulk and stood ponderously. "Madam." With a sateen-swathed arm, he made a sweeping motion that took in all the table. "Your service to Netaia in this trying time shall always be honored, whatever course we take from this juncture. Perhaps you alone could have led us through the Federates' temporary overlordship. Yet the situation is changing." He crossed his arms. "We must resist the Federacy with unified strength, or every minister here will lose his or her jurisdiction."

This was her Electorate. Months ago, she'd chosen some of these men and women because they seemed to respect the Federates. She'd hoped to ease the inevitable transition from occupation to Federate covenance. Yet to most electors, covenance was anything but inevitable. One high commoner, a professor wearing his dignified scarlet robe, nodded solemnly at Rogonin. How long did he think he'd last at this table if she stepped down?

Rogonin leaned on the table, knitting his sculpted eyebrows as if he felt compassion. "Madam, we sympathize with you. We know your concern for His Highness, and that you would prefer to stay with him." Rogonin glanced at the empty chair at Carradee's right side. "And, madam, you cannot keep his condition secret much longer."

Carradee blinked. Truly, she'd give up everything she owned if it meant having Daithi whole again.

"Majesty, you should not have sent your heiresses away." Rogonin smoothed the ends of his blue nobleman's sash. "Netaia must have a strong, confident ruler—even if only a regent-designate, acting on behalf of the Crown. There is a precedent, at the end of the first century of Angelo rule..."

Carradee let him expound. She knew the story of Grand Duke Tarrega Erwin. Everyone in the room should know it. Regent for the infant Queen Bobri, "Bloody Erwin" steered Netaia through the Coper Rebellion.

Her left leg ached, but she didn't move to ease it. That would look weak.

They were speaking of a long-term regency. Unlike her mother, Carradee never had enjoyed power. This meeting was forcing her to admit it—to herself, at least. Would it be best for Netaia if she followed Siwann's example and stepped down?

Surely not for the common classes!

Her stiff skirt rustled as she straightened under the Chamber's high dome, leaning into her leg braces. "Should a regency prove desirable," she said, "there is the matter of rank. First Lord Baron Erwin. Baron Parkai. Consider your positions. Have you weighed the responsibility that would be thrust upon you should one of you serve as regent for our daughter, Iarla?"

As she sat down, whispers passed around the table. These men and women obviously assumed that Rogonin, temporary regent while she cared for Daithi, would take any quasi-permanent regency. Suggesting these higher-ranking alternates should slow the proceedings to a fuddbug's crawl, giving her time to consider her options and plan a strategy.

Bualin Erwin stood on her left. A stooped man in his seventies, implant-young otherwise in his appearance, Erwin cocked one eyebrow. "Madam, my father's removal from this body after the Veroh War left somewhat of a stain on our family. At present, if called upon to serve as regent, I would decline for the sake of maintaining good relations with the Federate governor, until his departure... or overthrow."

"Oh," Carradee murmured, surprised to hear Erwin pass by the honor so quickly.

Beside Rogonin, young Reshn Parkai rose. "For the same reason, madam, my father's death at the Hunter Height debacle precludes my accepting the scepter."

And that left Muirnen Rogonin, Duke of Claighbro, who sat beside her with smug decorum. She wondered if the barons truly stood down out of honor, or if Muirnen Rogonin had made offers.

Carradee felt lightheaded, as if she were floating away from the world she knew. By sacred tradition, if she had a daughter ready to rule, her next task would be simple: Procure two doses of gentle, deadly Somnus, one for Daithi and one for herself. But four-year-old Iarlet could not ascend the throne for almost a decade and a half. Rogonin meant to have a long rule.

Still, noble suicide was an honored practice. Rogonin obviously felt ready to govern. Carradee jerked to her feet. "Noble electors, this body is recessed, to meet tomorrow morning at nine hundred. At that time, we... there shall be laid before you certain documents. That is all."

Her touch deactivated a transcriber at her place on the table. She stepped back from her chair and walked toward the gilded doors, followed by her personal servitor. Slowly—the electors could wait. She was still queen. The heels of her leather pumps clicked on the chamber's gold-shot black marble floor. Its high white ceiling echoed back the soft clicks. She imagined she could feel Rogonin's soft green stare follow her around the table.

He didn't expect to see her alive again. He would probably shed real tears at her state funeral. Was this tearful bewilderment how Firebird had felt when the electors issued her geis orders? She'd looked courageous, calmly kneeling at the foot of that table.

Two red-jacketed guards stood beside the gilt doors. They reached simultaneously for handles and pushed outward, letting Carradee through. The doors shut behind her: *boom.*

Numbly she stood listening to the faint scrape of chairs and a sudden rise in voices. She looked up and down both grand corridors of the palace she called her home. This building where queens lived, and worked, and died.

Clutching a handful of stiff skirt, she limped up the long curving stairs to Daithi's room. There, she lifted his arm that had once seemed so strong.

She lay down beneath it and let it fall across her back. "Daithi," she mumbled, "what shall I do?"

Heavily sedated, he could not answer.

• • •

Solicitor Merriam, whose forefathers had been legal counsel to queens for two centuries, came to her an hour later, carrying the tools of a time-honored trade in his paper case: recall pad, vellum sheets, long black calligraphy pens. He spread them on a spiral-legged table and pulled up a chair.

"I wish two documents made." Carradee sat stiffly on the other side of an antique table in the secure sitting room. After a long mental struggle with the cruel, fickle Powers under Daithi's limp arm, she'd bathed, put on fresh clothes, and made up her mind.

Truly, she wasn't strong-willed enough to rule effectively—because she didn't even have the courage to commit honorable suicide. Rogonin meant to break with the Powers by seizing the throne? Then she would break with them in her own way. Something else waited for her. She wasn't sure how she knew it, but she knew. She would carry Daithi to Danton on her back, if need be, and beg the governor to transport them to a Federate medical center, or maybe to Firebird. Then she would send for Iarlet and Kessie. They could all live together elsewhere—humbly, without palace servitors—and Muirnen Rogonin could manage Netaia without the Angelo fortune. That belonged to her blood relations, not the Electorate.

"Two documents," she repeated. "A new will, and a document of abdication."

Merriam laid down his pen. "I have no standard form for an abdication, Majesty."

"I know." She folded her hands. "We will create one together."

• • •

Eleven days dragged by after Brennen left Hesed. Master Dabarrah examined Firebird's turn several more times, always shielded, but they made no progress toward controlling it. Between sessions with him and quiet hours practicing and composing on her clairsa, she started another

new course, a detailed comparison of Federate regimes. That, and a
review for credit of the Transnational Government text she'd studied in
protective custody, kept her mind busy while her body ached for those
absent babies.

This morning, she stood at the waterside edge of Hesed's commons.
A white-haired couple lingered at one of the tables, sharing ching tea.
Something loaded with sugar and yeast was baking in the kitchens, but
Firebird had no appetite. In Dabarrah's study, a meeting was underway—
an evaluation of that new RIA technology, she guessed.

Anna Dabarrah stood close by, so Kiel and Kinnor must be with a
sekiyr. Only Jenner and Anna at Hesed knew that Firebird was on A-status
for deadly reasons. The others simply knew that she mustn't be accessed.
The sekiyrra didn't seem afraid. They coached her with essential Ehretan
vocabulary—words they had studied here, including "berries," "thorns"
and "leather-palmed gloves."

Firebird reached up to her throat and touched Brennen's medallion.
She wore it, a small comfort in her solitude. Anna had just reported
that earlier this morning Kinnor had changed from an alert, if difficult,
baby to the very embodiment of tension. Suddenly he couldn't keep still,
except in sleep. He demanded constant touching, comforting, stroking.
"I believe he's picking up your anxiety, Firebird," Anna said. "It hurts
him. For his sake, stop fighting the Holy One. You cannot bring Brennen
back by worrying."

Mistress Anna might as well have asked Firebird to stop breathing. By
her calculation, Brennen could've arrived only hours ago at Three Zed.
"Kinnor needs his father." Firebird glanced over her shoulder at the retir-
ees sitting peacefully at tea. "Brennen understood Kin's moods from the
first day. Brennen could help him. If he were here."

Anna stroked the white rail, and Firebird studied her profile. Hesed's
mistress, mother to five sekiyrra at any time of year because of the college rotation, had deep, intelligent eyes and a nose almost jewel-like in
symmetry, a little too long for beauty, but Anna's real beauty was internal.
One sekiyr called her "the holy woman."

"Sanctuary Master Dabarrah," Anna said, "will help Kinnor. You can
help too, by submitting your will to the Speaker. By learning to trust
Him. Besides," she added, softening, "many small crises come and go for
every child. Most problems vanish with time and tenderness."

But Firebird feared deeply for Brennen. Had he arrived... and survived
that? Would Phoena cooperate? *Help them, Mighty Singer!*

Anna flicked silvered brown hair behind her shoulder and gazed up
at the skylights. "Babies of strong epsilon potential can be difficult," she

said, "because they have no way of telling you what's disturbing them. I was ten when your Brennen was born. I remember the rumors."

What made Anna an authority on babies?

And if Firebird lost Brennen, how could she ever guide Kinnor and Kiel through their boyhood? She'd never even had a brother...

Anna bowed her head. "Firebird Mari, you're not listening. As soon as my husband finishes with this meeting, you must go to him again. Tell him I asked him to address your tension."

"I'd rather go back out to the garden. I won't disturb Kin up there." Finally, she had license to wander.

Anna reached for her hand.

Firebird pulled it back. "Don't touch me, Anna. I'll crack." Silently she prayed, *He can't die there! Singer, you wouldn't call him there just to let them kill him, would you?*

Anna lifted her hand. "You are disrupting the sanctuary. Brennen was sent to Three Zed, and following a sacred call is the safest place in the Whorl. Our Holy Speaker cares for His own."

Firebird backed away. "Don't comfort me with platitudes." Her wistful depression turned to anger, and she didn't care if the elderly couple sensed it. Every day she felt more of a misfit here, even after her consecration.

Anna's voice took on the subtle tone of command. "Firebird, calm yourself."

Firebird resisted. "Brennen has taken a virtually untested craft against an enemy that represents all we despise. He is the finest man Thyrica could've sent against the Shuhr, and he was probably the best intelligence officer the Federacy ever had." Her voice kept rising. "If he succeeds it won't be because of dreams or platitudes, but because of skill—and hard training—and perseverance—and prayers, including mine."

Her peripheral vision caught a lanky form striding along the waterside. She recognized Master Jenner and stopped speaking. Her cheeks felt hot, her throat tight. Compressing her lips, she stared at the water.

Anna's light footsteps hurried away.

Wonderful. Now she would face the psi healer. What was the treatment for anguish and anger?

He touched her shoulder. "Firebird," he said softly.

"I'm sorry," she muttered. "I shouted at Mistress Anna."

"She understands better than you know." The Sanctuary Master smiled ruefully. "She loves you, Firebird."

Love? Anna had peculiar ways of showing it.

Then again, she had once thought that of Brennen. "How are my children, Master Jenner?"

"Kiel is thriving," he said. "Healthy, contented. Gaining weight. Kinnor is just as strong, but restless."

"So I hear. Master Jenner, every day I'm without them, they feel less real to me, as if I only dreamed them. This can't be right. What kind of mother are you people... is this separation making out of me?"

"Firebird," he said softly, "be patient. They will be yours again. They will claim your heart. You will have a bond with them almost as deep, and just as real, as your bond with their father."

She stared at the water, feeling hollow. "I'm going uplevel for a while," she said. "Tell Anna I apologize."

She strode up the pavement to the golden double-doors of the ground-side lift. When she stepped off onto the broad lawn she halted, hearing music.

At least music still moved her. She followed the haunting melody up onto the hillside. It sounded like a kinnora, beautifully played.

Kinnor, she moaned silently, imagining the warm weight of her child in her arms. *What's wrong, little Kin? I'm sorry. I don't mean to hurt you.*

Halfway to the hilltop, she found the sekiyr. He sat cross-legged, with black hair falling into his face—the same youth who had played for her consecration service. This angle of his face gave her another heart-wrenching flash of memory. Lord Corey Bowman, her dearest wastling friend, had waved jauntily from the stepstand of his Netaian fightercraft the last time she ever saw him. Black hair had tumbled into his eyes, too, before he tipped head into helmet for the battle where he died. Her more-than-brother, black eyed and rebellious, wildest of the wastlings...

She stepped slowly, trying not to disturb the sekiyr and shatter the dear illusion. Everything had ended, everything changed.

Corey too... soul-tainted?

Brennen! Singer, protect him! If she couldn't do anything else, she could pray constantly.

The young man laid down his instrument and looked up with solemn blue eyes that dispelled all imagery of Corey Bowman. "Hello, Mistress Caldwell."

"Hello. You're...?" Firebird winced. "Forgive me."

"Labeth Kinsman." He swept one finger up the strings.

Wonderful, a relative of Ellet's. A cumulus cloud passed in front of the sun, but that wasn't what raised prickles on her arm. "Please finish, Labeth. That was lovely."

As he plucked another melody, she sank onto the soft, cropped grass and kicked off her shoes. When he finished the piece, he lifted the instrument from his lap.

"You play, don't you?"

"A similar instrument. And I dabbled a little with a kinnora." She wished Janesca were here. Or Carradee! She was unutterably lonely.

"I thought so, from the kind of attention you pay." He held it out to her.

Her clairsa was back at her room. On kinnora, she'd make an amateurish fool of herself...

Firebird, she told herself, *forget your pride. It's friendship he's offering!* She took the little harp, balanced its sound box on her thigh, and picked out a tune she often heard at chapter.

He smiled. "Self-taught?"

"On kinnora, yes."

He reached for the upper arch. "Let me show you the proper position."

"Please!"

For an hour she listened, watched, and tried to emulate Labeth. That afternoon, when Labeth reported for work, they harvested the first snow-apples together, Firebird at ground level and Labeth in the treetops.

The round white fruit felt heavy in her hands, and the rapidly filling basket promised food for months to come. *The Sentinels are right—it's good for the spirit here—whoops!* She bent to retrieve a dropped fruit, but before her fingers closed it flew to the basket, apparently of its own accord.

"I'm sorry," Labeth called down. "I should've seen that fall."

"It's all right." Gazing out over the valley, she leaned against the rough trunk and finally asked, "Labeth? How are you related to Ellet Kinsman?"

Autumn leaves fluttered as he laughed, rising from tenor to counter-tenor. With a rattle of branches, he dropped down to land beside her. "I'm her brother." He regained the mature timbre. "Not her favorite, I'm afraid. It's not easy, being the youngest in the shadow of such a grand lady."

Firebird thought of Carradee and Phoena. "Believe me, I know."

He flicked a net-winged insect off the basket. "But we correspond, and I heard about you a year ago. She never mentioned the clairsa, only General Caldwell. Ellet's a raptor on the hunt. She'll do well." Hefting a snow-apple, he bit into it noisily and grinned around the sweet mouthful.

"Labeth," she asked, abruptly curious. "Why do you think evil can exist? Why does the Speaker allow suffering?"

He shook his head. "I don't know why, but I see His wisdom and power and creativity." He gestured toward the garden, then up to the peaks, with his white snow-apple. "I've felt His love, and I know He is molding me to serve Him forever. When things go wrong, that's all I can cling to. I may not know why, but I know Him."

That, she understood. "I have so much to learn." She scuffed her feet in the leaf-strewn grass.

"Don't we all?" Labeth rose back up the trunk.

Firebird closed her eyes, letting her heart cry in longing and anguish. Brennen! Mighty Singer, help him!

• • •

Brennen walked up a golden corridor in a fog of epsilon silence. With his inner sense chemically blocked and much of his memory gone, he felt disoriented. Seventeen-year habits kept tripping him. He kept trying to shield but couldn't. He couldn't measure his captors' emotions or tell when they lied. But he mustn't stop trying. His memory wouldn't come back without outside help, but blocking drugs wore off. He must stay poised to escape.

A nameless escort walked ahead of him, Testing Director Polar behind. Two golden doors parted as he approached. The three men passed into a volcanic chamber filled with head-high, transparent museum cases. "Slow down," Polar ordered in the holy Ehretan tongue. "You'll want to see this."

Brennen couldn't get used to hearing that language spoken casually, sometimes even profanely. How naive his people seemed now. They forbade translating Dabar, hoping to hide prophecies from a people who still spoke Ehretan as their primary language.

He glanced into the nearest case. Inside, on a golden tripod, perched the mounted body of a long bird with pale blue breast and green back. He stared. On its wings, outstretched to fill the transparent cubicle, the colors intensified to brilliant indigo and emerald. Its wing tips splayed in two downy proto-paws. At college, in a class scorned by many older classmates, he'd studied Ehretan zoology as part of his heritage. That memory hadn't fallen behind the curtain. "That's genuine," he murmured.

"Of course."

The Ehretan creature had been perfectly preserved. Thyrica had no such relics. "Was it a pet?"

"Hunting trophy," Polar said. "Three of the Six took their favorite possessions shipboard before it became necessary to flee."

"The Six?"

"You aren't taught your own history?"

Brennen drew a blank. "Please explain," he said. Should he remember?

"The first group of babies to survive Altering. The first who could function as normally human, so weren't humanely killed. They were in their fifties when the war broke out. They led the Altered revolution. You aren't told?"

He hadn't forgotten. He'd never known. His forebears hadn't honored the war makers by naming them. "I suspect you know what we're told," he answered. He stepped to the next case, which contained six torso mannequins. Each wore clothing and jewelry he'd seen in the historical record: knee-length vests with formal headdresses, pleated tunics, gloves trimmed with the fur of animals that hadn't survived Ehret's destruction... or had they, in Three Zed's bioformed zones?

Slowly he turned a full circle. Three aisles were lined with enough cases to spend days standing and studying.

"It's our ancestors' hall." Polar rested a hand on his holster, casually reminding Brennen of their captive-captor relationship. "I'll bring you back shortly, if you'll answer my questions."

Then they'd only paused here on their way to an interrogation. Brennen had wondered how soon that would start. "What kind of questions?"

Polar smiled coldly.

Brennen barely shook his head.

"I'm glad," Polar whispered. "I like a good fight. Walk on." Brennen had been assured that Special Ops memory blocks couldn't fail. That guaranteed him a harrowing time.

The next double door led into a darker corridor, round-walled with an evenly poured duracrete floor. Three turns later, they approached several men and women waiting in a wider passway. All of them stopped speaking and stared as Brennen approached. One swept a hand toward an open door. The Shuhr guard led inside. Brennen's stomach churned. *You are never alone,* he heard, but his palms turned cold.

At the room's center waited a heavy black chair. Behind it stood a cart with resuscitation equipment and a life-signs monitor, and on its side he saw adjustments for a restraining field.

The others filed into the room behind him. Polar came last. Brennen parked himself just inside the door and let the others pass by. He wouldn't move toward that chair until they forced him. Polar halted too, watching him.

"Sit down." Polar raised a hand as if to command, then smiled narrow eyed and waved at an observer's chair.

Brennen guessed that he should recognize the technique: Frighten the prisoner, then accommodate him. Suggest you could show mercy.

Recognizing the technique didn't keep him from responding to it. As he took the small chair, tensed muscles relaxed with his immense relief. They wouldn't begin, not yet.

Most of the others sat down with heads tilted toward him, though three women carried on a silent conversation betrayed by their glances at one another.

He felt utterly alone. Even if Polar were the only one armed, anyone here could command him.

"General," Polar exclaimed aloud. "Welcome. Meet your eager students." Instead of introducing them, he gestured aside. On the wall behind him appeared an image of a Thyrian city. Another picture sprang up next to it, then another, until all four walls glowed with cityscapes or aerial maps. He knew them all.

Polar touched the near wall. On it, two gray cloud banks and a white-capped ocean framed cliff-side Base One in Soldane. "Thyrica, naturally."

He tapped the image twice. Brennen recognized the remote orbital image that appeared next, a complex of croplands and pastures surrounded by snowy peaks. "Procyel and your sanctuary interest us in the long term." He swept out an arm. "But first, we want to discuss Tallis." Images flashed around the room: ground and orbital bases, Regional command headquarters in the MaxSec Tower, satellite nets that surrounded the Federacy's Regional capital world. One diagram he didn't recognize at all.

The amnesia block was worth what it had cost him, then.

Polar extended a hand, offering Brennen a chance to speak willingly. Brennen crossed his legs, laced his fingers around one knee, and leaned back. They would discover the block soon enough. Meanwhile, he would enjoy what physical comfort was left to him.

Polar took a vacant seat across the circle, toying with him again, pretending he posed no threat. From that position, he could menace more effectively later. "There is an alternative, of course, to infiltration." He waved a hand in the air.

The room went dark. One new image appeared on the wall directly in front of Brennen. On Thyrica's western coast, between foothills and sea, a crater rimmed by fire-blackened ruins slowly filled with ground water. Brennen leaned forward, examining the image, grieving. This was more recent than any he'd seen.

"We could strike Tallis that way." Polar waved the image away and brought up the lights. "We have agents there, of course. I don't imagine that surprises you."

"No," Brennen said. He didn't try to recall his co-workers. He guessed at this technique too: Polar wanted to know who might be under suspicion. In his mind's eye, resisting Polar with a more edifying image, Brennen studied an exquisitely illustrated page of liturgy often sung in Hesed's underground chapter room.

Polar crossed his knees and swung one leg. "Answer one question, Caldwell, and we will send you home."

Brennen raised an eyebrow. He didn't dare hope Polar was serious. Polar's casual posture couldn't hide the deadly intensity in his voice. "How did you get into this city? Our force at Thyrica reported a new kind of disruptor field. Your arrival confirmed it. What is it?"

Brennen couldn't remember, but now he knew what Polar wanted most. "I am sorry," he said softly. "That information is classified."

Polar raised one eyebrow and nodded across the circle.

A thin, strong-looking young man rocked onto his feet. He sauntered toward the empty chair next to Brennen, staring all the while into Brennen's eyes. Feature by feature, Brennen catalogued the resemblance to a blackened-faced intruder who had leaped onto his bed at Trinn Hill.

Previously motionless observers uncrossed their legs and rocked forward. The wiry young man stared down at him for several seconds, then sank onto the empty seat. "My name's Shirak, Caldwell. Micahel Shirak. I'm the Eldest's grandson. I work in enforcement. Today's my last chance to speak with you. I've been assigned to an outlying area. A settlement," he growled, "while I study basic military tactics. But I helped plan a special reception for your mistress. I hope they use it."

Brennen stared at Micahel's full lips, cleft chin, and high cheekbones.

"They'll call me when she comes. I only hope I can get back in time. I don't want to miss the celebration."

Brennen wrested his mind to the liturgy.

"Give up, Carabohd." Micahel Shirak's nostrils flared. He stretched one fingertip toward Brennen's forehead and thrust an image into Brennen's mind. Brennen saw through Micahel's eyes, in Micahel's memory...

...a dim doorway, where he gripped the frame to listen cautiously.

The hall was almost dark, but in less than a second, Brennen recognized his brother's home. His own right hand gripped a blazer, thumb covering the safety. One glance over his shoulder... he was still undetected.

Brennen struggled to break Shirak's control, to raise shields, to fight free of Shirak's memory...

...Under rumpled covers, a small form sprawled on the bed. Tousled blond hair hid most of a sweet, feminine face.

Destia.

He shuffled closer.

"Stop." Brennen flung out both hands, and the image blurred into a rage-red mist. Micahel Shirak's leering face reappeared, framed with black curls.

Brennen's hands, seemingly possessed, seized his own knees and dug in. In his mind, though, he was choking this man who had terrorized his beloved niece. His cheeks flamed. He had controlled his anger, his temptation to hate, since Tarance's death. He couldn't hold it back now. It didn't matter that he was titillating his audience. He didn't even feel rational.

"It didn't start there, Carabohd." Micahel brushed his hand on one pant leg, as if he'd soiled it by touching Brennen. "My father killed your uncles. My grandfather, your great-uncle. Your family and mine have intertwined for years, and you didn't even know it."

So that was the explanation. "Why?" he demanded.

Shirak shrugged. "I think you can guess."

Brennen's thoughts fled for one uncontrolled instant to the sanctuary. Micahel shook his head. "We know where your sons are. Give us one boy," he suggested, "and we might spare the other."

Brennen forced himself to breathe slowly, to ignore the taunt. It was nothing more.

"Maybe." Dru Polar's voice startled Brennen. "But maybe not forever." Standing at Brennen's elbow, he glanced toward the heavy chair and life-signs monitor.

Did Brennen remember enough to betray Hesed's defenses?

• • •

Polar's prisoner crumpled forward, willfully unconscious as before. Micahel glanced up and sent, *Let me stay. Let me help.* He glared toward the interrogation chair. *That family is mine.*

You know your assignment, Polar reminded him. *Study your tactics. You're not ready for this one.*

• • •

When Brennen awoke in his stony cell, his shoulders and backside ached as if he'd been dragged back down the black-and-gold corridors. The room light had been dimmed. Around the massive black door, an arch of red striplights pulsed dully.

He clenched his hands, longing to crush Micahel Shirak's throat... or better, to thrust with epsilon might into the other man's beta centers, as the Codes absolutely forbade... to stir Micahel's physical energies into a vortex, creating heat, pressure, pain. Brennen would have paid for that attack with his life, whether he tried it here or on Thyrica, but what was that life worth here?

Amnesia blocks could cause personality changes. Brennen recognized despair, hatred's fellow destroyer. He rolled onto his stomach, clenched his hands, then begged a silent heaven to let him live long enough to avenge Tarance's family. *Why did you call me here?* he cried silently. *I've accomplished nothing!*

Again, the first answer was silence.

23

DEATH STROKE

con timpani sordi
with muffled kettledrums

Six days later, Brennen lay in his stone cell, too exhausted to sleep. All week, Polar had worked on breaking his amnesia block, digging for information that was still stored in his synapses. Now Brennen knew the misery of enduring interrogation without epsilon shields.

Faintly lit by the slowly pulsing red arch, this cell was never truly dark. He rolled over on his cot, which was as narrow and hard as a chapter room's altar. Seventeen years had passed since he had endured pain without the ability to block it. Now, when he willed himself unconscious, Polar shot him full of stimulants and kept probing.

At least he retained affective control, and he could forget the tortures after they ended. He shifted again and called up other thoughts. Unfortunately, Micahel Shirak's face rose to mind. Heartsick with hatred, he thrust it aside.

Holy One, was I mistaken? Did I follow a false vision here?

Not necessarily. Even holy men suffered. He remembered an Adoration—

• • •

My mortal enemies surround me;
I am caught, they have tracked me down.
They watch with sharp eyes,
They fling me to the ground, their teeth tear me.
I am their prey.

O Holy One, save me by your hand.
Come down, rescue me…

• • •

Rescue me, he repeated. Unless he could prevent Mari's coming, her death seemed as certain as his own. But he couldn't think of a way to warn her off. If she came, what kind of "research" would she endure? How would they use her if they found out she could kill… had killed?

He shut his eyes against the pulsing red lights and a buzzing headache. The blocking drug was wearing off early, and he must hide that fact from his captors. They'd underestimated their dosage.

My mortal enemies…

Micahel appeared again in his mind, leering as he forced the rest of his cruel recollections into Brennen's memory. Hatred boiled in Brennen's spirit. Unless he subdued that emotion, it would grow like malignant cancer. Micahel Shirak had deliberately poisoned him, and not just with memories. Brennen couldn't retain this lust for revenge and still live by faith, not here, not anywhere.

His black door slid open. Cassia Talumah stepped through. At each shoulder of her sleeveless jumpsuit fluttered a white streamer scarf, setting off her weirdly striped hair. He rose warily off his cot and greeted her. She'd come once already, with repellent suggestions.

"I'm not staying this time," she answered, "though I could still develop a taste for your kind. But if you want to eat tonight, I'd suggest you come with me to Polar's quarters. He's asked us to dinner."

"Us?"

She turned half away from him, displaying her provocative silhouette, brown beneath white gauze. "He asked me. But I'd rather not go alone. I'm choosing to bring you."

He backstepped. "No. But thank you."

Instantly, fire crawled over his skin like a hundred tiny demons. He gasped and hunched forward.

Cassia smirked. The burning sensation ceased without leaving even a sense of warmth.

He shivered. "What was that?"

"My wild talent. Synthesizing a heat response at nerve endings. Shall I call it up again?"

"No," he said.

"Then come." She reached toward his face. "General, I believe you're going to have a scar."

He touched his cheek, still tender where Phoena kicked him.

"I like it," she observed. "Very rakish."

He rubbed the roughening cuff of his tunic, fingers still twitching. "Polar," he said. "You fear him, Cassia. What has he done to you?" He remembered how Polar had leered, watching Phoena die. Cassia had probably seen worse. He trained the children here. What did he do to those who failed?

"Nothing yet. And he'll do nothing tonight." Cassia drew a shock pistol. "After you."

She directed him down golden passways. As he stepped into Polar's apartment with Cassia's hand arched on his arm, he blinked, visually hammered by riots of color. Each chair and lounger seemed to have been chosen to clash with its nearest neighbor, the floor underneath, or the walls behind. Above a long mirrored cabinet hung the trophy head of a huge cat, lips curled back to show six upper fangs. The room's openness appealed to him after seven days in a tiny cell, but it crowded him with brightness. Could Polar be color-blind, or was this his taste?

Polar wore a long shimmering shirt of magenta belted in black, and formfitting black pants. His hair, set in tight waves, glistened with matching magenta flecks. *Not color-blind, then, unless someone dresses him.*

Cassia caressed Brennen's arm. "A change of scenery could stimulate the prisoner's memory."

Polar's glance returned to Brennen. "Certainly, Cassia, if it will entertain you." He poured a glass of ruby-colored liquor. "Steen, my friends?"

"Naturally." Cassia took the cordial.

Polar raised one eyebrow toward Brennen as he handed Cassia her drink. Brennen shook his head.

The entry opened soundlessly. As Brennen took a fan-backed chair beside Cassia in the dining alcove, a hurrying youth set down a dinner that looked and smelled very different from the subsistence food Brennen had eaten on six previous nights. He dispatched the delicately spiced dishes quickly, without trying to hide his enjoyment. Cassia watched him, plainly amused, but he refused to notice. Even if kindness wasn't her motive, tonight he moved unfettered among the Shuhr. If he escaped, he would carry out knowledge no one else had reported.

As he sipped excellent kass, a second training-age youth removed platters. Even stripped of probing ability, Brennen could see that the young man radiated fear in Polar's presence, almost dropping a goblet in his haste to be gone.

Brennen thanked the Holy One that this man didn't train Sentinel children. He wondered if Dabarrah had given Kiel and Kinnor back to Firebird. That might keep her at Hesed.

Polar pushed back his chair, strolled to a wall unit, and opened a cabinet. "A fascinating thing." He twisted his hand. Brennen heard the familiar singing note of his crystace as Polar turned around. He rose from the table, wanting to wrest it from Polar's hands. Cassia laughed at Polar's vacant smile while Polar swung the shimmering, virtually invisible blade of the Sentinels' ceremonial weapon. "I tested it on a few substances: permastone, duracrete, sub-adults. I haven't been able to shatter it, but I suppose I haven't really tried. I'd rather keep it for my collection." Fingering off the sonic activator to return the ehrite crystal's molecular bonds to their stable length, Polar tucked it into tonight's black sash, then smiled.

Brennen sidestepped toward another pair of loungers. When he committed himself to one, Cassia pointedly joined him.

Polar crossed his arms. "Caldwell, your surface memory is cluttered with knife fighting drills. Have you been studying recently?"

"Not recently."

"Of course." Polar opened one hand and conceded, "It's more likely that you've been teaching someone."

"Not recently..."

"Cassia has been tutoring my son Jerric." Polar glanced from Brennen to Cassia. "Here we are with an hour to spare and a chance to try something novel. If the two of you held a practice match, I'd find that entertaining."

Unlimited wealth, uncanny power... and the man was bored. "Not him, Dru. This kind wants to hold back. I would waste too much effort," Cassia said, but as she spoke, she plucked the streamer scarves from her shoulders as if trimming for battle.

Polar flexed his arms. "Then I'll take you, Cassia, if you're willing. Too long without practice leaves even a knife edge rusty. Our pet Sentinel can referee."

Cassia and Dru reached for their boots. Each came up with a triangle-bladed dirk half the length of a Carolinian dagger. Observing no preliminaries, Polar sprang toward the lounger. Before Cassia had fully risen, Polar's blade flickered. Brennen stared, startled to see Cassia's bare arm bleeding below the elbow.

"Well?" She glared at Brennen. "That counts."

"Score," he murmured. "Polar."

Polar led Cassia to the cabinet and drew out a medical kit. In a minute, they returned to center floor.

"We'll try that again." Polar poured and drained another cordial. He had drunk freely during dinner. "There. Now we're more evenly matched."

"Ready." Cassia's tone defied him. This time they both looked at Brennen. "Begin," he said.

Now Cassia slashed fiercely. Polar hung back in a casual stance, all his weight on one foot. Suddenly she stepped in close, tripped him, and swung her dirk. He twisted as he fell. The blade sliced only shirt and skin, but it was a near miss of a major artery. "Score," Brennen said softly, sensing Polar's freely broadcast anger and surprise. "Talumah."

Cassia nursed Polar this time and then ignored him, walking instead to Brennen's lounger. Polar stayed behind, leaning against the cabinet with yet another goblet. He sipped delicately.

"Now, Sentinel?" she asked, flicking her dagger's edge. "Now that you know I can hold my own?"

He rose uneasily, suspecting he'd better not refuse. "All right, Cassia. Polar, will you lend me a blade? Mine is elsewhere." He glanced at the sash and his crystace.

Polar chose two more knives from his cabinet, another slender dirk and a long fighting blade. He extended the dirk to Brennen, grip first. In the moment both men held it their eyes met, and Brennen glimpsed hatred flickering there, not the least blunted by liquor. "That one's a handicap design." A corner of Polar's mouth twitched. "Watch your hold."

Brennen followed Cassia to the center of the room. Polar clenched his blazer in his right hand and the longer knife in his left, on guard.

Cassia crouched, eyeing Brennen hungrily. Brennen adjusted his hand around the unfamiliar grip. Its hold was perpendicular to what he considered normal, and he would swat with the flat unless he paid as careful attention to his hold as to Cassia. He didn't dare harm her, he didn't even want to bloody her, but he could see by the spark in her eyes that she would enjoy slicing him.

She sprang. He ducked and dodged but didn't counterattack. "Wake up." She planted her fists on her hips, reptile-striped hair draping her shoulders. "If you're not going to cooperate, give the knife back to Dru."

He nodded and stepped out clockwise to lead with a glaring feint, then parried her counterstroke with the flat of his blade. Metal rang.

She pulled back, wringing her hand. "What are you trying to do, disarm me? We don't play that way."

"You won't fight, Sentinel?" Brennen spun in time to see Polar drop his blazer, shift the long knife to his right hand, and lunge.

Hastily Brennen backed out of the Shuhr's reach. "Wait, Polar."

"You'd best defend yourself. You could serve our purposes just as well with one less—arm!" Polar lunged again, closer this time. Brennen sprang away, watching for the slightest opening. Polar offered none but crouched closer yet, steady on his feet: barely, dangerously liquor-relaxed.

Brennen prepared to leap in any direction as he turned, seeking his carrier across the gap that kept narrowing as the drug wore off.

There! The turn felt tenuous, but he could tap resources Polar expected him to lack.

Polar's attention flashed to Cassia for approval. Brennen unleashed his hatred and attacked.

Polar responded with astonishing reflexes. Fire bloomed on Brennen's chest. Automatically blocking the pain with familiar epsilon energy, he aimed a cut at Polar's withdrawing knife arm. Polar laughed as he sprang away. Brennen's hold on the grip had shifted, and what might've been an effective slice was a comical swipe.

The black-haired Shuhr returned to his crouch, gloating through lashless black eyes. "We'll tape you later. Say it, Cassia. Score. Polar. And here's a better." He charged again.

"Dru!" Cassia shouted. Brennen saw the knife homing for his shoulder. "Cool down!" He twisted aside. "Shirak will have your head if you maim him!"

Polar spun. He stabbed again from well within Brennen's guard, aiming for his chest. A death stroke.

Brennen's backward leap both saved and betrayed him.

Polar straightened. He stood breathing heavily, eyeing Brennen.

Brennen felt Polar's probe touch his epsilon matrix. He relinquished the turn too late.

"My mistake," Polar said icily. "I shouldn't have tried that. You're too valuable to kill." He turned aside. "Cassia, our guest needs his medication. Would you be so kind as to administer ten mls of DME-6?"

Cassia stopped circling. Her face clouded for an instant, then she tossed her head. "Oh. I'd enjoy that. Of course, Dru. I don't suppose you keep any in here?"

He gestured toward a black carryall on the floor.

As Cassia knelt to sort ampoules, Brennen tensed, wondering if he dared to resist.

"I wouldn't," Polar said quietly, very sober now. "I'm growing tired of your conceit."

Brennen fingered the thumb guard of his dirk and turned again. The carrier flickered. He hadn't regained solid enough linkage to depend on it.

Cassia snapped a cartridge of clear blue fluid into a long-needled venous syringe, tightened the barrel, and then flicked it almost casually. Brennen could feel her crowing as she stood up. *Hold him, Dru.*

Polar lifted a hand in casual command stance, strode forward, and took the odd knife from Brennen.

"I'm ready." Cassia stepped up. "Kneel."

Kneel? Brennen sent, hoping only to gain time.

There are other positions. But this is best for the spinal fluid.

Brennen swallowed hard. *Nonsense.* Even a dart-pistol dose, injected into muscle, could disable.

Polar's hand shifted. *On your knees, Caldwell.* Brennen's legs buckled. Cassia's talons tilted his head. A UV beamer kissed the hairline at the base of his skull. Then cold pain mocked his hope of escape, he grew dizzy, and Polar let him go.

He scrambled to his feet, fighting to retain contact with the carrier, though they watched and laughed. The pain of his chest slash intensified as his control slipped. He wiped salt water from his eyes.

Cassia flicked a fingernail across his shoulder. "I'll tape you. But you'd better get back to your room first. You'll be asleep in five minutes."

24

FUSION THEORY

attacca
continue from previous section without pausing

Firebird sat beside Tel, on a bench under a sweeping kirka tree. Around their small square island, the underground reflecting pool lapped quietly. As on the past four nights, they'd reminisced and shared hopes. Brennen and Phoena could conceivably return in as little as four more days. But Firebird's sense of disaster hadn't diminished, and tonight, when Tel mentioned Kinnor and Kiel—a month old today—she broke into long, racking sobs.

Unexpectedly Tel reached out and pulled her head to his shoulder. Sitting, he was barely taller than Firebird... but the gesture was comforting, his arms warm, and his shoulder already becoming too solid for a noble's. When she stopped shaking, he kept one arm tucked loosely around her waist.

At least she had a waist again. She'd lost all her pregnancy weight and then some.

"I should be shot, Firebird." He whispered so softly that she almost couldn't hear him. "I wish I had never left Netaia. Caldwell would still be here, if not for me."

On another small island, one she could see from this stone bench, they'd spoken their vows. She sighed, then saw the guilt contorting Tel's delicate features. "Don't talk that way," she said. "We made our choices, and not in ignorance."

"Firebird..."

She smiled at him fondly, but her tears gathered again.

"If neither of them comes back—I mean, if Phoena is... gone—then you're no wastling anymore. And if you ever wanted to go home—"

"It'll be a very long time before I stop hoping he'll be back."

"Let me finish." Tel laid his other hand on her arm, clutching with his long fingers. "Please. I couldn't bear to see you left a widow because of me. I'd owe you—well, anything I could give. If you wanted it."

Firebird saw that he too wavered near tears. "Thank you, Tel. I'll remember that."

The next day, a trio of Sentinels arrived at Hesed with messages.

Firebird heard most of the news over lunch from young Labeth, but Dabarrah called her into his private office to deliver another message. "We've had more bad news from Netaia," he said solemnly.

"Another attack? Is Carradee all right?" If one more thing went wrong, she might pack a duffel, snatch back her babies, and run off into the mountains.

"Not harmed, but deposed. The Electorate forced her to abdicate."

Firebird could've sworn her heart stopped for a moment. "She didn't suicide?"

"No. No, I'm sorry I didn't make that clear. She drove Prince Daithi to Governor Danton. His condition is more serious than we were originally told."

But she hadn't taken the Powers' way out. *Bravo, Carradee!* "Will Daithi live?" Again she thought of his brother Alef, alive somewhere in the Federacy. Daithi still thought Alef was dead.

Dabarrah eyed her closely. She wondered if he sensed the old deception, even though she hadn't lied out loud. "With care," he answered.

"Will Danton send them to Tallis? Or—"

"I would allow them at Hesed."

"Yes," Firebird urged, glad to help save two more lives. "Thank you." Then she had to ask, "Who rules?"

"The Duke of Claighbro. Not as regent for Carradee, but for a new queen, Iarla Second."

Carradee had named her first daughter for their great-great-grandmother, Firebird's heroine—a wastling who survived to be crowned Queen of Netaia. Firebird's own ballad for Iarla now took on a new layer of meaning. Its chorus flitted through her memory: *Iarla the compassionate, Iarla the queen—Iarla, doomed to die young.* "Is there any news on Carradee's daughters? Do we know little Iarlet is safe?"

"Governor Danton sent them to Inisi, one of Ituri's protectorate worlds. There has never been Shuhr activity there. We should have word of their safe arrival within days."

That would be a relief. But... "Rogonin." Firebird mouthed the hated name, and her throat tightened. Rogonin would undo everything Danton and

Carradee had accomplished. Where would that lead Netaia? "Master," she said urgently, "there's a simulation I worked with back at Thyrica. Can you call up what I left at Soldane University?" She had to know how this power shift would affect her home world, by the best Federate projection.

"I believe I can." He turned to his touchboard. She walked closer and watched over his shoulder as he routed a query. "We're updated by Soldane University whenever a messenger arrives from Thyrica."

"Don't look under my name," she warned him. "I took the course as Mari Tomma."

He touched in that name. A page appeared, written in academic jargon. She couldn't find even her name. Squinting, she leaned closer. "I turned in my final essay the day I went into labor. Did I pass?"

He touched a key, then smiled up at her. "Honorably. Congratulations. You were selected for University publication." Then he touched another series. The first page of her simulation appeared on the screen.

"That's it," she exclaimed.

"I'm transferring this," he said, still tapping keys, "to your data desk. Done. You're wise to follow events this way. It's a good use of your time."

"I can't leave it alone. But I'd rather have Kiel and Kinnor back. And Brennen. How can I stand this? I'm not simply half a person now. I'm less. I... can you tell," she blurted, "has he died?"

"He's definitely alive. I can tell by watching you that the pair bond remains intact."

Relieved, she pressed on. "You've accessed me ten times now. I haven't hurt you. I won't hurt Kiel or Kinnor. Please give them back."

"Firebird Mari." He steepled his fingers and raised both eyebrows compassionately. "There is too much at stake. We haven't solved your mystery, and you still cannot use that turn in any practical, controllable way. You must learn patience."

"I've stretched my patience to its end. It's gone."

His eyes softened. He pushed back his chair. "Then pray for strength and the will to go on for one more day. Our Speaker doesn't exempt His people from pain. He only enables us to bear it and be strengthened."

Firebird worked her fingers together. "I suppose you define impatience as a lack of faith."

Jenner Dabarrah held her stare with kind blue-gray eyes. "Your insight is excellent," he said, and she felt an assuring access-touch. "Faith and patience are closely linked."

Comforted, she found the courage to say, "Master, I have to get something off my conscience." She told him about Alef Drake and the lovely common-class woman who went into exile with him, and the wreckage she and Corey strewed in outer-system space, faking Alef's death. Her reluctance slowly turned to relief. "I don't know," she finished, "if it would do any good to confess this on Netaia. The electors would've killed Alef for no purpose. And I'd only be charged with another capital crime."

"I would advise keeping the secret a little longer." The master stood. "For now, confess it to the One."

From Him, Firebird could expect forgiveness.

"And write a song for them," Jenner suggested. "You have a gift for melody. You should use it more."

• • •

Tel leaned against the waterside railing and watched Firebird hurry away from Dabarrah's office.

He'd changed here. Like his muscles, his spirit had hardened. He actually enjoyed task work. The stable master claimed he showed a real talent with breeding animals. That work heightened his sense of identity, of a human dignity that came without aristocratic titles or pseudo-godhood.

But Phoena had left him.

She'd acted as if she needed him, as if she treasured what he could give her...

But now he knew better.

After Firebird vanished under an arch into her room, Tel stepped out across the stones. Firebird hadn't noticed his agitation. Other concerns consumed her, and this matter hurt his pride. This wasn't something to share with a woman.

He rapped at the master's door. Dabarrah called softly, "Come in, Your Highness."

The Sanctuary Master sat on the long white stone bench carved into his left wall. Tel sank into a still-warm wooden chair.

He dreaded that Dabarrah would ask, "What can I do for you?" How would he say it? How would he humble himself again to a Sentinel, as he'd done by asking Brennen Caldwell's help? He stared back at the serene master sentinel, whose hair shone white-gold under the skylight. On another occasion, he might have suggested painting the man's portrait.

"Good afternoon," Master Dabarrah master said simply. "Welcome."

Tel nodded slightly. "Thank you."

"You've been abandoned." Dabarrah spread his hands. "I will not—I cannot—eliminate your hurt. That would diminish you as a feeling person.

But if you came for healing, I could escort you back through some of your memories of Princess Phoena. You need to recall her accurately, knowing now what she has done. In doing that, you may gain a deeper understanding of her motives and your own. It would help prepare you for her return. It's a kind of access healing," he said. "Is it something you feel could help you?"

"I think I already understand my motives."

Dabarrah raised an eyebrow.

Tel reached for his sash ends, but he wore no sash now, only simple gray shipboards. "Muirnen Rogonin and I were friends before the Veroh invasion, before Hunter Height. I know you just told Lady Firebird that he's trying to take power on Netaia."

"How do you know?"

"The sekiyrra are buzzing with it," Tel explained. "And I knew weeks ago that he meant to try to talk Carradee off the throne. I... encouraged him, especially when he spoke about Phoena's natural nobility and about her sacrifices as our leader in the loyalist cause. I dreamed once of sitting beside Phoena as prince consort." The image promenaded through his mind one last time. "Now I know what Rogonin really wants. The crown. Just as Phoena did. Does," he corrected himself. He would not give up hope.

In the silence that followed, Tel heard water running beyond the arch. He shifted on the hardwood chair.

Dabarrah shook his head slowly. "Yes, Prince Tel. I agree with you about Rogonin, and so does Lady Firebird. I'll be contacting Governor Danton. Her Majesty and the prince should join you here in safety."

"Oh." Tel stared, considering. "Absolutely," he decided. "But Carradee will need to feel she has discharged her duty to Netaia, done her utmost, before she leaves. She would seek to fulfill that responsibility first. Yet..." He pushed upright in his seat. "Master, either Phoena or Firebird would have made a stronger queen."

Dabarrah stood. "You would be more comfortable in the inner room, if you still want the healing."

Tel pushed up out of his chair. "I'm ready," he said. "My conscience is clean."

• • •

An entry bell sent Three Zed's geneticist, Juddis Adiyn, hurrying past a terminal where his young technician sat keying in chromosomal data.

Many of the unbound raised their own children, particularly out in the settlements—but the best and most gifted came from this laboratory. Rows of softly humming cylinders nourished embryos and fetuses destined for birth. Another wall held shorter-term incubation tubes, one row for each Golden City resident, their cloned embryos awaiting harvest and ayin extraction.

Ard Talumah, trader in unusual commodities, stood outside the main door. He pulled a pair of sample cases out from under one arm and looked down his long nose at Adiyn. "Yours."

"Any trouble?" Adiyn took the small cold-cases. He'd filled identical boxes with tissue specimens from Phoena Angelo. Until these new cases received alphanumeric designations, their labels were neatly printed Casvah/Angelo, Iarla; and Casvah/Angelo, Kessaree.

"Think about it." Talumah lounged against the doorway. "Blasting a shuttle is easy. Leaving the passengers intact enough to get samples takes a little more effort."

"I would've preferred them intact. Alive." Adiyn sent a hint of displeasure on his epsilon wave. He'd looked forward to introducing two little girls to Three Zed's ways.

Talumah shrugged. "Hard vacuum isn't kind to the body. I pieced together what you wanted. Blood, deep tissue. All five types of nerve."

"Ayin?" Deep in the brain, those regions were difficult to harvest after a skull hardened. He hadn't taken Phoena's ayin sample until after her "execution," when they had carried her down to be cold-stased.

"I said all five."

Adiyn set the cases next to his tech. "Terza, designate and map these. Nuclear and mitochondrial. Priority. This is our new chromosome line."

• • •

Brennen struggled apprehensively to consciousness, fearing at any moment to feel the probe Polar had flung repeatedly through his alpha matrix. The lights had been brought up, and—he cautiously raised one arm—he'd been released from Polar's restraining field.

Then Polar had finished again.

It was the eighth day of interrogation. Yesterday, Polar had claimed he'd broken the amnesia block and flaunted a sheet of data. But Brennen saw nothing on it that Shirak's agents couldn't have learned from Harcourt Terrell's cohorts on Thyrica. Polar must have noted that thought, because this time he said nothing. That was a different kind of torment. Exhaustion and hatred weakened Brennen as Polar experimented with interrogation drugs that left him shaky and babbling.

The more power He gives us to wield, he heard in his own voice, *the more He must purify us.*

Have mercy...

Only footsteps, no sense of approaching mind, alerted him to Polar's return.

He opened his eyes and sat up on the edge of the steely slab, gripping its rim with both hands. That last defense, willing himself unconscious, had returned to his control when he discovered a way to counter Polar's stimulants. It weakened him, though. So did the fear of what Polar might do to his body while his mind was elsewhere.

Polar stepped close. "Come," he ordered. "I have something to show you."

In a second laboratory lay a recently opened cold-stasis crypt, a coffin-like apparatus designed to hold one severely injured patient almost indefinitely, until revival for treatment or permanent disposal. Beside the crypt, on a metal table that radiated warmth, lay a thin, dark-haired boy with a terrible head wound, inadequately bandaged. Brennen took a stool, double-guarded like the boy.

The boy groaned.

"Quiet." Polar rolled his own stool close. "I'll ease this for you if I can. And remember. There's a Caldwell watching. Carabohd. Do you understand?"

The boy turned dark eyes on Brennen, who saw mingled with his fear an awful hatred.

"Better." Polar reached for the boy's chest and let his hand lie there. "My real hopes are built on this, Caldwell. Today you'll see how fortuitous your arrival has been.

"This boy suffered massive brain injuries several years ago, fighting an age mate. We stabilized his condition, but he can't recover." Brennen glanced at the stasis crypt. Its corners and edges were rounded, and a net of some sort lay limp in its depth. "He knew when we stased him that he would serve our long-term plan by helping with research, instead of draining resources."

"I see he's no volunteer." Brennen clenched his stool.

"Watch your manners, Caldwell. He's unhappy enough. Now, let me explain. I place electromagnetic disruption probes here..." He slipped a hand under the small of the boy's back and taped on a wire. "...and here." He repeated the act at a pale, sweaty temple near the boy's wound. "Using a standard power source, I'll create a momentary reversal of his epsilon wave's electrical polarity. That will mirror-image its wave forms. Can you understand, brain damaged as you are?"

Brennen considered. Standing epsilon waves stabilized in uniform patterns, any of which was polarized in a particular direction, relative to the spine and ayin. Yes, he could understand.

Polar went on. "Any epsilon-capable subject reacts to the reversal with an involuntary turn. If at that instant I can access-link, that will superimpose my normal epsilon wave over his reversed-polarity wave. My theory is that this fusion should release a surge of wave-synchronous energy. I should be able to hold that energy as long as I can hold my own turn. The experimental evidence points that way, anyway. I do know it'll leave him little more than a husk."

"For certain?" Brennen asked dully.

"Yes. We've been unable to proceed past this point. You'll see why."

Brennen guessed Polar's "research" had proved more successful than he would acknowledge. "You're anxious to have me observe, then," he said, to mask another awful suspicion.

"Oh yes."

So this was his intended fate. If he didn't escape, he would be the next experimental subject, or the next. "But Polar, this boy couldn't have begun to exercise his potential. And the injury—"

"Does age affect potential?" Polar reached aside. "And his ayin was undamaged." He brandished a syringe filled with pale pink fluid. "From my clones," he explained. "Undifferentiated brain-tissue suspension."

Brennen's heart wrenched. "You kill your own children."

"We 'harvest'—we do not 'kill.' Embryos have no sentience." He stepped behind a fabric screen. Brennen reached toward the doomed boy's shoulder, but a guard stepped between them.

Polar returned with his head tossed back and his eyes gleaming. "You must try it someday," he said. "The most breathtaking sensation I know."

"Never," Brennen whispered. But they'd surely extracted genes from his own cells. Were reproductive technicians culturing his cloned embryos even now?

Polar settled back onto the wheeled stool. "Hold him." Guards seized the boy's wrists and ankles. Polar leaned over the boy's body. "Now," he barked.

For one moment, Brennen felt a secondhand surge of epsilon energy thrust through him... and then fade into familiar silence. The boy lay without breathing, his face gray and contorted.

Polar sighed deeply, straightened, and then whirled his stool. "So you see. None of my subjects have survived the reversal. I think they simply weren't strong enough to maintain mental function while I tried for fusion. I need a stronger subject. Just one." Polar smiled, showing a row of perfect yellow-cream teeth. He snapped his fingers at Brennen's guards, then pointed up the passway. "Take him back."

Keeping all thought silenced, Brennen walked with the guards to his cell. The door shut behind him soundlessly, and this time Brennen was grateful to be left alone. He dropped onto his cot.

What had really happened in that laboratory? Did Polar devour the boy's potential, as Brennen suspected? Or had the demonstration failed, as Polar claimed?

Polar thought he could create a surge of incredible power simply by accessing a subject whose epsilon carrier wave was forced to reorient itself in a mirror image, an unusual kind of standing-wave polarity.

Brennen's thoughts sprinted on. The isolated Casvah-Angelo line had picked up at least one hereditary disorder, the one that caused Mazo syndrome. Could there have been a second mutation too? Had Firebird Mari inherited a naturally reversed-polarity epsilon wave?

Could that have empowered her, when Harcourt Terrell forced access, to draw him into those horrific images? He stared at the black floor. Terrell's native abilities shouldn't have destroyed a normal Sentinel's beta centers...

But if Terrell were in the Shuhr's pay, they might've given him ayin-extract treatments, too much power to control... certainly, power enough to beat an access interrogation. If fused with a reversed-polarity carrier, that power could have been doubled, tripled, amplified enough to destroy him. Also, Terrell had meant to murder her. Maybe she turned his own intention back on him.

The data fit perfectly. That didn't mean his theory was correct. *Oh, Mari...*

He sat up straight, imagining it again, picturing Firebird's vivid vision of darkness linked to Polar's notion of fusion power. If such fusion could really be created, and if Terrell and Firebird were both turning at the moment he tried to destroy her, without any shielding static between them, then Terrell's accentuated epsilon strength—and the wave fusion—

might have blasted back through his mind, which was focused on death—
and killed him.

He rubbed his stubbled chin. Or maybe the solution was simpler,
and that energy surge always killed the weaker partner in link. Polar had
destroyed all his subjects, though he tried to keep them alive.

All theories, just theories. Brennen understood only one thing. Polar
meant to use him, too, for a research subject, after trapping Firebird and
forcing him to kill her. In bereavement shock, he'd be truly undone.

Not if he escaped! But his captors kept him locked down and guarded.
This cell was as secure as any at MaxSec.

Knowing the worst possible fate gave him an odd sense of calm. Yes, they
would suffer if Mari came here... but that would end. Even Destia hadn't
suffered long, compared with the peace she now enjoyed. And maybe Mari
would stay at Hesed after all.

He had broken despair's stranglehold. Now for his hatred: He drew a
deep breath and called up the final image Micahel Shirak had poured into
his wounded memory—Destia's gentle blue eyes, terror wide in a last silent
scream.

He imagined, then, those eyes as they widened farther with wonder,
opening again beyond the Crossing, seeing first all her family—together—
and then the One who had brought them safely Across.

Any pain we endure as we die, he had read, *is the last we will suffer, forever.*
He sighed deeply.

Another thought shattered his momentary peace. If Dru Polar achieved
this fusion, how did he mean to use it?

25

FOR BRENNEN

con molto affetto
with deep feeling

Late that afternoon, two Special Operations ships reached Hesed's perimeter. After watching them glide in on the grassy strip, Firebird seated herself in the commons for dinner with Tel. He listened, frowning, while she explained the Federate simulation's projections for Netaia under Rogonin's regency. Barring unforeseen circumstances—outside attacks, natural disasters, significant scientific discoveries—their home world might slip back toward stability for a few years. "But at what cost," she exclaimed, punctuating the sentence with her soup spoon. Behind Tel's shoulder, two uniformed Sentinels strode across the stepping stones toward the commons. "You know Rogonin. He'll strip the low classes of everything Danton gave them. When they finally stand up and resist him, when they've stockpiled weapons and recruited disgruntled military people, the uprising will be much worse than if—"

She fell silent. The uniformed Sentinels reached the waterside commons—bulky young Air Master Dardy, followed by a tall black-haired woman with proud eyes, a shapely but prominent nose, and slightly concave cheeks. Could that be—?

Tel craned his neck around, following her stare.

Groaning, Firebird scrambled to her feet. "Ellet!" What brought her here? Firebird reluctantly thrust out a hand. "Hello, Dardy. Join us."

"Mistress Caldwell," Ellet Kinsman returned smoothly. Her face looked pale, her eyes red.

Tel stood too. Firebird laid a hand on his shoulder. "This is my sister's husband, Ellet: Prince Tel Tellai-Angelo. Tel, this is Captain Ellet Kinsman of the Federate forces and Air Master Damalcon Dardy of Thyrica."

"We know of you, Prince Tel," Ellet said. "We've come from Master Dabarrah's rooms."

Firebird sat back down. Dardy seated Ellet, then walked off to find a sekiyr to bring two more bowls. Firebird's stomach clenched so tightly that she hoped her soup would stay down.

"I've had the news," Ellet said quietly, "from Master Dabarrah. I'm sorry. For all of us."

Of course she was sorry. And had Ellet asked him why Sentinels were told to shun Firebird?

Tel checked the silvery pitcher. "I'll get more kass." He hurried toward the servo, leaving Firebird and Ellet alone.

Firebird took a deep breath. She ought to tell Ellet it was good to see her, or make some other insincere small talk. She'd never been good at that.

Ellet glanced darkly at Tel as he bowed gracefully to a sekiyr and then turned back to the table. "Tonight," Ellet muttered. "We need to talk."

• • •

Firebird sat on her bedside, clenching a slick red-and-blue audio rod in frustration.

"He's alive, then," Ellet remarked as confidently as Master Dabarrah had done. "And since he hasn't come back empty-handed, we can assume his RIA unit took him past their fielding."

"Then he's been taken prisoner." The constant cascade poured down the wall, and beside Firebird and Brennen's bed a luma globe shone dimly. "I can't do nothing, Ellet," said Firebird. "If I thought I could break out of Hesed's perimeter and pass the fielding at Three Zed, nothing could keep me here. You've seen Mistress Anna, and everyone else, with the twins. Even if I failed, Kiel and Kin would be raised as lords—or princes." Her chest no longer ached when she thought of them. Only numbness remained.

"Never doubt that."

Firebird raised her head. "Yes. I've been to the altar now. I know."

Ellet mumbled, "Congratulations."

Firebird sighed. "What can you tell me about the Three Zed situation? They attacked Thyrica. Does the Federacy intend to do anything?"

"Oh yes. They sent the Fleet to Soldane."

"That's not what I meant." *...and you know it, Captain Kinsman. Will they give Three Zed what it deserves? What they did to Netaia?*

Ellet compressed her lips. "There's been debate, but several representatives are stalling. They're afraid. They want to stand back and let us settle the problem."

"So now we're a liability to other Thyrians. If the Shuhr were to attack us again, they might find themselves in the middle." Firebird bowed her head. "Regional command... are they still angry with Brennen?"

"They never were," Ellet said dryly. "They simply enforced regs."

"What about the Special Ops agents who came with you?"

"They're headed out. Covert."

Surprised to get so much information, Firebird absently tapped the audio rod against her bedside table and stared around the room. "What kind of ship do you have?"

"Dardy and I brought a four-seat J46 transport with a RIA system."

Firebird's breath caught. She felt as if Ellet had handed her an armed missile. "You have RIA?"

Ellet barely smiled. "So you know about that too."

"Brennen showed me. Here."

"Claggett found a way to make RIA catch a carrier," Ellet explained, "to spare effort for finer work. There are five RIA ships now, still concealed from the Federacy. As we were coming to Hesed, we were allowed one."

If a RIA unit could *catch* an epsilon carrier, whatever that meant technically, she might not even have to hold a turn. "Why did..." No. Firebird shouldn't ask that. Ellet's business here was her own.

But Ellet answered, holding one hand near her mouth. "Damalcon has asked for my hand, and he wants Master Dabarrah to bless our bonding ceremony. I haven't consented, but I agreed to consider it. For the master's advice, and for news of... you and Brennen, the run to Hesed was worth applying for."

A detached part of Firebird's mind understood Ellet's machinations. "Might I look at your RIA ship?" She didn't turn to meet the tall Sentinel's eyes.

"I would have been surprised if you hadn't asked. You've undoubtedly been wanting to get back into flying."

Firebird spun to see Ellet's face, solemn and knowing.

So. Ellet meant to give her a chance to slip to Three Zed. Ellet also knew it would probably kill her—in a worthy cause, as before—this time, a chance Brennen might escape alone. A long shot, but Ellet would risk anything to free Brennen from the Shuhr... and from Firebird.

Firebird slid a finger up and down the audio rod's gleaming surface, and for one moment, she sympathized with her rival. Undoubtedly Ellet also suffered from visions of Brennen in Shuhr hands. Brenn imprisoned, abused.

Ellet's cheek barely twitched. "I wouldn't even be surprised to find Damalcon willing to check you out in it tomorrow. There'll be time before we meet with Master Dabarrah."

• • •

Ellet strode out across the stepping stones, deeply satisfied. Although untrainable and unstable, Firebird now was determined to go—and would unquestionably fail at Three Zed.

But she might get a RIA ship to Brennen before they killed her. Dardy had brought the J46 from Thyrica to Regional HQ at Tallis, never suspecting Ellet hoped to send Firebird after Phoena. Today's news, that Brennen had already left for Three Zed, had nearly crushed Ellet.

So she would send Firebird after Brennen instead of for Phoena. Obviously Firebird wanted that. *I would want it too,* Ellet admitted.

Tomorrow, Firebird would commandeer that transport. To keep a RIA craft from falling into Shuhr hands, she and Dardy would be justified in taking a fast Brumbee messenger ship and chasing her—before they had time to forge a pair bond! Dardy was a good man, attractive and certainly connatural, but he wasn't Brennen Caldwell.

They couldn't intercept her in slip space, but in a Brumbee they could beat her to Three Zed. The two trained Sentinels would then free Brennen. Assisting another Sentinel in danger was allowed by the Privacy and Priority Codes, regardless of risk or expense. Ellet and Brennen—and hopefully, Dardy—would return with both ships. That was how she would justify it to Dabarrah.

They'd save Firebird too, if they could.

But if Firebird and her ship were destroyed there... Brennen would need comforting.

• • •

Firebird did find Dardy willing to check her out in the new transport ship, though she had to wait for the next evening, and her cautious attempt to run up the RIA unit was less than encouraging.

But when she returned to her chamber, she found not Ellet but Jenner and Anna Dabarrah standing at the foot of her bed... with her babies. Master

Jenner cradled Kinnor over his shoulder. Anna held fair little Kiel in front of her like a shield.

"Firebird," Master Jenner murmured, his voice heavy with concern. "I can think of only one reason you would have gone out with Sentinel Dardy."

Firebird stepped closer. A force more powerful than gravity drew her to those blanketed bundles.

"This is your son," Anna said hoarsely. "The image of your husband and the promised of your God. How dare you consider leaving him? How dare you, Firebird?"

She ached to touch him, hold him. Would Anna let her?

Let her? She was his mother! "You've already taken him from me, Anna." Firebird's voice shook. "And you, Master Jenner."

"Do you consider yourself more of a match for the Shuhr than Brennen, who was called there?" asked Anna. "Do you wish these children orphaned? Never to know mother or father?"

Firebird crossed to the cascade. She parted the watery curtain with one finger, but she couldn't take her eyes off the child Anna held. Image of his father... yes! Gently squared chin, even beneath his baby-round cheeks—sapphire eyes—and not far from Kiel, Kinnor slept so peacefully, curled around Master Dabarrah's shoulder. "Never to know the horror their mother found inside herself?" she reminded them.

"It lies in everyone, Firebird." Mistress Anna caressed Kiel's plump cheek with her nose, then looked up, softening. "We simply can't see it. But Firebird, you're so frightened. That's why you anger so easily nowadays." Anna appeared to relax, though Firebird never felt certain of most Sentinels' real emotions. They controlled so Powers-blessed well. "Don't leave them. You cannot. You must not."

Firebird sank onto the bedside and looked up into Master Jenner's compassionate eyes. "Will you make me a prisoner again, then? That's what it would take to keep me here."

"No," Jenner said.

Startled, she looked from Jenner to Anna. Anna pursed her lips and clung to Kiel.

"Firebird," Jenner said, "if you mean to go, we have no right to contain you. I ask only that you let me know your decision. Let me send help with you."

"I... will," she said shakily. This gracious capitulation was the last thing she expected. "Thank you." Then she stretched toward Mistress Anna. "Give him to me. Please. Let me hold him."

"I cannot. Shamarr Dickin—"

"You can. I'm his mother. I've never broken your unnatural prohibition. I'd never harm him." After fourteen uneventful sessions with Master Jenner, she believed it was true. Terrell's death must've been coincidental. "Give him to me."

Frowning, Anna stepped to the bedside. She laid the wriggling child in Firebird's arms.

A familiar warmth pulled Firebird's shoulders forward and her head down, curling her body womblike around an infant she'd longed to hold again. He felt heavier than she remembered, with a faint, milky smell. "Kiel," she whispered. "Precious one." She clutched tightly.

Squirming, he gave a short cry. Firebird stiffened. She'd forgotten what to do. Her very instincts seemed to have died.

Anna arched her eyebrows. She reached down again. Kiel started to whimper.

"I am not hurting him." Firebird sat motionless for a moment longer, then raised her child back up to Anna.

Anna seized him, pressed him possessively to her shoulder, and rocked from side to side. Kiel quieted instantly.

Firebird felt as if she'd been stabbed. She stood and tiptoed around Master Jenner to look into Kinnor's elfin face. He scowled in his sleep.

She backed away, not wanting to wake him. "Thank you," she whispered dully.

As the Sentinels carried the twins out her door, she sank onto her knees on white flagstones. They wouldn't keep her here, after all! She could leave freely—

Then she shuddered. Leave her children? What was she thinking about, going to that place? Clenching her hands, she curled forward. *Holy One, help me. Show me. They've given me the choice. What shall I do?*

For several minutes, she prayed. Then she listened. She prayed again, focusing this time on His nature, His love, His will, and the song she had heard in her vision—the primal music of creation. *Show me,* she begged again.

An incredibly strong urge hit her. She must leave. She must leave *now.* Without delay. She felt no fear, only an unshakable conviction.

She sprang to her feet.

• • •

Master Dabarrah entered his office. Mistress Anna followed him, bowing her head.

"She still means to go," Anna murmured. Her tightly guarded tone and facial expression said nothing, but on the resonance of the pair bond Dabarrah felt shock and reproof. "Even knowing all she now knows. I thought her heart would change when she saw the children again. When she held Kiel in her very arms."

Closing the outer door and dimming his office lights, Dabarrah shook his head mournfully. "Anna, remember. Firebird was raised by servants, not her mother. Her own mother ordered her death. She never experienced the mother-child bond we take for granted."

Anna folded her hands against the skirt of her long blue gown. "Reconsider, Jenner. Send a sekiyr to watch her rooms. Guard her. Keep her here, under gentle restraint."

"No. I gave my word."

Dabarrah felt her disappointment. Immediately it turned to waiting steadiness. How he loved this godly woman!

"Yes, we could keep Firebird here," he said. "She is welcome."

"But she unsettles the Sanctuary with her misery," Anna admitted.

"That would only grow worse."

"Maybe she too is called there. Kiel and Kinnor have been given life. They are safe, and the line will continue. Imagine her pain, giving them birth and then having them wrenched away."

Sadness, sympathy, and pain flooded the bonding resonance. He laid an arm across Anna's shoulder. "I know two full Sentinels here who would willingly join Firebird in her mission. Tomorrow morning I'll speak to them, choose one, and send Firebird with our help and blessings." He sank with Anna onto the stone bench, careful not to sit on her long straight hair.

"You know her willfulness," Anna answered. "She'll bring him back or die."

He wrapped her in his presence, comforting her. "There is the matter of Sentinel Kinsman," he added.

Anna's eyes clouded. "How does that follow? Does she guess what Firebird means to do with her ship?"

"Ellet came to Hesed precisely for that purpose. To lure Firebird to her death and launch a rescue effort for Phoena... and then Brennen." Dabarrah visualized, for his bond mate, the sum of Ellet's actions that led him to this conclusion.

Anna tilted her head, indignant. "So thanks to Ellet, we must send at least one more Sentinel into the trap at Three Zed, to protect the RIA secret." He nodded. "I wouldn't have thought it of Ellet," Anna said. "She's the responsible one, Mistress Firebird the volatile one."

"Neither is so simple as that." He knew them both too well. "Firebird has shown me moments of surprising wisdom. Ellet's sense of responsibility vanishes where the Caldwell family is concerned."

"Is she still chasing Brennen?"

"She has made herself ill with jealousy."

"Why did she come here with Sentinel Dardy? Is she deceiving him as to their compatibility?"

"No, they're deeply co-natural. In denying him, Ellet is probably resisting her only chance for bonded happiness."

Anna slipped out from under his arm. "You must discipline her, then, as Sanctuary Master. 'Reproof is painful, but love requires it,'" she quoted. "Ellet is a wonderful woman with many talents."

"Yes, and she can be cured. Restored to useful service. Would you bring her—and Air Master Dardy—to the office, my love?"

Anna stood silently for a few seconds, fingering her skirt. Then she squared her shoulders. "Ah," she said. Smiling, she nodded. "Indeed." She turned toward the door.

• • •

Two minutes later, Anna Dabarrah stood outside that same doorway. Inside, Ellet Kinsman and Damalcon Dardy occupied all her husband's attention and half of hers. Ellet's voice rose, arguing vehemently.

Anna wanted to call a sekiyr to attend Kinnor and Kiel. Yet she'd just checked their alpha rhythms, and those infant heirs to the prophecies slept deeply. For half an hour, they wouldn't need her.

Only half an hour. That much time, I can give Ellet and Damalcon. She opened the office door and went in.

• • •

Firebird halted outside that office door and raised a hand to knock. She heard voices through the door and hesitated. The conversation sounded low and intense. *Don't interrupt.* It felt like the same Voice, and it roused not fear but a deep, holy awe. *Don't delay.* If she waited for Dabarrah's help, that might take hours.

One minute, she begged the Voice. *Just one.* She whirled toward the next door, which led to the Dabarrahs' private rooms. For the first time since the prohibition had been laid on her, she stole inside.

By the dim light of a round ceiling luma, she found two tiny warming cots. She bent and kissed each child, her heart aching under a load of guilt. *Little sons of destiny,* she crooned silently. *Forgive me for going.* If she didn't come back, they wouldn't even remember her. One tear splattered on a tiny cheek, but fortunately it was Kiel's. He wriggled but didn't cry out.

Oh Singer, she pleaded, *watch over them. Keep them safe, help them grow, let them know that I… loved them, I loved them as well as I could.*

Then she wrenched away from her sons' cribs, crept along the pool, and rapped quickly on Tel's door.

It took less than a minute to explain her intentions. "Meet me at the hangar in five minutes," she finished, "or I'll be gone."

"Fuel banks are charged? And there's room for four, to make our escape?" He jumped toward his bureau.

She nodded. "The question is whether I can learn to control that projection module well enough to matter before we reach Three Zed. It's only a twelve-day slip, and I have no RIA training. I can't even turn every time I try. I'll have to do it mostly on instinct."

"I have every confidence in your instincts, Firebird." Tel threw a handful of clothing onto his bed. "I can practice piloting in slip on the override sims, so I'll be able to help if you need it."

"We do have to leave quickly. I… prayed about it," she said self-consciously, "and that's the answer I heard. Master Jenner actually offered to help us."

"He did?" Tel stood up straight.

"Yes, but he's busy, and I don't dare wait for him to finish."

"That would make a difference?"

"Probably hours." Hours, she mourned, that she could've spent with Kinnor and Kiel. *Singer, I really could use Master Dabarrah's help—*

Go now.

Tel tossed a duffel onto his pile. "I'll be ready in two minutes," he said. "Go pack."

• • •

"I'll fly it out." Firebird slip-sealed the craft and harnessed in. A four-seater with bunks aft, this light transport smelled of damp soil and kirka trees. At the edge of her peripheral vision, Tel stowed and secured their satchels. She worked through the preflight check, sinking her maternal depression deep down. "We're going to alert someone no matter what we do, so we'll make this fast. It's a straight shot out the valley. I'll accelerate the second we hit the bay's main door. Ready?"

Tel swung into the other front seat and secured himself. "Ready." On his face she saw hard determination, and though she despised the object of his affections, in that moment she knew she'd learned to love Tel.

They blasted into a starry sky. Firebird punched in the fielding drop code she'd seen Dardy use and set a vertical course, and the speedy little ship responded as designed. By now, she guessed, Jenner and Anna had found the message she left, thanking them for their offer of help, explaining the urgency she felt, begging their forgiveness... and asking that if she didn't return, the twins would be raised together. Soon the transport passed out of Procyel II's gravitational interference. Firebird fed her computer the celestial coordinates she'd researched from the Sanctuary database. The onboard translation program turned those into a slip heading. Firebird took a confirming readout, shot off one more prayer—for the only help that really mattered—and then pressed the jump bar. The slip-shield activated, the translight drive pressed her spine against the seat's frame, and they were away.

"Just like that?" Tel asked.

Firebird smiled down the console, wishing she could give him a friendly kiss but not daring to offend his sensibilities. She sighed and stretched, then sat fingering Brennen's medallion on its chain. "Just like that. Now the work begins. Unless I can learn to ride this RIA unit in twelve days, we'll do just as well ringing the bell and asking the Shuhr to take us in."

26

ONE CROSSING

allegro sussurando
quickly, whispering

On his bed in an emerald-encrusted chamber, Juddis Adiyn lay staring at his obsidian ceiling. A bedside field generator projected threads of light—blues and purples, yellow and pale red—onto the glimmering blackness. Their hypnotic flickering helped him reach a trance state, in which he could call the elusive shebiyl to mind and glimpse the future.

…The young woman he knew from tri-D images to be Firebird Caldwell, sleeping in a spacecraft bunk near an effeminate young man sprawled on a flight seat…

Then she was on her way, or shortly would be! Sentinels were fools not to use the shebiyl. Perhaps they thought it caused pride. But he'd seen his own death too many times, in too many ways, to grow proud of this work. He used all his skills to serve his people. He was as committed to their purposes as any Sentinel was to the Federacy. Unfortunately, only one group could win the long war.

He closed his eyes again.

The path branched. He pressed his awareness down one stream of possible events—

…She lay at his feet. That striking auburn hair masked her face as she writhed out the last breaths of her life. Caldwell clutched the dendric striker in shaking hands. Anguish and shock hammered him to his knees…

Excellent! And from the clarity of this branch, highly probable. Polar would want to see this. Smug despite his self-warning, Adiyn pressed his point of consciousness across the gap between branches, toward another gleaming vision—

...An explosion filled his brain, fire and blinding light... and then darkness...

Another possible death! Hastily he probed backward up that stream, hoping to see what went wrong. He'd evaded deadly danger three times that way.

The branch vanished before he could manipulate it. He rolled on his bed, cursing the shebiyl that afforded such clear glimpses but would not always yield to skilled handling. What event had opened that branch? Where was the nexus point? How to prevent disaster?

He forcibly slowed his own pulse. Once, he'd foreseen his death as a high probability, at Dru Polar's hands. He had avoided the confrontation and still managed to get his own way. Now he sent epsilon signals throughout his body, gradually calming its shaking and perspiring. Then, though the shebiyl faded, he pressed his point of focus across emptiness toward another strong branch.

...There too, she lay at his feet, writhing...

She was an attractive woman, in agony. Very much like her sister. And just as they could keep using Phoena Angelo's ruined body for genetic research, they would take Firebird Caldwell's... though in Lady Firebird's case, they would allow full, irreversible brain death. Phoena's stasis crypt would preserve the princess for decades, irreparably crippled but medically alive, available for sampling or further experiments. Adiyn's tech also had gene preps well under way for both dead child-princesses. Adiyn owned the Casvah chromosomal line now. It was one more step in his people's self-evolution.

Smiling, he waved off the ceiling lights. The shebiyl faded as he drifted toward sleep.

• • •

Brennen lay restrained on the contoured couch. Today it felt ominously comfortable. In his cell last night, Polar had mounted a device that screeched every few minutes and kept him awake. He couldn't guess what Polar meant to try. He blinked his aching eyes as the long-haired Shuhr steered a cart toward the head of his couch. On it rode a device that was roughly cubical and vented, with a conical protrusion.

"Yesterday evening," Polar said, "I remembered that natural amnesia can result from an alpha-matrix discontinuity. One of our researchers worked on that topic several years ago. He developed this to restore alpha function."

A hard point pressed against the top of Brennen's skull. Caught in the restraining field, he couldn't move away.

"First, we'll read your alpha frequencies. Scan the matrix to produce a map."

The device hummed. Polar stood over him, looking first at his face, then past him, then at his face again. After several minutes, he reached toward the device. "Yes," he said softly. "There's the gap. It looks as if something cut a scoop right through your associational grid. Want to see?"

"Why not?" Brennen muttered. Maybe Polar would release the restraining field for a few seconds. If Polar watched the grid instead of his victim's thoughts, Brennen might catch him off guard...

A red image appeared on the ceiling, shaped like half a melon and crisscrossed inside and out with yellow lines. One area flickered even as he watched, while another faded. Brennen recognized the standard first-year college visualization of the complex alpha matrix.

"See it?" Polar asked.

Deep inside the hemisphere, an asymmetrical slash disrupted a major area, separating it from every line in the main grid. It did look like a dark scoop. No lines crossed that terrible disruption. Inside it, the alpha grid had turned a grayed, inactive shade.

That was his conscious mind, the resource that made him a Sentinel—made him human. He'd done the damage himself. But as long as that area held his most sensitive memories, keeping them isolated from the surface of his mind, no interrogator could access them.

"All I need," Polar said, "is to restore one link, one crossing. Amused, Caldwell? Today, I hope to cure you."

"You can't." Only an access healer like Dabarrah could restore amnesia blocks.

"I think that this time, I'll prove you wrong." Polar shut off the projection, fiddled with the device, and then stepped away. "Feel anything? Warm spot?"

"No."

Polar shrugged. "According to my records, this device worked best during natural sleep. So relax," he murmured. "Pleasant dreams, Caldwell. Pleasant, healing dreams."

He strode out, pausing only to wave off the room light, leaving one guard on watch.

Brennen struggled briefly and uselessly against the restraint field, then blinked up into drowsy darkness. It would be easy to sleep. If he just shut his eyes and surrendered, he'd sleep deeply.

Hoping only to stay awake, he prayed.

Father and Speaker of the Eternal Word... Creator... Sustainer... you fill the universe with glory, and all time bows to you. Thank you for calling me your servant. Holy One, I have nothing left to give you but my life. If there is no other escape from this place, lift me into your presence. Keep me from betraying my people and the family you promised to honor.

"Mari," he whispered. *Mighty One, mercy! She thinks she found complete love in me, and I let her think it. Forgive me! Don't hold my arrogance against her. If you have to remove me to bring her close to yourself, I am your willing servant. Let her die to pride, as I should have done. I depended too much on my abilities and too little on you.*

Had he rushed into this trap? No... he'd come as the Speaker called, motivated by mercy and faith, but believing that the call confirmed the Holy One's faith in him. *She knew, Lord. She saw my pride because she is proud herself. Spare her. Show us both, willful as we are, how to obey you.*

Shamarr Dickin had told him long ago that any place the Speaker called a believer was a place for an altar. Now, the truth of that statement shattered the last of his pride.

And finally, he heard the Voice. *I have asked all that you are. Are you ready to give it?*

"Yes," he whispered. "Take me. Only spare Mari. Please, Holy One." Her image rushed into his mind, as when he first saw her... her delicate chin and soft red cheeks, that sweat-soaked auburn hair clinging to her forehead... dying by poison, by her own hand, as ordered...

...the image shifted to a dusty sky, and his mission to defend Veroh. He had to be dreaming. Mari flew as his wingman, and their wing tips almost touched. Her voice sang over his headset interlink, a song he didn't remember.

• • •

Wing to wing,
O my love,
Touch me, take me—

• • •

A hot light blasted him awake. Dru Polar settled into his usual seat near the couch's right shoulder. The silvery rod protruded from his sash belt. *Dendric striker,* Brennen realized. No world calling itself civilized participated in that weapon's manufacture. It scanned a victim's reflex-arc frequencies, then launched a cascade of motor-nerve firings. Poor Phoena!

"Welcome back," Polar purred. "One thread. One crossing. I told you that was all it would take."

He recognized the weapon! What was this treatment device? Special Ops needed to know it existed... but he wouldn't be the one to bring back that information. He must cue another amnesia block. He drew a deep, shaking breath. The alpha matrix wouldn't tear as cleanly as before. He would cause worse damage—deeper, and more likely to prove permanent. Polar would restore one more thread, and Brennen would be forced to create another block. After only a few cycles, he would be truly helpless.

But useless to Polar as an intelligence source. And, maybe, as an experimental subject.

I will ask all that you are. Now he understood. This too was an altar.

At least he'd awakened refreshed enough to remember the Voice.

Polar couldn't make him sleep again, not naturally, for several hours. He might not break today. After tomorrow, though, there might be little left of his mind. *If this is your tempering for eternity, Holy One, strengthen me to face it. If not, guide my fight!*

"Don't do it, Caldwell," Polar said. An image flashed onto the ceiling: the tall, angular MaxSec Tower, the Federacy's stronghold on Tallis IV, headquarters of Regional command. "You're finished, and you know it. We'll start here."

"No," Brennen whispered. "You won't." He winced as he cued the second block.

• • •

A red stone valley carpeted with brown grass and graceful animals cantering on low hills: These, and a cold sky veiled by wisps of cloud, framed Carradee's first glimpse of the Hesed Valley.

A lanky Master Sentinel introduced himself as Jenner Dabarrah. He escorted her underground and showed her the vast pool rippling under its skylights, then they saw Daithi revived from travel sedation in a warm, impressively modern special-care cubicle. This underground hall felt oddly familiar, as if she'd dreamed it.

Dabarrah took her into his office and offered a simple wooden chair, then apologized that he must deliver unsettling news.

Carradee crossed her ankles under the chair and gripped her hands in her lap. "Very well," she said. "Tell us, Master Dabarrah."

His voice conveyed real pain. "To our best knowledge, the shuttle carrying your daughters has not arrived in the Inisi system. We should have had word five days ago. A search has been mounted, madam."

The edges of Carradee's vision darkened. Her throat tightened. "Master Dabarrah, do you think they are alive?"

"We have no way of knowing," he said gently. "Accidents in slip-state are rare but not unknown."

"Abduction?" she asked, pressing a hand to her chest. "Murder?"

"Majesty, our people are checking all sensor records of arrivals and departures in Inisi space. It could be some time until we receive word." He extended a hand. "I can at least ease your worry. In our terms, let me place a site block in the alpha matrix that carries your thoughts and emotions. You will accomplish nothing by suffering. May I help you this way, while others help by searching?"

When she shut her eyes, she saw a small, trusting face rimmed with curls bent over her bedside to kiss her good-bye. Exhausted from travel and from worrying about Daithi, Carradee gulped tears down the back of her throat. Truly, her misery wouldn't solve the mystery, heal Daithi, nor bring back Firebird, General Caldwell, or Prince Tel.

You are weak! she berated herself, but she nodded. "Yes, Master Dabarrah. Please help me."

Dabarrah rose from his chair, stood over her, and laid both hands on her head.

An hour later, after stopping briefly in a room that adjoined the medical suite and had been assigned to her, she joined Master Dabarrah and his wife at a circular table near the waterside. Young men and women ladled out bowls full of fragrant stew as a young couple sat down next to Master and Mistress Dabarrah. The master introduced them as Sentinel Dardy and his bride, Ellet. Ellet's dazed, joyous stare never left the Sentinel's boyish face, and they waited on each other with tender deference.

"Bonding shock." Dabarrah leaned toward Carradee, his smile full of compassion. "It lasts only a few days. It's good for the Sanctuary to have them here. All of us feel their love and wonder, and they don't mind our company. They scarcely notice us."

Carradee stared a little longer at the oval-faced woman. She certainly seemed happy. Was this what had happened to Firebird?

Dabarrah had dulled her grief from a frantic, serrated knife edge to this calm sadness. These truly were good, kindly people. Governor Danton hadn't deliberately sent Iarlet and Kessie into oblivion, either. If they were alive anywhere in Federate space, Federate searchers would find them. If not—

O Mighty Powers, receive them into bliss. And comfort me. But the Powers never comforted. She had defied them, refusing to suicide—sending her daughters offworld—coming here.

"After dinner," Anna Dabarrah said, "please join us at a vespers service. We will offer thanks for your safe arrival and prayers for your daughters."

Had the woman read her mind? "Thank you. You surely know that I've worshiped other gods all my life. I betrayed them by coming here."

"You are welcome to join us at service," said Master Dabarrah. "At Hesed, we speak a language of grace."

Carradee spooned the last drops of brown broth from her bowl. *A language of grace.* That sounded so comforting. "I... want to know more, Master... Mistress. But first, please, may I meet my nephews?"

• • •

Firebird's onboard computer brought her out of slip-state near Three Zed. As she anticipated, it seemed all too soon. Tel had helped her experiment with the RIA apparatus. A Sentinel probably wouldn't have let him try, fearing a loss of secrecy, but she couldn't have done this alone.

It took hours to navigate through the unexpected asteroid debris, using only touches on steering thrusters, but finally she approached the planet. Then, grasping Tel's hand in unspeaking understanding, she gave him control of the ship.

She slid on the splayed-finger RIA headset. Edging inward to turn, she felt strangely composed. The flaming terror no longer frightened or called to her. It was only a pseudo-mythical memory... she hoped. She passed through its familiar horror storm, secured her carrier, and then reached back out for the RIA harmonic. The new technology snatched and held her crippled epsilon carrier.

Instantaneously, her senses extended outward, passing through the ship's bulkheads into space. Using the RIA unit, she found she could focus them in any direction. She exhaled in relief and listened toward Three Zed while watching for motion in high orbit. "There," she murmured to Tel. "I've found their fielding net. But don't go in yet."

To her altered perception, the fielding satellites felt like dozens of disembodied intelligences glaring into space, poised to destroy an approaching mind. How to blind one of those satellite eyes? She could rely only on instinct, on her barely adequate control of the RIA unit, and a remark made long ago by her traitorous old instructor at the Planetary Naval Academy. Vultor Korda had heaped scorn on a Sentinel who could only "push a few electrons along." If phase control was a simple skill, then maybe in concert with the powerful RIA unit she could kill a satellite.

She'd also experienced, kneeling in front of Master Dabarrah, how it should feel to listen with her epsilon sense. She extended her probe a little farther and touched one solar-sailed cylinder. Passing inside its metal walls, her amplified senses heard a cacophony of electrical activity, hissing and buzzing in staccato rhythms.

Like the visualization that let her turn, this sparked an idea. Maybe, if she had learned to hear this way, she could also sing.

Imagining a note at utter tritonal disharmony from the satellite's fundamental pitch, she willed that note to sound, using the satellite's circuitry as her instrument. It vibrated at the frequency she commanded. The satellite howled around her, every surface a sounding board. A series of harmonics built, tone on shattering tone, that made her cringe and almost flee. Then it fell absolutely silent.

She wrenched her awareness back across kilometers of vacuum into the pilot's seat, and the universe seemed to shrink. "I got one, Tel," she gasped. At last she appreciated how exhausting the outlay of mental energy could be. "There." With the computer's light wand she set a spark onto the fore screen and covered one smoothly moving point of light.

"It's too far ahead of us now." He pulled one hand off the controls. "We've fallen back in orbit."

"Chase it! I don't want to do that again!"

The transport shuddered as he accelerated, pursuing the corridor of marginal safety. Firebird snugged her harness, leaned back with her eyes closed, and forced herself again into accord with RIA. Pressing the RIA sense forward, she scouted for the weird music of those satellite eyes. She waited seemingly forever for the ship to drop, all the while trying to hold blinders over the darkness that rose with her carrier. To distract herself, she hummed the melody she'd written for Iarla, her niece's namesake. That tune made her feel brave.

"We're through their orbital altitude," Tel whispered loudly. "Where do we set down?"

She too wanted to whisper as she eyed the sensor screens. "Squill," she exclaimed softly, "I don't know." Extending the RIA probe one more time, she scrutinized the black sphere for "sounds" of life. "Take us as low as you can," she mumbled, and she swept her point of awareness along the planet's distant surface. "We don't know if those fielding satellites see downward as well as up." Had Jenner's? She hadn't paid attention. She'd lost all her old training habits. "This could take a while."

Finally, she spotted the largest colony by its cackle of enharmonic voices. "That peak. There. Don't get too close."

He cut speed and dropped lower yet, into the shadow of a volcanic crag. "Here, Firebird?"

"Good."

He set down with a jolt that Firebird ignored. Gladly she pulled off the headset and shook out her hair, shaking free, too, of a sickening dread at the pit of her stomach. For a while she would be glad to avoid contact with that tainted epsilon carrier.

Tel unharnessed first. "Hurry, Firebird. Powers go with you."

"Do you still—"

"Go. I'll guard the ship."

"You're sure?"

"I'd only trip you up." He looked away, and she knew how badly he wanted to storm the citadel. "Can we keep in touch?"

"If I transmitted back to you by interlink, they'd find us both. I don't dare."

"Well, then... go."

She unclasped her flight harness and stood. Working quickly but deliberately, she checked the gear she'd scavenged from the ship's emergency supplies: food concentrates and painkiller jellies, a little electronic tap circuit, two doorbreaker charges that would send their pulse to a panel's edge and detonate there, and two recharges for the Federate-issue blazer she'd brought from sanctuary.

No shock pistol this time.

She unclasped her web belt and slid the pouch around to ride on her left hip, then made sure the dagger Brennen had given her was bedded securely in its forearm sheath. *Doesn't look like much,* she observed. She hoped, though, to depend not on gear but the bond link to find Brennen, and then on his abilities to escape.

Just before she debarked, she embraced Tel awkwardly through her gawky pressure suit. "Give me one day," she warned as she opened its helmet clasps. "I probably won't survive even that long if I don't find Brennen, but give me a standard day. If I'm not back, or if you see any sign they've found you, get offworld fast. I can find another ship." *I hope.*

"Firebird." He sniggered, a most ungentlemanly sound. "Do you think I could do that?"

"Tel," she growled, knowing they couldn't threaten each other anymore.

He shrugged.

Raising one eyebrow, she smiled. "You're right. I can't order you away. Be careful, then, if you come in. Chances are, Brenn and I will be dead together."

He bent and kissed her cheek. Firebird stood a moment bowing her head, searching for words to apologize for the hatred she had once nurtured for him and his kind. She couldn't. She could only turn back and salute him ten minutes later when she neared the edge of the craft's visual range.

Struggling against the too-large vacuum suit, she crossed a boulder field under a starry firmament in sense-deafening silence. She needed to enter without being seen or setting off an alarm.

But why would their airlocks be alarmed? As far as they knew, no one could pass their fielding net. RIA changed everything. She bypassed two sizable airlocks, circling the obviously inhabited area, flitting between boulders that provided good cover, and finally found a minor entry that appeared unguarded.

She stole nearer, keeping to shadows, until she felt sure she'd spotted the external monitor. She steadied her blazer on a rough boulder and fired once. The monitor didn't spark, sputter, or give off any other sign of damage. *Go?* she asked the Voice she was learning to trust.

When she heard no other leading, she walked straight to the small side airlock, stepped inside, and brought its air pressure up. No audible alarm went off. Once inside the entry bay, she stripped off her suit.

The bay looked volcanic, and it vibrated with the sound of air-cycling machinery. Firebird tiptoed across. Then she peered down a long inbound corridor, twitching at the safety stud on her blazer. At her first sight of the golden passway, she blinked, awestruck. Then she ignored it. Gold had no value to her now.

It wasn't difficult to sense the colony's layout. Like the tunnels under Hunter Height on Netaia, curving passages ran parallel to the outside, straight ones led in or changed level. She halted at the first junction. Now where? And how to stay hidden?

A powerful hunch, vaguely like the bonding resonance, told her Brennen would be nearer if she took the left straightaway.

But was it a trap? A psychic defense invented by the Shuhr, luring a careless intruder to her death?

Again, why would they bother? They thought their fielding defense was impenetrable.

Resolutely, she turned left and followed the hunch inward, straining to hear footsteps. The corridors remained uncannily quiet. At every junction and lift shaft the sensation repeated, until after several minutes she stood before a blackened, forbidding metal door sealed to solid stone. Its lock panel was arrayed with colored tabs and an alphanumerical coder. It looked fit to contain a powerful, valuable prisoner.

She hesitated, fighting the panicky sense of being one minute too late. Every beat of her heart sounded like approaching boot steps.

Flattening a hand on the door, she tried to relax. After her panic faded, she kicked the door three times with a metal-tipped boot, then waited—then did it again. After another second she felt a faint, thrilling surge of awareness as if she'd awakened—

Brennen?

Was this him? Something felt wrong, something fundamental and deep. She felt... otherness. It could be a pretender, keeping her here with some mockery of Brennen's presence.

His first instant's welcome turned to utter confusion. Firebird gasped as if he'd sliced her. Tempted to turn and run, she begged, *Singer, where*—

Before she finished framing the prayer, an answer rang in her mind: *Stay.*

She forced herself to relax into the pair bond, loosening her right hand to let it rise in Brennen's epsilon control. Surely he'd observed the unlocking sequence on that panel... if this was Brennen.

Nothing happened. Fear seeped into her soul. Only deadly determination kept her moving. From the gear pocket at her belt she pulled one of the little explosives and pressed it to the door. It seized hold with a soft *chunk* she hoped Brennen recognized. Then she set the delay for four seconds.

She stepped up the corridor as far as she dared to go, drew her blazer, and trained it on the door. If this were a Shuhr impostor, she must kill without hesitating.

A wild crackling noise made her flinch. The panel fell outward, clanging like a gong, and she steadied her blazer arm again.

A man leaped through the frame, over the fallen door. He looked right—and she felt whole again! Though the otherness baffled her, she let his presence flow over and through her, penetrating and completing her—

Something inside the cell screeched. Brennen seized her hand and pulled her up the corridor, heels pounding. At the first corner he palmed a panel and pushed her into a tiny service room. He pressed in after her, palmed the uncoded closing panel... and then shrank away.

"Brenn," she gasped. Hastily she holstered the blazer. "What's wrong?"

In dim orange half-light, he shook his head, arching his dark eyebrows. "Forgive me," he murmured. "Forgive me. I feel who you are, and what you are to me.

"But I don't remember you."

27

FUSION FIRE

stretto
climactic section in faster tempo

Firebird gasped. She wanted to kiss and caress Brennen, despite the desperate need to escape and the certainty that others had heard that door fall. But finally she recognized the new sensation as a deep irrational terror. Like her phobia of needles and injectors, it was far stronger than his affective control. "What have they done to you?" she demanded.

"They didn't. It's a..." He firmed his lips. "An amnesia block. I've had to induce it twice, at least." He eyed the bird-of-prey medallion hanging over her shirtfront, furrowing his forehead as if he knew it but couldn't guess why she wore it.

"Is phobia a side effect?" she asked.

"I don't know. I don't r-remember."

Heart-wrung, she circled his waist with both of her arms and laid her head against his chest. He returned the embrace hesitantly. His hands trembled against her shoulders. *Hurry,* a voice urged in her mind. *Hurry!*

Was that wisdom or impatience? She needed Brenn's help. She had to bring his memory back. Otherwise, how could they escape? She looked up. His face looked thin—he'd lost weight. A dark scar marked his left cheek where some injury had gone untreated. They'd stolen his master's star, and he wore ill-fitting blue shipboards. But under the tiny orange luma, amid deep lines of pain, fear, and exhaustion, she saw gleaming blue eyes that were still windows to the soul she loved.

He was in there somewhere. Their bonding resonance still pulsed faintly at the depth of her mind. "Do you remember that you're a... Sentinel?"

He nodded grimly. "Master. I haven't lost everything. But they've been drugging me. I can't touch my carrier."

That alone would explain his anxiety. "You know I'm your bond mate."

He nodded. "My name's Firebird. You call me Mari."

"Why?"

"It's... an endearment." *Reason enough.*

"Mari," he repeated. "You're one of us, aren't you?"

Mighty Singer, has he forgotten me completely? "Not... no," she admitted. There was no time for posturing. What could she say that might bring back his memory, his Special Ops skills? "I've just started turn training."

"How in the Whorl did you get here?"

"In a RIA ship. With Tel. Prince Tel. Do you remember RIA?"

His eyebrows arched, and she felt a fresh spasm of fear. "Forgive me, Mari. No."

"New technology. Projects an epsilon carrier. Like fielding."

"F-fielding," he muttered. "I remember that. Vaguely."

"That's something." She wished she could sense his emotions more plainly... or did she? He'd tried to help her fight her own phobia. If only she'd persisted! "Tel, Phoena's husband, is guarding the RIA ship. Let me tell you where it is, in case you get out but I don't."

"I doubt that'll happen," he said bitterly. Still, he listened closely as she described the way back.

Then he drew a ragged breath, and her worst doubt fled. With that breath came intense, uncompromising gratitude. Even now, without the full bonding resonance and half of his memory, she could read that. And he'd helped her through terrorized moments. Surely she could distract him, reassure him.

"You can turn?" he asked. A light seemed to come back on in his eyes, despite the service room's dimness.

She was on the right track! –she hoped. "Sometimes. It's intermittent."

At least now he seemed focused. "I've been blocked," he explained, "but if you could turn and open completely to me, your carrier and the bonding resonance might take me across the chemical blocking to my own. I might be able to function for as long as I could hold a turn."

That might bring back his memory too. "Good." Firebird tried to feel confident. "Here." She took several deep breaths and shut her eyes.

Did she really believe she wouldn't hurt him, even kill him, as they thought she'd killed Harcourt Terrell?

She hadn't harmed Master Jenner. Both their lives—and Phoena's and Tel's—depended on this one turn. She was relaxing against his shoulder, envisioning the wall, when approaching footsteps brought her alert.

"Easy," Brennen whispered. He slipped her blazer from its holster and trained it on the door's edge.

That was the Brennen she knew... except that his hand shook. The footfalls passed.

"Try again. It's worth the delay." He closed his arms around her, one hand at her waist and the other arm crossing her shoulders. The quivering blazer tickled her spine.

A minute later, tears streaked her cheeks. "You're trying too hard," he whispered, and she felt his fear rise again. "It should be like falling asleep."

"I know. I just can't do it that easily." If only she could! "Where's Phoena? We've got to find her. Do you remember—"

"Dead," he murmured. "The Shuhr executed her the day I arrived. I've forgotten her, but they love to remind me why I came, and that I failed."

She felt kicked in the chest. "Poor Tel!" Faintly, like an echo of the resonance they'd known, she felt his anger. It didn't seem possible for Phoena to be dead. She'd always been there. "Well," she said, "we need a way out, and a distraction—some way to keep them from hunting us down."

He shuddered. She had to steel herself against his fears again. This was like facing a battery of immunizations! "I do have a f-feel for this part of the city," he told her. "As for distraction, my instinct is to sabotage their nearest power source. It's night shift here. The best time to try." His face darkened. "I wish we had another blazer."

"Keep mine." He would feel less helpless that way. His marksmanship had been just better than hers. "Generator, then. That'll kill their fielding and energy guns too, so we can take off." Airlocks also used power, but she'd never seen an airlock without emergency reserves.

She shook off her fears. Brennen needed her... and more. *Help us, Singer,* she pleaded. *We can't do this alone. Give us back what he was. What he still should be.*

With two fingers he pried open the sliding door. He peered through and then motioned her into the passway ahead of him. "There's a drop shaft," he whispered. "End of this hall, turn right. It'll be on the left. I'll cover behind."

She stretched back to plant a kiss on his stubbled neck, then sprinted down the gleaming corridor. Her heart started pounding again. As her blood flowed harder, she began to believe they would escape.

Careening around a tiled corner, she practically flew into the arms of a tall stranger in black. She recoiled, flailing for balance. This was a Shuhr, a renegade! His hand angled upward into command stance. He hissed one unintelligible word. Her body froze wide-armed.

He smiled with his mouth, but his dark eyes narrowed. "Mistress!" he greeted her with an odd, throaty accent. "Mistress Caldwell! Oh, don't be afraid, not of me." He took a step forward. "I won't harm you. Shirak's orders are 'alive and unhurt.' Have you found him?"

Brennen rounded the corner. The Shuhr's glance darted away, his hand changed angle, and just as at Trinn Hill and at college, Firebird felt her assailant's command shift away from her. Her arms and legs came back under control.

Brennen sprawled on a slick tile floor, though. Galvanized, she pulled her black dagger from its hidden sheath and lunged.

The stranger seized her arm. She twisted away. She wished she could kill again, deliberately this time, the way she had killed Harcourt Terrell. If she'd killed him!

Come in short! she admonished herself, remembering that bruise Brennen had given her in training. The Shuhr struck her elbow aside. Insistently, he kept his free hand at a peculiar angle, holding Brennen under command.

Firebird tightened her hold on her dagger. He grabbed for her. She wriggled out of a half headlock, but he dove forward to pin her. Brennen had beaten her that way several times, in training—but Brennen had never fallen with all his weight, and she'd never done this with a real blade. She spun, clenched her dagger two-fisted over her ribs, and let him come down on her.

He seemed not to see it, intent on driving her to the ground hard enough to stun her. She felt the dagger slide home. His shriek tore at her ears. Her spine hit the floor, and they rolled sideways together. Skull ringing, she pushed away two-handed and then pressed to her feet. Her ribs hurt, her head still rang... and her dagger protruded between the Shuhr's clutching hands. She shuddered violently.

Released from command as his captor lost consciousness, Brennen hurried up and drew out her dagger. From point to hilt the black blade shone wetly red. Firebird retched, surprised—after all she'd been through—to find herself sickened by a bloody knife. She had a sudden flash of memory: her hands, plunged wrist-deep into an innocent creature's lifeblood... but this man was no innocent. In the next instant, she realized that her nausea came secondhand, from Brennen. He stared at the blade, eyes fixed, exactly the way she'd stared at Master Spieth's injectors.

Enclosed spaces. Blades. What else terrified him?

She wrested the dagger out of his grip, then wiped it on the stranger's stained tunic.

Recovering in an instant, Brennen murmured, "Well done, Mari. You're quick with a d-dagger."

She fumbled it back into its sheath, turning away to hide it from him. "I had a good teacher," she answered, trying to sound confident. "You."

Brennen's eyebrows arched, and she felt a low rumble of worry as he tried searching his memory.

"Forget it," she said. "Go."

He gave back her blazer. "I can't use this." Then he broke into a run again, leading up the passway toward that drop shaft.

Firebird came close behind, running hard to smother her shock and fear. Shouldn't she feel guilty too? But she didn't—only worried that Brennen might not remember the way.

She jumped down the shaft after him. Knees bent, she landed. Then, sprinting like racers, they pounded along a lower-level passage.

Brennen vanished around a blasted-out corner. Firebird felt his sudden surge of terror, and… was this hatred? She skidded to a halt barely around the bend.

In the wide access to an obsidian chamber, two men and a woman stood as if they expected her, each holding one hand at the angle to voice-command. She knew she was caught, even before she felt the invisible cords draw tight on her body.

They looked ordinarily human, and yet—yet—their eyes betrayed them. Quick-moving and suspicious, those eyes trusted no one. She didn't dare try her epsilon turn, didn't dare even to hope she might use it against them. These were no Sentinels to respect her mind's privacy. They watched her like hunting kiel.

First one stepped closer, then another. Then the third. They all wore battle gray, except for the younger man's wide sulfur yellow sash belt. That one grinned at Brennen, triumph lighting his lashless eyes. Brennen stared back. Loathing contorted his features.

"Good evening, Caldwell. Couldn't sleep?" The older man's voice echoed with a weird twang off shining black walls and a mass of humming machinery. He took another step on long legs.

The woman paced closer to Firebird, separating her from Brennen.

Firebird stood panting and didn't try to flee, staring instead at the woman's bizarre striped hair.

"Mistress Caldwell." The elder's voice flowed like honey. He was a handsome man, silver haired at his temples, with a broad mouth and a strongly cleft chin. "We heard you'd arrived. We've been expecting you."

The younger man stood with his head high, as arrogant as any Netaian nobleman. He chuckled. "My lady, you're surprised? Certainly you didn't think you arrived unnoticed. Your strike at our satellite was charmingly original, but I would have thought the woman of Brennen Caldwell's choosing would remember to deal with our mass detectors."

Mass detectors? *Oh, squill...*

He folded his arms. "I had to call a special training session to keep the security division from interfering with the drama we're about to play. We'll recall it for them." He glanced at the older man, back to Brennen, then smiled wickedly and said, "Poor Micahel. He can't get in from Cahal for at least an hour—"

"We're not waiting," the other man interrupted.

Firebird's hand tightened convulsively on the grip of her blazer, but her arm hung useless down at her side. Her finger rested far from the firing stud.

"Oh. Forgive our lack of manners." The handsome older man stepped back. "I'm Eldest Eshdeth Shirak, director of this outpost. My colleagues, Testing Director Dru Polar and Cassia Talumah. Polar, in particular, has looked forward to meeting you. He and your sister were close."

"Very close." Polar touched a hand to his forehead and bowed. "To the depths of her subconscious mind, to the very moment... when she died. So you see, I know you well, as she knew you."

Firebird shuddered. What little pity she'd felt for Phoena died right along with her uneasiness over knifing that Shuhr. Phoena had come willingly to Three Zed. She'd started this deadly bait-and-switch.

Cassia Talumah stepped closer, her fluid movements accentuated by military-cut shipboards and framed by ripples in her snake-striped hair. She raised a finger and laid it at the bridge of Firebird's nose. "Mistress of the faithful master," she mocked, turning the fingernail and then drawing it down, scratching deeply. "What do you think of him now?"

Still caught in command, Firebird couldn't pull away. Her eyes teared with pain. She glanced at Brennen. He took long, slow breaths, his expression closed, his eyes hostile.

Polar strode to him, drawing from his yellow sash a rod as long as her forearm. "Take it!" he barked. Brennen's hand jerked out. Firebird trembled at the sight of her Master Sentinel voice-commanded. "You remember this, don't you? Throat pressure point..."

Brennen seized the haft an inch from the weapon's orange thumb stud. Polar's hand slipped along its surface, touching and sliding controls. A long needle thrust from the other end.

Firebird's throat closed. She gasped.

"Ooh," breathed Cassia. "She's phobic, too!"

"So I see." The corners of Polar's mouth twitched.

Eldest Shirak hitched his thumbs into the side pockets of his elegantly tailored shipboards. He glowered at Brennen. "Wait. You're surprised. How could you not know Lady Firebird was already phobic?"

"Ha! It's his amnesia block again." Polar batted Brennen's ear. "You don't remember her, Caldwell. Do you?" he taunted. "You pitiful slink. You've spoiled this for us."

"Not entirely," Shirak said. "He'd have to know what she is. That can't be disguised." He turned back to Firebird. "And we have no real use for you alive, milady. So let me explain precisely what Master Caldwell will do with that dendric striker… for your education."

The scar along Brennen's cheek darkened as his fair skin grew pale. The silvery rod shook with his hand. She stared at it as Shirak spoke. "It causes all the central motor neurons to fire. Every muscle contracts, every synapse sparks as if it were insane. It will tear your muscles from the bones, and eventually stop your breathing… but it leaves sensory nerves intact to the very end. Enjoy this honor, Lady Firebird. When your breathing stops, we'll take our guest back to his quarters."

"He won't last long." Polar's smile broadened. "We'll crack the amnesia block now—enough of it to pick out some threads of what he used to be. He's done too much damage, though. You never would've gotten him back. Not the way you knew him. You understand that now, don't you?"

Horrified, Firebird finally tried to break command. She couldn't.

"So I suggest we enjoy the pleasure at hand." Smiling, Dru Polar tapped Brennen's shoulder with the weapon. "Even with amnesia, when you die he'll experience—good, you've heard of bereavement shock. I think that will work in our favor. I'll help him to sense the pain of your dying too, since he's less than fully able."

Now Firebird understood why Brennen hated Polar. She gritted her teeth, trying to project to Brennen—through her fear and defiance—trust, and complete forgiveness, and the hope he'd escape. The Singer would want it that way.

"Acch," Cassia hissed. "That's vulgar! You can do better than that. Don't you believe Polar? Give this murdering master the end of your blazer!"

Firebird's right hand jerked up, still holding the weapon. Automatically, her forefinger slid off the safety circuit and took up the slack on its firing stud. Three meters down her sights were the glacial-ice blue of Brennen's eyes.

She fought to swing it. If only she could sight on Dru Polar instead! *Singer,* she pleaded, *distract them! Please—just for a moment—let me try to turn.*

"Maybe I'll let you do it," Cassia blurted. "Save your true lover from watching you die, and from Polar's experiments. He'd rather die now. We could bargain. Maybe you'd like to hear what happened to your nieces."

Iarlet and Kessie? But Governor Danton sent them to safety! Firebird gasped. "No, I would not."

"Cassia," Polar growled, "he's not yours to kill."

Cassia paid no attention. "But my brother Ard brought in the tissue samples. He said they were such pretty little girls."

"No!" Firebird cried. She would trust nothing the Shuhr woman told her.

Cassia shrugged and stepped away. "Fine." Tossing her head, she made her hair ripple again. "You're as ungrateful as the rest of them."

"Caldwell," said Polar. "Go to her."

Firebird felt Brennen resist, but he approached step by reluctant step, holding the rod low with a quivery arm, while her blazer—Cassia's toy— followed his eyes. When he'd crossed the distance, it touched the bridge of his nose. Still Cassia left Firebird's forefinger free to move. *Please,* she begged. *Help us!*

"Cassia!" Polar called again. "No! I have research to finish." The two young-looking Shuhr glowered at each other.

It was the distraction she'd prayed for.

"Can you turn?" she read on Brennen's lips.

Drawing a deep, shaking breath, Firebird tried to blank out her surroundings: the humming generator, the Shuhr hungering for her agony, and the promise of death in Brenn's trembling hand. She tried to picture the granite wall, hoping the bickering Shuhr wouldn't sense her effort.

Brennen's nearness distracted her. She could ignore everything except the presence she'd missed so desperately. Everything but Brennen, though he stood there disabled. She would've loved him if he'd always been as powerless as Tel Tellai.

Tel! Had they found him too?

Gasping, she let her eyelids fly open. Her blazer still rested on Brennen's nose. Down at her side, he brandished the silvery horror.

She mouthed, "I can't."

"Try again." She felt no anger from him, no impatience, only hope... and a faith deeper than his terror.

Polar gestured angrily, turned away from Cassia, and stepped closer. "Now," he ordered, and Firebird lost her chance. Brennen's arm lifted and jabbed the contact into the angle of her throat. Panic seized her. She already couldn't move. Now she could scarcely think.

"Do it, woman," Cassia urged from her other side. "Kill him! Kill him before he can kill you! He'd thank you for doing it."

"Cassia!" Polar shouted. "Follow orders or you will be breathing vacuum!"

"You low-blooded, empty-headed half-watt!" Cassia shrieked, and Firebird still could've fired. "You don't rule the Talumahs!"

"And you have no right to kill a Caldwell!" Shirak bellowed. His hand twisted violently. Cassia fell away from Firebird and crashed against a corner of the volcanic corridor.

Firebird gasped, released from command but held helpless by the terror piercing the skin at her throat. Brennen's quivering hand made the needle shake.

Polar laid one hand on Brennen's shoulder, one on hers, and shut his eyes, smiling.

Firebird narrowed her focus and clung to Brennen's love, still pressing into her mind. He knew why she'd come. If he remembered only that, he loved her for trying. *Strengthen my will, Mighty Singer,* she prayed.

No, not my will! Do yours! I don't know why... but I know you. Labeth's words flushed her with strange excitement. She bowed her head and murmured, "Mighty Singer, take us to you."

—And turned.

A flicker of terrorized strength licked through her. Back upon it flowed an indescribable surge of energy. It had to be Brennen's carrier, resonating with her own.

Her throat skin tore as he flung the striker away. Roused by pain, she let go of her turn, wheeled, and fired. She wanted Polar—ferociously—but Shirak was there. He fell backward, eyes wide in disbelief.

Something landed on her back. Strong hands seized her head and twisted her neck, gouging her scalp with long, cutting nails. "Brennen!" she choked, falling hard. Where had he gone? Had she killed him with her turn?

Cassia's voice seethed unintelligible words into her ear. Flaming anguish erupted all over her body, from no visible source. Every nerve insisted she was burning, her skin turning crisp. Hatred and nauseating otherness throttled her mind. Pinned to her enemy, Firebird flailed for her turn. Cassia clung snakelike to her point of awareness, tightening her arms, painting deeper patterns of crippling heat onto and into Firebird's body.

Firebird fled inward through the ancient wall. Black spouts of flame, the deepest heart of the Dark that Cleanses—flames just as black as this evil chamber—illuminated the greedy darkness inside her. Smoke filled her lungs.

Evil, evil!

In that instant, she knew the truth. Dabarrah was right... this was evil, not memory! It had held her prisoner to the unholy Powers. It had tried to destroy Kiel and Kinnor as they were born and had even reached out to seduce her during her consecration.

Cassia's psychic coils loosened. Firebird sensed the other woman's startled terror.

Despairing, Firebird dove toward a black depth. Ravenous flames thickened as she plummeted. She drew a last cool breath. Cassia's fear flooded her senses. She thought she heard a long, quavering scream. *Save Brennen!* –She shot away the prayer and then called up one truly evil memory. In a Netaian tagwing fighter, she accelerated toward death on a black Verohan pinnacle. This time, she took Cassia with her.

But could she really choose to die?

At the last possible instant, she wrenched the EJECT lever... punched out... and then seized her carrier. She felt Cassia ride the plunge to—

Impact! The pain of disintegration lasted less than a heartbeat. The fireball caught Firebird from behind.

Then she felt nothing at all.

• • •

As Firebird seized her epsilon carrier, Brennen grabbed the spark, a desperate strength that shocked him with its intensity. He drove that spark across the drug-induced chasm between control and his own carrier—and found it! Shouting triumph, he turned. The stuffy chamber seemed to broaden as he mastered the terrors. He could breathe deeply again! Access-linked with Firebird across a doubled carrier, he glimpsed her blazing core of white energy and black anguish, like nothing he could remember.

Then a swell of power rose through him, shock waves blasting through trained checks and controls, so much energy that he couldn't direct it—or had he forgotten how?—but he didn't dare stop its flow and return to his blocked state. Throwing both hands wide in bewilderment, he sent the hideous striker flying and stood stupefied.

Polar tackled him to the ground. Energized by adrenaline, Brennen rolled away from the Shuhr, breaking his fall while he struggled to bring this inward explosion under control. From too little epsilon strength he'd passed suddenly to far, far too much!

Polar sprang up and flung out a hand. From Shirak's lifeless palm, a blazer flew to him.

Brennen forced back the energy storm to keep it from paralyzing him, the way the phobias had weakened him until he turned. He willed a wisp of power into his voice and pressed up from the floor. He stretched out a hand. "Down!" he commanded Polar.

The Shuhr fell sideways. His blazer glanced against stone and fell loose. Still minimizing the frenzy of power, Brennen directed the excess inward on itself, holding energy with energy, and let free a kinetic burst to call that blazer.

It slid past him, out of control.

Polar staggered to his feet and reached into the air to gather and focus power. Around the black-haired Shuhr condensed a massive epsilon shield. Brennen loosed the energy storm in a desperate strike at Polar's mental centers, but even against this, Polar's shield held unbreached.

Brennen gasped, fighting despair. Against such an adversary no mental attack had any hope. Its only weakness was Polar's human body. He must strike Polar physically, cut him down, but he had no weapon.

From his sash, Polar pulled and activated a crystace that had to be Brennen's own. Its whine filled the chamber. "You can't escape," Polar roared. "You're finished." He held his arm high over his head, poised to fling the crystace. "You, and your Speaker!"

Roused by fury, Brennen sent a last word of command. The torrent of energy burst its gates, and he flung it—not at Polar, invulnerable behind that shield, but at his own weapon. "Down!" he commanded it. Power flowed up, and through him, and was gone. He couldn't hold his turn one second longer.

Polar vanished with a crash. The chamber seemed to shrink.

Crushed by the weight of returning fears, Brennen fought to keep breathing. The suffocating silence was eased only by the piercing note of a crystace and the generators' steady bass hum.

Brennen lurched to the spot where Polar had stood. An impact crater half a meter deep and wide, bisected by a slender trench almost a meter long, had been blown into stone. His crystace lay in the trench. Burying most of the terrible blade's length...

Turning away, Brennen swallowed hard. He'd glimpsed a width of gray sleeve darkening with moisture. Under that, in the crater's depths, lay an unrecognizable mass of crushed flesh and bone.

His crystace, powered by the incredible force of fusion energy, had crushed pommel first through Dru Polar's body, creating a shock wave so powerful that bone and muscle were reduced to jelly. Only the stony floor stopped its travel. The crystace lay across Polar's remains, intact, humming softly.

That's got to be a new use for a crystace. Brennen gasped down another breath.

Then he saw Firebird and Cassia lying near the chamber's black wall, auburn hair and striped hair twisted like silken rope around both their throats.

No! he cried silently, stumbling forward. This small, beautiful stranger was his bond mate, his beloved for life. He dropped to his knees, then rolled her onto her back while he quested for echoes of her consciousness.

He felt nothing. He inhaled to shout his fury, not caring who would hear. Let them come! He'd bury her body under corpses—

Realization slapped down his anguish. He was chemically blocked. Of course he felt nothing! Cradling Firebird's head, he fumbled at her throat and searched for a pulse.

At the carotid it throbbed, weak but steady. Relieved but more confused than ever, he searched her body for other injuries. He found only scratches and the crusting cut at her throat, where the striker's probe had torn free.

He stretched a shaking hand toward Cassia. At no angle could he find a pulse, either in wrist or throat.

Had Firebird killed her?

Their enemies were dead. They must flee.

Generator first. Then... outside... someone waited in a RIA ship. She'd tried to explain RIA.

The thought of squeezing into an even smaller enclosure stopped his breath again. He would almost rather die than attempt space flight. But for her sake, he had to try. She couldn't turn for him now. He must do this phobic and powerless.

He fumbled in the narrow trench that his crystace had blasted in the stone floor, crossing Polar's crater like a grave marker. He plucked out his weapon, deactivating it while he looked elsewhere. Polar's "training session" might keep other Shuhr away until he reached that ship. But if they'd seen her coming, had they impounded it? They wouldn't have known about its special features. They might have left it alone for the moment.

• • •

Tel straightened in the pilot's seat, blasted upright by the sense that someone had found him. He examined his external screens. Sweat broke out on his forehead. None of the glimmering forms outside had changed position. This had to be—

Welcome to Three Zed, visitor, a voice boomed.

He sprang off the seat and grabbed his belt holster. They'd found him. But how?

We're nowhere near you, visitor. There are three of us watching, the voice taunted, and sure enough, he felt a kind of echo. *We would have greeted you sooner, but all the fielding teams were detained in a training session.*

He drew his blazer.

They laughed inside his brain. *Put it down, visitor. We can destroy your mind or send you screaming out the hatch into vacuum—but we'll just put you to sleep for a while, until it's convenient to come out and take you and your ship. It must be a remarkable ship, visitor.*

He shrank against the galley servo. "Cowards," he cried. The longer he distracted them, the better chance Firebird might have to save Brennen and Phoena. "Cowards and bullies. I've known people like you. I've had friends like you," he added, bitterly remembering his faithful service to Muirnen Rogonin. "Come out here. I'll lay down my weapon if you'll switch off your—"

Again he felt laughter. *We're so frightened. Sleep well, visitor.* Limp and blind, he collapsed.

• • •

Brennen spotted a control board high on the generator. He wanted to jump to its metal-grate service platform. Instead he pulled himself up a long ladder with shaking arms. He glared at a glasteel cover bolted over rows of relays, then reactivated his crystace. Again the sight of a blade made his throat constrict. Averting his eyes, he sliced the cover away. Then he cut again, deeper. The chamber plunged into blackness.

That would put down their weapons, their scanning capability, even the fielding team. He hastily touched off the humming crystace.

Tormented by silent darkness, toeing gingerly for each rung, he descended to the floor, then dropped to his knees. He groped cautiously back across the chamber, not wanting to pitch headlong into Polar's remains.

Another minute's creeping brought him to the labored wheeze of Firebird's breathing.

Had Shirak called her *Lady* Firebird? What should he remember?

Gently he lifted her over his shoulder, but when he tried to step, his legs buckled. He let her fall, cushioning her impact as well as he could. Infuriated by his weakness, he gripped her slender shoulders and shook her, first cautiously and then harder. "Mari," he pressed. "Mari."

She didn't rouse. "Mari," he whispered. "Get up!" He couldn't believe no one had heard the commotion in here. Sliding his hands down her arms, he found her wrists and dragged her up the space-black passway.

28

EMBERS

rallentando
gradually slowing

Tel groaned. He lay on the deck near the galley servo. Someone was shaking him—

Caldwell! Suited for vacuum, the Sentinel let a smaller suited figure slump on the transport's deck. *Phoena?*

No, Tel realized. Through the faceplate he saw Firebird's darker eyes, open but blank. He sprang up. "Where's Phoena?" He lunged toward the remaining vacuum suit.

"Stop!" Caldwell wrenched off his helmet. "I couldn't save her. We have to take off. Now."

Pressing the heels of his hands into his eyes, Tel folded forward. She was dead after all—his Phoena, gone forever...

"H-help Firebird," Caldwell gasped. "Secure her, please, hurry. We're dead too, if we don't move fast."

Shaking, Tel knelt. He fumbled an unfamiliar helmet off Firebird's head, then wrestled her onto one of the aft bunks and belted her down.

Caldwell fell against the airlock, slip-sealing it with one hand, then flinched away from a bulkhead. Dark lines and circles surrounded his eyes.

Tel sprang to his feet. "But how long has Phoena been...?" He couldn't say it.

"I-I can't count days," Caldwell stammered. "I tried to save her. Forgive me. Please."

Tel glanced at the airlock. Caldwell couldn't stop him from going back, from trying to claim her body—

And what would that accomplish? "Then take off," he said, slumping again.

Caldwell passed a hand over his eyes. "I've forgotten how to pilot. I've forgotten your name. I've forgotten... almost everything."

What had they done to him? Tel finally realized that Caldwell kept glancing at bulkheads as if he expected them to collapse. "What about the RIA unit?" he cried, springing forward onto the pilot's seat. "Can you use that?"

Caldwell sank down beside him. "Does it take epsilon skills?"

Tel punched up the generator. "Just the turn, and not even a strong one. That's all Firebird can do, anyway."

Caldwell shook his head. "Then I can't use it. They've blocked m-my turn too."

Tel gaped.

"Lift off," Brennen pleaded. "Hurry, before the fielding team gets its power back!"

• • •

Juddis Adiyn backed against the star tank and eyed the Golden City's new Eldest, Modabah Shirak. Modabah was a taller, more glamorous, but oddly stooped version of his father Eshdeth. Moments before the generator-room fiasco, Adiyn had spotted disaster on the shebiyl. He'd summoned Modabah to the Eldest's office even as Eshdeth Shirak's body stiffened.

Modabah slammed a hand onto his new obsidian desk top. Some tech in the waste-processing facility was taking the brunt of his fury. "If that generator isn't running in five minutes, your corpse will be waste too! Am I understood?"

An organic odor filtered from Shirak's air vent. Most of the City's auxiliary life-support stations had come on line when main power winked out, but not at waste processing. The Golden City was filling with a foul stench.

Modabah waved off the circuit and barked at his com unit, "Give me main generator."

Adiyn stepped closer to listen. "Update," Modabah ordered.

Seconds later, someone answered. "They're installing the new panel now. We expect switchover in six minutes."

Adiyn glanced at a surveillance image on Modabah's data desk. In six minutes, the tiny spark fleeing Three Zed would be out of range, both of ground-side guns and of the fielding satellites. "What happened in there?" Modabah demanded.

Yes, what? Even Adiyn hadn't guessed until the last instant that they stood at the brink of disaster. Eshdeth, gone. Polar, gone too! Even young Cassia. Unavoidable. Why, though?

Maybe the Sentinels' god gave explanations. The shebiyl never did.

"We don't know," said the downside voice.

"I never trusted Polar's research," Modabah declared, turning aside. "I warned him he'd destroy himself someday."

Adiyn eyed his new Eldest through narrowed eyes, careful to keep his thoughts shielded by epsilon static. Polar might have created an epsilon-power mishap and destroyed his own body, but plainly—from the profound satisfaction in Modabah's alpha matrix—the new Eldest had also suspected that Polar meant to seize leadership. Maybe Modabah Shirak was paranoid, or maybe he was right—but who would train the young people now?

A gilded door slid open. Micahel Shirak charged toward his father, tight-lipped, clenching both fists. Spotting Adiyn, he spun aside. *Did you foresee this?* he demanded subvocally. *Didn't you warn Security? Why didn't you delay them until I got here?*

"Not even you," Adiyn said evenly, "could've saved this situation." His imagination now filled in the blanks from his glimpse of the shebiyl. Polar's self-destruction could've distracted Eshdeth Shirak and Cassia Talumah long enough for their prisoners to strike, reach the generator, and then escape.

They're gone, aren't they? Micahel glared with wide eyes. His jaw twitched.

Modabah Shirak pointed at the surveillance screen. "There they are. But we're weaponless for five and a half more minutes. The fielding team can't even put Mistress Caldwell's backup pilot back into tardema. Fielding's without power."

Give me a ship, Micahel pressed. *I'll pursue.*

Adiyn eyed Micahel and Modabah. Eshdeth Shirak, a sensible leader and a stable strategist, had always followed his own brilliant father's long-term plan. Eshdeth would be missed. The Ehretan unbound had suffered a staggering blow.

At least their genetics would stay in competent hands.

"Adiyn?" Modabah caught his attention. "I need a shebiyl reading. Now. How can we use what's left of the Angelo princesses to settle this? What about Caldwell's gene samples? Or our agents in Citangelo?"

Father! Micahel's epsilon sense seethed like a boiling pot. *I said give me a ship.*

Modabah turned aside, glaring. "You will follow my orders," he shouted, "or you will be executed."

Adiyn guessed that at this moment, Modabah would love to see someone die. Micahel must've understood too. He stood clenching his fists for two seconds, then stomped out. Adiyn watched him go, wondering behind his deepest shields if it would be best for his people if *he* stepped in and took over, wresting power away from Modabah Shirak.

Perhaps later.

He sat down in a chair near the star tank. Staring into its depth, he searched his mind for the elusive shebiyl, hoping to glimpse what the future might hold for the Golden City under Modabah... or himself.

• • •

Tel stepped out of the RIA transport's hatch into a predawn wind. Under the lights of Hesed's grassy landing strip, beyond Master Dabarrah, a tall woman waited. Master Dabarrah had warned them over the interlink to anticipate Carradee. He'd told them about her new grief for the missing princesses.

Tel glanced back into the ship's darkness. "Go ahead," Brennen's voice said. "I won't drop her."

Squaring his shoulders, Tel stepped down the ladder. Hesitantly, the woman waved.

He hurried toward her. "Carradee. Majesty." Kneeling on damp grass, he took her hand and kissed it.

"Prince Tel. It is you. You look different in shipboards." Beneath loose blond curls, her forehead wrinkled. "Are you all right, Tel? Phoena... they tell me... I'm so sorry."

He sighed relief. The Sentinels had spared both of them from having to inform each other. "I will be all right. Caldwell and I have... talked. At least I know, Carradee. I can hardly imagine your pain, wondering—"

Carradee gave a little gasp. Tel sprang to his feet. Brennen had emerged from the transport, carrying Firebird. She lay in his arms, legs dangling, hair hanging over his elbow. Carradee shivered and pulled her woolen coat close.

Nodding a somber greeting to Carradee, Brennen passed them. Dabarrah hurried toward him.

As Tel stepped out behind Brennen, Carradee took his arm. An image of Phoena exploded into his mind: Phoena as he'd known her, the paragon of all nine Powers: Strength, Valor, and Excellence... Knowledge...

He faltered.

The fifth Power was Fidelity.

No, he realized, humbled by his sorrow. No, that virtuous image was Phoena as he had imagined her, and she never existed.

A sekiyr strode toward them, carrying a warm jacket. Tel slipped into it. "At least Firebird's condition didn't deteriorate en route," he told Carradee.

"Since she survived this long, Dabarrah will surely heal her." He stared at Brennen's back. Caldwell, the invulnerable, implacable Master Sentinel, had also existed only as a façade, a controlled image that concealed a good man. They'd talked for hours, returning together. Tel had helped set up the shipboard blood-cleansing equipment that filtered the blocking drugs from his system and brought back most of his epsilon powers. As long as he could hold a turn, he could hold down his crippling new phobias. But he could not sleep, and his memory survived in tatters.

Tel pressed Carradee's hand. "I'm glad you came, Majesty. This is a good place." He stared up at the shadowed red rocks over the Hesed Valley. "Was Rogonin unkind to you?"

"Yes," she murmured, but to his surprise, she smiled with sad eyes. As they walked toward the downside lift, she related the electoral mutiny. Procyel's sky lightened over her head, and curls blew into her face. Carradee Angelo Second, whom he'd rarely seen happy since she acceded to the throne, looked rested... ready to lead the search. "It's peaceful here," she said, glancing around. "And Daithi is so much better. The first time he saw Firebird's babies, something inside him came back to life. Come with me, Tel. Come see him. Would you?"

What a courageous woman. "Of course, Majesty. It will be good to see Prince Daithi again."

● ● ●

Master Dabarrah laid down his recall pad. "This is encouraging," he said.

Brennen tried to sit up. His arms still shook, and he couldn't pull a deep breath.

"No," Dabarrah insisted, "lie still. I'm going to put you back down in just a few minutes. But first, I want to assure you that there's been no shift in sensory, critical, or moral judgment." He touched the recall pad. "Your personality profile still fits the imprint from when you tested for training, if I adjust it for age."

At that news, Brennen's skylit bed seemed to grow softer. "Brain damage?" he asked.

"Physically, none. Alpha matrix..." Brennen heard calming overtones in Dabarrah's voice now. "Yes. Memory patterns, associational ability, and especially recall. I can help you with those, to a certain extent."

"I haven't just lost old memories. Tellai had to tell me his name twice." The realization had devastated him.

"Your powers of recall are damaged. With retraining, we can probably improve what you still have."

"You're saying it won't come back?"

Dabarrah laid a hand on his shoulder. "All things are possible."

That was scant comfort. Brennen squeezed his eyes shut. "And th-the fears? The stammer," he added, disgusted by his own voice. "What am I so afraid of?"

Dabarrah's forehead furrowed. "Most of your terrors seem related to Three Zed. Darkness, solitude, locked or enclosed places."

"Sleep," Brennen suggested.

"Yes, loss of consciousness. Certain weapons. I found odd fears too. Red lights, and anything made of gold."

The suggestions made Brennen choke. Dabarrah's access touch lightened the sudden weight on his chest. "What do you remember of *Dabar?*" the Sanctuary Master asked. "Of *Mattah?*"

Brennen shut his eyes and concentrated. Isolated phrases sprang to mind, chapters and verses that ended in blank spaces—

"Stop. The problem is there, Brennen. The Holy One has not forsaken you, but you've forgotten much of what you knew about His commandments. Including those against fear."

Brennen groaned. "At least I know where to start studying." *Be my courage until then, Holy One.* He stared at the stone ceiling. This was still worth all it had cost him, if he'd saved the sanctuary. Using deep access, Dabarrah had refreshed his memory of that dream, of the call he had followed so confidently. Evidently Dru Polar's colleagues had meant to strike Hesed House. Apparently they would have succeeded. He would've died here. He, Mari, Kiel, and Kinnor...

But had the amnesia block held at Three Zed, or had he betrayed secrets he no longer remembered? He must've broken at least once, to need a second block. How had Dru Polar pierced his amnesia?

"Without perfect recall," Dabarrah said, "you must learn as others do, with study and repetition. It will be slower than you're accustomed to, but you'll still have unusual advantages. I urge you to access people who've held key positions in your life, to regain your own past. I will gladly serve you. I would also suggest accessing Sentinel Dardy. And Lady Firebird, when I awaken her."

"How soon will that be?" He dreaded the deep, healing sleep he'd been promised. He feared lying alone, even here where nothing could harm him.

"Her psychic shock demands total rest, so I'll keep her down for several more days. But I'll move her in here," Dabarrah told him. "You won't be alone."

"Jenner," Brennen whispered, "is it possible they tricked me, that Phoena isn't really dead? I ... don't remember what happened."

Dabarrah pursed his lips. "I probed first for that, Brennen. You do have a deep, unaltered memory. You saw her die. Be at peace about this. You did not betray Tel."

One more thing— "I've lost carrier strength too. I can feel it, right now. I'm not as strong as I was."

"That may not be permanent."

Brennen shut his eyes. The ayin complex, and epsilon power, had been created by their ancestors in disobedience. Over the decades, it had caused more evil than good... on war-blasted Ehret, and now stretching out from Three Zed. Someday it might be a relief to lay down that power.

But not yet, if he could help it! Tomorrow he would step out on a new branch of the Path.

● ● ●

There had been pain, and terror. They haunted the region between dreaming and dozing, but Firebird felt strong again. Strong enough to wake.

Something warm lay on her chest. She raised a hand to touch it and felt silky hair on a firm skull. Longingly, she threaded her fingers into that hair.

An even warmer sensation invaded her inner awareness, the essence of a tropical sea that smelled of incense...

"Brenn," she whispered.

Then she came fully awake. Should he be inside her mind? They must escape! She struggled to sit upright.

"Rest, Mari," he said softly. "I remember you. We're safe."

She exhaled and relaxed on the bed. The Shuhr, the chamber, her horrible revelation—that Dabarrah's claim had been true and her inner darkness was essentially evil—all seemed irrelevant.

Brennen was back.

"Not completely," he said. His smoky-sweet access probe shifted at the back of her mind. "Dabarrah did all he could for my memory, but I still have gaps. I'm filling them in. Studying. Accessing others."

She rolled her head, looking around. White stone shone above her. Beyond one wall she heard water whispering and splashing. A skylight glowed with the soft orange-red of sunset or dawn.

She'd been carried from horror to Hesed. She caught a breath of damp kirka trees as Brennen's delicate epsilon touch danced through her memories. It paused here, lingered there, to relearn what they'd shared, and as it did, some of the strangeness in him faded away. "The blocking drugs they gave you at Three Zed. You beat them!" she exclaimed.

"There's medical equipment aboard all our craft," he murmured. "Blood cleansing. I see that we did it once to you, at Veroh."

"You'd forgotten?"

She felt his sadness. "I had," he admitted.

Should he be doing this? Wasn't she still on avoid-status? "Where are Kiel and Kinnor? Are they all right?"

Distracted, he opened his eyes, though she felt his probe linger on the moment when she'd told him of her pregnancy. "They're close, and better than all right." He arranged her long hair around her shoulders. "Master Jenner has promised to take you off A-status and give them back to us as soon as I finish this." He raised her chin with one finger, leaned close, and brushed his lips against hers. The touch at the back of her mind shifted again, stroking as it comforted.

Firebird savored the pleasure she'd missed so intensely. "Be careful, Brenn," she whispered. "There's evil inside me."

He hesitated, then answered, "And in me. But Mari, the darkness is only a taint on us. Years ago, I came to the Holy One needy. To faith. And He covered that taint. He met my need, just as He met yours."

Master Jenner had tried to explain all this. Perfect holiness couldn't even look at evil, not the slightest shadow. But the Holy One had found a way to let offenders stand in His presence. Not by the ancient sacrifice, but by her faith in it... no, in Him... He could lay a covering over her, like a garment.

"I think," she said softly, "I'm starting to understand."

"And someday there'll be no need for covering. He'll take the evil from us and sweep it away."

She relaxed completely. If Brennen remembered that much of his faith, everything else would fall into place eventually. Sweet sensation rose in every niche of her body and mind.

"You once asked," he said, "why He allows suffering and evil. Now you'll ask why He called me to Three Zed and nearly let me be destroyed."

She looked deep into weary blue eyes. "Yes."

"I don't know why He let the Shuhr kill Tarance and Destia, but for myself... answering the call is everything. We're forbidden to tell others about the obedient life, so we must show them."

"That's all?" she whispered.

He took her hand. The skylight over his head glowed brighter.

"What did you change?" she murmured. "What saved Hesed?"

"We unbalanced the Shuhr, Mari. We killed two of their strongest leaders. And... there was more. Let me try to remember..."

She'd never seen him struggle for memory before. It felt almost like pain.

His head drooped, and a strand of hair fell toward his face. "For a while, they were moving toward confrontation. I think we've won a respite. The One who called me there is sovereign, and He accomplished His purpose. Mari, I had to trust your help at Three Zed, in the same kind of faith—I only knew what you are to me. I know what He is, in a greater, deeper way. So I trust Him."

She pressed his hand against her cheek. "Finish what you're doing for Master Dabarrah."

He nodded. "Don't turn, Mari. I'm going to go deep."

His warning cued up an image of the rough, cold granite wall, but the epsilon power deep inside no longer held any allure. She had nearly died at that wall... again.

Suddenly Brennen straightened, exclaiming, "Polar's research!"

"What?"

His eyes lit with smile lines, and the tension smoothed out around his mouth. "Polar would've created his own version of RIA. Then there would have been no stopping him, here or anywhere. The Shuhr would have taken the Federacy."

Firebird nodded. Brennen had saved the Federacy... and Regional command would never even know! Unfair—yet even more vitally, he'd filled in a memory gap without any help. Maybe more of his past would return.

He laid a hand on her shoulder. "Mari, when I stop turning now, my fears will come back. I have so much to relearn. Until I do, you'll feel them."

She covered his hand and squeezed. "Thank you for warning me."

She braced herself. Slowly, gradually, he pulled his probe away. As he did, she felt an eerie change come over Hesed House. The room seemed to shrink, the light dimmed. Brennen's hand trembled. She gripped it harder.

His eyebrows lowered. "Are you all right? Can you deal with this?"

"As long as you're here," she said firmly. *Don't you dare avoid me just to spare me from sharing your pain!*

He smiled again. Straightening, he leaned toward a wall panel and switched on an interlink. "Done, Jenner," he said. "She controls her response beautifully." He rubbed the dark mark on his cheek with his free hand.

Had that been some kind of test? If so, she'd obviously passed. She eyed his left cheek. Maybe every victory left scars, visible and invisible.

"I had a message yesterday from Regional command." He turned away from the link panel.

"They want you back," she guessed.

"Yes. An offer of full reinstatement. I wouldn't even have to return my severance pay—"

The door opened silently. Anna Dabarrah glided through, followed by a slender sekiyr. A kicking blond baby gazed toward Firebird, held around his waist by Anna's arm. "Kiel!" Firebird exclaimed, and she would've leaped off the bed if she'd felt stronger.

Anna gave Kiel to Firebird, who took him as carefully as crystal. His warmth, his musky smell, his tiny curled fingers... all seemed as familiar and right as her own face in the mirror, or Brenn's.

The sekiyr laid auburn-headed Kin on her lap. To her shock, Kin worked his jaw and plump cheeks in his sleep. "He's been so content since you came back," Anna admitted. Firebird fingered his fist, marveling at its smoothness. "Somehow, he made peace with the world. Your worry disturbed him, but now your presence comforts him."

In her arms, the blond twin hiccupped, stared a little longer, and then broke into a broad smile.

Firebird tightened her arms, drawing that pink-gummed grin even closer. "Kiel!" she exclaimed. "Do you know me?"

"Ghh," said her son. He tangled her hair in flailing fingers and dragged it toward his mouth.

Helpless to do anything else, Firebird pressed her cheek to Kiel's. The sanctuary women left the room, and Brennen's arms tightened, folding Firebird, Kiel, and Kinnor together. "I suppose," she mumbled, "I'm in trouble with Thyrica for taking that RIA ship." She didn't even care. Kin arched and wriggled, and she rolled him toward her shoulder. There had to be some way to cradle them both.

Brennen shook his head. "The transport was Jenner's to send, from the time Ellet brought it here."

"Ellet," she muttered. If only she could forget that woman, or make Ellet forget Brennen! *Just one touch of amnesia…*

Brennen carefully pulled Kiel out from under his brother. At last, his eyes came alive with mischief. "Mari," he said, "I have something to tell you about Ellet—and Damalcon Dardy."

ACKNOWLEDGEMENTS

Amy, Andrew, April, Basia, Bill, Dr. Bob, Brett, Chris, Diann, Eddie, Gayla, George, Jane, Janna, Jo, Kevin, Marjorie, Marlo, Martha, Matthew, Mike, Sharon, Tana, Vance, and Wynne—thank you for critique, encouragement, and ideas.

Steve, thank you for breathing fresh life into these books.

The best words on these pages belong to all of you... and to One who has given me the desires of my heart. Inconsistencies, impossibilities, and weak wording are all mine.

ABOUT THE AUTHOR

Kathy Tyers published her first science fiction novel in 1987 and she has been at it ever since. She has been accused on two counts of writing Star Wars novels (and pleads guilty on both counts), but she also likes being known for her original "Firebird" series. *Firebird, Fusion Fire,* and *Crown of Fire* (volumes 1-3) were later combined into one book as *The Annotated Firebird,* Volume 4 is *Wind and Shadow,* and the messianic *Daystar* rounds out the series.

She has also published three other science fiction novels, a travel book, and co-authored a book with classical guitarist Christopher Parkening.

Kathy lives in southwestern Montana.

Visit her web site: www.KathyTyers.com

TRAVEL THE
FIREBIRD UNIVERSE

WITH

KATHY TYERS

ENCLAVE PUBLISHING

WWW.ENCLAVEPUBLISHING.COM